Secrets of Ravensbarrow

TEDDY vs. the FUZZY DOOM

Braden Hallett

Read at your own risk, filthy ape-pups!

toronto · berkeley

© 2024 Braden Hallett (text and illustrations)

Cover art by Braden Hallett
Cover design by Braden Hallett, Sam Tse, and Rachel Nam
Interior designed by Braden Hallett, Sam Tse, and Rachel Nam
Edited by Claire Caldwell
Copyedited by Dana Hopkins
Proofread by Mary Ann Blair

Annick Press Ltd.
All rights reserved. No part of this work covered by the copyrights hereon may be reproduced or used in any form or by any means—graphic, electronic, or mechanical—without the prior written permission of the publisher.

We acknowledge the support of the Canada Council for the Arts and the Ontario Arts Council, and the participation of the Government of Canada/la participation du gouvernement du Canada for our publishing activities.

Library and Archives Canada Cataloguing in Publication

> Title: Teddy vs. the fuzzy doom / Braden Hallett.
> Other titles: Teddy versus the fuzzy doom
> Names: Hallett, Braden, author, illustrator.
> Description: Series statement: Secrets of Ravensbarrow
> Identifiers: Canadiana (print) 20230510094 | Canadiana (ebook) 20230510108 | ISBN 9781773218557 (hardcover) | ISBN 9781773218564 (softcover) | ISBN 9781773218571 (EPUB) | ISBN 9781773218588 (PDF)
> Subjects: LCGFT: Novels. | LCGFT: Illustrated works.
> Classification: LCC PS8615.A392458 T43 2024 | DDC jC813/.6—dc23

Published in the U.S.A. by Annick Press (U.S.) Ltd.
Distributed in Canada by University of Toronto Press.
Distributed in the U.S.A. by Publishers Group West.

Printed in Canada
annickpress.com
bradenhallett.com

Also available as an e-book. Please visit annickpress.com/ebooks for more details.

Thank you to my parents who long ago bought me a monumentally stupid but nigh-invulnerable hamster and then later a dog. Though I loved the hamster, I much preferred the dog. Also thank you to Claire and the other fine folks at Annick Press for all their advice and support (and for deciding to print the book even after learning what it was about). —B.H.

Table of Contents

Chapter 1	Hi. I'm Teddy.	1
Chapter 2	Hamster-Girl	14
Chapter 3	Ravensbee	19
Chapter 4	HAMSTER-GIRL!	28
Chapter 5	Just Blend In, Teddy	34
Chapter 6	Welcome to the New Class, Same as the Old Class	42
Chapter 7	Well, Same as the Old Class Except with Evil Hamsters	49
Chapter 8	Weird Kids	63
Chapter 9	Ms. Mint	73
Chapter 10	Scrufflechops	77
Chapter 11	Milk. Ick.	83
Chapter 12	The Hamster Plan	93
Chapter 13	Our Plan (with Puppets)	103
Chapter 14	We Need an Adult!	114
Chapter 15	Just a Silly Little Story	125

Chapter 16	The Gauntlet	136
Chapter 17	Frekizor	144
Chapter 18	The Milk Heist	160
Chapter 19	AAAAGHBLURGLURGLURLGAAARGHTHPTH!	171
Chapter 20	Heart-to-Heart	179
Chapter 21	The Fuzzy Menace	187
Chapter 22	The Fuzzy Evil	193
Chapter 23	Desperate Times	203
Chapter 24	Operation Hamster Bath	209
Chapter 25	OHMYGOSHTHEY'REGONNAEATUS!!!	216
Chapter 26	Scrabbles	223
Chapter 27	I Suck	231
Chapter 28	AAAAGHBLURGLURGLURLGAAARGHTHPTH! (Part 2)	243
Chapter 29	Don't Leave Anyone Behind, Teddy	250
Chapter 30	Family Traditions	261

Hi. I'm Teddy.

That's right. Teddy. I'm an anxious kid.

Seriously anxious.

"This is me, too..."

How anxious? Well, the "I bite my nails" kind of anxious.

That doesn't help, Teddy. Explain it better.

Okay, you know that feeling like you're at the very top of a roller coaster and you're JUST about to go over the edge... and you KNOW that the ride's gonna break and you're gonna plummet to your doooooom?

That feeling like you're about to go on stage and you know, you KNOW, that you've forgotten all your lines?

Or like that time you did something really, REALLY stupid in front of your classmates and it was the kind of thing that's gonna follow you all the way from elementary school to middle school and then to high school and then into your first job and noone's–evergonnaletyouliveitdownfortherest...

of your LIFE!

"I'm kinda mean to myself."

Sorry. Mom calls them tangents.

Anyways, I'm an anxious person. I feel like that all the time. I don't like it either. Sorry.

Stop apologizing, Teddy!

So you know just as well as me that when my family had to move from our home in Kamloops (dry, dusty, and oh so nice and warm) to Ravensbarrow (way up north and ALWAYS RAINING) I was gonna have a hard time.

Also, there was that whole thing about evil hamsters trying to take over Ravensbarrow Elementary. I had a hard time with that, too.

Come to think of it, maybe I should just start there.

Yeah. Forget you read that first bit. Let's start with the evil hamsters.

Well, I didn't KNOW that there were evil hamsters when I showed up for my first day at Ravensbarrow Elementary. Gosh, that's a mouthful. I should call it something else. Oh, wait. Hamsters first.

Behold, the ULTRA-EVIL hamster!

Now, the school. Maybe one of those things where you just use the letters? A whatchamacallit... ac-ro-nym? Yeah. An acronym. Something like R. B. E.?

Nah. Too many "E" sounds.

Barrow Elementary? Still not right. Apparently "barrow" means "grave." I don't like thinking of graves. Death freaks me out. I mean, it freaks everybody out, right? It's DEATH.

Maybe something shorter but with less barrow. Ravens-Bee Elementary? Maybe just Ravensbee.

It was my first day at my new school, Ravensbee (yeah, I like Ravensbee a lot better!). My mom had grown up here. She'd gone to Ravensbee. I had cousins who went here, too, but they were out of town this week. I was all alone.

I stepped out of my dad's car and slammed the door behind me. It was raining. A lot. All the other kids were wearing heavy-duty rain gear and I was already soaked to the bone in my cotton hoodie. I thought rain gear would make me look nerdy (more nerdy, I guess). Real smart, Teddy.

A shack in the middle of the endless pine forest that makes up this part of Canada.

"So you've got everything you need, Teddy? Not missing anything?" Dad had rolled down the window, but not much. If he'd rolled it all the way down, the car would have filled up in seconds from all the rain.

Geez, I hate rain . . .

"Yeah, Dad, I've got everything."

"Pencils?"

"Yeah."

"Paper?"

"Yeah."

"Polybarometric oscillating thumb-whacker?"

"Yeah."

"Good. You kept forgetting about it in Kamloops."

Dad's a weird guy.

Dad started to roll up the window. "All right, Teddy! Have a great day! I gotta get to work."

That feeling in the pit of my stomach flared and I

This is Dad

There are many like him, but this one is mine

grabbed the window before it closed.

"Dad, wait!"

Dad kept glancing at the clock. "What's up?"

"I... Well..." Oh, geez... Dad had to get to work. If he was late on his first day, he'd get fired. If he got fired, we'd lose our house! We'd be homeless! We'd be stuck on the streets in this awful, wet, dim place filled with nothing but pine trees, rotting leaves, and ugly cinder block shacks that they called elementary schools! What would we eat? We'd have to eat my cat! I like my cat!

"Teddy?" Dad raised an eyebrow and bit his lower lip. He only did that when he was worried. Now my dad was anxious!

"Sorry, Dad. No, I'll be fine. I think. I hope."

Dad kept biting his lip. He looked really worried now! I wasn't helping. I should say something weird. Dad likes weird things.

I rustled my hood a little, spraying raindrops everywhere. "I mean, what if all the kids are part of some dark secret conspiracy aimed at removing the brains of all the adults in order to power a supercomputer?"

Dad smiled. He likes jokes like that. He likes to run with them. He rubbed at his chin and looked me in the eye, all super-serious. "I wouldn't worry about it. Kids around here aren't into evil science, Teddy. Besides, adult brains aren't good for supercomputers. All we're good for is meat and skin."

"What would kids use human skin for?" I forced a laugh. I knew this was all just a joke, but the thought of someone hunting my dad to use him for leather started to worm its way into my mind.

Dad shrugged. "Shoes? I wonder if my unicorn tattoo would be a good thing or a bad thing for cannibalistic child-cobblers . . ."

"You have a tattoo?!"

Dad did a double take at the clock. "I gotta go, Teddy! I love you! Have a good day! Make good choices!" He drove off, leaving me alone.

In the rain.

"I hate the rain."

Hamster-Girl

I jumped. There was a girl standing right behind me like we were waiting in line for ice cream or something.

She had a glazed look in her eyes, kinda like she was trying to look at both of my ears at the same time. Unfocused. **"Also, you'd need to use a slow cooker."**

I was not ready for this conversation. "I . . . I beg your pardon?"

Her voice had a strange, cold, breathy echo. **"Adult meat. You'd need a slow cooker. Adult meat is stringy."** Her tongue licked around her mouth like it was trying to dislodge a bit of leftover breakfast.

I froze up. I froze up like I always do when I try to talk to new people. Then again, maybe it was okay to freeze up if someone was trying to talk to you about the finer points of eating your parents. I had to say something!

"Thank you for the . . . advice?" Good one, Teddy. Excellent response. Genius.

This girl was WEIRD.

But the REALLY weird thing about the girl was her hamster. She held a hamster ball (that's fine, totally normal). There was a hamster inside (once again, not surprising). A remarkably calm and collected hamster (a little strange for a hamster). A Zen-like hamster (getting weirder). It stared at me with its beady red eyes and then held a little paw over its muzzle to cover it (really weird!).

She lifted the hamster ball up to my face. I froze. I always froze in new situations, and this situation was certainly new. I mean, is it impolite to refuse to greet a rodent in Ravensbarrow? I didn't know! I could see the hamster was ready to pounce. It kept one paw covering its mouth and the other brandished needle claws.

"You should say hello to my hamster." There was that strange breathy echo again, like two voices were speaking. Was her backpack wriggling?

She unscrewed the top of the hamster ball.

"My hamster wants to say hello." Was her hoodie wriggling?

The hamster flopped out of the hamster ball and landed with a SPLORT.

"I should go." I moved toward the school. "I don't want to be late for class."

The girl stared off blankly. The hamster, though . . . The hamster stared at me with the most intensity I've ever seen from a rodent (not that I've seen a lot of intense rodents). I had no idea what to do.

"It was nice to meet you?"

The hamster stared.

"See you inside?" I walked toward the school.

The girl stayed standing near the road. Staring. Just standing and staring in the rain.

The HAMSTER stayed standing near the road. Staring. Just standing and staring in the rain.

I shuddered then hurried inside toward my new classroom.

I bit at my fingernails.

I was getting anxious.

Ravensbee

Well, at least it wasn't raining in the school...

I looked behind me out the window. Hamster-Girl was gone, but I couldn't shake the feeling that her hamster was lying in wait to sink its teeth into my neck like a tiny adorable vampire.

AGH!

I couldn't think about it! I had to get to my classroom. I shook the rain out of my hair and looked around. No one really tells you this, but most elementary schools are pretty much the same. They even smell the same. Well, Ravensbee smelled just like my old school in Kamloops, anyways.

Does this count as a tangent? I mean, I'm describing the school, which you kind of need to know about. Maybe a map would be better...

A gravelly old voice barked at me. I looked over at the tiny office window that all elementary schools seem to have. A little old lady in a loose-fitting deep-blue tracksuit leaned out and glared at me. Not a normal little old lady with a tray of cookies, I mean a little old lady crossed with a wolverine.

"I don't recognize you, pumpkin." The wolvagranny raised her glasses to get a better look at me. "Who do you belong to?"

"Um... I..." I froze up. AGAIN. She was the secretary, not a hungry bear (maybe), so why did I get the feeling that she wanted to tear me to shreds?

"Simple question, honey."

"I... Um..."

I started to nibble at one of my fingernails.

"Don't bite your nails, dumpling," growled the granny. Did I say something wrong? Did I do something wrong?!

AGH!

A short, wide gentleman with a majestic caterpillar mustache walked up to us.

The angry granny shrugged. "Not intentionally, Mr. Spinnaker. I think this one's just jumpy."

"Don't worry," Mr. Spinnaker said to me. His whiskers pulled his cheeks up into a smile. "Mrs. Sergeant doesn't bite. Well, not anymore."

Mrs. Sergeant snapped her teeth at me. I jumped. She laughed. I could only imagine how many students she'd intercepted and eaten before anyone had noticed.

"We're JOKIN', cupcake! Don't worry, I ain't gonna eat you," Mrs. Sergeant said.

She was lying. Obviously.

Mr. Spinnaker chuckled and looked down at me (but not too far down . . . he was pretty short). "And YOU must be my new student. This one belongs to me, Mrs. Sergeant. Welcome to Ravensbarrow, Teddy."

My new teacher! This was my moment to make a good impression!

"Hi."

Well, that could have gone better, Teddy.

Mr. Spinnaker raised his eyebrows. He was waiting for me to keep talking. I jammed my hands deeper into my hoodie pockets and looked at a nearby bulletin board. Did I forget to mention that I'm a really REALLY anxious person?

The awkward pause stretched on.

Mrs. Sergeant adjusted her glasses and coughed into her hand. "Just a reminder, Mr. Spinnaker, Teddy's got an appointment in the learning assistance room first thing today."

I'm not the best at math. There's nothin' wrong with that, but I wished that I wasn't singled out because of it. I HATE being in the spotlight. Ugh. Multiplication is sorcery.

"I have a memory like a bear trap, Sarge, but thank you!" Mr. Spinnaker tapped his head with a finger and grinned.

Mrs. Sergeant raised a single eyebrow. "Maybe I'll swing by to check on things just in case."

Mr. Spinnaker clapped and smiled at me. "Well, let's give you the grand tour, shall we? Over there is where we keep the ankle-biters." He pointed to the primary wing and then leaned down like he was sharing a secret with me. "The last new kid to go down that hallway was found days later buried in the sandbox, so I'd stay out of there."

Roger that, Mr. Spinnaker.

He steered me down the hallway. "The gym is over there. That's where I will pretend to know how to play sport-ball or sport-puck depending on the time of year. I've never bothered to learn the rules. I just blow the whistle and things seem to happen."

I'd never learned any rules to sport-ball either.

"Through that door"—Mr. Spinnaker motioned grandly—"is the teacher lounge where all us educators take off our human-suits and relax in our true forms."

This. Teacher. Was. STRANGE.

He was strange like my parents, though . . . He was doing the same thing my dad did where he just kept talking. Dad did it to keep my mind off things. I'm not sure why Mr. Spinnaker was doing it, but I started to

26

feel a little better. The roller-coaster feeling in my stomach started to fade a bit.

I wondered what a teacher's true form was . . .

I stopped biting my fingernail.

Maybe this wouldn't be so bad?

Mr. Spinnaker stopped and turned toward the front door. "Oh, hello, Heather!"

I turned to see who Heather was. My stomach lurched.

HAMSTER-GIRL!

"Teddy, this is Heather. She's in your class."

AGH!

"In fact, I think she's your class buddy for this semester."

AGH!

"That means you'll be partners for any group work, proofread each other's writing, and generally work together a whooooooole lot."

AAAAGH!

Mr. Spinnaker continued down the hall. He talked as he went. Hamster-Girl sidled up behind me, JUST out of sight. You know that awful feeling where all your hair stands on end and you can almost feel something breathing down your neck? Like something's hunting you?

Hamster-Girl was hunting me.

Mr. Spinnaker had a spring in his step. "I hear you've brought your hamster to show the class again, Heather!"

Her breathy echo whispered in my ear. **"Yes. I have brought my hamster. I have brought my hamster to show the whole class."**

"It's always nice to see Scrabbles, Heather. You've brought him by"—Mr. Spinnaker counted on his fingers—"at least once a week for the whole year now!"

"Scrabbles likes the school. Scrabbles likes the children. Scrabbles wants to be everyone's friend."

"How many hamsters do you have now, Heather? The last time I talked to your parents they said that one of your hamsters had given birth!" Mr. Spinnaker gracefully dodged a sandwich someone had dropped in the hallway.

ONE of her hamsters? Out of how many?!

"Many. Hamsters." I heard a dry, breathy cackle behind me ... It sounded like it was coming from the hamster ball still clutched in Hamster-Girl's arms ... "There are now MANY hamsters."

I started to get that roller-coaster feeling in my stomach again.

"Well, I hope you brought enough for the whole class!" Mr. Spinnaker smiled. He obviously enjoyed that joke.

I could feel Hamster-Girl grinning behind me. **"Ha. Ha. Ha. Ha. If you insist."**

I started to bite at my nails. Again.

Mr. Spinnaker's class was the last one on the right. I heard the class buzzing away. Mr. Spinnaker gestured grandly once again.

"Head on in, Teddy. Your seat is well-marked."

I stepped through the door then turned around to say thank you. I stopped dead.

Hamster-Girl was still staring at me.

The HAMSTER was still staring at me.

It kept its paw over its adorable little muzzle but glared at me like a starving tiger. Geez, those eyes were red. It whipped its head up to look at Mr. Spinnaker.

Hamster-Girl jerked her gaze over to Mr. Spinnaker in unison with the hamster. **"Mr. Spinnaker. I would like to talk to you in private. It is important. It is very important. Very. Important."**

Mr. Spinnaker furrowed his brow. He actually seemed worried. "Sure, Heather! You go find your seat, Teddy. I'll be in soon."

I hesitated.

Mr. Spinnaker smiled.

The hamster smiled.

Mr. Spinnaker made a little shooing motion with his hands. I hiked my backpack up on my shoulder and shuffled into my new class.

A bit of my fingernail came off in my mouth. I tasted blood.

Ow...

Just Blend In, Teddy

Okay, so at this point you probably know something's off with the hamster.

You're probably thinking, "What the heck is wrong with you, Teddy?! How could you have not seen this coming?!"

Seriously, Teddy.

I am OBVIOUSLY evil.

Blood-red eyes? Fangs?

I mean, come on.

You've gotta remember, though, that I was in full panic mode. I'd have been in full panic mode WITHOUT the weird hamster. Have you ever had to move to a completely new school? It's TERRIFYING. Besides, it was just a hamster! They don't run hamster drills in schools!

Stop tangenting, Teddy!

Sorry.

Stop apologizing, Teddy!

Ugh.

I jammed my hands back into my hoodie so that I'd keep my finger out of my mouth. If there's one thing that kids will notice right away it's if you bite your nails, and I did NOT want to stand out.

I wanted to be one of those kids that you forget about. I wanted to be part of the herd. I just wanted to be a kid. An unnoticeable kid.

You're probably thinking, "That sounds really lonely, Teddy." It is. I've never really had friends. Never ever.

But it's better than standing out. If I stood out then the other kids would notice me. If the other kids noticed me then they'd figure out that I'm a weirdo.

They'd figure out that I'm a freak.

And if kids figure out that you're a freak, they can get really REALLY nasty about it. Even if they say that they're your friends. Blending in is safer.

Right now, you're probably being very nice and thinking, "Oh, Teddy, you're not a freak. You're a perfectly nice young man."

Okay, how about an example of just how weird I am, then? Something other than biting my nails? Or having a fear of milk?

Or needing to go back and check that you've flushed the toilet, like, a hundred times?

Yeah, there's that, too.
Or your big ol' teeth?
Teef!
Maybe let's leave my appearance out of this?
Okay, how about your unnatural hatred of geese?
Mr. Bitey
HONK!

SNAKE-NECKED MURDER CHICKENS, you mean? And no, I had something else in mind.

Making new friends is scary, right? That's normal. What's scary for me is BEING friends with people.

That's pretty weird, Teddy.

I know, right?!

To me, being in a group of friends is like being in a play. Heck, just having a conversation with anyone at all is like being in a play.

You're probably thinking that this doesn't sound too bad. Everyone knows their lines. Everyone says their lines at the right time. The audience claps. Everyone bows. There's a cast party with pizza and kittens. Hooray.

I don't know my lines.

Not a single one.

Nooooooone.

Not only that, but I've missed all the rehearsals and the director has changed the play from *Cinderella* to *Hamlet*.

> Alas, poor Yorick. I kn' him, Horat

> GOSH, Cinderella! Those sure are nice slippers!

I bet you're thinking that NONE of this makes sense because I had a perfectly normal conversation with my dad about making shoes out of his skin. When I talk to my mom and dad, it's not scripted. It's improv (fancy talk for makin' stuff up). It's fun. Every other conversation has rules and scripts that I don't know. Conversations are hard for me. Yeah, I know. It's weird. Everyone at my old school thought so, too. I did a pretty good job of keeping things secret by blending in, but then . . . then I got that stupid STUPID nickname.

If I did something like freak out about a hamster on the first day at my new school, I DEFINITELY wouldn't fit in. If I didn't fit in, then the other kids would figure out just how weird I actually am. If the other kids figured out just how weird I actually am, then I'd be torn apart like a chicken slowly lowered into a cage of starving ferrets! Ferrets with chainsaws for claws!

AGH!

Seriously. How is this scary, Teddy?

BUT I DON'T NEED TO WORRY ABOUT THAT! New school, new Teddy. I'm good at blending in. I am very happy to try to be Captain Conformity.

Geez, you're weird, Teddy.
I know. I don't like it either. Sorry.
Stop apologizing, Teddy.
Okay.
Back to the hamsters.

6
Welcome to the New Class, Same as the Old Class

Mr. Spinnaker's class seemed pretty normal. A little loud, maybe, but pretty normal. No fires, blood, or broken bones. Lots of smiling faces. Everyone was working on something at their desks even though they were talking.

There was lots of flannel. Lots and lots of flannel. I needed to buy some flannel.

There were two empty seats near the front. One of them had a name tag with "Teddy" in fancy calligraphy along with a neat little pile of worksheets. The other featured a name tag with hamster doodles covering the name. Heather's, obviously.

I sat down and slid my backpack under my new desk. All the other kids kept talking. Now I just had to stay quiet until Mr. Spinnaker got back and I could avoid talking to any . . .

HI!

Just a TAD jumpy

New classmate

Friendly

Aggressively friendly

SCARILY friendly

I turned around to see a boy with freckles and giant teeth. He reached out and patted me on the shoulder, trying not to laugh. "Oh wow! I'm sorry, I didn't mean to scare you!"

So you know how I said that it was like everyone else knew the lines to the play and I'd missed all the rehearsals? This was one of those times.

Freckles McToothyface waited for me to remember my lines.

Nope. Nothin'. I wasn't sure what play this kid was in, but it definitely wasn't *Cinderella*.

"Sooooo you're from Kamloops, right?" Toothy Freckle-face rested his chin on his palm, lounging on his desk. "I hear it's hot down there!"

Say something, Teddy!

"Uh... Yeah." I turned back around in my chair and started fiddling with the straps on my backpack. I'm certain I've mentioned that I'm really REALLY anxious, right?

Freckle-facey-toothy-mouthy got out of his desk and walked in front of mine, smiling. "It doesn't get hot here. It rains all the time. Doesn't even snow all that often. Just kinda keeps raining."

Delightful. I could look forward to never seeing the sun again.

Freckles lounged on my desk just like he'd done with his. "My name's Parker, by the way. And your name iiiiiiiiiiis . . ." He grabbed the fancy name tag. "Teddy!"

Parker looked at the pile of worksheets on my desk. "Ick. Morning work. Mr. Spinnaker makes us work ALL THE TIME. We start every morning with worksheets. Math, mostly. Other than that he's nice, though."

"Yeah?"

"Too nice sometimes, if you ask me." Parker pointed at Hamster-Girl's desk. "I mean, I know he had to put you somewhere, but next to Heather?"

Apparently I wasn't the only one who got a weird vibe from Hamster-Girl. I looked down at my backpack straps. "Yeah?"

"Mr. Spinnaker really REALLY wants Heather to

have friends, but she's just so . . . so weird! Nobody likes her. I'd stay away from her if I were you."

I had kind of been like Heather until I learned to blend in. People can smell when you're desperate for friendship. It turns them off. It's better to not try.

Parker moved from lounging on my desk to sitting on it, kicking his legs. "Don't worry. Mr. Spinnaker changes the seating plan pretty often. You won't have to worry about her for too long. And . . ." Parker trailed off and looked at the door. Mr. Spinnaker's heavy footsteps could be heard moving back toward the classroom.

Parker whispered as he scooted back to his desk, "I'd start on those worksheets if I were you, Teddy!" I pulled out a pencil and looked at the first one on my desk. Ugh. Math.

Mr. Spinnaker walked back into the room.

Wait . . . No . . .

Something that LOOKED like Mr. Spinnaker walked back into the room.

7

Well, Same as the Old Class Except with Evil Hamsters

Bonjour!

I dropped my pencil on my desk as a puppet of my new teacher shuffled into the room.

Its eyes were blank and unfocused. Its feet were lead. The mustache drooped, sad and defeated. Hamster-Girl was nowhere to be seen.

There was, however, a hamster poking out of the Spinnaker puppet's shirt pocket. It wasn't Hamster-Girl's hamster, but still, there was an adorable little rodent poking out of the shirt pocket. It grinned then covered its mouth with a paw.

What. Was. HAPPENING?!

Heather has brought her hamster, Scrabbles, to show the class.
ALL BOW BEFORE HIS FUZZY MUZZLE!
Ugh.
Groooooan
Not the hamster again!

There was a stunned silence.

Mr. Spinnaker now had a high-pitched, squeaky echo. "Also, Heather has a surprise for all of you. Heather has made cupcakes." Mr. Spinnaker reached down and grasped at the class attendance list (still staring dead ahead). The hamster in his shirt pocket

51

made pawing motions toward the list as well, leaning out of the pocket. Mr. Spinnaker crumpled the sheet and brought it up to the hamster. "You shall receive cupcakes one at a time."

Someone said, "Ooh! Cupcakes again!"

I took a deep breath. Maybe this was normal. No one else seemed worried.

"The first to receive the blessing of cupcakes is . . ." I could see the hamster in the shirt pocket tracking its little claw along the attendance list. "Parker Allen. Come, Parker. The cupcake awaits with Heather."

Parker hopped up and scooted out the door. Everybody loves cupcakes.

There was a muffled squeak from just outside.

Parker walked back into the classroom.

No, something that LOOKED like Parker walked back into the classroom . . . There was a hamster poking out of the collar of Parker's shirt. It gripped the flannel with both hands like it was driving a car.

At this point, I really should have said something, I know. But I had to be normal! I couldn't stand out and risk being the next hamster-kid! Besides, no one else seemed to notice that Parker was acting weird.

What a great choice, Teddy. Dad would be real proud.

The Spinnaker puppet smoothed the attendance list. The hamster tracked its claw along the paper.

"**Bethany Carson.**" A girl with pigtails stood up and moved to get her cupcake. There was a spring in her step.

Bethany returned, slumped and blank, a hamster at the helm.

More names were read off the list. Each time a happy student left for their cupcake, they returned with shuffling feet and slack jaws.

I started to hyperventilate. Something. Was. WRONG.

Should I say something? Should I do something? I didn't know! I tried to calm down. I told myself that this was normal. No one else thought something was wrong.

More and more students returned, staring blankly. Some bumped into desks like they didn't quite know how to walk.

There weren't many kids without hamsters left. They were all focused on their morning work.

Why hadn't my parents told me something like this might happen? All these years teaching me to wash my hands, brush my teeth, and smile when someone takes my picture and they'd NEVER ONCE mentioned that my class might be taken over by hamsters!

I took a deep breath. I had to get out of here. I had to do something.

I tried to stand up, but I couldn't. What if this was totally normal? I couldn't do anything weird. I HAD to blend in!

But it was OBVIOUSLY dangerous here!

But it was dangerous to stand out!

I couldn't just leave!

I couldn't stay here!

AGH!

Wait, what if I needed to pee? Leaving to pee was a totally normal thing to do!

Yes! Urine to the rescue!

Ew. Teddy, that was a weird thing to say.

I took a deep breath and went to raise my hand...

But by then it was my turn...

I looked around the room. Every single kid stared at me with blank eyes. Hamsters poked out of collars, sagged in chest pockets, and snuggled into nests of hair on top of heads.

The room was dead silent.

This definitely wasn't *Cinderella* anymore...

"And now..." Mr. Spinnaker and his hamster put down the attendance list. "Our new student... For him, a very SPECIAL cupcake." The hamster grinned, flashing its little teeth.

There was a chorus of squeaking from all around me. Hamster applause.

I guess I DID say that I wanted to blend in...

"HEY, TEDDY!"

Every single head in the class whipped around. Mr. Spinnaker rotated his body to match his head.

Mrs. Sergeant didn't have a hamster! She put her hands on her hips. "Memory like a bear trap, eh? I TOLD you that Teddy's scheduled for group time with Ms. Mint first thing today!"

"And . . . And . . . ?" Mr. Spinnaker rolled his head to the side.

"Means he has to go practice math!"

I'm bad at math! I was so happy to be bad at math!

"Now is not a good time, madam." The hamster leaned forward. Mr. Spinnaker lurched.

58

"Tommyrot!" Mrs. Sergeant scowled and waved at me. "Come on, Teddy, let's go to the mathematics torture chamber."

PERMISSION!

I grabbed my backpack, stood bolt upright (knocking my chair back with a BANG), walked (well, frantically scrambled) out of the classroom, and nearly ran straight into Hamster-Girl.

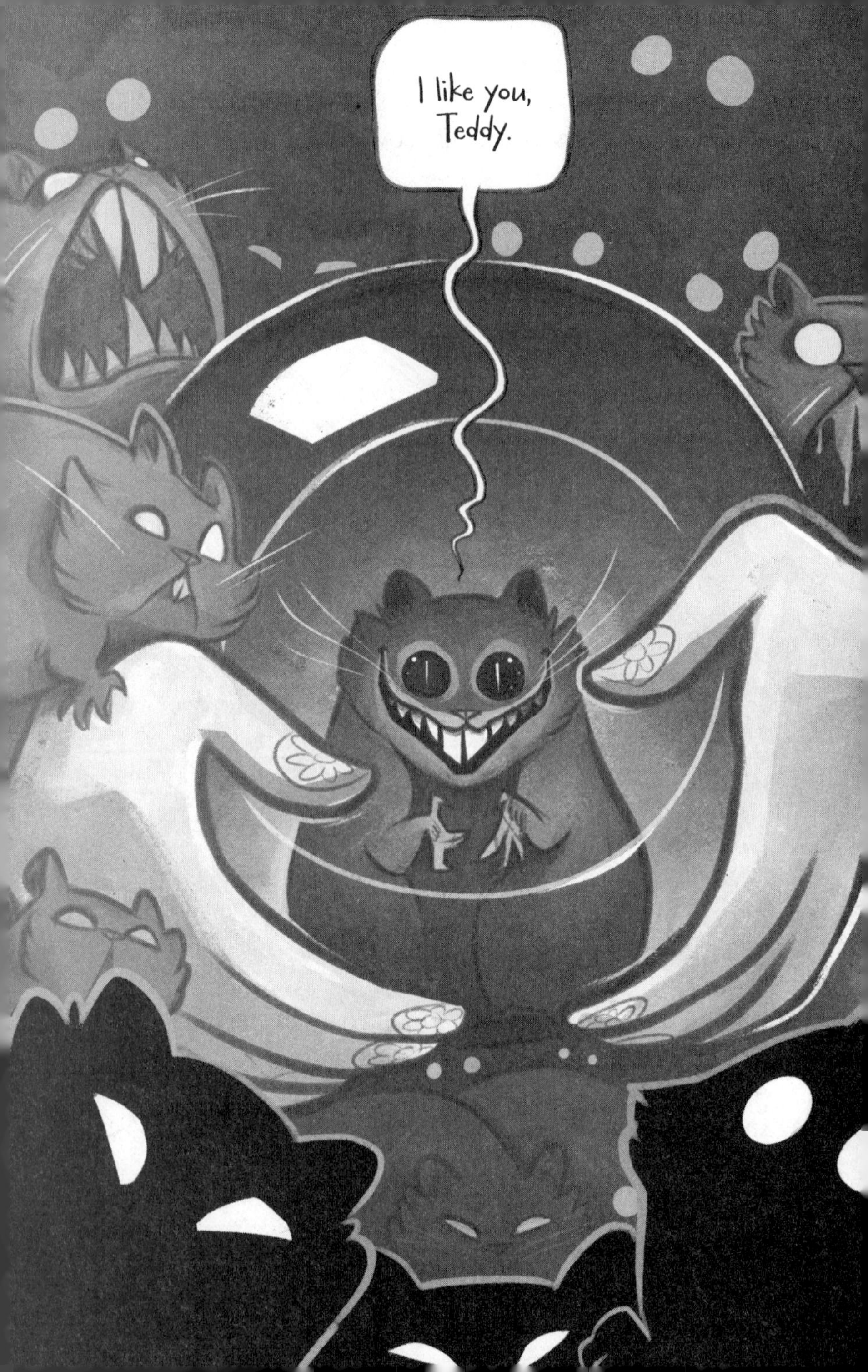
I like you,
Teddy.

AAAAAAAAAA

I dropped my backpack and ran into the hallway, bouncing off a locker and coming to a skidding halt against a water fountain.

I wanted to throw up.

I put my hand over my mouth. I didn't want everyone to know me as the kid that pukes in the water fountain . . . again . . . Geez, I hated that nickname.

Teddy! You're tangenting again!

Oh, geez, I am!

Right!

Back to the hamsters!

AGH!

Mrs. Sergeant picked up my backpack and strolled over to me. "Teddy, it's math. There ain't no need for theatrics."

Weird Kids

I don't remember much about the walk to the learning assistance room. I didn't say a word. I was too busy thinking of those evil little hamster teeth... eating things...

The smell of mint snapped me out of it. The learning assistance room smelled like a toothpaste factory.

The room had one hexagonal table surrounded by shelves and counters stuffed with every game, activity, and learning toy imaginable. There was a kettle with steam wafting out in a happy little column. I'm pretty sure I could have counted a thousand different kinds of minty teas scattered around the kettle. Through a door at the back of the room there was a desk, an ancient couch, and a chair that appeared to have been upholstered with one very fat sheep. Even more boxes, papers, games, and toys littered the back room, along with an old pet cage.

Three kids sat at the hexagonal table. A boy with round glasses, tan skin, and a braid down his back doodled in a sketchbook.

A girl with blue hair who was dressed to run a marathon was spinning her pencil like a baton. They both looked a little older than me. Another boy, skinny and dressed in purple-gray flannel, was reading a comic. He looked a little younger.

The boy with glasses and the sporty girl looked up at Mrs. Sergeant. The kid with the comic kept reading.

Mrs. Sergeant gave me a gentle pat on the back.

"Good morning, crew! I've got a new kid for you. Name's Teddy. Make sure he doesn't get into trouble until Ms. Mint gets back, will you?"

The boy with glasses smiled. "Sure, Mrs. Sergeant!"

The sports-girl ripped off a crisp salute. "You got it, Sarge!"

The boy with the comic kept reading.

Everyone looked at me. I'm pretty sure I could hear crickets.

Mrs. Sergeant never bothered raising her voice. Instead she managed to pour every single ounce of irritation and exasperation into the tone of a few simple words. "For Pete's sake ... Sit. Down. Teddy!"

I scurried forward and sat in the empty chair beside the sporty girl.

Mrs. Sergeant shook her head. "Well, at least I know you can hear me." She turned to leave. "Teddy's new here, crew, so watch out for him. He's part of your gang, understand?"

The sporty girl saluted once more. "Yes ma'am!"

Mrs. Sergeant returned the salute with her fingers. As she left, I saw a cluster of hamstery shapes scuttling along the base of the lockers in the hallway outside.

I bit my nails.

Skitter Skitter

"Don't do that, Teddy. It's gross."

"Don't just grab his hand!" The boy with glasses smacked the sporty girl's hand. "Personal space, Tienna!"

Tienna rolled her eyes and waved her hands sarcastically. "Ooh, look at me! My name's Shane and I love my personal space!" She scootched her chair over to Shane, leaning in close. "I love my personal space sooooooo much."

Shane said nothing but made that awful horking noise that everyone makes when they're about to spit. Tienna leaned back.

"So what are you in for?" Tienna turned toward me and rested her cheek on her palm. Shane leaned in beside Tienna, eyebrows raised. Comic boy kept reading.

Normally I'd be able to keep things moving by saying "yeah" or "sure" or "math" or "banana." You know, words that kind of fit in everywhere. Something. Anything. But there was only one thing on my mind. One fuzzy, evil little thing.

Shane cocked his head to the side. Tienna raised a single eyebrow.

Hamsters

Fuzzy

Terrible

angy

Talking

Evil...
Little...

MONSTERS

I really wanted to say, "Hamsters have taken over the school for unknown nefarious reasons! SAVE YOURSELVES! FLEE!!" But . . . I didn't want to be the weird kid going on about a hamster invasion. I had to be normal. Normal was safe!

Yup. Reeeeeeal safe, Teddy. Dork.

Shane and Tienna looked at each other. Shane shrugged. The boy with the comic book was looking at me now, too.

Usually people just kept talking instead of waiting for me.

I heard a squeaky chittering noise from the hallway.

"Math!" I blurted. "I'm here for math." I turned in my seat and eyed the door to the hallway.

=Chitter=

"Are you sure you're not here to work on your language skills?" Tienna said.

"No, I . . ." I turned back to the table. "Look, I need to tell you about—"

"Because that's what Shane's here for. Shane can't reeeeeeead," Tienna said in a sing-song.

Shane blushed just a bit. "I *can* read, just slowly!" He sat up in his chair. "Tienna's here because she doesn't understand what 'no,' 'stop,' and 'don't throw that rock' means."

I could hear scrabbly little claws at the door.

"Um... There's... I need to..." I tried to get a word into the conversation. Shane and Tienna didn't notice, and that other kid was STILL reading his comic. I took a deep breath. I didn't want to seem weird, but I also didn't want the hamsters to get me! Besides, these kids seemed pretty odd themselves.

Claws!

"What does Ms. Mint say about you, Tienna? Poor impulse control?" Shane grinned.

Tienna folded her arms against her chest. "I'm perfectly in control!"

The chittering in the hallway got louder...

"You threatened to skin a kindergartner alive and burn his house down!" Shane said.

"Well, he made fun of my hair!" Tienna started to raise her voice.

I could smell hamster shavings...

So smelly!

"INEEDTOTELL YOUABOUTTHE HAMSTERS!"

Well, that got everyone's attention.

"Sure did, Teddy. Now what?"

Good question...

Ms. Mint

The boy with the comic book looked at me.

"Uuuuuuuh..." Tienna leaned away from me.

Shane cocked his head. "Sorry, what?"

"The... the hamsters," I said, slower this time.

"Yeah, we heard you." Tienna hopped her chair closer to Shane. She kept her eyes on me.

"Something happened in my class. There... There were a bunch of hamsters."

"Wait, are you in Mr. Spinnaker's class?" The boy with the comic book raised an eyebrow.

"Oooooooh..." Shane said. "That's a good point, Duggy. You're in HEATHER'S class. Yeah, she really likes hamsters."

"Yeah," I said, "I KNOW. Look..." How was I supposed to explain this? "There are a bunch of hamsters, okay? Like, lots and LOTS of hamsters and they're doing something..."

"Doing something?" Tienna said.

"Yes, they're... They're doing something to people's minds! They did something to my whole class."

"Okaaaaaaay..." Tienna turned to Shane and whispered, "Dude. Switch seats with me."

Wonderful. Now I was the weird kid. I was gonna be the new hamster-kid for the rest... of... my... LIFE.

"Looks like someone's here for math AND for being a compulsive liar," Tienna said.

"I'm not lying!" I said. "I—"

The door opened.

Tienna smiled and sat up in her chair. "Hi, Ms. Mint!"

"Good morning! Tienna, darling, would you please get the multiplication game off my office desk?" Ms. Mint, dressed entirely in comfy green, strolled into the room.

"Sure, Ms. Mint!" Tienna jumped up and scooted to

the back room. I could hear her tossing boxes around.

Ms. Mint turned to me. "You must be Teddy, our new—"

Something in the open doorway squeaked.

Ms. Mint turned around. There was a hamster standing up on its haunches.

She leaned down toward the hamster. "Oh, goodness me! Did the kindergarten class lose its . . ."

Squeak.

Ms. Mint stood up.

"Ms. Mint?" Shane said. "Are you okay?"

Ms. Mint turned around. Her eyes were blank. The hamster from the doorway clung to her left earring. It grinned.

"I'm more than fine, children . . ." Ms. Mint didn't speak. The hamster did.

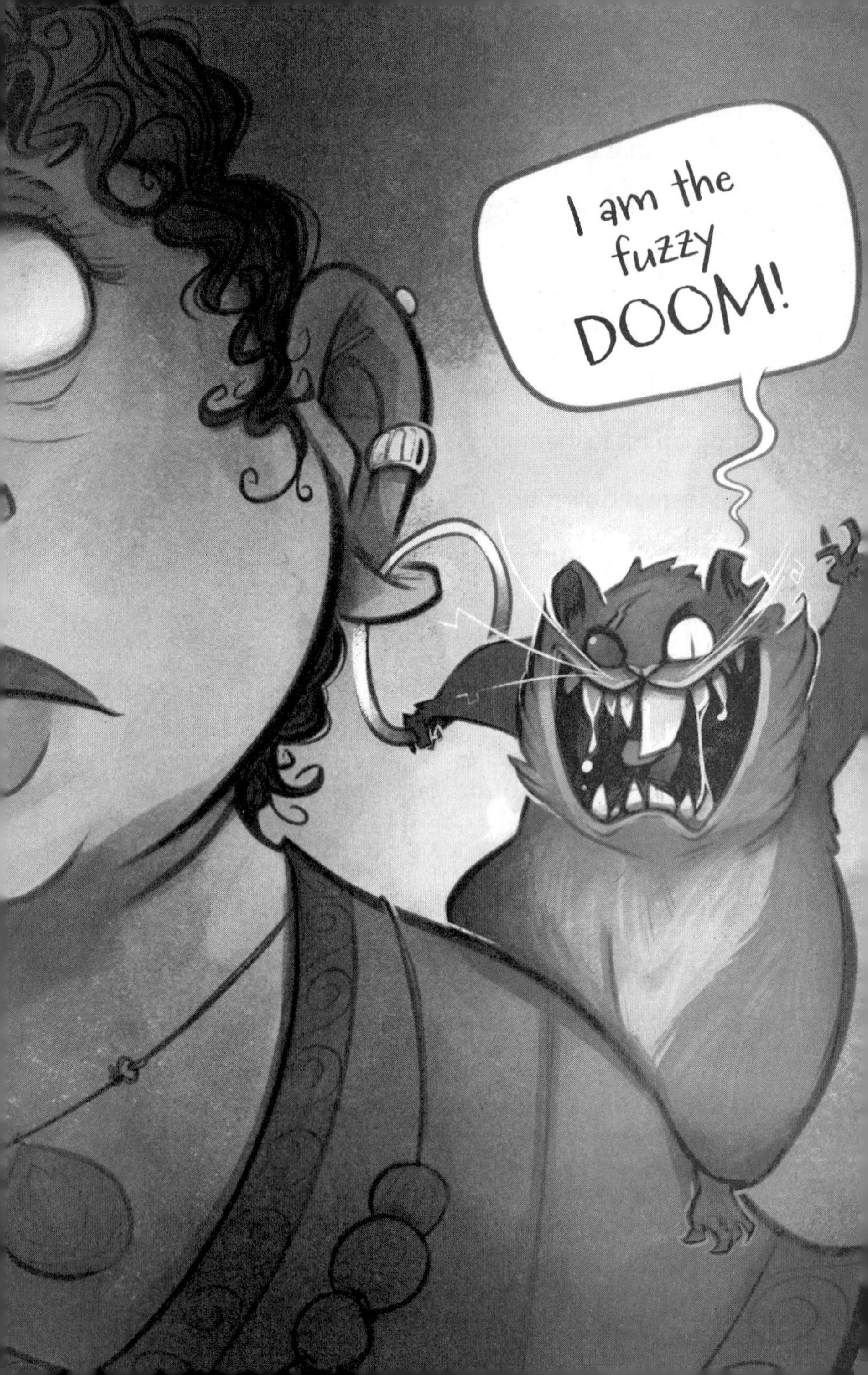
I am the fuzzy DOOM!

Scrufflechops

Ms. Mint plodded closer. "I, Scrufflechops the fuzzy, have been sent for the one called Teddy!" The hamster pointed at Duggy. "But you, I think, will make a fine prize as well."

"Me?!" Duggy edged behind Shane. His lip trembled. "Why . . . Why me?!"

The hamster twitched its nose and licked its scruffy chops. I guess its name made sense, at least. "Because you smell of apples. Tasty, tasty apples. Worry not, little human. The process is quite painless! Only a gentle touch, and then the voice of Scrabbles shall soothe you."

"Teddy, what the heck is going on?! What the heck is going on, Teddy?!" Shane grabbed my hoodie and shook me. He was scared (duh, Teddy). "TEDDY, WHAT THE HECK?!"

Scrufflechops and his Ms. Mint steed advanced.

Behind Shane, Duggy asked, "Guys, what do we do?" His voice quavered. He was scared, too (DUH, Teddy).

"I dunno!" Shane said. He held his sketchbook and backpack in front of him like a shield. "I dunno!"

We'd been backed into a corner. Ms. Mint and Scrufflechops spread their arms wide like they were about to hug us (to death, I'm sure).

The hamster licked its chops and blinked its beady, dead little eyes. I heard Duggy start to cry, but I couldn't rip my eyes away from the hamster and its Ms. Mint zombie. Its Mintombie. Its Zommint?

Teddy! Tangent!

This was it.

MWAHAHAHA!

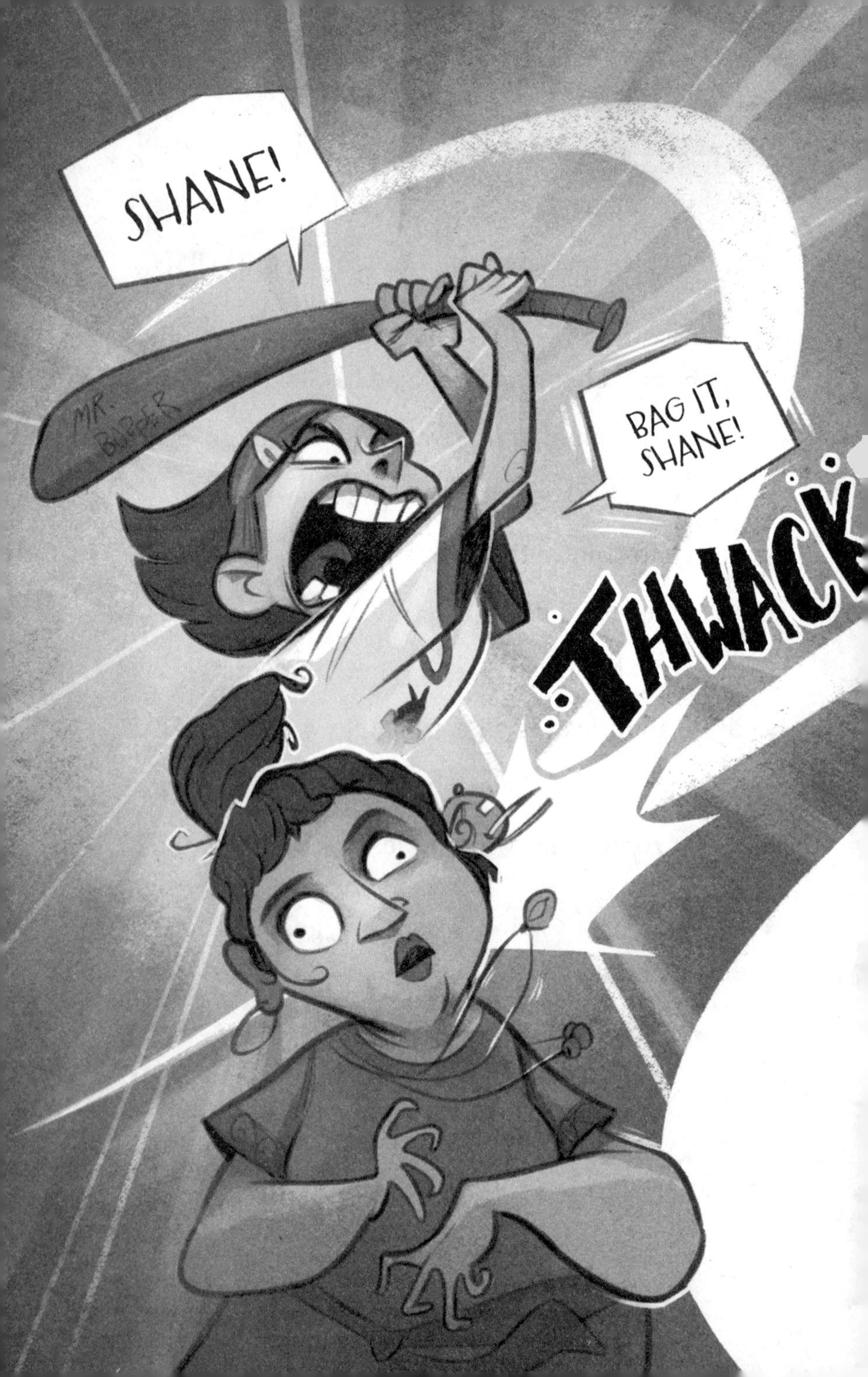
SHANE!
MR. BUDDER
BAG IT, SHANE!
THWACK

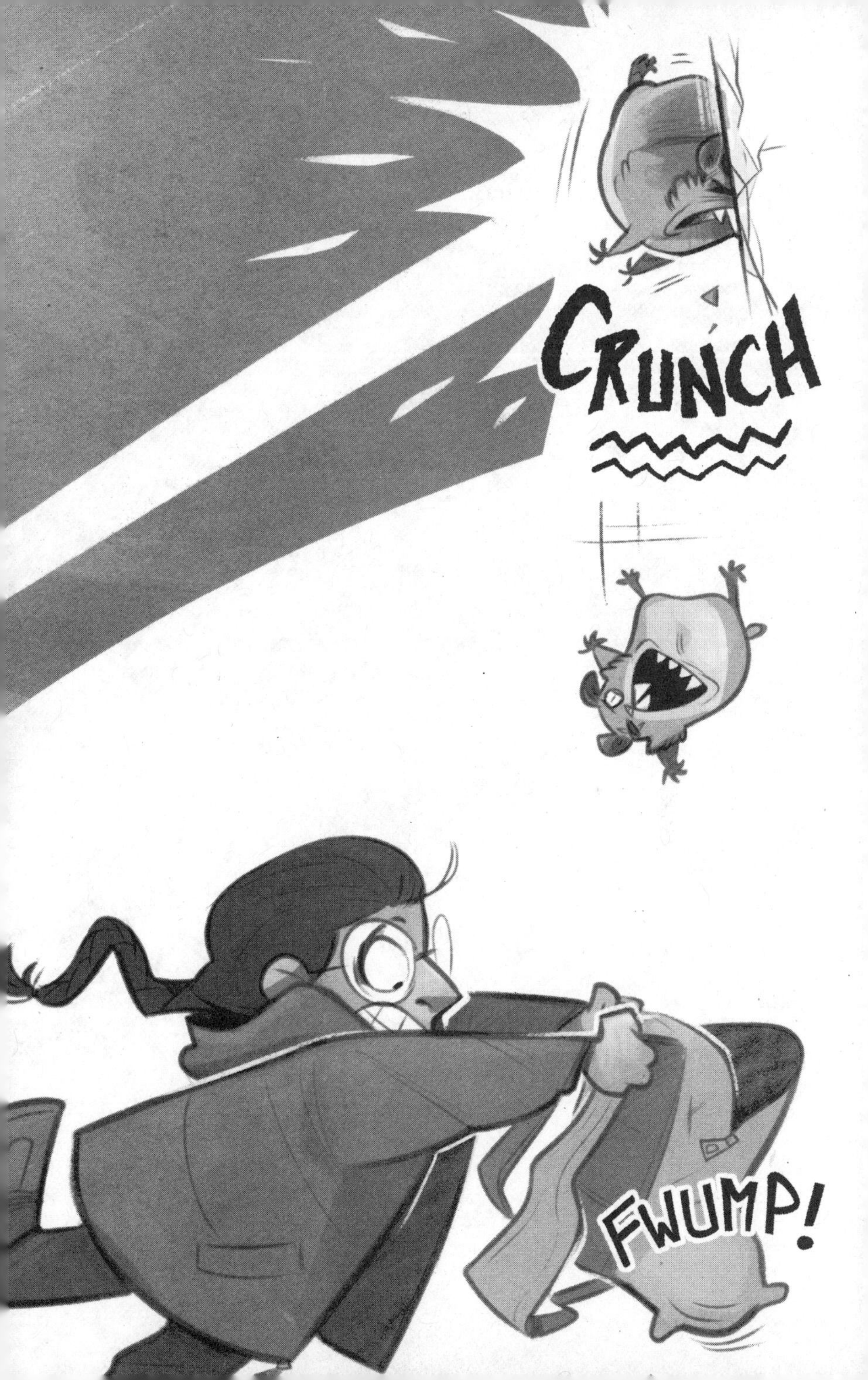
CRUNCH
FWUMP!

Yup. Hamsters.

Milk. Ick.

Shane looked down at the struggling bag he was holding.

You guys... There's a hamster in this bag.

A HAMSTER!

Tienna tugged on Ms. Mint's shirt. "Ms. Mint? You okay?" Ms. Mint stared.

"You guys, there's a TALKING hamster in this bag!" Shane shook the bag at Duggy.

"I know, Shane!" Duggy yelled. "It said I was next, whatever that means!"

"Ms. Mint?" Tienna waved her hands in front of Ms. Mint's face. Ms. Mint didn't even blink.

Shane placed the bag in the middle of the table. Scrufflechops squeaked in rage, thrashing about like a cat trapped under a toilet seat. Don't ask me how I know what that's like . . . Let's just say that little cousins are the worst sometimes.

Duggy's hands were shaking. "Oh my gosh. I'm . . . I'm hungry. I need to eat."

"You might as well." Shane waved his hand in front of the Mint zombie's face. "I don't think Ms. Mint is gonna mind."

Duggy started digging through his lunch kit.

Tienna took one of Ms. Mint's hands and gestured

at me. "Teddy! Come help me with Ms. Mint!"

I hurried over and took Ms. Mint's other hand. Her eyes were blank.

Ms. Mint didn't say anything, but she responded to our movements as we steered her into the back room. It was like pushing a human-shaped shopping cart around. I could hear Scrufflechops tearing at his prison in the other room.

Tienna sat Ms. Mint in the sheepskin chair. "Why don't you have a nap, Ms. Mint? I think it's time for your nap."

Sheep

Glazed, blank eyes

Ms. Mint no longer

Limp like a ragdoll

Like a puppet with its strings cut

Ms. Mint sat in the chair. Ms. Mint stared. She hadn't blinked in minutes.

Geez, that was creepy.

Tienna motioned for me to follow her back out to the other room. We closed the door behind us.

Shane had dug an old wire cage out of the piles of educational supplies. Duggy was sipping on a juice box, hands trembling. The remains of a sandwich and two apples were spread around the table.

He WAS hungry . . .

Shane positioned the bag over the top of the cage.

"What are you doing?" Duggy's voice was shaky. "You're not gonna let that thing out, are you?"

Shane glanced over his glasses. "No, I'm gonna put it in a cage so I can look at it."

"It's a hamster!" Duggy exclaimed. "An evil little hamster! Why would you want to look at it?"

"What if it's not actually a hamster?" Shane asked.

We all glanced at each other. I mean, taking over people's minds was definitely not normal hamster behavior. I didn't think so, anyways. I'd never owned a hamster. I owned a cat. I hoped that Mr. Fuzzikins was okay... He doesn't do well without me around... No one else scratches his ears right.

Teddy! Tangent!

Okay, yeah, that was definitely a tangent. Sorry!

Tienna picked up the wiffle bat. Duggy sank further into his chair, slurping his juice box, his eyes glued to the struggling bag. I backed up to the window. Tienna nodded at Shane, and he dumped Scrufflechops into the wire cage and slammed the lid down in one quick motion.

Shane leaned down and peered at Scrufflechops. "Looks like a hamster." He poked a pencil through the bars of the cage, and Scrufflechops bit down so hard that it snapped in two.

"I look like a hamster because I AM a hamster!" Scrufflechops sprayed slobber and little bits of pencil.

Tienna tightened her grip on the wiffle bat. "Hamsters don't talk."

"We do now." Scrufflechops grinned, baring his little teeth. "We, the children of Scrabbles the all-father and followers of Heather the great provider, are a new breed."

"Why are you doing this?" Shane asked. He got out another pencil and started to sketch Scrufflechops. Good question, Shane. I never think of good questions.

"I'll never tell! Loyalty to Scrabbles and faith in Heather! Besides, you will find out soon enough, ape-pups! There is no hope for you. 'Tis better for you to walk yourselves into the hallway and surrender. No point in drawing everything out!"

Duggy made a slurping sound. The juice was gone. His hands were still shaking.

"Duggy, are you okay?" Shane asked.

"This is my first experience with talking evil hamsters and I am NOT DOING WELL." Duggy put the empty juice box on the table along with the rest of his lunch wrappers. He'd eaten everything. "Apparently near-death experiences make me hungry. I'm STILL hungry!"

Come to think of it, I was doing pretty well considering everything. I mean, I was anxious about the whole thing, but I'm ALWAYS anxious. Yeah! I could handle this! Good job, Teddy!

Tienna put the bat down and dug through her backpack. "You're not gettin' my sandwich, Duggy, but you can have my milk."

MILK!

GROSS!

EW!

MOO!

DISGUSTING!

Liquid chalky DEATH!

I backed up against the shelves behind me and knocked a few books to the floor. Scrufflechops recoiled against the bars of his cage so hard it nearly fell off the table.

Tienna stared at me in disbelief. "Teddy . . . It's just milk."

I . . . HATE . . . milk. Normally I don't freak out at the sight of a carton of it, but what with moving to a new school and the EVIL HAMSTER INFESTATION, I was a little off my game.

Wait a minute . . . I looked at the cage. Was Scrufflechops afraid of the milk, too?

I edged along the bookshelf. "I just . . . I really, REALLY hate milk," I said. "Look, I know it's weird . . ." Wonderful. Now everyone would know about the milk thing. "But considering everything else that's going on can you please not give me a hard time about it?"

Tienna rolled her eyes. "I don't like milk either, Teddy, but you can't be afraid of it! It's just milk!"

Duggy had opened the milk carton. Scrufflechops flinched.

"I don't think it's just me," I said, pointing at the hamster.

The Hamster Plan

Duggy's hands kept shaking, spilling a little bit of milk on the table next to the cage. Scrufflchops hissed, baring his teeth and clawing at the bars.

Tienna grinned and grabbed the carton. She moved it closer to the cage, inch by inch. "And what if we give you a niiiiiiiiice milk bath, Scruffy?"

Scrufflechops shrieked. "No! Please no! I'll talk! I'll talk!"

Shane raised an eyebrow. "Really? That's all it takes?"

"Yes! Just no milk!" Scrufflechops clasped his little hands together, pleading.

I kept my distance. I really felt sorry for him. Milk is unnatural.

Tienna kept grinning as she tipped the carton little by little. She was obviously enjoying this.

Please... Kind ape-pups! Be reasonable!

Do not do anything drastic!

Shane had found another poking-pencil and he jabbed at Scrufflechops. "What are you planning to do with us once we're, uh, hamsterfied like Ms. Mint? Why are you doing this?"

Scrufflechops didn't take his eyes off the most disgusting of cow-based drinks. "Please! Move it away! Even the smell hurts my soul!"

Me too, Scrufflechops. Me too. Blech.

"Not until you tell us something that we wanna

knooooooooow," Tienna said in a happy little sing-song.

"I was sent to bring Teddy to the gym! All will be gathered there, hamsters and students alike!"

"Why?" Shane asked. Tienna giggled. She let a few drops spatter in the cage and Scrufflechops screeched in dismay.

"The great ceremony! All will be gathered for the great ceremony!" Scrufflchops sobbed.

Well, that didn't sound ominous at all.

Duggy put his head in his hands. "CEREMONY?! Ceremonies are never a good thing!"

Tienna rolled her eyes, put down the milk, and walked over to Duggy. "Duggy, this is real life, not a comic book. I promise that nothing bad is gonna happen to you." She picked up the wiffle bat and motioned at Scrufflechops. "You saw what I did to Scruffy with Mr. Bopper, right?"

Duggy sniffled. "Yeah."

Tienna gave Duggy a hug. "I promise that if any of these monsters get near you, I'll bop 'em so hard that they'll turn back into regular hamsters."

Tienna was a lot nicer than I'd expected. Kinda like a really angry big sister. Wait a minute. I was scared! Where was MY hug!

"Oh, and Duggy?" Tienna patted Duggy on the back.

Duggy wiped a tear away. "Yeah?"

"If you freak out like this again I'll give you the worst snake bite of your life, just like I did to Fletcher Cartright last week."

Maybe I was good without a hug.

Duggy stopped crying.

"Remember that, Duggy?"

Duggy nodded.

"Remember Fletcher going home early? Because he was crying so much?"

Duggy nodded again.

"That's because I'm pretty sure I twisted his skin off." Tienna made little twisting motions with her hands. "Clean off, Duggy." She put her hand on his shoulder and smiled. "You good now, bud?"

Duggy nodded and folded his arms tightly across his chest. He didn't look good to me. I wondered if Fletcher Cartright had deserved it.

"Good stuff!" Tienna grabbed the milk carton, drank a sip, and poured a little bit onto her hands. She started rubbing milk along her arms like sunscreen.

Ew.

"That's a good idea!" Shane said. Tienna gave him the milk carton and he took a sip. Then he rubbed some milk onto his arms and his neck.

EEEW!

"That's weird, you guys," Duggy said.

I wanted to say, "You're right, Duggy, that's super weird and also the most disgusting thing I've ever seen," but I was too busy holding back my gag reflex.

"It's hamster repellent!" Tienna moved her milk-covered arm toward Scrufflechops. The hamster screeched and backed away. Shane breathed into the cage with his milk-breath. Scrufflechops covered his snout and squealed.

"That's so cool!" Duggy said, splashing some milk on his arms.

EEEEEEEEEW!

"You need some, too, Teddy!" Tienna said. "Here!" She started to move toward me with the milk carton. "Have a sip!"

I'm really not proud of what happened next.

I ... um ... I aggressively defended my need to not drink or be splashed with milk.

That's not true, Teddy.

I'm not proud of what happened next either.

But that's not what actually happened.

No ... It's not.

I freaked out.

Dad calls them lizard-brain moments. It's when your body needs to do something even if you don't want it to.

Lizard-brain moments often involve screaming and the thrashing of limbs.

I really REALLY hate milk.

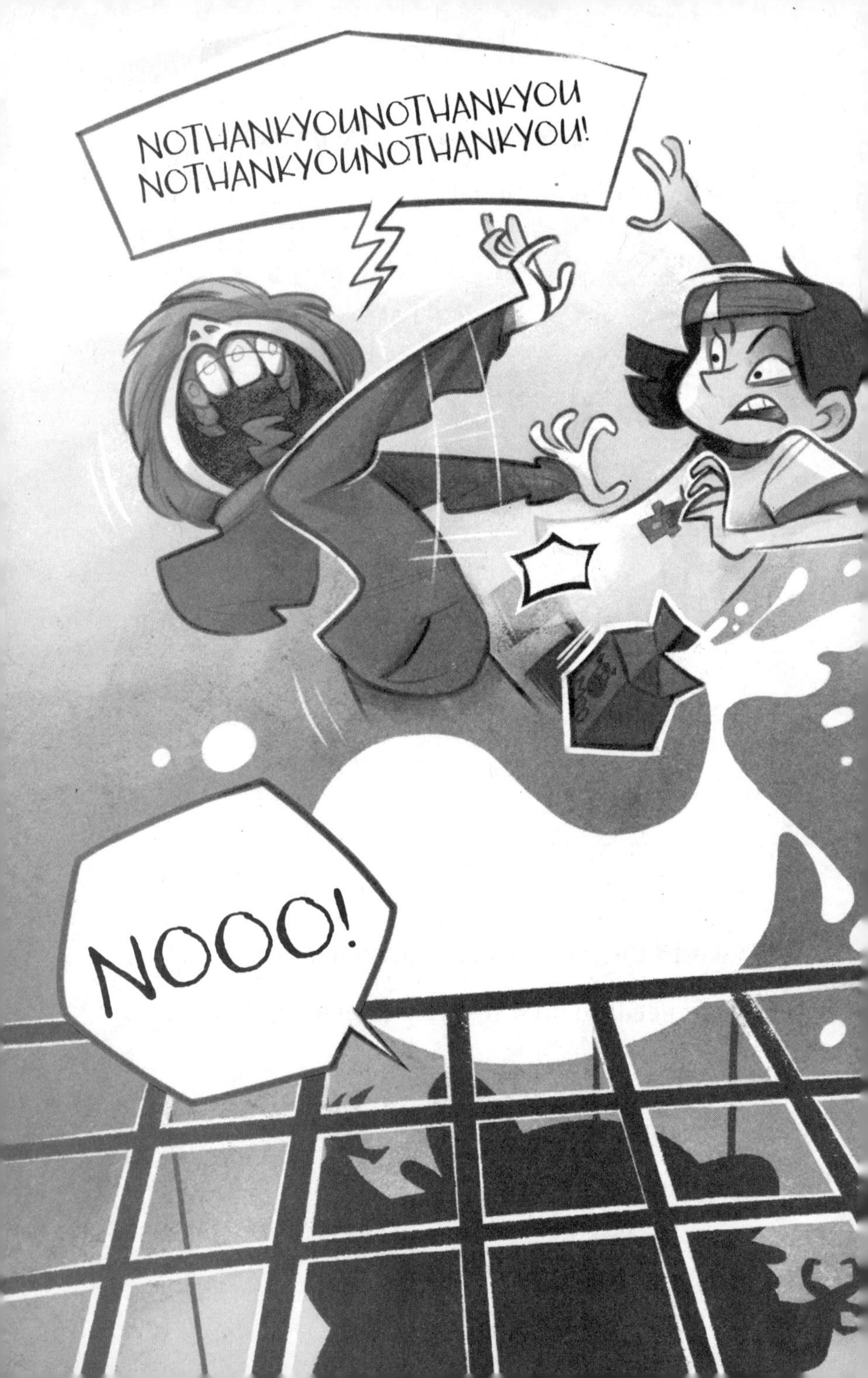
NOTHANKYOUNOTHANKYOU
NOTHANKYOUNOTHANKYOU!
NOOO!

"What the heck, Teddy?!" Tienna looked like she was about to hit me.

"I'm sorry!" I blushed. Geez, that was embarrassing. "I'm sorry! That was just too fast for me! I . . ." I gagged a little bit. "I really really REALLY hate milk."

"Dude . . . Are you going to throw up?" Tienna backed away and kicked a garbage can toward me.

"No," I said between gags. "No, I'm not." I was totally lying. "But if I drink it"—gag—"If I drink it or if you splash it on me, I sure will. At least give me some warning next time."

"Warning?" Tienna said. "It's milk!"

Milk. Ew. Don't throw up, Teddy!

I managed not to hurl.

"Guys, shut up!" Shane said. He was leaning down, staring into the cage at Scrufflechops. "Come here and take a look at this!"

Tienna peered at the hamster cage with Shane. Duggy and I looked over their shoulders.

Scrufflechops was no more.

Our Plan (with Puppets)

"Huh," Shane said. "Neat." He started to scribble notes next to his drawing of Scrufflechops.

Tienna reached into the cage and picked up the hamster. It sniffled and cuddled into her palm. "I can see why he was so afraid of milk!"

Shane poked the hamster. It squeaked. "For sure. But why MILK?" he asked.

"Because milk is an awful, terrible substance produced by the nastiest, ugliest monsters on the planet, and you've all been brainwashed into thinking that drinking their fluids is normal," I muttered. I'd stopped gagging. Finally.

Everyone turned to look at me.

Wrong line, Teddy.

"I'm just saying that milk turning talking hamsters into normal hamsters isn't the only weird thing about this whole situation. Also, is the 'why' important right now? What are we gonna do?!"

"Why is ALWAYS important, Teddy." Shane looked at me over his glasses.

"No, it's not." Tienna put the hamster back in the cage. "Besides, I know exactly what to do!" She picked up the wiffle bat and swung it. Duggy ducked. "We start smashing hamsters! Everyone grab a hamster-smasher!"

I remembered Heather, CRAWLING with rodents. "There's a literal horde of them!" I said. "We won't stand a chance."

"Let's run, then!" Duggy hopped in place, eager to start running. "We can run away and get help!"

I looked outside. I could see at least a dozen figures lurching around in the rain and the mist. They all had hamster riders. I thought of us running across the field while hamsters (with human steeds) chased after us with their sharp, gnashing little teeth. "I think the hamsters thought of that," I said, pointing out the window.

Tienna closed the blinds. "Don't point, you dork! So what do you suggest we do, then? Give up?"

The intercom crackled to life. **"Today is an indoor day, boys and girls. An indoor day. Do not go outside,"** said a deep, buttery voice (with a squeaky echo) through the speaker. **"Also, it is National Hamster Day. A day of hamster celebration. Find a hamster and embrace it. Embrace the hamster."**

The bell rang. It was recess.

"Something tells me that they got to the principal," Shane said.

"We have to do something!" Tienna said. "We can't let this 'great ceremony' or whatever it is happen. I still say that we get to smashing!"

"I don't want the hamsters to get me," I said.

Tienna glared at me. "Or for the hamsters to get anyone else!"

I nodded. "Or that. But if the hamsters know that we're on to them, then we don't stand a chance! We can't just go smashing hamsters. I guess . . . I guess we need to blend in?" It certainly worked with kids. Kids and monstrous hamsters are pretty much the same thing, right?

Tienna laughed. "And how are we supposed to do that, Teddy?"

Someone knocked on the door. We all jumped. A girl poked her head in. "Is Ms. Mint here?" she asked. The girl didn't have a hamster.

"She's, uh . . ." Tienna looked at the back room where Ms. Mint sat bolt upright in her sheep chair. "She's napping."

The girl shrugged. "Well, when she wakes up, tell her that there's an emergency staff meeting. All the teachers are supposed to be there." The girl skipped away, leaving the door open. We could see kids walking around the hallway. Talking. Laughing. In fact, if we weren't looking for the hamsters (and the glazed, zombie-like expressions) we might have not noticed that anything was wrong. The hamsters were blending in, too.

"And now they can get to the rest of the teachers," Shane said. "But I guess we could just act normal." He looked at the hallway. "There are lots of kids without hamsters out there."

Tienna walked over and closed the door. "Okay, but at some point we're gonna come across a group of hamsterfied kids! What are we gonna do, ask them nicely if we can pass by them? We don't have hamsters! We're not zombified!"

"Hamsterfied," Shane said.

"We're gonna have to fight!" Tienna punched the table. She really really wanted to go hamster-smashing.

Duggy raised his hand. "Doesn't Ms. Mint have a hamster puppet? That might help if the hamsters don't look too closely."

"There's only one puppet!" Tienna said.

Duggy scooted over to a bin of craft materials labeled "puppet supplies." He reached in and came out with a handful of fuzzy socks. They were a perfect hamster color. "We just need to add eyes and a mouth!"

"And those weird little nubbin ears and a stubby tail," Shane added. "We gotta be accurate."

"Okay, fine." Tienna crossed her arms. "But—"

"You just wanna go hamster-smashing," Shane said, rolling his eyes. "It's the salmon run field trip all over again."

"I do not!" Tienna said. "Even with hamster puppets, we don't look like zombies!"

Duggy tucked his puppet into his shirt collar, rolled his eyes into the back of his head, and shuffled across the room. The sock hamster curled its little claws and twitched its ears.

"I'm Scrufflechops and I'm gonna eat your skin like bacon, ape-pups! Grr! Argh!" the hamster puppet squeaked. I couldn't help but laugh a little.

"How are you so good at that, Duggy?" Shane laughed, too.

Duggy shrugged. "I like acting. My teacher doesn't like it. No one in my class likes it either, but I do. I do voices, too!"

109

Tienna rolled her eyes. "If I were in your class I wouldn't like it either, Duggy! Fine! No hamster-smashing. But even if we can sneak around, what are we actually gonna do about these little monsters?"

"Get milk," Shane said. "Lots and lots of milk."

I stopped laughing. Milk. Ew. Gross.

"And douse them!" Tienna grinned. "I like it!"

"But we can't just go splashing random hamsters with milk. They'll swarm us! We need to find a LOT of milk."

"Easy," Tienna said. "The hot lunch today includes milk. Let's go get it."

"AND"—Shane peered over his glasses—"we need to know how to help people that have been hamster-fied. Do you want Ms. Mint to stay a zombie?"

"FINE!" Tienna crossed her arms and leaned back in her chair.

"I still say that we need to find help." Duggy pulled out glue and googly eyes and got to work on our sock puppets.

"Who?" Tienna asked. "All the teachers will have hamsters by now!"

"Not Monsieur Lambert," Duggy said. "He won't have a hamster. He's not a teacher."

"Who's Monsieur Lambert?" I asked.

"The custodian," Duggy said. "I play card games with him at lunch. He might actually believe us!" Duggy had finished a sock-hamster already, whiskers and all.

"Well, recess is over in ten minutes." Tienna glanced at the clock. "We'd better move!" She shouldered the wiffle bat. "Shane, do you have milk in your lunch?"

Shane dug through his backpack and tossed a carton of liquid monster-chalk to Tienna. She walked toward me.

Tienna made a calming gesture. "I understand that this is hard for you, Teddy, but it's just milk!"

I nodded, arms still out. It WAS hard. Milk. Ew.

Milk is never just milk. Milk represents all that's wrong and awful in this world. Filthy cow excretions.

Tienna rolled her eyes. "I'm not gonna splash you with it, Teddy. But if we're all gonna go out in the hallways together, then you've gotta at least hold onto the carton."

I looked at Tienna. I looked at the milk carton. Milk. Ew.

"Just showing it to them might make them think

112

twice," Shane said. "Do you want to get hamsterfied?"

"Hmmmmm..." I scrunched up my face. "Maybe I'll just stay here? Lock the door?"

"Alone?" Tienna said, hand on her hip. "In a room with no exits? No. We're not leaving you behind, Teddy. We might as well throw you to the hamsters."

My face scrunched even more. "Hmmmm..."

"Sometimes you've gotta do something you're afraid of, Teddy," Tienna added. "Sometimes you've just gotta drink the milk!"

Milk. Ew.

14
We Need an Adult!

And so there I found myself, walking down the hallway in my new school with a sock puppet poking out of my hoodie and a carton of milk (ew) clutched in my hands. Kids around us went about their business. They were smiling. Laughing. Mostly. But occasionally I saw the telltale blank expression of hamsterfication (totally a word) or a fuzzy little hamster along for a ride.

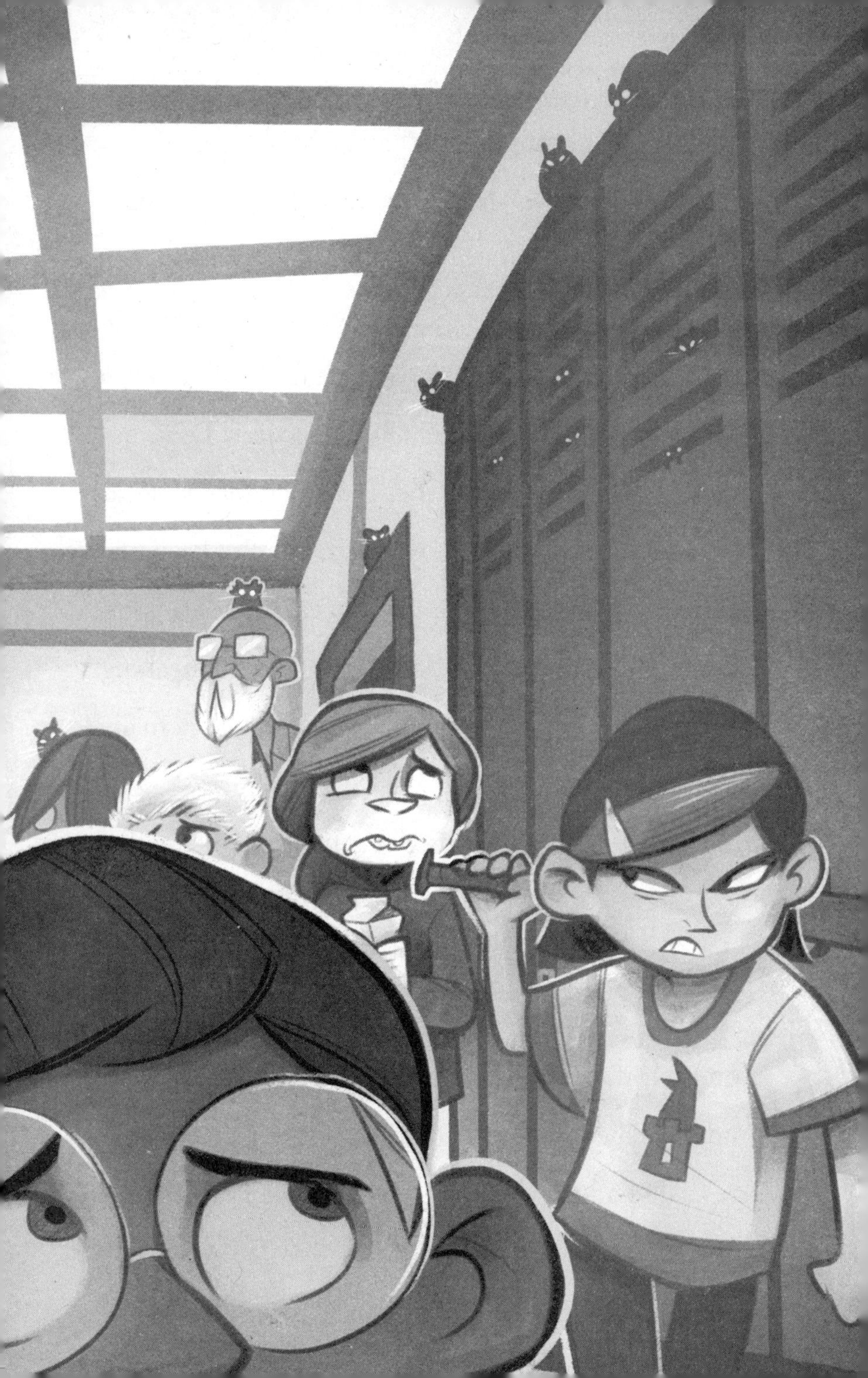

"Aww!" A group of kids had gathered around a hamsterfied classmate as we passed by. "Cute hamster! Can I see it?"

The hamster in question smiled and covered its mouth. Their human automaton said, **"Of course you can... All the cool kids have hamsters. Lean in closely and say hello."** There was a muffled squeak.

I shuddered and kept walking. I had to keep up with my strange new acquaintances or I'd be a goner for sure. A hamster scuttled over my toe, squeaking in irritation. I began to realize that this was actually happening.

Wait a minute... This was actually happening!

I started to hyperventilate. I didn't need to do this. I could go back and hang out with Ms. Mint! She wouldn't mind! Tienna, Duggy, and Shane could go on their doomed hamster mission and I could wait until the bell rang so I could go home!

All I had to do was turn around and walk back to Ms. Mint's room.

Why did this new school have to be so small!

Tienna turned to Duggy. "So you play cards with Monsieur Lambert at lunch?"

"Yeah, sometimes," Duggy said. "He swears *en français* when I win. It's neat!"

At my old school I'd have been worried about being singled out if I'd hung around with the staff. "Don't the other kids give you a hard time?" I asked.

Duggy shrugged. "They give me a hard time anyways. None of the other kids like me much."

Tienna frowned. "What? Why? There's nothing wrong with you."

"I dunno. They never have. I've tried to fit in, but . . . they just don't like me."

I'd seen this before. Sometimes classes just wanted someone to pick on. I'd managed to avoid being that kid for a while, but then the pukey incident happened . . .

"That's ridiculous," Tienna said, sneering. "Why try fitting in? Just be yourself. I've never tried to fit in."

"You hit people and start fires in trash cans." Shane rolled his eyes. "If anyone should try and NOT be themselves, it's you."

Tienna put her arm around Shane's shoulders and poked him in the ribs, grinning. "Good advice from someone whose ONLY FRIEND 'hits the other kids and starts fires,' oh wise one."

"There's no point in trying, anyways," Duggy said. "No one likes to hang out with the weird kid. Monsieur

Lambert's my only friend, really."

"Darn right there's no point in trying!" Tienna said.

I had an opinion about this! I had a line! "I dunno... I don't think there's anything wrong with trying to fit in. It's kinda nice. People don't give you a hard time if you fit in."

Shane gave me a weird look. "That's not the ONLY reason you wanna fit in, is it, Teddy?"

"There are other reasons, too..." I said, trailing off. Well, maybe there weren't a lot of other reasons, but not being picked on was a pretty big one!

"Well, Duggy, you've got three friends, now!" Tienna put down the wiffle bat and dragged Duggy close. "Friends forever, you little weirdo!" She reached out to grab me by my hoodie, but I stepped back. Her hands were like bony vices. Also, being friends wasn't that easy, was it? Acquaintances but not friends. I think. No. Not friends.

"Be careful what you wish for, Duggy," Shane said, rolling his eyes. Duggy gasped for breath.

The door shot open. I looked up. I looked up further. Monsieur Lambert was TALL.

"*Salut*, Duggy, Shane, Tienna!" Monsieur Lambert leaned down and looked at me. "And small person I don't recognize!" Then he grabbed a wheeled wooden chair and sat down. Well, he didn't really sit but more folded his legs like a cricket. His knees nearly came up to his chin. "What may I do for you and your friends, Duggy?" Monsieur Lambert had a French accent. "I don't think we have enough time to play a round of cards during recess."

We all looked at each other. Tienna poked Duggy. "Tell him!"

I was glad that I wasn't the one trying to explain a hamster invasion to a giant.

"Please, sit down!" Monsieur Lambert pointed at a set of chairs held together with duct tape. "My office is always open. Mostly because I'm too lazy to fix the lock!"

Monsieur Lambert
Taller than the door!
Tall
VERY tall
ike, SUPER tall
Hands like shovels
Legs are close to two Teddys high!
MR. BOPPER

We sat down. Monsieur Lambert's office was taken up almost entirely by a workbench that ran the whole length of the room. The surface of the workbench was utterly clean. Spotless, in fact. My dad's workbench back in Kamloops had been a minefield of dried glue, bent nails, and abandoned projects. Here, tools and clamps and other things hung above it on a pegboard. A lone, rusty pail served as a garbage can.

A pile of random mechanical things was clumped in the corner behind the trash can. Under the pegboard was a shelf stuffed with ragged paperback books with titles like *Invasion of the Rhizome Monsters*. In the back was a door marked "boiler room." An old light bulb hung from a wire. It flickered.

"Uhhh . . ." Duggy scratched his head. "You like weird stories, right, Monsieur Lambert?"

"Oui!" Monsieur Lambert smiled and gestured at his library. "I am a huge fan of weird fiction!"

Are any of them about evil hamsters?

Who are afraid of milk?

And can control minds?

Just a Silly Little Story

There was an awkward silence. Monsieur Lambert raised his eyebrows. "I must admit I was waiting for your new friend to add something else to the list," he said, pointing at me. Agh! It was my line!

"Sorry," I said.

Monsieur Lambert laughed. "I was joking!" He leaned in, waiting for me to say something.

Oh, geez. It was my line. AGAIN.

Tienna poked me in the ribs. "His name is Teddy."

"Welcome to Ravensbarrow, Teddy." Monsieur Lambert smiled. "And no, I don't think I have any stories that have all three of those things." He started flipping through his books. "Most of the time adversaries that control your mind are aliens. Are these hamsters aliens?"

"They say they're just hamsters," Shane said.

"Interesting!" Monsieur Lambert muttered. "And often these mind-controlling things do have a weakness of some kind. Germs. Extreme cold. Fire. Salt. Explosives."

"Do you have any explosives?" Tienna asked, perking up.

"Not since I dealt with that marmot, no." Monsieur Lambert snapped the book shut and scowled.

"Darn," said Tienna, snapping her fingers.

"So I suppose milk could be a weakness." Monsieur Lambert scratched at his stubble. "It wouldn't make very much sense as a weakness, though. I don't think real hamsters are afraid of milk."

"These ARE real hamsters," Duggy said.

"Yes," Monsieur Lambert agreed. "In your story these are real hamsters, I understand."

Wait a minute . . . Monsieur Lambert thought we were writing a story!

Tienna started to say something, but I cut her off. "In . . . In the story they want to gather everyone for something they call the great ceremony."

Tienna poked me in the ribs again. Ow.

"They've taken over everyone's minds and gathered them in the gym," I continued.

"Yes, but why?" Monsieur Lambert asked. "In this story, have the heroes tried talking to the hamsters? There's a hamster in the kindergarten class! Perhaps they could ask that one?"

"We . . . The heroes have tried asking one of the hamsters, but they were only told that it's called the great ceremony," I said. "All the heroes know is that they need to stop the hamsters."

"With milk?" Monsieur Lambert asked.

"Are you sure you don't have explosives?" Tienna asked.

"*Non*, Tienna, I have no explosives."

"Well then, milk seems to be our only option," Shane said, fiddling with his glasses.

"Hmm . . ." Monsieur Lambert leaned back in his chair. Springs screeched and cushions groaned. "And you want to know what I would do?"

"Yes," said Duggy. "Yes, please."

Monsieur Lambert laughed and he tousled Duggy's hair. "I must admit you children give me hope for the future. All the other kids in this school are so boring. Evil hamsters indeed!"

Duggy smoothed out his hair. "So what would you do?"

"Well, they are all going to gather in the gym, *oui*?"

We nodded.

"So they're all going to be in the same place at the same time?"

We nodded again.

"And does it take much milk to deter these ravenous rodents?"

"Just a splash, apparently," Shane said.

"Well then, I would find a way to hose them all down once they'd gathered in the gym."

"That's perfect!" Shane exclaimed. "We could hide behind the stage curtain until the time was right! All we'd need is something that can spray the milk!"

A water gun!

A sprinkler!

A bucket of milk and a stick of dynamite!

Monsieur Lambert laughed and clapped his hands. "Like I said. All the other children in this place are so boring! Dynamite indeed! None of these things are likely to be found on short notice, however."

I peered into the back of the room. Poking out of a pile of debris I could see a bright red nozzle, kind of like a water gun. It was attached to a hose that led to a backpack held together with black screws.

"What's that?" I asked.

Qu'est-ce que c'est?

Liquids go here?

Firehose nozzle?

Industrial!

Backpack straps?

Looks ANGRY

Electric motor?

Monsieur Lambert raised his eyebrows. "Good eye, Teddy," he said. "I had forgotten about that!"

"What is it?" Tienna asked, walking to the back of the room and yanking on the object.

"It is a backpack sprayer," Monsieur Lambert said. "It uses a battery to pressurize whatever you put in the tank and sprays a long stream!"

"Does it work?" Shane asked.

"If anything, it works too well," Monsieur Lambert said. "That thing could probably strip paint off a car. Too dangerous for me, though. I'll be returning it."

"Can we have it?" Tienna asked, shouldering the backpack. A bit of water sloshed out.

"*Non*. Of course not."

"Why not?!" Tienna dropped the backpack and put her hands on her hips. I got the feeling that not a lot of people said "no" to her.

"Because," Monsieur Lambert said, "I KNOW you, Tienna, and spraying down an assembly with milk while screaming about mind-controlling hamsters is something I can see you doing just for fun."

Tienna stood silent for a moment. "Yeah?" she said, finally. "And?"

The bell rang (the tinny old thing) and I jumped in my seat. Recess was over.

Monsieur Lambert heaved a heavy sigh and unfolded back onto his feet. He stretched his arms up. They almost touched the ceiling. Geez, he was tall!

"And now," he said, "it is time for you four to go."

Duggy reached out and grabbed his jeans at the knees. "Wait, Monsieur Lambert! Do you think that you could maybe stay in your office? You know . . . take a day off?"

Monsieur Lambert gently batted at Duggy's hand. "I have many duties around the school, Duggy. I can't just stay in my room."

Duggy didn't let go. "Just . . . please be careful, Monsieur Lambert. Watch out for hamsters."

Monsieur Lambert laughed, then ushered us into the hallway and closed his door. Tienna leaned against a locker and motioned for us to huddle down.

"So milk's not a problem," Tienna said. "The lunchroom is full of the stuff, but how do we steal the sprayer?"

"I don't know," Shane said, "but I don't think it matters right now. We need to know more. We need to talk to a hamster again."

"No, we DON'T, " Tienna growled. "We know milk turns them back into hamsters, we know the sprayer will work, and we can't waste any more time!"

"But milk doesn't help the people who were hamsterfied!" Shane said.

"You always do this, Shane!" Tienna's grip on the wiffle bat tightened. "You always make problems more complicated than they need to be!"

"I think Shane's right," Duggy said.

"It feels like we're still missing a part of the puzzle," Shane continued. "We can't do anything drastic until we know more."

Tienna turned to me. "And what do you think,

Teddy?! I say we go find milk!"

My stomach lurched.

"And what are we supposed to do, huh?!" Tienna snarled. "Ask nicely? We got lucky with Scrufflechops and you know it!"

"Yes, but Monsieur Lambert already told us how," Shane said.

We all looked at each other then back at Shane. Shane rolled his eyes.

"Guys, he literally told us to go talk to the kindergarten hamster. He told us to talk to Frekizor."

The Gauntlet

The school was empty. Well, empty of everyone except the hamsterfied. Peering into the hallway, we could see several groups of hamster servants blocking all the exits.

"Everyone got their hamster puppet?" Tienna asked.

Shane nodded. Duggy rolled his eyes into the back of his head and made his hamster puppet do a little salute. Geez, he was good at that. I glanced down at my own little hamster puppet. It looked like a sock with googly eyes. This was never going to work. Socks were not hamsters.

DEFINITELY not a hamster!
Googly eyes
Paper nose
Paper ears
My thumb
SOCK!
My inkie
No legs?
Cottonball tail
Definitely a sock!
My arm!
So he gets the real puppet
Duggy is the master puppeteer

Oh, geez! This was never gonna work! We'd be overrun by hamsters in seconds!

AGH!

Everyone lurched, zombie-like, around the corner. I didn't move. Tienna turned around and glared at me.

"Teddy!" Tienna whispered. "Come on! We don't have all day!"

"I . . . I can't!" I whispered back. I leaned against the wall and started to hyperventilate.

"Teddy, blending in was YOUR idea!" Tienna fumed.

"I know, but . . ."

"Teddy, we're all scared!" Shane said, adjusting his glasses. He didn't look scared to me.

"I'm terrified!" said Duggy's puppet waving its hamstery little paws. Duggy's lips barely moved. GEEZ, he was good at that.

"Remember how I said that sometimes you've just gotta drink the milk?" Tienna asked.

Milk. Ew. I gagged.

"Don't you dare puke, Teddy!" Tienna put her arm around my shoulders. "I meant meta... meta-for..."

"Metaphorically?" I offered.

"I knew that!" Tienna snarled. Wrong line again, Teddy. "Sometimes you've gotta do scary things!"

"I can't!" I said. I bit at my nails.

They didn't get it. This was pointless! We were kids! There was no way we could do this! We were gonna walk up to the first hamsterfied zombie squad in our path and they were gonna pounce on us and sink their adorable little hamsterteethintooursoftfleshandtheyweregonna...

Eat...

Us...

ALIVE!

AGH!

"You're gonna need to take a little sip of metaphorical milk here." Tienna patted my shoulder.

I shook my head and tried to be one with the wall.

She looked at Shane and Duggy and started a whispered chant. "Drink the milk. Drink the milk."

Shane joined in. "Drink the milk! Drink the milk!"

Duggy's hamster puppet chimed in. "Drink the milk! Drink the milk!"

I knew what they were doing. It wasn't gonna work. Teachers always try this kind of encouragement and it's so easy to see through! They could chant all they liked, but there was NO WAY that I . . .

I hadn't noticed that Tienna had started walking me down the corridor.

This was happening!

AGH!

A hamsterfied kid and his goons walked into our path. It was Parker and a few other kids from my class.

The hamster mob leaned their kid mounts forward, crowding around us. Their whiskers twitched. I put on my best hamster-zombie face.

There was a moment of silence. Parker's hamster wrinkled its nose and spoke. "You reek of milk."

Tienna's hand tightened on her wiffle bat.

I felt like a twisted elastic band wrapped tight enough to snap.

"These filthy ape-pups ALL reek of milk!"

Duggy's hamster rubbed its adorable ears. "Though these ones were having a milk fight when we chanced upon them, grotty little monsters that they are!"

"Indeed!" Parker's hamster chittered. It didn't bother speaking through Parker so there was no squeaky echo. "It is good you brought them into the fold, then. Can't have that awful stuff spraying everywhere. Though soon we won't have to worry about milk anymore, eh, sibling?"

"I agree!" Duggy's hamster cleaned its whiskers. How was Duggy doing that?! "And now we must away! We go to guard the exit near the kindergarten!"

"Proceed, then! Loyalty to Scrabbles and faith in Heather!"

"Indeed!" Duggy's hamster puppet did a little salute. "Loyalty and faith and . . . and . . . and fresh apples!" Duggy called over his shoulder as we lurched away.

That was close.

Too close.

17
Frekizor

"How do we know Frekizor isn't part of the plan?" Duggy asked. "How do we know he's not the one behind it all?"

"Yeah!" Tienna agreed. "Duggy's got a point!"

"I guess we don't." Shane shrugged.

What if Duggy was right? What if this... this Frekizor (such a sinister name!) was the one pulling all the strings? What if we were walking into the spider's web?! What if there was an army of hamsters waiting just behind the door? We'd be drained of all our blood and left as dry little skin husks to be used as beanbag chairs!

AGH!

"But Frekizor's always been here," Shane continued. "He was here when Tienna and I were in kindergarten.

I'm pretty sure if he wanted to start a hamster uprising, he could've done it a long time ago."

"I liked Frekky," said Duggy. "He's warm and soft. He used to sit on my lap during story time."

Shane smiled. "I used to draw him riding in spaceships."

"I tried to flush him down the toilet." Tienna chuckled. We all stared at her.

"He looked like he wanted an adventure!" Tienna said. We all continued staring at her.

"I didn't actually do it!"

Shane rolled his eyes, then knocked on the kindergarten door.

After a moment, the door was opened by a tiny boy with shaggy black hair. "Hi, Shane!" The boy grinned. "Are you here to read with us?"

Shane blushed. "Uh, no, Ryder. We're actually looking for your hamster?"

The boy nodded and then wandered back into the classroom. He waved at us to join him.

The room was brightly lit, and the curtains were closed. It looked like a normal kindergarten classroom. The boy tugged on the dress of his kindergarten teacher. She turned toward us. Her eyes were blank. Her expression was dead.

She was hamsterfied.

Mrs. Rose
But where's the hamster?!

Blank soulless staaaaaare

Hamsterfied

Hamster in long hair?

Super deep pockets for hamster hiding

Hammy claw hands

The kindergarten teacher lurched toward us and we all backed away. Tienna gripped the wiffle bat. The hamsterfied body leaned forward like a puppet on bad strings, and we heard a sniffing noise. Something was smelling us. After a moment, the teacher leaned back up and spread her arms wide.

"Welcome, Tienna, Shane, and Duggy!" The echoey voice was a deep bass under the teacher's light tone. **"I remember you well from your time in my garden! Come! Join the fun!"**

We all looked at each other. We were expecting a fight, not an invitation to play. There was definitely a hamster controlling Mrs. Rose, though. Somewhere.

"Um . . . No thanks, Mrs. Rose," Tienna said.

"Nonsense!" The hamsterfied Mrs. Rose waved a hand dismissively. **"Stay here! You will play all day! Many blocks for stacking. Many books for chewing!"**

Tienna nudged Shane but kept the wiffle bat handy. "You were the one who wanted to talk, Shane!"

"We actually wanted to talk to Frekizor?" Shane asked.

"Oh?" Mrs. Rose leaned in again but quickly straightened up after another sniff and took a couple of steps back. "And why would that be?"

"We wanted to talk to him about the hamsters?" Shane said.

"Hamsters don't say much. What exactly would a hamster be able to tell you about itself?"

This was obviously a trap. Obviously. Any moment a wave of hamsters was going to come spilling out of the ceiling, or the walls, or the shelves, and the only thing that would be left behind were our picked-clean, slightly bloody skeletons!

"Well . . ." Shane shrugged. "If he's like the other hamsters around the school, he can talk."

Mrs. Rose glared at us with her blank eyes. "Follow me to the back room," the voice of the hidden hamster rumbled alone. "There is much to discuss."

Much to discuss about how she was going to eat us alive!

148

Mrs. Rose took a bell out of her pocket and rang it. All the kindergartners fell silent and looked at her. "You are all amazing and wonderful, my kindies! If you continue playing so nicely you will all get a Rose dollar!"

"Thank you, Mrs. Rose!" the kindergarten class chanted.

Perfectly behaved five-year-olds?! This was unnatural! But they definitely weren't hamsterfied.

"Keep that milk handy, Teddy!" Tienna whispered in my ear. Milk. Ew.

We moved into the dark room and the door closed behind us. The lights flicked on. We were in a small supply closet.

The deep bass of the hidden hamster seemed louder in the tiny room. "Now, my curious friends..." Mrs. Rose began to turn. The light flickered, making her blank eyes flash. "Now that we are alone..."

Tienna edged forward, wiffle bat in hand.

Mrs. Rose's hair rustled.

Duggy and I edged back toward the door.

Greetings, friends! We meet once again. I am Frekizor, protector of the Ravensbarrow kindergarten.

How may I assist you?

Twirly whiskers AND mustache?!

Safety-pin clasp

A gentleman pirate in hamster form. Gentlepiramster!

Cape and pin sword!

So dashing!

We all looked at each other. I'm not sure what we were expecting, but it certainly wasn't this.

"WHAT THE HECK IS GOING ON?!" I waved my arms. "HAMSTERS! INVASION! AGH!" I didn't care if it wasn't my line, I had to know! I bit at my nails.

Tienna grabbed my hand. "Don't do that, Teddy! It's gross!"

"She is correct, my jittery new friend. You must keep your claws sharp in these uncertain times. And as for 'what is going on,' you summed it up quite nicely. There has been a hamster invasion."

"But HOW?!" Shane asked. Good question, Shane. "Hamsters don't talk! Hamsters don't turn people into zombies! Hamsters don't hatch evil schemes! Hamsters are just . . . just hamsters!"

Frekizor shrugged once again. "Strange things whisper in the woods. The magic of this place is ancient and unknown. All sorts of things are possible in the misty rain of Ravensbarrow."

Once again, I'm not sure what we were all expecting to hear, but it certainly wasn't that.

"No, no, NO!" Shane yelled. "There's no such thing as magic!"

"Well..." Duggy raised his hand and peered over Tienna's shoulder. "Maybe?"

Shane glared at Duggy. "Come ON, Duggy. Really? You're just going to believe that these are... MAGIC hamsters?!"

Tienna lowered the wiffle bat and grinned at Shane.

"Maybe they grant wishes?"

"Or shoot lasers out of their eyes!" Duggy laughed.

"IT'S NOT MAGIC!" Shane shouted, squeezing his eyes shut. "Haven't you guys seen *The Secret of NIMH?* These hamsters escaped from a lab! Or . . . or some machine at the mill bathed them in radiation or something!"

I am NOT a lab hamster.

And I assure you that I am NOT radioactive.

"Then it's something in the water!" Shane shook his head. "But it's not magic!"

"But it may as well be." Frekizor reached out and put his paw on Shane's hand. "I am very sorry that you are having a hard time with this, Shane. You have always found working without clear instructions difficult."

Tienna leaned over and loudly whispered at me, "He needs an instruction manual to play make-believe."

"Shut up, Tienna!" Shane yelled. Tienna grinned.

Frekizor rang Mrs. Rose's bell, and the clear tone cut through the shouting. "Do not fight! We are all friends here," Frekizor said. "The 'how' is not important. What is important is that this IS happening and that something must be done about it. Something must be done about the great ceremony. The ceremony of friendship with Heather."

"Wait," Tienna said. "This is HEATHER'S fault? She's doing this?!"

"I don't think so," I said. "This morning when I met her she seemed hamsterfied and absolutely crawling with hamsters." I shuddered a little.

"Indeed," Frekizor said. "I remember Heather from her time in my kindergarten. She is a kind and generous person. She has no rotten fruit in her cheeks. She would never allow this to happen."

Shane rubbed at his eyes. "Look. It doesn't matter whose fault this is. We need to know how to stop it! We know that milk makes hamsters normal again, but we don't know how to help the people that are hamsterfied. And don't you dare tell me that we have to do some weird magic ritual, Frekizor! This isn't *Dungeons & Dragons!*"

"No, Shane, there is no magic ritual. You must find and defeat the first of the hamsters. The father of this new talking horde. Heather's pet, Scrabbles. Only when Scrabbles is defeated will the people AND hamsters under his control return to normal."

"But how do you know that? How do you actually know that Scrabbles is the key to this whole thing?"

"Because Scrabbles told me so after I dealt with

the miscreant that hamsterfied Mrs. Rose. He bragged about his power to hypnotize people through the touch of his hamster children and his ability to keep them under his claws for as long as he wishes. He even offered me the life of our fair teacher here if I joined his cause."

"Her life?" I asked. "Like Scrabbles . . . Scrabbles would kill her?"

"No, my jittery friend. She was hamsterfied before I could intervene, and then Scrabbles offered her to me. He said that her life to live would be mine. I could take Mrs. Rose's place as the school kindergarten teacher."

"How exactly would that work?" Tienna asked. "No offense, but you're a hamster. Hamsters can't be teachers."

"As I said, Tienna, I am not entirely sure how it works. However, what matters is that it is through Scrabbles's power that everyone remains hamsterfied."

"But if Scrabbles is the key to this whole thing,

won't you go back to normal, Frekizor?" Duggy asked.

"Perhaps," Frekizor said. "But perhaps not. As I said, the magic—"

Shane talked over Frekizor. "The magic of Ravensbarrow is ancient and dark. We heard you."

"You're still throwing a tantrum over the possibility of magic," Tienna said, "but you're ignoring the fact that now we have to try to find a hamster in a haystack! I say we start smashing!"

"Do we, though?" I asked. Tienna rolled her eyes. She really REALLY wanted to go murder all those hamsters. "Won't he be at the great ceremony?"

Tienna glared at me. "I hate to sound like Shane, but how do we KNOW that, Teddy?"

Wonderful. Wrong line, Teddy. Even with this group of oddly inclusive weirdos, you're still in a different play.

> Actually...
>
> Teddy is correct.

> It is through the touch of Scrabbles that the great ceremony will be carried out. He will be there.

Wait a minute... Oh my gosh, I hit my line!

"Then we stick to the plan," Tienna said. "Find milk, get the sprayer, and hose 'em all down. Even if we don't get Scrabbles, we'll get most of them!"

Frekizor bowed. "I thank you from the bottom of my heart, Tienna. You are all braver souls than I. True hamsters.

I wish that I could help, but I must stay here and defend my kindies. They, at the very least, will not be present at this great ceremony."

The bell rang. I jumped.

Shane sighed. "Well, at least we know there's milk at lunchtime."

As everyone left, I hesitated. "Hey, Mr. Frekizor. Why milk?" This was the first time in my life that I'd known anyone else who hated milk as much as I do, even if they were a hamster.

Frekizor wrinkled his nose. "I do not know, young Teddy, and I hope I never have to find out."

18

The Milk Heist

Easy to find? Yes.

Easy to get at? No.

"I knew it . . ." Tienna said. She glared at a boy who was wandering around the common area. "I KNEW it would be his fault somehow."

"No you didn't." Shane rolled his eyes and cleaned his glasses. "You just love to hate him."

"That's because he's so easy to hate!" Tienna snarled, still glaring at the boy. "With his poofy fletching hair, and white fletching teeth, and stupid smarmy fletching smile."

"And his cute fletching eyes?" Shane said, leaning in and batting his eyelashes.

Fletcher Cartright (hamsterfied) was wandering the cafeteria with a backpack full of pop and offering to exchange it for milk that kids had brought from home.

He'd then bring it to the cafeteria attendant (also hamsterfied) who would (at arm's length, just like I would have) dump it down the sink. Flats of the stuff sat in the kitchen. The attendant was disposing of those, too, bit by bit.

"And of course," Tienna muttered, "everyone wants to do what he says, even though he's awful. He'd have been happy to help Scrabbles if he'd been asked."

I watched as a kid pointed out the hamster in Fletcher's shirt pocket. Fletcher picked a hamster up off the floor and handed it to the kid. I wondered how many other students had been hamsterfied because they'd wanted to be one of the cool kids . . .

The Spinnaker thing's "cupcakes" hadn't fooled me earlier, but if someone like Fletcher had called me into the hallway? I'd have followed him to seem normal. Maybe everyone else was trying to do that, too?

Tangent, Teddy!

Yeah. Let's not think too hard about that.

"What are we gonna do?" Duggy asked.

"We're gonna hit Fletcher with a chair." Tienna glared at Fletcher.

Shane rolled his eyes. "And what will that do for us?"

Tienna grinned. "It'll make me feel better before the hamsters get me!"

"We need to do more than that!" Duggy said. "We need that milk, and it's all goin' down the sink!"

Milk. Sloshing and splashing all frothy down the sink. I shuddered.

"We need to distract them," Shane said.

Milk, swirling, gurgling, and smelling like old cow. My stomach churned.

"Yeah, but how?" Duggy asked. "Just standing up and shouting won't do anything. Half of them are hamsterfied!"

Mucky, yucky milk.

"Like I said," Tienna said, "I could hit Fletcher with a chair. That'd be distracting."

Probably moldy milk. Blech.

"Only for the normal kids," Shane said. "And you'll get marched to the office real quick. What do you think, Teddy?"

Miiiiiiiiiiilk. Ick.

"Teddy? Teddy?!"

Milk. Blech.

Tienna punched me in the arm. "TEDDY!"

"OW!"

"Teddy, we're trying to come up with a plan here and you're off in la-la land!"

Half the time I forget my lines and half the time I miss my cue entirely. Good one, Teddy.

I rubbed my arm. "I'm sorry, guys. It's just . . . all that milk really makes me need to puke."

Duggy perked up. "Remember that time Cooper Wiggins got food poisoning and puked everywhere?! Everyone was running and screaming and pointing and then the principal slipped in it?!"

Shane nodded. "Yeah, everyone gets distracted by someone getting pukey sick."

I started to bite my nails. I shook my head and shut my mouth tight.

"Think about it, Teddy!" Duggy bounced in his seat. "It's perfect!"

"Not only will everyone be distracted," Shane said, "but Monsieur Lambert will come to clean up the puke!

He'll be distracted, too! Duggy could run and grab the backpack sprayer!"

Tienna leaned in. "He's so good at acting hamster-fied no one will suspect a thing!"

Shane whipped out his sketchbook and doodled a quick diagram. "Duggy can grab the sprayer, and Tienna can heist the milk. I'll stay here to watch your back. It's perfect!"

The roller-coaster feeling in my stomach got stronger, and it was joined by the shame and guilt gremlins. This plan was perfect! I could save the day! But . . .

"It makes sense," I said. "It's just . . . I can't . . ." I was letting my friends down. I was the worst.

"Sometimes you've gotta drink the milk, buddy!" Tienna put her hand on my shoulder and started chanting quietly, "Drink the milk. Drink the milk."

Wait . . . These kids weren't my friends. Having friends wasn't this easy. Was it?

"Drink the milk! Drink the milk!" Shane started chanting, too.

I had friends?! Like, real friends?!

"Drink the milk! Drink the milk!" Duggy's hamster puppet joined in the chant.

Oh my gosh, we WERE friends. They'd learned more about how much of a freak I was than anyone other than my parents and Mr. Fuzzikins, but they were still sticking by me.

I was letting my friends down . . .

SHAME.

A speaker in the ceiling crackled to life. **"This is a special announcement."** The voice was deep and buttery with a squeaky echo. **"Today there will be an assembly in the gym soon after lunch. It is the day of the great ceremony."** Several students (hamster-fied) cheered. **"THE GREAT CEREMONY! All will attend. All. Will. Attend."**

I wept.

Tienna put an arm around me. "Heeey. Hey, Teddy, it's okay."

I sniffled.

"We know that milk's something you can't handle," Tienna said. "There's nothin' to be sorry about."

I wiped a tear away. "Really?" I sniffled some more.

"Really," Tienna said. "Even if there were something to be sorry for, we'd forgive you. And that's why I'm really REALLY hoping that you'll forgive me."

"For what?" I asked.

"For this."

SPLASH!

19

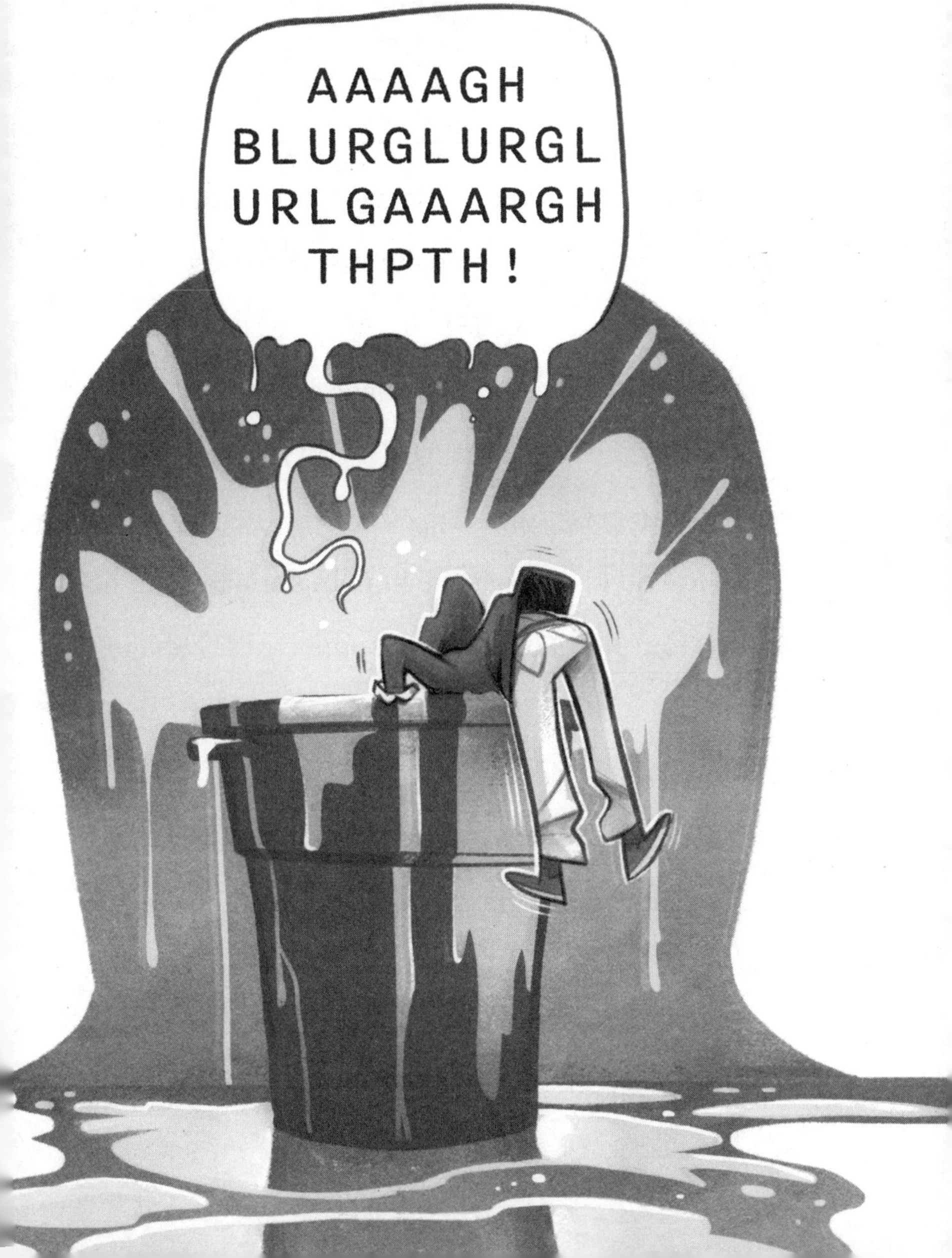

I had a lizard-brain moment.

I don't remember many details about what happened next. When things came back into focus I was leaning over a trash can that was clear across the common area from where I started. Someone patted me on the back. It was Shane. He had a carton of milk in his hand and was watching the crowd of kids who had gathered around us.

"How you doin', Teddy?" Shane asked.

"BLUUUUUURGHLURGLURGLURGL!" I replied. Not great, Shane.

"Did you know that the human stomach can hold almost four liters of liquid in some cases?" Shane asked.

"BLARGARGLARGLARGL!" I replied. I was unaware of this amazing fact, Shane.

"I think you may be a special case, though, Teddy," Shane said.

"HRUUNGATPPPHHTTTTHHHBPTBPT?" I replied. Really, Shane?

"Yeah," Shane said. "That's gotta be way more than four liters!"

"FLAAAAAARGLARGLARGLARGL!" I agreed. Fascinating, Shane.

He was right, though. I had no idea where this was all coming from. My breakfast that morning had been toast. Toast and only toast!

I leaned against the rim of the garbage can. From the crowd around me, I could hear kids talking . . . *Is that a new kid? Eeeeeeew! Gross! What's his name? Teddy. Like a teddy bear? More like a pukey bear! Eeeeeew! Pukey Bear!*

Wonderful. The same nickname as at my old school. I could kiss blending in goodbye. I was gonna be an outcast. The pukey kid. Good ol' "Pukey Bear Tyler-Meier." I could look forward to never fitting in and being the butt of every easy joke for the rest . . .

of . . .

my . . .

LIFE!

I slumped against the garbage can. "I wann' go hommm," I muttered. Words are hard after throwing up. Dad calls it post-puke fatigue. Ugh.

There was a hush from the crowd of kids, and I heard scattering footsteps. An adult had arrived. I knew better than to turn my head from the garbage can, though. There's always that last little bit of . . .

"BLAAAAAAAARGHLTHPBPTBPTBPT!"

Yup. Every time.

"Oh *mon DIEU!*" I recognized Monsieur Lambert's voice. "Teddy! What happened?!"

"*Oui!* I can see that!" Monsieur Lambert surveyed the pukey aftermath. "This . . . this ALL came from you? How?!"

"Mihllllk," I said.

"*LAIT?!* Milk?! What?!"

"I don' like m'lk," I said.

"THEN WHY DID YOU DRINK IT?!" Monsieur Lambert began scattering sawdust. He scattered a LOT of sawdust.

"Ah diddunn drnk itt!" Drink milk? Ick.

"Did you get any *in* the garbage can?!" Monsieur Lambert lifted me up from under my arms. I hung there like a wet cat.

"I thnk zo . . ."

"Why'z my hoodee wett?"

"I'm pretty sure it's ALL on your hoodie," Monsieur Lambert said, flicking one of his hands. I heard a splattering noise. Ew. I heard snickering and gasps from the kids.

"Guys!" Tienna sidled up to Shane. She had two backpacks, one in each hand, stuffed with milk. "We're good! Let's go!"

Tienna! The milk-splasher!

NNNNNO!

Ah'm not goin' anywhere wiv YOU!

"Oh come on, Teddy," Tienna said, rolling her eyes.

"Teddy!" Monsieur Lambert struggled to hold me upright. "Keep calm!"

"She splasht me!" I jammed my head back in the garbage can. "She knew I get pyoowkee and she SPLASHT me anyways!"

Monsieur Lambert looked at Tienna with a heavy sigh. "Oh, Tienna . . . And things were going so well today."

Tienna blushed and looked away. "Teddy, we'll help you get cleaned up. Come on."

"NNNNNNO!" I shouted, my voice echoing in the garbage can.

"I will help Teddy!" Monsieur Lambert said.

"But . . ." Tienna said.

"I know Monsieur Quint, our fair principal, is very eager to hear about your behavior these days, Tienna!" Monsieur Lambert handed me a towel. I was gonna need a bigger towel.

"Teddy, we'll wait here for you," Shane said.

"Don' bother!" I said, wiping my face with the far-too-small rag.

"Come with me, Teddy," Monsieur Lambert said. "Let's get you some new clothes."

Heart-to-Heart

I sipped at a cup of water. Monsieur Lambert had stuffed my hoodie (soaked) and shirt (also soaked, somehow) into a garbage bag. He'd found me a T-shirt to wear and was rooting through the lost and found in search of another hoodie. The carton of milk that traitorous Tienna had given me sat on the floor beside me.

"I don't see why you want to keep that milk, Teddy. It's warm. Also, it makes you throw up. A lot. A freakish amount, Teddy!" Monsieur Lambert tossed a random lost sock over his shoulder.

"I know," I said, "I'm sorry about that . . . But Tienna was the one who splashed me!"

"Yes, but why?" Monsieur Lambert said. "Tienna is many things, but she's never NEEDLESSLY cruel."

"Well . . . Remember the hamsters?"

"She splashed you with milk because of the hamsters?" Monsieur Lambert laughed.

"Because of the hamsters," I said, nodding.

"Hamsters indeed! It is quite the story you and your new friends have come up with," he said. "And I must thank you for that."

"Thank me?" I said. "Why?"

"I was worried about those three," Monsieur Lambert said. "Tienna and Shane are friends, but they can bring out the worst in each other." Boy, could they ever. I'd never trust Tienna again, that's for sure.

Monsieur Lambert pulled out a hoodie with cat ears. Wonderful. I'd be Pukey Cat instead of Pukey Bear.

"And Duggy?" Monsieur Lambert put the cat-eared hoodie back. Phew. "Duggy was alone. Playing cards with an old janitor at lunchtime cannot replace a friend. And now they seem to have come together. Because you are their friend. So thank you!"

"I'm NOT their friend!" I said. I brought my knees closer to my chin and sipped my cup of water. "Thanks to Tienna, now I'll never fit in. Now everyone knows that I'm a freak!"

What?

A freak?

Because you threw up?

"Even you said it was a 'freakish' amount! And it was! Because I AM a freak."

"No, Teddy . . ." Monsieur Lambert furrowed his eyebrows in concern. "You're not."

"Yes I AM!" I looked Monsieur Lambert in the eyes. "I've just gotten really good at hiding it."

Monsieur Lambert sighed. "I apologize, Teddy. 'Freakish' was a poor choice of words." He went back to sifting through the lost and found. "I wouldn't worry, though. By the end of next week, I am willing to bet that no one will even remember what happened."

"That's not true. Kids remember. A thing like throwing up an ocean out of an empty stomach is never, EVER forgotten. I'll be the odd one out forever. Being lonely is one thing, but now I'll be a target! They already gave me a nickname. Pukey Bear. Nicknames NEVER die."

"If this is true, Teddy, why do you WANT to be part of this group?"

"It . . . It feels safe. It feels safe to fit in. And if you're not part of the group, you're alone. You said it yourself about Duggy!"

"Fair enough." Monsieur Lambert tossed clothes left and right. "I agree, it can feel safe. And sometimes it IS safe. But..."

"But that's not all!" I cut in. "If you're not part of the group, then you're NOT part of the group. You're an easy target. Pretty soon you're the kid everyone can look down on and make fun of, and nothing will ever change it even though you try. You suffer completely alone with everyone laughing at you until you just crawl into a locker and cry yourself to DEATH." I didn't care what play I was in anymore. "I've seen it happen!"

Monsieur Lambert scratched his chin. He looked worried. "Teddy, I don't think that—"

"And don't tell me it's not true!" I hugged my knees closer and looked at the ground. "Think about Duggy! Think about Heather! EVERYONE knows her as Hamster-Girl. The first kid who talked to me in my class told me to stay away from her! That's gonna be me! Stay away from Pukey Bear Teddy, everybody!"

"You obviously think deep thoughts about this kind of thing, Teddy . . . So, if you're so worried about fitting in, why would you spend your time with these kids who don't fit in at all? I watched the four of you today. You were inseparable. What happened?"

"They . . . They just wouldn't leave me behind, I guess. No matter what happened, they wouldn't leave me behind."

"You make that sound like a good thing, Teddy." Monsieur Lambert was near the bottom of the lost and found.

"It was . . . It is."

"Would this larger group you want to be a part of leave you behind?"

"Well . . . yeah."

"Well then, I suppose you need to make a choice, Teddy. I can't tell you who to be friends with, but if Duggy, Tienna, and Shane refused to leave you behind, then here's your chance to do the same for them."

I looked off to the side. Geez, this was embarrassing. Why was this embarrassing?! Monsieur Lambert continued to rummage.

"Aha!" he said. He pulled out a gigantic dark purple, checkered flannel hoodie.

Voilà! You'll grow into it, I'm sure!

I grinned. He was a good guy. "Thanks, Monsieur Lambert." I tucked the carton of milk into the gigantic front pocket of the hoodie. I could've worn the pocket instead and it still would have been big on me. "I'm okay now. I should get back to the others."

"You are welcome, Teddy." Monsieur Lambert grinned back. "You mean back to your friends?"

I jammed my hands in the massive pocket of my new hoodie. "Duggy and Shane are okay, I guess."

Monsieur Lambert leaned down and patted me on the shoulder. "Go have lunch with your friends, Teddy."

I began to walk away.

"After all, you wouldn't want to miss the great ceremony **ceremony**," Monsieur Lambert said.

No . . . Something that LOOKED like Monsieur Lambert said that. His voice had changed. I recognized the cold, breathy echo underneath it.

Scrabbles.

21
The Fuzzy Menace

Little fuzzy figures with beady eyes popped up from the lost and found and twitched their whiskers. I didn't see Scrabbles, but I heard his voice from the entire hamster horde. They didn't bother speaking through Monsieur Lambert. A chorus dark and hamstery.

I froze up. I froze up like I always do. Although maybe this time I was allowed to freeze up. I was talking to a hamster that had somehow managed to take over most of my new school with a legion of hammy minions for unknown, guaranteed-to-be-awful reasons. Anyone would have frozen up.

I mean, for all we knew, the hamsters were doing all this so that they could eat everyone.

Oh my gosh, were they gonna eat me?!

THEY WERE TOTALLY GONNA EAT ME!

AGH!

"I just want to talk, Teddy," Scrabbles said. "I wanted to thank you."

WHAT?!

"This morning you were very kind to Heather," Scrabbles said. "It had been quite some time since anyone had spoken to her in a nice way."

"I . . . Um . . ." THIS WAS NOT THE PLAY I'D REHEARSED FOR! Oh my gosh, what HAD I said to Heather this morning? Something like "It was nice to meet you."

"I think we can be friends, Teddy. We are very similar, you and I."

"We are?" I said. I found a wall and put my back to it.

"I have been watching you all day, Teddy, and you remind me very much of my children." The chorus of hamsters squeaked happily as Scrabbles spoke. "You are small and easily frightened." The hamster chorus sniffed at the air. "Yes, even now you smell of fear. You live in a world where to be noticed, to stand out, is to be eaten alive. But, like we the honorable hamsters, you press on. You care for your friends, as we care for Heather."

Praise be to Heather, provider of apples!
Even your name is of fine hamstery origin.

"I... what?" I asked.

"Have you not heard of the teddy bear hamster?"

My full name is Theodore. It's definitely not called a "Theodore hamster." I wasn't about to correct Scrabbles, though.

"I... uh... I am indeed named after the teddy bear hamster." I got the feeling that I was swimming in the ocean talking to a shark. Maybe walking through the forest talking to a cougar? Nah, it was worse than that. I was talking to a bomb and everything I said was changing the time left on the countdown. I was talking to a shark cougar bomb and I had no idea when it was gonna go off.

A shark cougar bomb? Really, Teddy?

You know what? You be quiet! Now is not the time for this!

"Fine and hamstery," the chorus squeaked, bobbing from side to side, twitching

Shush!

their whiskers. **"I want to be friends, Teddy. Can we be friends?"**

"Um ... Sure?" I said. Maybe if I kept Scrabbles talking, the others would come looking for me. Maybe I could splash Scrabbles with milk! No ... I knew what would happen. I'd open the milk and I'd puke everywhere and then I'd be standing in the hallway covered in puke and all the hamsters would laugh at me and then ... they'd ... EAT! ME!

"And now that we're friends, Teddy," Scrabbles said, **"I wish to offer a deal."**

Uh-oh.

"You and your friends are up to something. You have been working to stop the great ceremony."

Uh-oh.

"I would expect nothing less, Teddy. You and your friends are brave and tenacious."

Okay ...

"And that is why they would make excellent friends for Heather. I wish to offer a compromise."

22

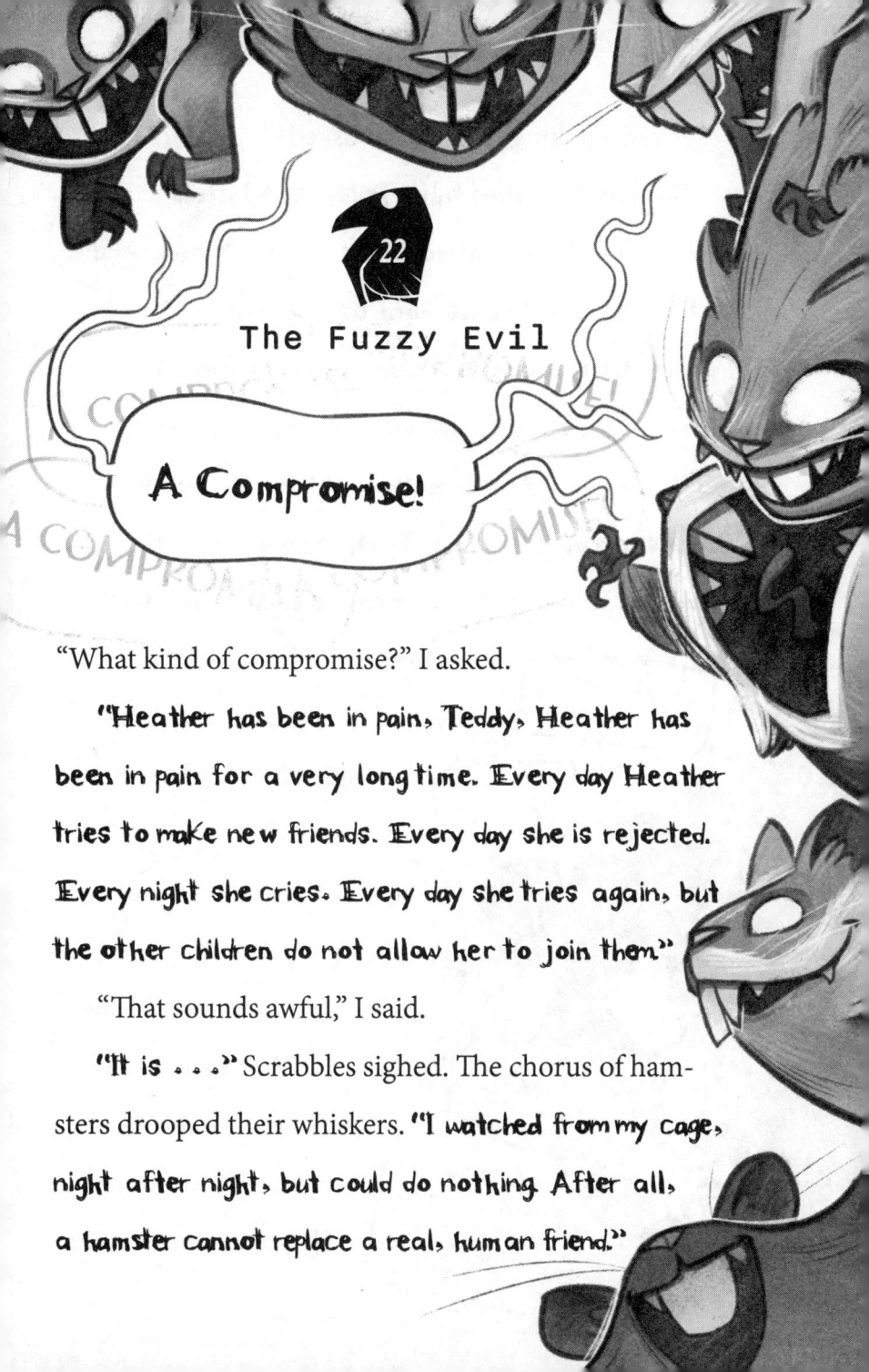

The Fuzzy Evil

A Compromise!

"What kind of compromise?" I asked.

"Heather has been in pain, Teddy. Heather has been in pain for a very long time. Every day Heather tries to make new friends. Every day she is rejected. Every night she cries. Every day she tries again, but the other children do not allow her to join them."

"That sounds awful," I said.

"It is . . ." Scrabbles sighed. The chorus of hamsters drooped their whiskers. "I watched from my cage, night after night, but could do nothing. After all, a hamster cannot replace a real, human friend."

"Even a talking hamster?" I asked.

"I couldn't always talk, Teddy. But I could always feel. I could always feel Heather's pain. And so I wished. I wished as hard as any hamster could. I wished that I could somehow be a real friend to Heather... That I could somehow be a person at her school... And something in the rainy woods of Ravensbarrow heard me, Teddy. Something in the rainy woods of Ravensbarrow helped me to become what I am now."

> Thing in the woods?!

> Helped?!

> What have these hamsters become?!

Frekizor had said the magic of Ravensbarrow was dark and ancient. What kind of awful place had my parents forced me to move to?!

"And now here we are, Teddy, and we wish to fix things. We wish to make sure that all children are accepted into the group. We wish to be everyone's friends."

Friends? That actually didn't sound too bad. I mean, Scrabbles was going about it the wrong way, but maybe he was trying to do the right thing.

"With us in charge, you won't have to be afraid anymore. You won't have to worry about hiding who you really are just so that the crowd won't pick you apart. You will be SAFE with us, Teddy. Everyone will have a place in this new school. All will be accepted. None will be excluded."

"And you're not gonna hamsterfy us?"

"I really wish you would call it something else," Scrabbles said. The hamster chorus pouted.

"Sorry," I said. "So, we won't be forced to have hamsters?"

"Of course not," Scrabbles said. "You do not need hamsters. Most children don't. Most children are very nice."

"But all the other kids will?" I asked.

"Some but not all. Don't worry. I have a plan."

"Okay ... This ... does sound really nice ..." All would be accepted? None would be excluded? No one ... well, almost no one would be hamsterfied? It DID sound nice. Maybe I wouldn't have to blend in anymore. Maybe I wouldn't have to worry ...

"Then we will all join Heather in friendship!"

"I'd love to, but ..." Something still didn't seem right. "But HOW are you going to do this?" I asked. "I know that you can control people with your hamsters, but they're not really people anymore. They're like zombies."

"You misunderstand, Teddy. Once my children have touched someone, I can whisper in their minds. Once I can whisper to them, I can calm them. They are not zombies, they are merely very ..." The Monsieur Lambert puppet drooled a little bit. **"Very sedate. Very suggestible. Easily led. Puppets. Once we are finished today, most will be released from my control."**

"Most? Some kids keep their hamsters? Why?"

"For the great ceremony, Teddy."

"What... What happens during the great ceremony?"

"We will gather everyone in the gymnasium..."

"Okay..."

"Those rotten children who refused to be Heather's friends, even though she BEGGED, will be brought to the front..."

Uh oh.

"And then we're going to hollow out their skulls, eat their brains, and make nests in their heads."

"Wait..."

"What...?"

Our master hamster plan, Teddy, is to . . .
Hollow out their skulls.
BURP
Eat their brains.
And make nests in their heads.
WHAT?!

"**Well, we need to gain their memories somehow, silly.**" Scrabbles chuckled.

Brain-eating hamsters...

"**There, in those warm, hollow nests, we will take their place and be Heather's new friends.**" The hamster chorus all rubbed their paws together and grinned. "**We will be real boys and girls.**"

"But that doesn't make any sense!" I blurted out.

"**It makes perfect sense if you're a hamster.**"

Scrabbles was an evil little monster.

"That won't work!" I shouted. This fuzzy goblin wasn't going to solve any problems. He was just going to kill a bunch of people! "It's impossible! People can't live without their brains!"

"**Impossible?**" Scrabbles chuckled. "**You're arguing with a hamster who is talking to you through the hypnotized body of a Quebecois custodian.**"

The Monsieur Lambert puppet and his hamster chorus crept forward and closed in on me. The voice of Scrabbles had an edge to it, now.

"The magic of Ravensbarrow is dark and ancient, Teddy," Scrabbles hissed. "And though I don't fully understand it, I assure you, it IS possible. What we do, we do in the name of Heather, and it MUST be done."

"Frekizor told me that Heather was a good person! Would Heather want you to eat everyone's brains?!"

"Of course not! Heather is far too gentle and kind. But when she wakes up, what happened here today will all be a bad dream and those who once hurt her will be her friends. She will have many friends. WE will be Heather's friends."

"But . . . But . . ." I made myself as small as possible against the brick wall behind me. What could I say? What could I do?! DO SOMETHING, TEDDY!

"And if anyone does NOT want to be Heather's friend . . . I can think of more than a few hamsters who would." The hamster horde chittered happily, flashing their sharp little teeth.

"So everyone at the school will be friends with Heather . . . or you'll eat their brains?"

"But not you, Teddy!" Scrabbles chuckled. **"We're friends already."** The Monsieur Lambert puppet bent down, bringing its face inches from mine.

Aren't we?

Aren't we?

Aren't we?

Aren't we?

"Right," I said. Oh my gosh, I had to get out. I had to run. I couldn't stay here. SAY SOMETHING, TEDDY!

"May . . . May I go tell Tienna, Duggy, and Shane the good news?" I asked. "Tell them that we're all friends now?"

"Of course, Teddy!" The hamsters melted away, scurrying about. The Monsieur Lambert puppet stood up and walked away. "We'll see you at the great ceremony."

A thousand squeaky little voices chuckled from all around me, their voices fading as they scuttled into the walls, ceiling, and floor.

"We'll save you front-row seats."

Desperate Times

Oh my gosh. They were brain-eating hamsters. Brain- eating hamsters. BRAIN! EATING! HAMSTERS! Evil scruffy demonic rodents! Pint-sized monstrous murderous quasi-gerbils that participated in sorcery!

I nearly ran into Duggy as he hurried back to Tienna and Shane. He had a garbage bag slung over his shoulder stuffed with something I hoped was the backpack sprayer. It dripped water.

"Duggy!" I said, hyperventilating. "Duggy, oh my gosh! Duggy, they..."

Wait a minute. Duggy looked different. No, he

wasn't hamsterfied (I mean, that would've been obvious). He had a look on his face that I knew well. Duggy was anxious.

Duggy was really really REALLY anxious.

"Duggy, what's wrong?"

He gave his head a little shake and bit his lower lip. "I . . ." Duggy heaved the garbage bag to his other shoulder. "I had a close call with some hamsters. I barely got away. I'm okay now."

That would have freaked me out, too. "Okay," I said. "Okay okay okay." I hurried toward the common area and motioned for Duggy to follow. "We've gotta get back to the others. I've got something to tell everyone."

Tienna and Shane had found a bench just out of sight of the rest of the common area. Tienna looked angry. Shane was glaring at her.

Shane poked Tienna in the shoulder as Duggy and I hurried up to them. "Tell him!" Shane said.

Tienna gritted her teeth and then glared at me as I slid onto the seat beside her.

"What?! They're gonna eat us?!" Tienna gasped. "That's ridiculous! I mean, how many kids could they even eat? Wait, maybe we can just feed them Fletcher."

"They're not gonna eat our meaty bits, they're gonna eat our BRAINS!" I whisper-shouted. "They think they can eat memories and take over everyone's bodies with hamster magic so that Heather will have human friends! Hungry-hungry-hamsters would have made some weird kind of sense! Carnivorous hamster necromancers don't make any sense at all! THIS IS SO MUCH WORSE!"

There was stunned silence.

A tear rolled down Duggy's cheek. "You guys, we can't do this! We have to run away!"

Tienna looked Duggy in the eye. "Duggy, do you remember what I said about the snake bite?" He nodded. "Those hamsters are nothing compared to me. I'll twist your skin clean off. Stop freaking out. We're all scared!" Tienna took a deep breath.

Wait. Did Tienna say she was sorry? I couldn't imagine Tienna apologizing for anything. I looked at her. "Did you just say you were sorry?"

"Yes, she DID say she was sorry, Teddy." Shane poked Tienna in the ribs. "And WHY are we sorry?"

Tienna crossed her arms and looked up at the ceiling. "Because we could have figured out a different distraction."

"Aaaaaaaaaaand?" Shane looked at her over his glasses.

Tienna glared at Shane. "Look, Shane, milk's hard for Teddy and apologizing is hard for me, okay? And you were in on it, too! Where's your apology?!"

Shane shrugged and turned to me. "Sorry, Teddy. I didn't know it would be that bad. It won't happen again."

Maybe Monsieur Lambert was right. "It's . . . Well . . . I guess can see why you did it," I said.

Tienna rolled her eyes. "Of course apologizing is easy for you, Shane. Whatever. I'm forgiven. Let's move on. These hamsters need a bath!"

"Guys!" Duggy raised his hand and leaned in. "I had to get the sprayer out of the boiler room."

"The basement?" Tienna asked. "Why?"

Yeah. The sprayer wasn't in the basement . . .

"I dunno," Duggy said. "That's just where it was, okay?! When I was down there I saw some windows. They're hidden by plants on the outside. They're not guarded! We could squeeze out and sneak away!"

No," Tienna said. "We can't let the hamsters get away with this."

"I agree," Shane said.

"I know taking on the hamsters is the right thing to

do," Duggy whined. "It's just . . . We're kids!"

I agreed with Duggy, honestly. I wanted to run away, too. We were way out of our depth. The hamsters were gonna catch us and eat our brains! How would they even get at our brains? They were hamsters! Did they have a cute little bone saw or something? Were they just gonna gnaw their way through?

I bit at my fingernail. Tienna grabbed my hand and yanked.

"Don't do that, Teddy. It's gross."

But I knew that Tienna and Shane were right, and I knew that they were gonna try it with or without me. What had Monsieur Lambert said? Don't leave them behind . . .

I took a deep breath. Still nervous, but . . . "I say we try the plan."

Operation Hamster Bath

"This is the last carton," Tienna whispered. "Don't you dare throw up, Teddy!" I heard milk sloshing into the backpack sprayer. I'd had to move to the far end of the stage and turn my back to everyone.

I gagged. "There's nothin' left to throw up."

"Yeah, I heard it was spectacular!" Tienna grinned. "I was too busy heisting milk to watch!"

"There was so much of it!" Shane said.

"You know that throwing up hurts, right?" I said, glaring at Tienna over my shoulder. "It's not FUN, guys!"

"Buuuut you forgaaaaave meeeee," Tienna sang.

Just on the other side of the heavy stage curtain was

the gym. From the sound of things, it was packed. Everyone had arrived for the great ceremony. The sprayer was in the middle of the stage, sitting in a puddle of water that Tienna had dumped out. Duggy stood at the rope to open the curtain. He looked anxious.

The gym went silent.

"Welcome, boys and girls," said a deep, buttery voice with a telltale hamster echo. Mr. Quint I supposed.

We all looked at each other.

"Today is the day of the great ceremony," Mr. Quint continued. "Or, as some people call it, the great feast."

Tienna nodded at Duggy.

"Today we gather in friendship." Mr. Quint chuckled.

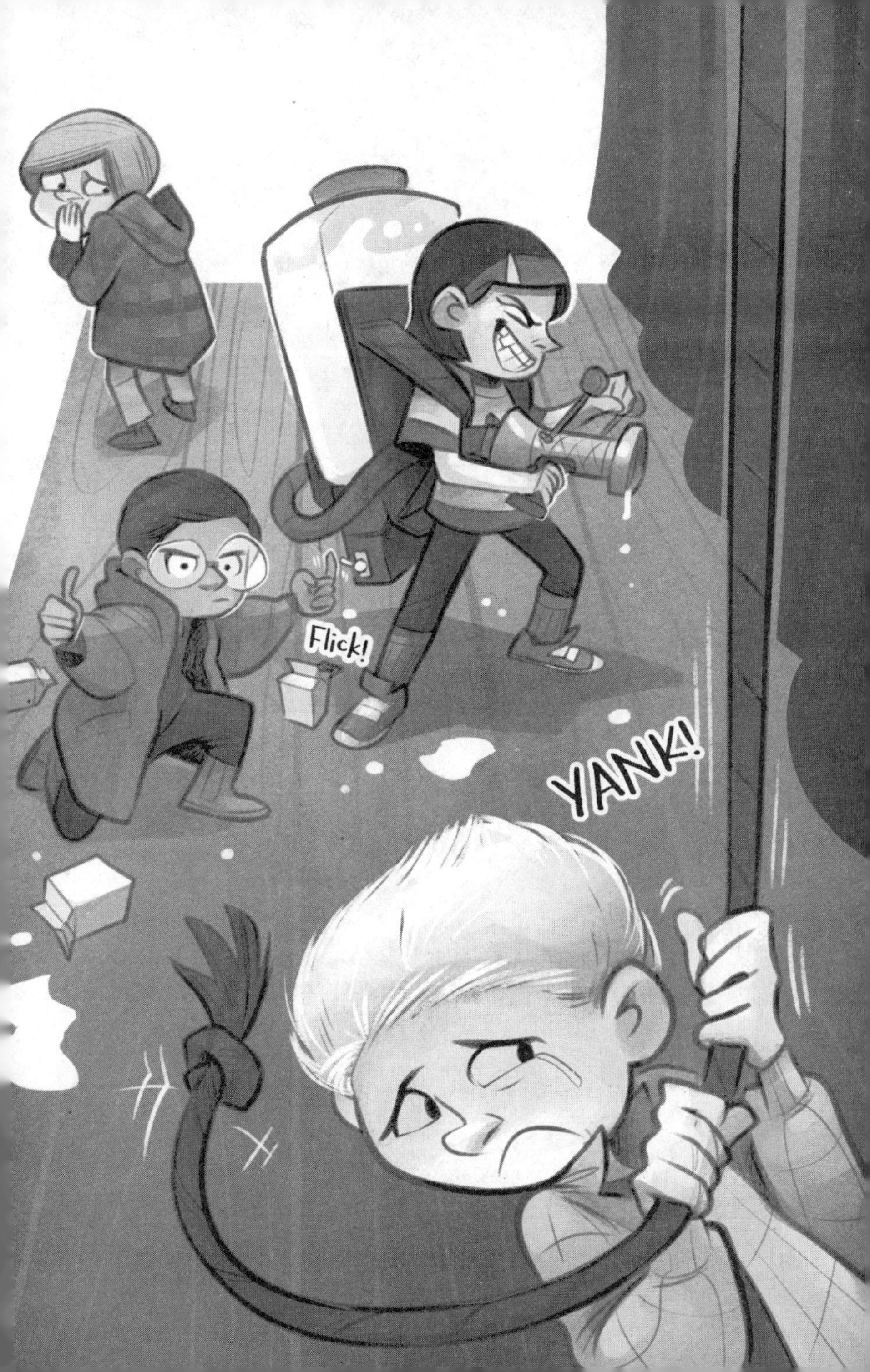
Flick!
YANK!

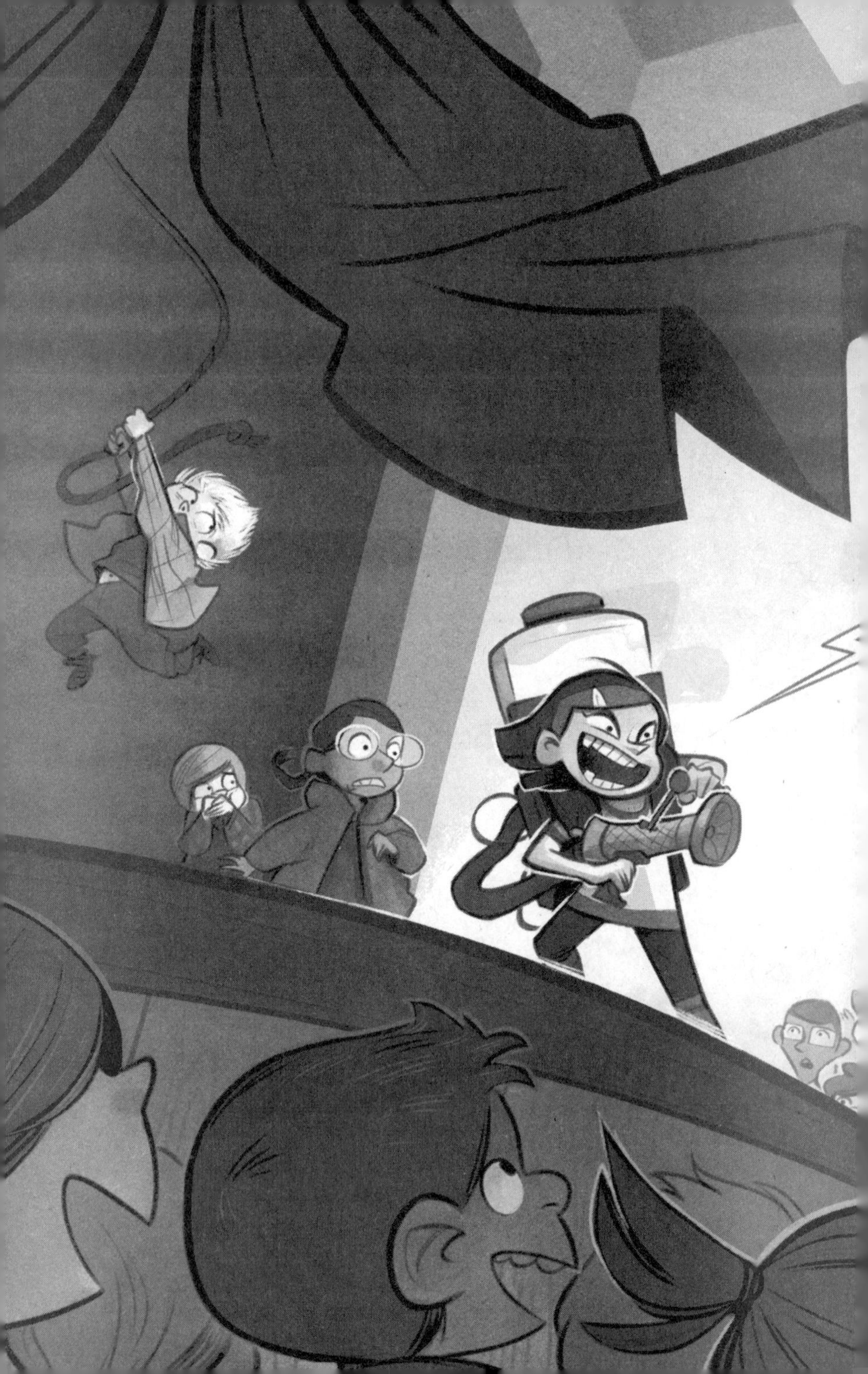

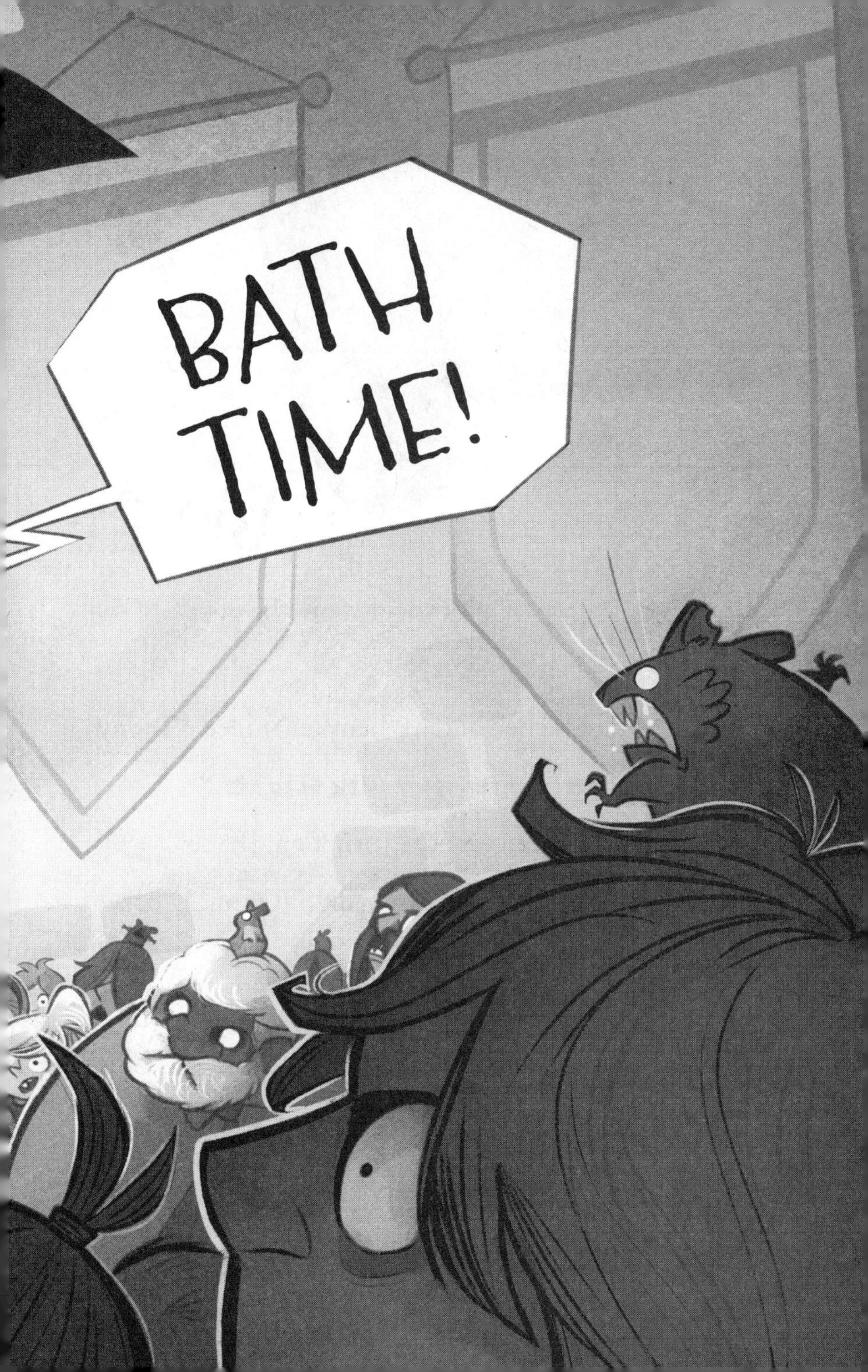
BATH TIME!

Bloop.

A single drop of milk trickled out the nozzle of the sprayer.

Mr. Quint turned and his hamster smiled. **"Today we ALL gather in friendship with Heather."**

"Shane!" Tienna yelled. "Turn it on, Shane!"

Shane flicked the switch madly. "It *is* on!" Flick flick flick!

"Guys!" Duggy pointed out at the gym, trembling.

The sound of ten thousand chattering rodent teeth echoed through the gym as a wave of evil hamsters began to sweep forward. Every kid the hamsters rolled over was left with a blank stare as they were hamsterfied. They all laughed (kids AND hamsters!), filling the gym with a horrid atonal song to the rhythm of gnashing hammy fangs.

"Shane, why isn't it working?" Tienna's eyes widened.

"I don't know!" Shane yelled back.

"GUYS!" Duggy pointed.

What was my line again? Oh yeah. "RUN!" I yelled.

25
OHMYGOSH
THEY'REGONNAEATUS!!!

AAAAAAAA

We screeched into the hallway, Tienna sloshing milk from the backpack sprayer. I slipped and bounced off a table. Shane helped me to my feet. The sound of the rodent tide roared behind us and then the fuzzy horde of ravenous hamsters spilled out of the gym doors.

There must have been millions of them!

MILLIONS!

We ran. We tried to find a way out, but all the exits were blocked by the hamsterfied.

"Shane!" Tienna yelled as she ran. "What the heck is wrong with this stupid sprayer, Shane?!"

Shane looked over the sprayer as best he could as we all tried to keep up. Geez, Tienna was fast! "I think it's missing some parts!" he said.

"I think... I saw... parts downstairs!" Duggy panted.

Tienna veered around a corner and then poked her head back so that she could yell at Duggy. "What is WRONG with you?! You didn't think to mention that before?!"

I screeched around the corner and saw Tienna running into Monsieur Lambert's office. We all piled into the room and Tienna slammed the door behind us. There was a sound like angry hail as hamsters hurled themselves against the steel door.

BANGBANGBANGBANG!

Shane jammed a chair under the door handle then started cramming the space under the door with rags as hamsters tried to squeeze through.

"I'm... SORRY!" Duggy panted. He leaned against the door to the basement. "I saw the... the parts downstairs!"

Tienna shoved Duggy aside and hurtled down the stairs toward the boiler room. Shane ran after her. Duggy held the door open.

I looked around the room. Everyone else was doing something to help. Everyone else seemed to KNOW how to help! What could I do to help?! We needed to fix the backpack sprayer. What do you use to fix things? Tools? Yeah! Tools. I went over to the workbench. There were screwdrivers, saws, clamps, and a large puddle of water. Someone had taken something apart recently.

Wait a minute . . . The bench had been clear before. Spotless. Now it was wet and filthy.

Duggy waved at me. "I found the sprayer down under the windows I told you about." I kept staring at the workbench. "Teddy, the parts are downstairs!"

The sprayer had been leaking water all this time. "I think the parts are up here!"

"No!" Duggy insisted. "The parts are downstairs! Come on, Teddy, let's go! That door won't last long!"

It sounded like the hamsters were trying to chew their

way through to us.

There were little slide marks where someone had brushed something into the trash can.

"I . . . I took them downstairs, okay?!" Duggy said, motioning me to come through the door. "I took them downstairs!"

"Why?" I asked. I looked in the trash can. There were jet-black screws and bright red pieces of plastic and machinery.

The sprayer parts were in the trash . . .

"Duggy, there's nothing down here!" Tienna yelled from below.

Duggy reached out, grabbed me by my massive oversized hoodie and threw me down the rickety wooden stairs to the basement.

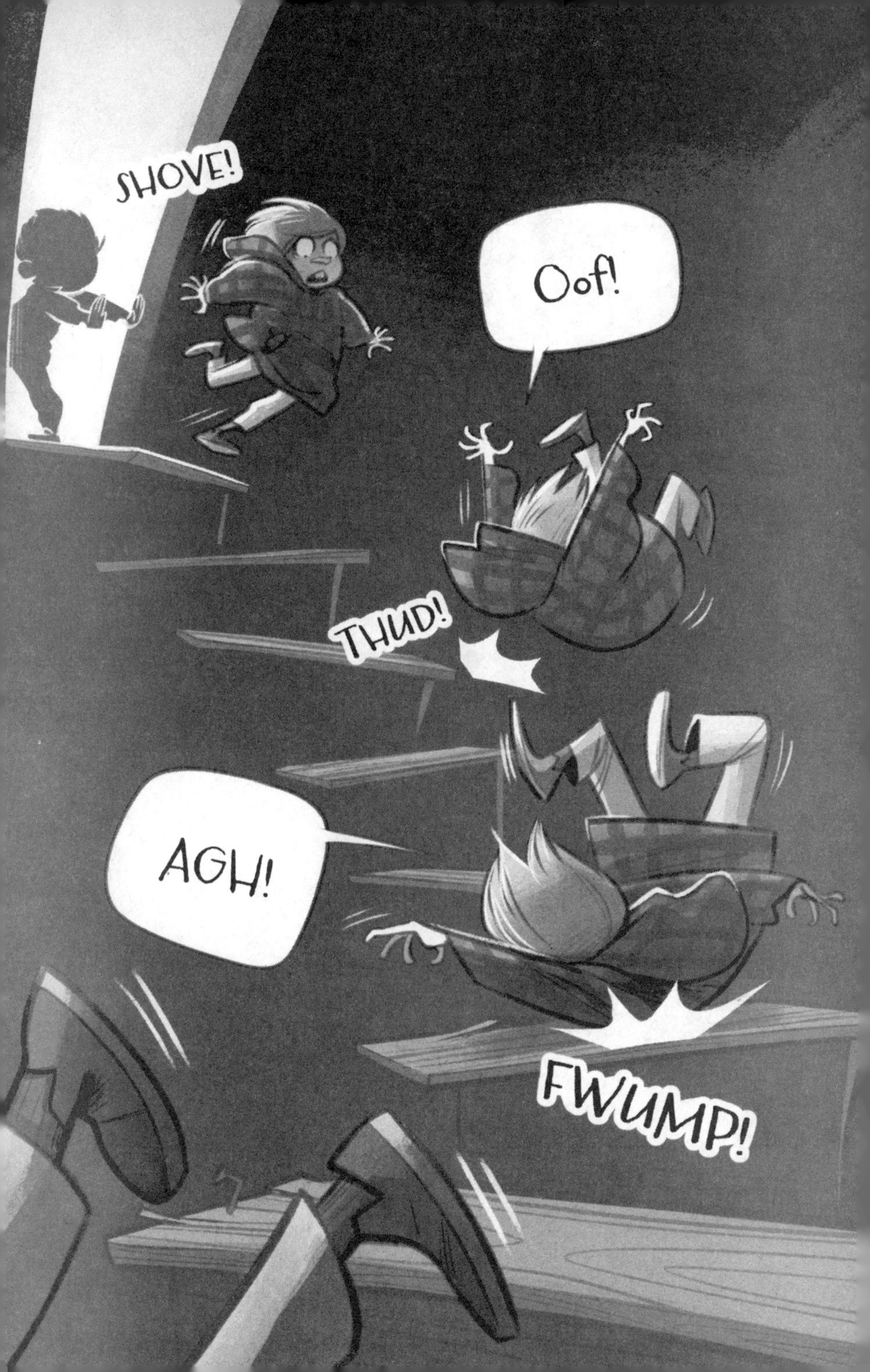
SHOVE!
Oof!
THUD!
AGH!
FWUMP!

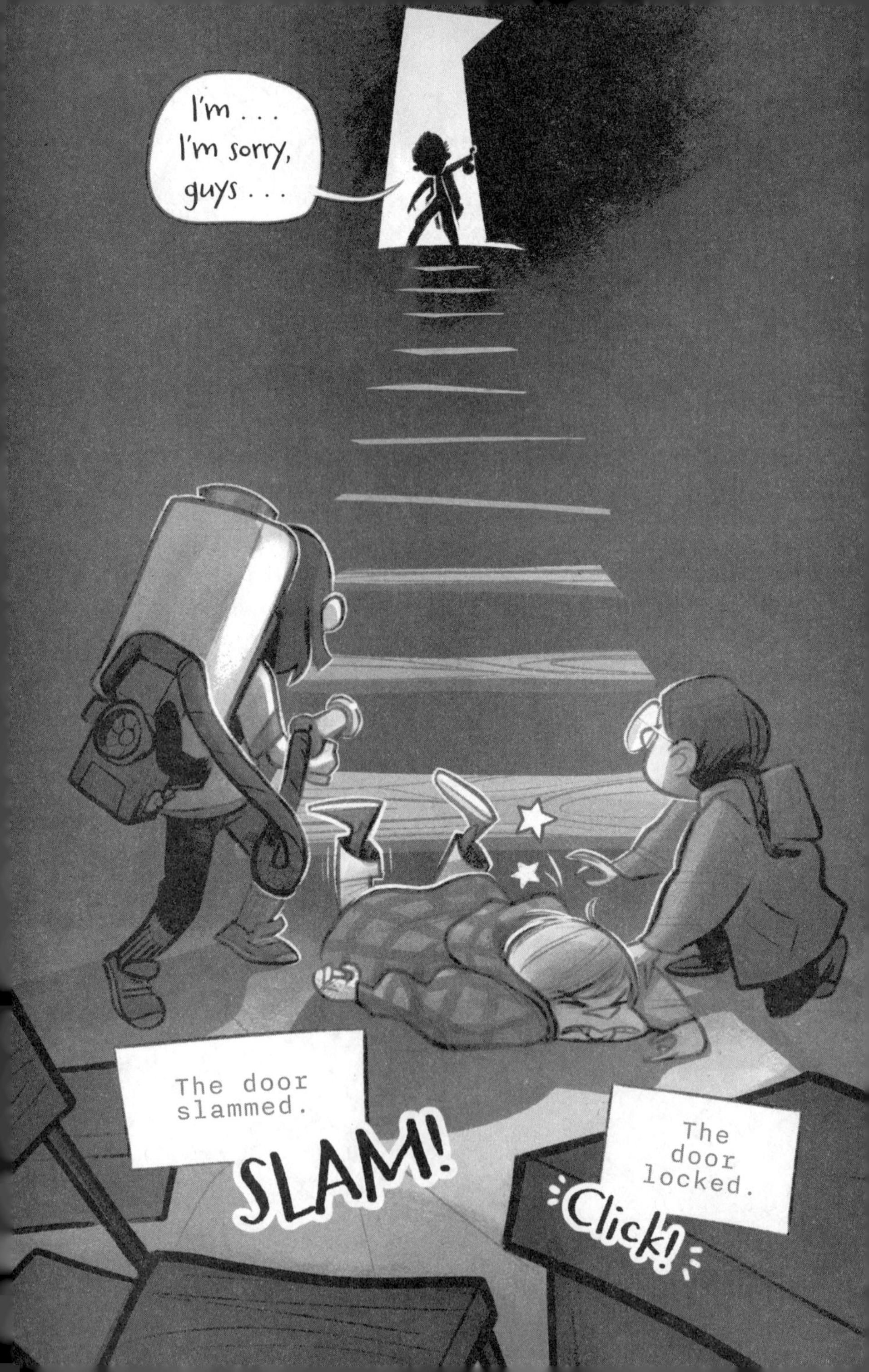
I'm . . .
I'm sorry,
guys . . .
The door slammed.
SLAM!
The door locked.
Click!

26

Scrabbles

Tienna tripped over me as she scrambled to her feet. She turned on the stairwell lights, raced back up the stairs, and pounded on the door. Shane ran up the stairs too, leaving me alone.

I looked around. The windows were tiny little things, barely a few inches high. They were all along the basement, which ran the length of the whole school. Just enough light was let in to make out the tangled storage that was the Ravensbee basement. Chairs, tables, old theater sets, and ancient gym equipment.

This was a place where things were thrown away and forgotten.

"Duggy, you open this door RIGHT NOW or I swear I'll snap your little neck in half!" Tienna's fist left a dent in the door.

I looked around. Maybe something down here could help us.

"Scrabbles... Scrabbles said it won't take long..." Duggy sounded like he was crying. "Scrabbles said that if I broke the sprayer and locked you in the basement he wouldn't eat our brains."

"Scrabbles was LYING, Duggy!" Tienna yelled. "Scrabbles can do whatever Scrabbles wants now because YOU betrayed us!"

I heard skittering... skittering from tangled pipes that led to an old boiler.

"And Scrabbles said that if I didn't do what he wants"—I heard Duggy slide down the door on the other side—"he'd eat Monsieur Lambert's brains first!" Duggy sobbed. "And then he'd eat yours!"

"Duggy," Shane said in a low, calm tone, "Please let us out. If you let us out we can still win!"

In the little bit of light from the windows, I could make out tiny shapes moving among the forest of discarded furniture and theater sets.

Hamsters...

"Monsieur Lambert's my friend!" Duggy cried. "He was my only friend. You're my friends now, too! I was so scared that I'd lose you just after I found you!"

"Well, you can kiss your friends goodbye because they're all gonna be replaced with hamsters now!" Tienna yelled. "You spineless, hamster-kissing stupid little dingus!"

I backed up to the bottom of the stairs. "Guys!" I yelled over my shoulder. "Guys... The hamsters!"

Shane flicked the basement lights on. A few ancient flickering bulbs sputtered to life.

= Flick!

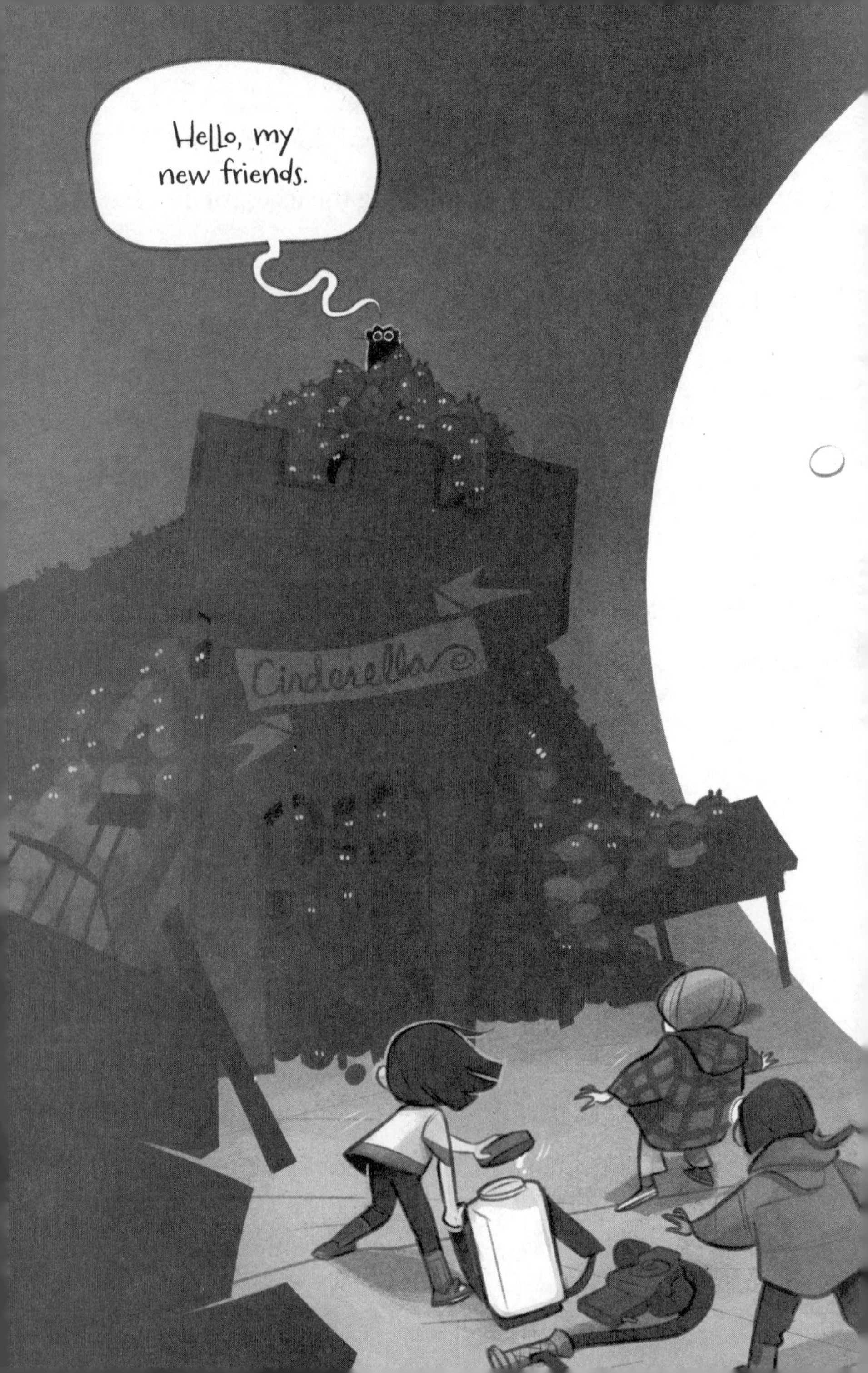
Hello, my new friends.
Cinderella

Tienna yelled at the top of her lungs and ran at Scrabbles, lifting the backpack sprayer over her head as she ran so that she could douse the leader of the hamsters.

AAAAAAAAGH!

MWA HAHAHAHAHA HAHAHA!

As she got close and hurled the milk, a wave of hamsters swirled over Scrabbles, forming a ball to shield him. A LITERAL hamster ball. The milk got a few of the hamsters, but there were too many. I heard Scrabbles safely inside, laughing.

The ball swept over Tienna and rushed toward me and Shane.

Tienna was left behind, lying on the ground. Her eyes were blank and unfocused. Hamsterfied...

The colossal ball of gnashing teeth and scratching claws bore down on us as Scrabbles cackled madly. Shane pushed me out of the way. I tripped over a box of magazines.

"Run, Ted—" Shane managed to yell before the hamster ball swept over him.

I ran through the maze of old theater sets and broken desks, and I hid...

With nothing but a tiny carton of milk...

And a horde of brain-eating little monsters...

In the dark, damp, cold basement...

Of Ravensbee Elementary...

Alone.

27
I Suck

Over the rain that pelted the tiny windows I could hear the ball of hamsters rolling about. Hamsters flowed around everything in the ball's path.

It was only a matter of time until Scrabbles found me.

"It's time to become Heather's friend, Teddy." Scrabbles chuckled. **"You will be a very, very special friend to Heather... Like I said, Teddy, I think Heather will like you. Heather will want to be your friend. And so we'll be her friend together, Teddy."**

Uh oh...

"I will be Heather's friend through you, Teddy."

Oh no...

"You will be mine."

I was gonna be Scrabbles's own personal Teddy skin suit... Well, actually, no. I probably wasn't. Scrabbles was gonna eat my brain and I was gonna die. I mean, that's what happens when something eats your brain!

"There's nothing you can do..." I heard Scrabbles getting closer. The skittering of ten thousand little claws scuttling across the floor was impossible to miss.

I was doomed...

I bit at my fingernails.

I was so stupid. I was so selfish. My friends, my REAL, actual, live friends had worked so hard to protect me, and what had I done? I'd run away. I'd left them. The hamsters were gonna win and it was all...

Because...

Of...

ME.

The hamster ball rolled closer.

A bit of fingernail came off in my mouth. I could taste blood. Ow.

Don't do that, Teddy. It's gross.

That's what Tienna would have said. Then she, Shane, and Duggy (well, maybe not Duggy anymore) would have tried to help. They'd have tried to help me get over what was scaring me. They'd have told me to just drink the milk.

The gnashing ball of hamster teeth came closer.

I felt the carton of milk in my hoodie pocket. There was no way to splash Scrabbles with it. The hamster ball was too thick. My friends would have told me to try anyway. They'd have told me to just drink the milk.

The ball of little hamster tongues licking fuzzy hamster chops rolled closer.

I took the carton out of my hoodie. I couldn't even open a carton of milk. Though maybe I'd have been able to if my friends were here.

They'd have told me to just drink the milk.

I hear you breathing, Teddy.
They'd have told me to just drink the milk.
It'll only hurt for a moment, Teddy . . .
Just drink the milk.

And then it will all be over . . .
Drink the milk!
Friends with Heather . . .
Drink! The! MILK!
Pop
Forever . . .

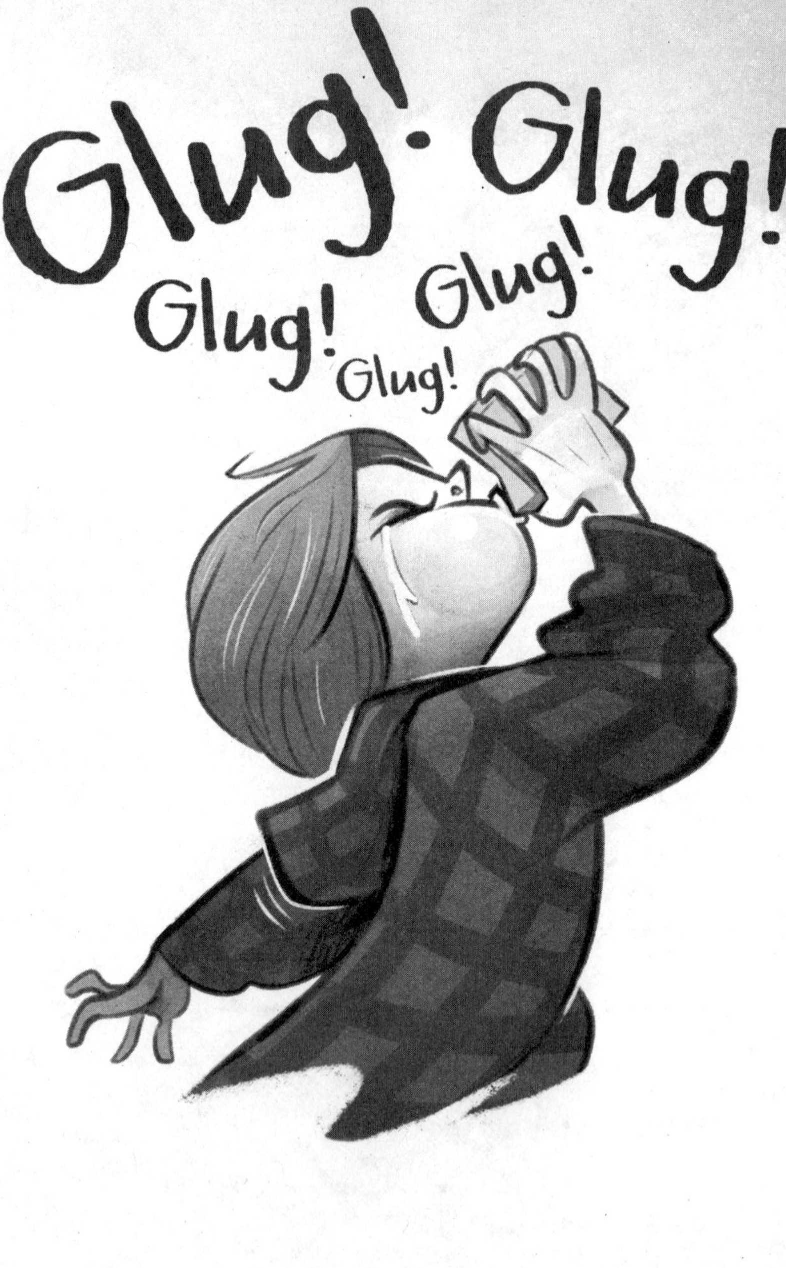
Glug! Glug!
Glug! Glug!
Glug!

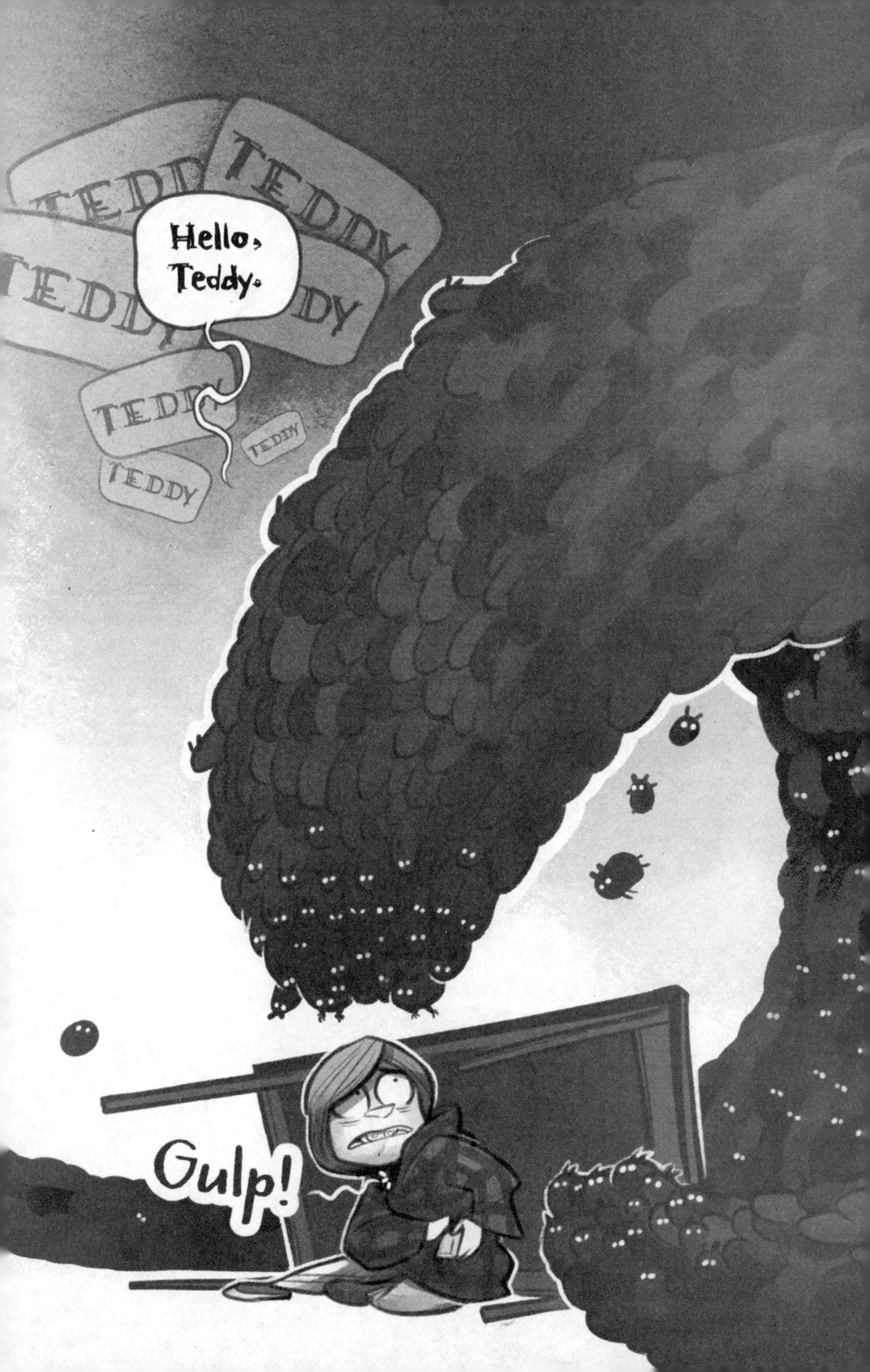
TEDDY
TEDDY
TEDDY
TEDDY
TEDDY
TEDDY
TEDDY
Hello, Teddy.
Gulp!

The hamster ball fell on me like a wave.

Open hamster mouths.

Cackling hamster voices.

Flashing hamster teeth.

Grasping hamster claws.

A million ghostly

hamster eyes.

And then...

The red eyes
of Scrabbles.

I threw up.

28

> AAAAGH
> BLURGLURGL
> URLGAAARGH
> THPTH!
> (Part 2)

AAAAIEEEEW!
FLEE!
ALL IS LOST!
Cough *Cough*
SCRABBLES HAS FALLEN!
FLEEEEEEEE!

The ball of hamsters melted away, leaving me lying there in a lake of milky throw-up (ew) and a doggy pile of regular old happy, hammy hamsters (well, not TOO happy, considering they were soaked in milky vomit).

I tried to move but just kind of rolled around. Post-puke fatigue is awful. It felt like I'd just gotten out of the pool after jumping into the water with all my clothes on.

"You have not heard the last of us, ape-pups!" a furious voice squeaked.

A hamster waved a clenched fist at me from the top of a Santa head from an old theater set.

"We will be back! We will learn the secret of the great Scrabbles, and we will return to—"

CRASH!

Someone threw a chair at the hamster, shattering the Santa head. I rolled around in the milky puddle and looked behind me. Tienna was picking up another chair to throw, but the hamster was gone.

Tienna was Tienna! She wasn't hamsterfied anymore! In fact, apart from the pile of poor little hamsters rolling about in the puddle with me, the basement was free of rodents, too!

Had we won? I mean, at the very least if there were any hamsters trying to hollow out anyone's skull upstairs, people could fight back.

"Teddy!" Tienna said, eyes wide. She rushed forward but came to a dead stop at the edge of the milky puke puddle. "Teddy, what . . ." She gagged. "Ew, Teddy, what did you do?!"

I tried to get to my feet but slipped. Splat. Ew.

cough Ah throo upp.

Shane picked his way gingerly toward me and helped me to my feet. "Well, you can't be mad at us this time, Teddy." He wrinkled his nose but helped me to the stairs. He tried to wipe his hand on Tienna's shirt. She smacked it away and clambered up the stairs.

"Keep an eye out for hamsters!" Tienna said, banging on the door leading out of the basement. "They're still smart enough to talk!"

"I thingk dehr gonn, tho," I said, slumping on the stairs. I felt a rustling in my hood. I reached behind me and pulled out a bedraggled little red-eyed bundle of wet fur. Scrabbles. "I gott the bigg wun."

Shane poked Scrabbles. Scrabbles squeaked. "Yup! That's just a hamster!"

The door at the top of the stairs opened.

"What are you three doing in my basement?!" Monsieur Lambert said. He was okay! "And why are there hamsters everywhere?!" He looked down the stairs at me and Shane. "Teddy! You threw up? AGAIN?! HOW?!"

"Miiiiilk," I said. I hiccuped. Milk. Ew.

"AGAIN?!"

Hiccup. My mouth tasted like bad cheese. Ick.

"You're like a dog with a jar of chocolate frosting, Teddy! How did this happen twice in one day?!"

"Mm sorreeee!" Disappointed adult shame is the worst. I slumped against the wall of the stairway.

"*Mon DIEU*, Teddy!" Monsieur Lambert rolled his eyes and grabbed a broom. "I'm not angry, I'm just amazed!" He snatched a dust pan and a trash bin. "I will have to leave you in the care of your friends, Teddy! I have much work to do! On top of being a custodian, I must now be a hamster wrangler!"

"Monsieur Lambert!" a deep buttery voice with an edge of panic called from out in the hallway. "Monsieur Lambert, we really need some help here, please! They're everywhere!"

"I hear you, Monsieur Quint!" Monsieur Lambert yelled over his shoulder. He turned back to us. "Tomorrow we will all be having a discussion as to why the hallways are filled with hamsters! Hamsters everywhere! And where my sprayer is! AGH! I don't know exactly what happened, but I know it was because of you three somehow. We will talk tomorrow!"

Monsieur Lambert hurried away.

We all looked at each other.

"Did we do it?" Shane asked. "Did we win?"

"I think we did!" Tienna said.

They both looked at me. I hiccuped. "H'ray!"

29

Don't Leave Anyone Behind, Teddy

We made our way toward the lost and found to get me something less pukey to wear. Cold, vomity clothes are the worst. The hallways were a tangled mess of teachers trying to clear the school of thousands of hamsters and hundreds of confused students (many of whom wanted to play with the hamsters).

"That hamster talked!" I heard a kindergarten kid say. "It called me a 'milk-sodden ape-pup'!"

"It said no such thing," a teacher replied. "Now get outside and DON'T TOUCH THOSE HAMSTERS."

Little clusters of scurrying shapes fled out the open doors, and students milled around the field outside. Nobody was hamsterfied. Frekizor had been right. Scrabbles (who Shane had insisted on washing off in the water fountain on the way to the lost and found) had been the key to the whole thing. Tienna left and came back with three cartons of milk. Just in case.

Tienna and Shane dug through the lost and found and we eventually settled on the hoodie with the cat ears. Scrabbles chilled out in the front pocket next to the carton of milk (he really was a nice hamster, now).

We walked out onto the field with the rest of the school. The hamsters were gone, for the most part. Some stopped to squeak in rage and shake their tiny fists at me, but I only noticed one or two scurrying little shapes among the crowd of kids.

"I still say that we should drown Scrabbles," Tienna muttered as we walked toward the bus loop. Tienna and Shane's bus was here, and apparently the driver didn't like to wait.

I petted Scrabbles. "He's just a hamster, now. I'm pretty sure he's safe. Also, we can't kill him. He belongs to Heather. And I don't wanna kill anything in general!"

Shane bent down to take another close look at Scrabbles. "Besides," he said, "if it ever does start to talk again, I've got so many questions for it! How did it control people? Where did all the hamsters come from? Why milk?!"

"Yeah," Tienna said. "Yeah, the milk is the weirdest part..." Tienna trailed off then sprinted through the rain and crowd of kids. I looked over to where she was running. She'd spotted Duggy!

After a second, Shane took off after her. "Tienna!" he yelled. "Tienna, you'll get suspended again!"

Tienna tackled Duggy and they both hit the ground. Just as Tienna was about to start swinging, Shane managed to drag her away.

"You splattery pile of wet dog crap!" I could hear Tienna's teeth grinding as she snarled at Duggy. "You were gonna let everyone have their brains eaten!"

The small circle of kids who'd gathered to watch the fight rolled their eyes and wandered away.

"Not everyone!" Duggy said, pleading. "They promised to spare you guys and Monsieur Lambert! I had to do it!"

Shane tugged at Tienna. "Tienna, you're right, but the bus is here! We've gotta go! Come on!"

"You didn't HAVE to do anything, Duggy!" Tienna yelled over her shoulder. "What you did was wrong, and you know it!"

Duggy blushed and looked at the ground.

"You're a terrible person, Duggy!" Tienna yelled as Shane pushed her onto the bus. She glared at Duggy from the back window as the bus rolled away.

It kept raining. Geez, I hate the rain.

Duggy sniffled and turned to me. "I suppose you hate me now, too . . ."

Scrabbles snuffled about in my pocket. I took him out and petted him. Duggy saw the hamster and started to cry (Scrabbles was a reminder of his betrayal, I guess.). I didn't know what to say.

"It's okay." Duggy said, turning to leave. "Tienna's right." He sniffled.

What had Monsieur Lambert said? Don't leave them behind? I reached out and put my hand on Duggy's shoulder.

"Scrabbles offered me the same deal, Duggy," I said.

"I didn't say yes, but . . ." I thought for a moment. "If Scrabbles had threatened to eat my DAD'S brain, I might have." Scrabbles snuffled at my hand. "What you did WAS wrong, but I can see why you did it."

Duggy stared at the ground, ashamed. After a moment he looked up at me.

Are we still friends?

"I . . . Um . . ." I said. "You made a bad choice, Duggy, but like I said, I can see why you did it. Let's talk tomorrow, yeah? After we've all had some time to think things through?"

Geez, I was good at remembering my lines right now! Apparently the problem all along was that I'd read the play titled *Hamsters Devour Everyone's Brains* instead of whatever everyone else had read.

Duggy smiled. "My bus is here. I'll see you tomorrow."

I waved as Duggy wandered off. Scrabbles clawed at my palm. Ow! The hamster was trying to get free. Scrabbles peered over my hand and squeaked. I looked in the same direction.

Heather.

Well, he WAS Heather's hamster. I walked toward her, Scrabbles in my hand, and her eyes lit up.

"Scrabbles!" Heather laughed as she snatched him up. "Oh my gosh, Scrabbles, I'm so happy you're okay!" She pocketed him then hugged me, nearly crushing my rib cage. "Thank you thank you thank you!"

"You're welcome!" I managed to gasp out. "I'm Teddy, by the way."

"Teddy!" Heather maintained the bear hug. "Thank you, Teddy! I was so scared! His hamster ball was here, but Scrabbles was missing! I was so SO worried!"

"I'm your new class buddy," I squeaked. I think my ribs cracked.

"Oh my gosh, that's amazing!" Heather squeezed harder. "I'm so happy to meet you!"

"Can you let me go, please?" I wheezed with the last of my breath.

"I'm sorry!" Heather said, letting me go. "I'm sorry, I just get excited is all."

You know that the other kids are gonna see you with Heather and they're gonna talk, right, Teddy? You're gonna be the new Hamster-Boy! You're gonna be the new Pukey Hamster-Boy and no one will ever let you live it down for the . . .

rest . . .

Of . . .

You

Lif

Hey!

Hey!

Hey!

SHUT. UP.

This isn't working, okay? I know it's not gonna be easy to change this, but we can't keep beating ourselves up. Besides, we really have much worse things to worry about than what everyone thinks of us at school.

What?! What could be more important than blending in?!

Well, for starters what ELSE in this town wants to eat our brains?

Fair point.

A car honked near the bus loop, and I saw my dad waving at me.

"Thanks again for looking after Scrabbles," Heather said.

"It's no problem at all. I gotta go," I said. "But... Heather?"

"Yes?" Heather snuggled Scrabbles.

"If Scrabbles starts talking about taking over the school, or eating people's brains, just make sure to give him a milk bath."

Heather wrinkled her nose in disgust. "Milk? Ew. Absolutely not. Milk's gross. Makes me SICK."

I smiled. "I'll see you tomorrow."

30
Family Traditions

"That's okay," Dad said. "It happens. So what did you do today? Did you make good choices?" We pulled away from the school, the rain pelting the windshield.

"We stopped a bunch of brain-eating hamsters from turning everyone into zombies and taking over the school."

"Brain-eating hamsters?! Really?!"

"Yeah."

"REALLY?!"

"Yup."

There was a moment of silence as Dad digested this

information. "Neat!" he said.

"Not really." I stared out the window at the rainy pine forest.

"No?"

"No. It was awful. It was really REALLY awful. It was scary and violent, and we almost didn't make it."

"I mean, there were brain-eating hamsters," Dad said. "Nothing about that sounds nice!"

"Yeah . . ." I sighed. I was really tired all of a sudden. "We got the big one, though, so everything's okay." I yawned.

"How?" Dad asked. "Teddy, did you murder some poor hamster? Hamster murder is never a good choice, Teddy!"

"What? No!" I said, closing my eyes. I could have a nap right here. "We used milk. Milk turned the evil hamster in charge into a normal hamster, and the others ran away."

"Milk? Really?"

"Yeah. Weird, right?"

"Teddy, has Mom been telling you scary stories again?" Dad glanced at me with a worried expression.

"No," I said. "She agreed not to do that anymore. Why?"

"Well, you know that your mom grew up in Ravensbarrow, right?"

"Yeah. Her and Auntie Morgan grew up on a farm here."

"More of a ranch, actually. A dairy farm."

"Ew."

"Yeah, I can't imagine you having to grow up on a dairy farm," Dad said, laughing. "But anyway, your mom's family had a little ritual. Whenever there was a new cow born, or a kitten, or puppy, or any animal on the farm, they'd splash it with a bit of milk. Heck, I think she even gave you a sprinkle of milk when we got you home after you were born."

"Really?!" Oh my gosh, MORE milk?! "WHY?!"

Dad shrugged. "It's just a weird Meier family superstition. Maybe she mentioned it a long time ago and you forgot about it."

"Maybe . . ." I shrugged and snuggled down against the car window. "But I guess it doesn't matter. It's all over now."

"Because you got the big one?" Dad asked.

"Yup!" I yawned.

"Are you sure?"

"Yeah." I could feel myself drifting off.

"Are you really really sure?" Dad pulled the car off to the side of the road.

I started to get anxious. ". . . Yeah?"

Dad stopped the engine. "Well, Teddy, I have a question for you."

I opened my eyes and looked over at my dad. "Okay . . ."

Yup, I was definitely getting anxious.

Dad looked out his side window for a moment then turned back toward me.

No . . . Something that LOOKED like my dad turned back toward me . . .

I had a lizard-brain moment.

"AAAAAAAAAAAAAGHGETAWAYFROM-MYDADAAAAAGH!" I ripped open the carton of milk in my hoodie and splashed my dad in the face.

Dad wiped the milk off. "I gotta admit, Teddy, I wasn't expecting that! Message received, though. Sorry! Just a joke, but I won't do that again!"

Dad started the engine and put the car in gear. "I'll clean this up when we get home. Wait a minute..." Dad glanced over at me. "Teddy, this car is soaked in milk and you're not throwing up!"

I really wish Dad hadn't pointed that out...

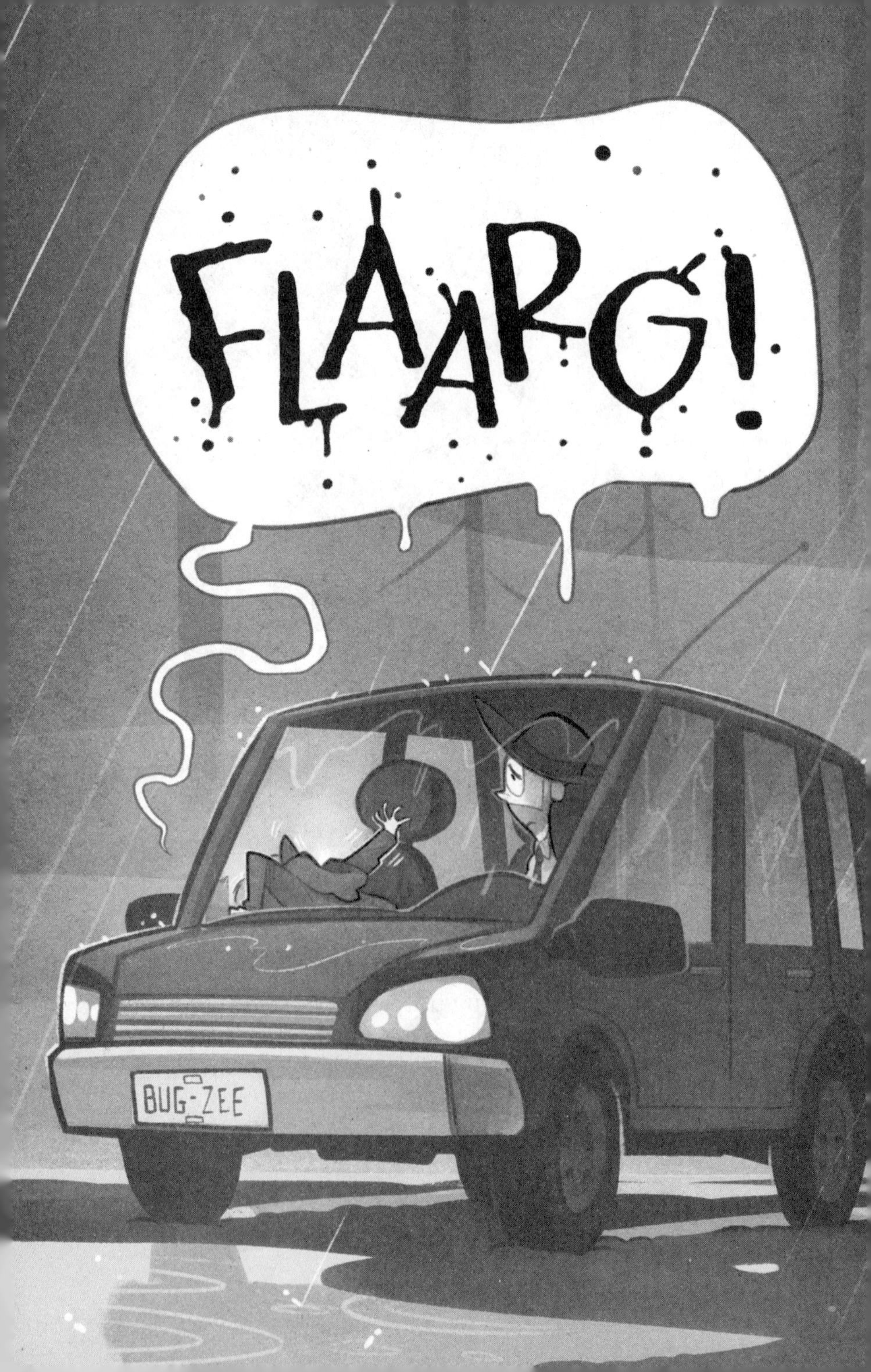
FLAARG!
BUG-ZEE

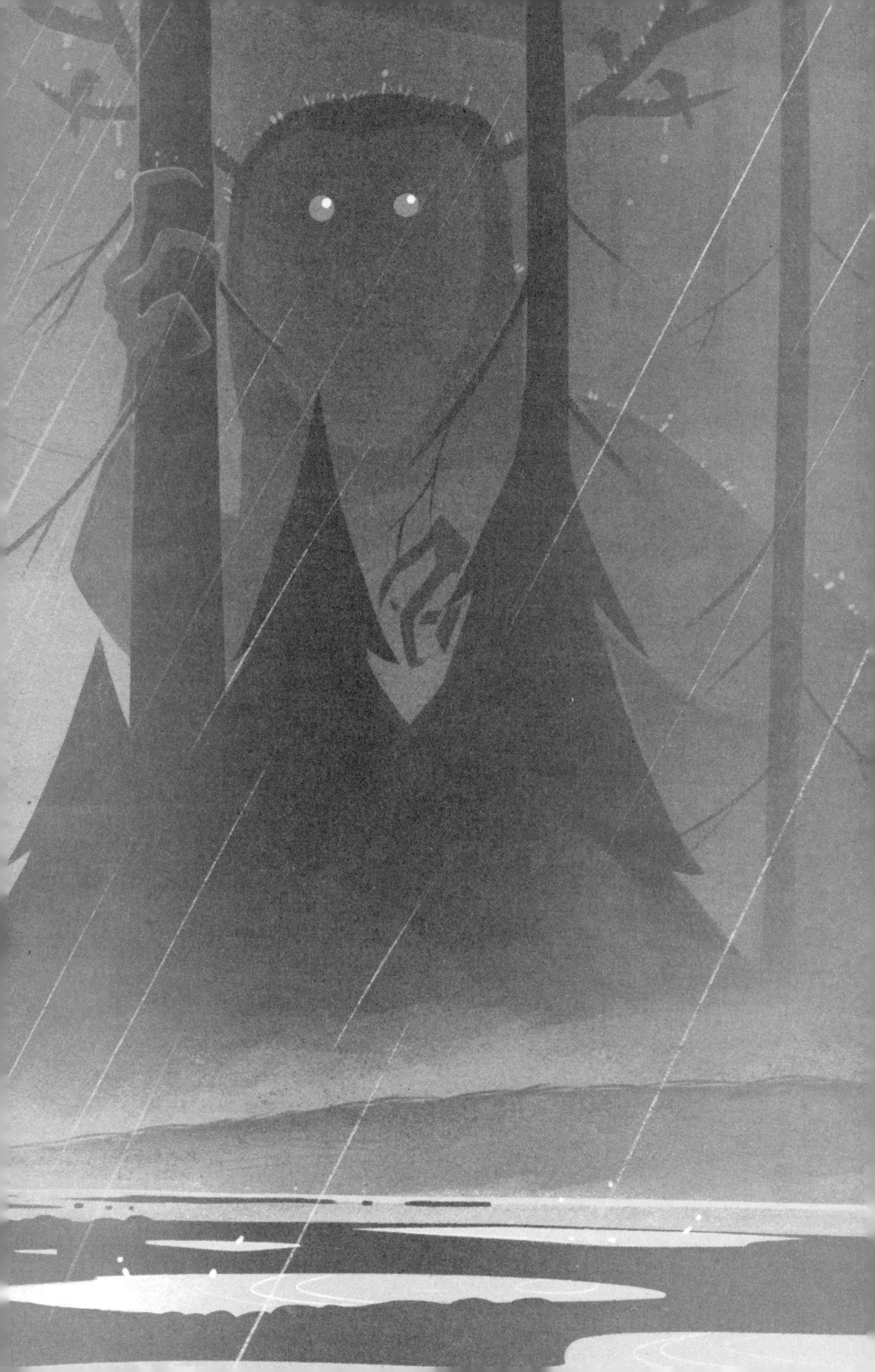

About the Creator

© Samantha Foraie, 4A Photography Kamloops

Braden Hallett, much like Teddy, lived through a hamster uprising in Kamloops, BC. The school in which the uprising occurred recently reopened. You can still hear their scratchy little claws in the walls... But let's not worry about that! Braden still lives in Kamloops and likes drawing oodles of doodles, writing more books that will still feature evil hamsters, playing lots and lots of role-playing games like *Dungeons & Dragons*, and occasionally playing board games with his many nieces and nephews. His dream is to keep illustrating and writing.

COMING IN FALL 2024
Secrets of Ravensbarrow Book 2

Teddy will return in:

Teddy vs. the Slimy Evil

Ravensbarrow
Note: not to scale
Like, at all
N
W
E
S
Deep evil scary lake
Farm
TRAILS

New school
Dark forest of endless doooooooom
Downtown
My house

Ravensbarrow
Note: not to scale
Like, at all
N
W
S
E
Deep evil scary lake
Farm
TRAILS

Holy Caster | Amelia No

"Stephenne Veronide. You are indeed Stephenne Veronide, yes? I hate to tell you this before you've even entered, but please stay out of this casino."

Stey's eyes instinctively go wide. She has no idea what's going on.

Scout | Sanya Chatre

"?!"

Holy Caster | Stephenne Veronide

DEFEATING THE DEMON LORD'S A CINCH

IF YOU'VE GOT A RINGER

VOLUME
5

TSUKIKAGE

Illustration by **bob**

YEN ON
New York

Translation by Caleb DeMarais
Cover art by bob

Defeating the Demon Lord's a Cinch (If You've Got a Ringer), Vol. 5

TSUKIKAGE

This book is a work of fiction. Names, characters, places, and incidents are the product of the author's imagination or are used fictitiously. Any resemblance to actual events, locales, or persons, living or dead, is coincidental.

DARENIDEMO DEKIRU KAGE KARA TASUKERU MAO TOBATSU
Vol. 5
© Tsukikage 2022
First published in Japan in 2022 by KADOKAWA CORPORATION, Tokyo.
English translation rights arranged with KADOKAWA CORPORATION, Tokyo through Tuttle-Mori Agency, Inc., Tokyo.

English translation © 2023 by Yen Press, LLC

Yen Press, LLC supports the right to free expression and the value of copyright. The purpose of copyright is to encourage writers and artists to produce the creative works that enrich our culture.

The scanning, uploading, and distribution of this book without permission is a theft of the author's intellectual property. If you would like permission to use material from the book (other than for review purposes), please contact the publisher. Thank you for your support of the author's rights.

Yen On
150 West 30th Street, 19th Floor
New York, NY 10001

Visit us at yenpress.com
facebook.com/yenpress
twitter.com/yenpress
yenpress.tumblr.com
instagram.com/yenpress

First Yen On Edition: September 2023
Edited by Yen On Editorial: Rachel Mimms
Designed by Yen Press Design: Andy Swist

Yen On is an imprint of Yen Press, LLC.
The Yen On name and logo are trademarks of Yen Press, LLC.

The publisher is not responsible for websites (or their content) that are not owned by the publisher.

Library of Congress Cataloging-in-Publication Data
Names: Tsukikage, author. | Bob (Illustrator), illustrator. | Kerwin, Alex, translator. | DeMarais, Caleb, translator.
Title: Defeating the demon lord's a cinch (if you've got a ringer) / Tsukikage ; illustration by bob.
Other titles: Darenidemo Dekiru Kage Kara Tasukeru Mao Tobatsu. English
Description: First Yen On edition. | New York, NY : Yen On, 2018– | v. 1: translation by Alex Kerwin ; v. 2–5: translation by Caleb DeMarais.
Identifiers: LCCN 2018023883 | ISBN 9781975327354 (v. 1 ; pbk.) |
  ISBN 9781975327378 (v. 2 ; pbk.) | ISBN 9781975303709 (v. 3 ; pbk.) |
  ISBN 9781975303921 (v. 4 ; pbk.) | ISBN 9781975370251 (v. 5 ; pbk.)
Subjects: LCSH: Fantasy fiction.
Classification: LCC PL876.S853 D3713 2018 | DDC 895.63/6—dc23
LC record available at https://lccn.loc.gov/2018023883

ISBNs: 978-1-9753-7025-1 (paperback)
        978-1-9753-7026-8 (ebook)

10 9 8 7 6 5 4 3 2 1

LSC-C

Printed in the United States of America

CONTENTS

Defeating the Demon Lord's a Cinch
(If You've Got a Ringer)

Part Five

Prologue
A New Strategy — **007**

First Report
On the Holy Warrior's Whereabouts
and Forthcoming Objectives — **021**

Second Report
On Acquiring Legendary Equipment and
Fortifying Battle Power — **081**

Third Report
On Utilizing an Ancient Legend — **163**

Fourth Report
On Encountering God — **223**

Fifth Report
On the Holy Warrior's Debut — **289**

Epilogue
Setting Out Anew — **319**

Special Story
What Happened to Amelia — **337**

Part Five

Let's Begin

The sea demon Heljarl: ruler of the ocean and among Demon Lord Kranos's top officials. Capable of calling upon storms and freely controlling aquatic monsters. This fearsome specter and his military might—the reason why humanity was losing ground—was what awaited Naotsugu Toudou and her party when they visited the water capital in search of a grand water elemental spirit.

In order to establish a covenant and obtain the power of such a spirit, one must first perform an ancient ritual within the water capital's sunken temple.
To this end, Toudou needed to obtain the cooperation of a gifted, curmudgeonly dwarf and magic-item craftsman, Zolan. With the Church's support, Toudou succeeded in obtaining an item that would allow her to explore the ocean floor. Through the power of the magic item, Toudou reached the bottom of the ocean, a place that normal beings are not allowed to visit.
Here Toudou was greeted by a fortress built by the powerful sea demon of ill repute who had slain umpteen heroes that fell before him and sunken countless ships, completely shutting down maritime traffic. At his side was an army of ocean demons waiting vigilantly for their next invasion.

Among all the members of the Demon Lord's army, the sea demon Heljarl had dealt particularly heavy damage to humanity and was an especially loathed beast. After causing massive damage to the ocean kingdom, Heljarl's whereabouts had been unknown, and nobody was able to lay a hand on him. If they could take Heljarl down, maritime traffic would resume, and individual kingdoms would be able to strengthen their cooperative activities.

Further, while embroiled in many twists and turns, Toudou learned that the innocent mermaids who inhabit the ocean floor, alongside the water spirit she had formed a covenant with, had been captured by the sea demon Heljarl.

Toudou needed to make a decision. Her opponent was a fearsome, powerful demon controlling a demon army that had obliterated a number of supremely high-level heroes before her. Even with divine protection, facing these foes with just four party members was simply too dangerous. However, only those recognized by Zolan are able to explore the world under the sea. The party wouldn't be able to call for reinforcements.

After vacillating for three days and three nights, Toudou reached a decision: She would fight. Yes, Naotsugu Toudou, without fear for her own life, made the decision to fight for the lives of the innocent. When the Holy Warrior displayed this level of nobility, suited only to her, the gods did not forsake her.

Before Toudou could head toward the sunken temple to face the sea demon, a young girl in a hooded cloak appeared before her: a monster researcher named Rabi. With Rabi's words of encouragement, Toudou was prepared with the wisdom and strategy to pull Heljarl's minions away from him, successfully bringing them into battle one by one.

In a fierce struggle for victory, the Holy Warrior wielded her holy sword with courage and the power of divine protection in the face of the sea demon Heljarl, who controlled dark weapons in the form of ocean monsters at his beck and call. The sinister forces Toudou was up against were unfathomably massive, and the battle

"The overdone sense of justice is a crime."

raged fiercely for hours. The ocean was rocked to the core by the powers of light and darkness colliding with fervor, and the sunken temple, having lain on the ocean floor since antiquity, shuddered and trembled.

The deciding force—which determined the outcome of the battle—was the water spirit that had been captured. While Toudou was engaged in battle with Heljarl, her compatriots had come to her aid. With the water elemental spirit's support and a powerful beam of light, the sea demon, who had felled so many heroes, was finally defeated.

In this way, some ten years after the Demon Lord Kranos had raised a flag of revolt against the gods, the smoke signals of counterattack by humanity had finally gone out.

Despite entering a covenant with the water spirit and defeating the sea demon, Naotsugu Toudou's perilous journey must yet continue. That said, she no longer needed to fear demons or monsters that were imbued with powers from evil gods. This was clear as day on the Holy Warrior's face.

Look ahead with clear eyes—that powerful light is right before us at all times.

Defeating the Demon Lord

Prologue
A New Strategy

The royal capital Ruxe is the center of the Kingdom of Ruxe and one of many large cities therein. A powerful knight corps stands watch along the robust rampart that encompasses the entire city, famous for never once being breached since the foundation of the Kingdom. Located in the heart of the capital, Ruxe Kingdom Royal Castle is austere yet profoundly beautiful, and its pure-white facade has led many to call it Castle Immaculate.

The Kingdom of Ruxe is one of the largest of its kind. It has enjoyed a long period of prosperity thanks to the rich, fertile soil and encompassing mountain ranges. The royal family descended from the Holy Warrior summoned long ago counts itself among the Church of Ahz Gried's patrons.

Ten years have passed since the Demon Lord's army began encroaching upon the human world. The situation remains tough for humanity, but the capital is quite far from the front lines, and the people walking its streets are beaming to an extent that is unfathomable for those who have actually seen combat. This sheer ignorance is because the demon army's encroachment hasn't spread like a massive fire but rather slowly and silently like a termite infestation.

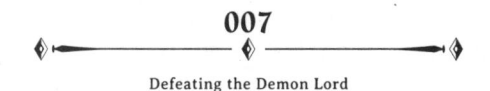

That said, Ruxe understands one thing: The battle with this Demon Lord is highly undesirable. For this reason, the Kingdom of Ruxe petitioned the Church to perform the miracle of hero summoning. After successfully getting Toudou to enter a covenant with an elemental spirit in Cloudburst, my party and I switched gears and returned to the royal capital.

We were able to forgo the annoying entry process through the influence of the Church of Ahz Gried, getting into the city proper via horse-drawn carriage. Most of the places we've visited so far were barren. Golem Valley and Purif go without saying, but even the renowned water capital of Cloudburst pales in comparison to the hustle and bustle of the royal capital.

Throngs of carriages pass us as we proceed along the well-kept main street, which is overflowing with open-air shops. Order is kept by soldiers in polished armor and helmets. Most people here are humans, although some have features of other species as well.

A bustling scene characteristic of a major city. The crowds continue to grow, and Amelia pokes her head out from the carriage's canopy toward the driver's seat. When she sees the street teeming with people out and about, her eyes widen slightly.

"...I've never been in a city this big before. I was always in the Church headquarters."

"This place is nothing like HQ."

The Church of Ahz Gried headquarters is merely a massive church; it's not a city in itself. Behind Amelia, Sanya and Rabi sit huddled together, draped in thick robes and clutching their knees. They're clearly not keen on drawing attention to themselves in a crowd like this, given recent events.

Thankfully, the chances that they'll be of any need here are quite low.

"Okay," I said. "Once we make an appearance at the Church, we'll hit the inn and rehash the current issues and come up with a game plan."

"More or less the same as usual, then..."

Amelia's reply is blunt. She furrows her brow and sighs quietly. This...isn't helping.

"Ares, isn't there something else we could do?" she asks.

Rabi mumbles a suggestion, shifting only her gaze toward me

"The overdone sense of justice is a crime."

Prologue: A New Strategy

from under her hood. "Boss... Perhaps a break would do us some good. We just took down a massive foe..."

Indeed... The entire group seems a bit downtrodden from our long journey. Nothing really happened during our travels to the royal capital, so perhaps their sense of urgency dwindled as a result.

I speak flatly, starting straight ahead from the driver's seat. "If we stop even once, we might not be able to get back up again, you know..."

"......"

"If only holy techniques could treat mental anguish, too..."

"Yeah, boss... Mind if you stop trying to exacerbate our pain even further?" Sanya says with utter disdain. Seems she agrees with Amelia and Rabi.

"Your master told me that you and Rabi don't need breaks," I reply.

"?! This is tyranny. We're goin' on strike!"

If they go on strike and we fail to defeat the Demon Lord, I doubt I'll be the only one on the chopping block. I sigh deeply and make sure my next words sound wholly unexpected.

"I understand. Once we leave the carriage at the inn, we'll take a three-day break."

"What? Are you sure?" Amelia asks, scrutinizing my face like she's just noticed something exceedingly bizarre on it.

Keeping my subordinates motivated is another part of my job. I planned on taking a few days of total rest and relaxation in the safety of the royal capital from the outset. It's a good thing my party demanded a break; I owe them a debt of gratitude.

Rabi lifts her head; her ruby-red eyes bore into me.

"But don't even think about running away," I joke with the group. "If you try, I'll bring you right back down to the depths of hell."

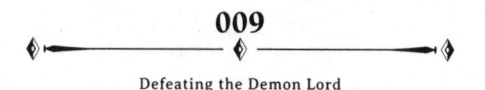

The sea demon Heljarl was exceptionally troublesome, even among the innumerable demons allied with the Demon Lord's army. An adversary of humanity as a whole, he was public enemy number one worldwide, particularly for nations along the coast. Toudou's defeat of Heljarl (granted, Rabi was the one who dealt the final blow) was such a spectacular achievement that he and his party were summoned back to the Kingdom of Ruxe.

The Holy Warrior, Naotsugu Toudou, is currently at level 43—relatively accomplished for a warrior, yet still underprepared for the hero who intends to defeat the Demon Lord. It's hard to know when that fact will become public knowledge, yet in the background, while the elites of the Kingdom were becoming impatient regarding the progress of our current journey, they must now be relieved by our most spectacular victory.

With the ocean free from Heljarl's control, an even vaster area is now available to us since Ruxe has a port. The wind is blowing in our favor.

I wonder if the Demon Lord's army has already learned of Heljarl's death. It was an arduous battle; we destroyed every foe that came our way, but I'd be hard pressed to say that we eliminated every last one of Heljarl's minions. If Toudou was fully developed in his skillset, we would have had the option of riding the wave of victory and pressing the attack, but that would have been premature. The demon army we're up against is entirely unprecedented.

I also can't stop wondering about the human turncoat that Heljarl was running his mouth about. There's no such thing as being too cautious.

It's tricky enough canvassing the movements of the Demon Lord's army; investigating the purported traitor is a tall order. Our intel is severely lacking. We don't even know if this person has infiltrated our circle or if they're an operative of the Demon Lord's army in earnest. The fact that Toudou's name hasn't yet leaked prompts me to believe it isn't someone in the top ranks of the Kingdom or the Church, but assumptions can have dire consequences.

This is truly a time for cooperation. Focusing too hard on the lurking threat of suspicion is unwise. Moving forward, we must instill

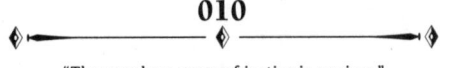

"The overdone sense of justice is a crime."

Prologue: A New Strategy

our battles with greater vehemence. We have learned a few things from barely surviving battles like in Cloudburst.

What we need the most right now is people. We wouldn't have been victorious without Sanya and Rabi. And if we had even more members, I wouldn't have had to fight hand-to-hand after being stabbed with a spear and getting covered in my own blood.

I separate with Amelia and company at the inn and head to the mercenary dispatch center, the Bar, where we originally came upon the chance to hire Sanya and Rabi. Many pairs of eyes fall upon me when I open the door, but this is my second time here, so I don't mind. It looks like I'm the only outside customer here again. A man standing at the counter who I recognize looks at me, and his eyes flare wide open. I immediately hear a number of ominous murmurings from the bar tables.

"Look, it's him again."

"I heard Bran's fairy-tale girl had a real rough time of it."

"Yeah, her reward for fighting the sea demon was a single golden carrot..."

"Mermares..."

What the—? Who just called me Mermares? Their information is clearly bunk.

Never mind the accuracy of their web of information—there are few people who actually know my name, after all.

"It...would appear that Sanya and company had a need to keep their mouths shut."

Flippant Sanya and Rabi, it's hard to say what they'll muck up next... Which one of them is the culprit? Theoretically, it could have been Amelia, too... Forget it. The actual chance that one of them is the betrayer is very low.

I gather my wits about me and place the trunk I've been dragging along on the counter. It contains 200 million lux. Two-hundred-goddamn-million lux. Including Stey, this is pay for two. On the basis of the achievement of defeating the sea demon Heljarl, Creio procured these funds—it's a veritable treasure trove.

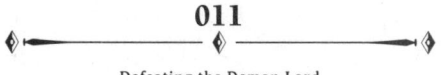

I won't let anyone tell me I'm broke ever again. If I obtain more party members and continue defeating the Demon Lord Army's top officials, we'll continue to acquire capital for use as we see fit. This will allow us to become even more prepared.

This is business. I whirl around and stare at the mercenaries seated at the tables before making my demand.

"Despite my obligation to dress as a merman to explore the ocean floor, and despite being made into a human shish kebab by a spear, I remained dedicated to my duty and strong in body and spirit, as well as impeccably resilient to such dirty work. I took a top-level demon on headfirst and hereby proclaim my prowess to defeat said demon, in addition to being particularly adept regarding the spiritual magic arts... Now, all that I'm looking for are some beautiful female soldiers—anyone have an idea?"

"......"

Everyone in the room falls silent as if the air was pushed out of their lungs. The reaction I had expected. I knew my absurdity would be perceived as such. That said, this worked flawlessly last time, so I see no reason why it shouldn't work again.

"Also," I add with a straight face, "any respite will come on an unplanned basis. There might not be any at all... But let's not beat around the bush. The job: defeating the Demon Lord."

Okay—who's ready to start some new business with us?

§ § §

"We are so glad you've returned unharmed, Naotsugu Toudou, you who hath received the blessings of Ahz Gried."

A mature man wrapped in a pure-crimson robe speaks in a clear voice. He has deep-indigo hair and a clean-cut goatee, and he is a full size larger than Toudou. Even with his robe on, it's easy to tell that he is in fantastic shape.

The crimson robe indicates the organization that governs over the Kingdom of Ruxe's military—it's proof of membership in the

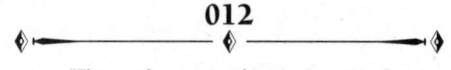

"The overdone sense of justice is a crime."

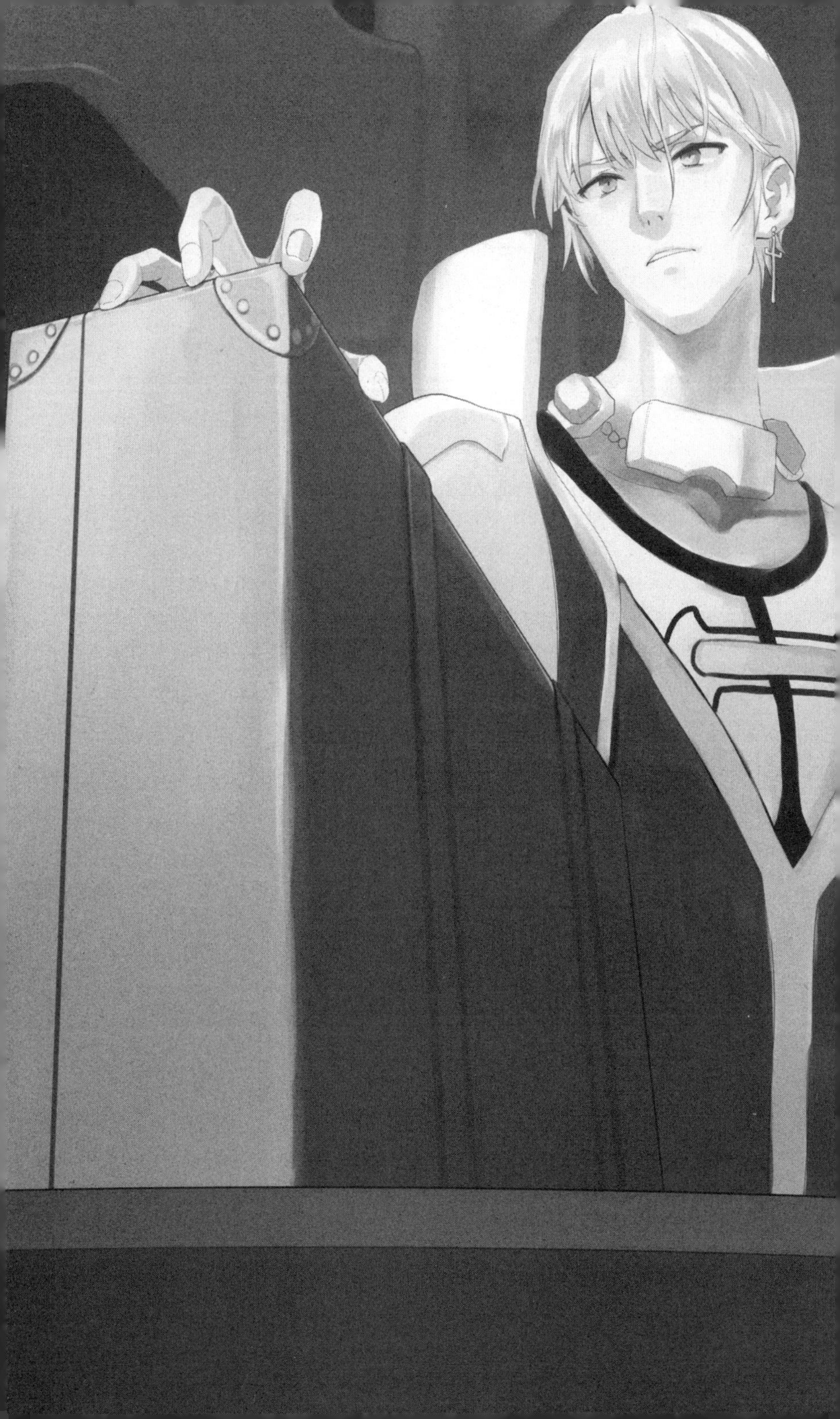

School of Swordsmanship. Both left and right walls are lined with knights in shining silver armor, aligned so systematically they could be statues.

They are the cornerstone of the Kingdom of Ruxe's defenses—members of Ruxe's mightiest chivalric order, the most skilled individuals this world over, each one boasting a high average level born from unflagging discipline: the Order of Radiance.

There are a number of chivalric orders in Ruxe, but in this one, military prowess and valor are held above all else. Status matters not within their ranks, and there isn't a weakling found among them. Their average level is around 70. Judging by level alone, they are a strictly elite group.

The man standing before Toudou oversees Ruxe's entire military force, including this elite corps. Norton Rizas—the current Grand Swordmaster, who Toudou met just after she was summoned. He is also the father of Aria, who was specially selected to join the hero's quest to defeat the Demon Lord.

In the face of this man standing proudly, Aria, standing next to Toudou, casts her gaze downward slightly. Norton does not look toward her but rather narrows his eyes and looks upon Toudou.

"I have heard of your accomplishments. Heljarl has been felled? Ruxe faced terrible tribulations thanks to that foul demon. No one was able to take him down—this is a phenomenal achievement quite suited to the name of Holy Warrior."

"...As previously mentioned, I didn't defeat Heljarl single-handedly."

Toudou furrows her brow, recalling the battle with Heljarl. The fierce battle at the sunken temple remains a bitter memory.

The high-level demon was even more formidable than expected. He possessed powerful attack magic that would overwhelm even high-level spirits, and his majestic appearance was truly formidable. Despite having gained some levels through battle experience, Toudou could barely move a muscle when the time came.

The shock that struck Toudou when Heljarl repelled a single

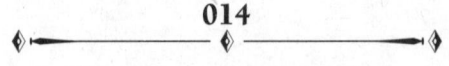

"The overdone sense of justice is a crime."

Prologue: A New Strategy

swing of her holy sword Ex, capable of ripping through anything... She can still feel it in her hands.

No matter how many times she replays the scene in her mind, she can think only one thing: It's a miracle she made it out alive. Plus, Heljarl had been alone without minions to accompany him back then, and he was wounded. Toudou can scarcely fathom what the sea demon must have been like at full strength.

Seeing Toudou's listless expression, Norton crosses his arms and nods deeply.

"Aye. Your opponent was a high-level demon, so your burden must be heavy right now. Nonetheless, even if you didn't take him down directly yourself, there is no doubt in my mind that he was felled as a result of your bravery."

Toudou's eyes go wide. She assumed she was going to be berated, and Norton's words are unexpected. He's right—Toudou made the decision to take Rabi to the sunken temple. In that sense, Heljarl wouldn't have been defeated without Toudou's involvement.

However, Toudou doesn't have the forethought to simply say, "Oh really, do you think so?"

Her expression hasn't changed. Norton purses his lips and smiles.

"The only thing that matters is the result, not the process. If you felt that you were underpowered, then it's time to devote yourself even further to training. Heljarl is only one of Demon Lord Kranos's subordinates. There will absolutely come a time when your blade is needed. Right now, you are tortured with thoughts of powerlessness, no? A high-level demon is a powerful foe, but a warrior that practices discipline and increases their level accordingly can sufficiently stand up to one. And you have this accomplishment under your belt."

"Do you mean that?!"

"Indeed, I do. There are only a few, but some accomplished mercenaries and warriors specialize in pursuing high-level demons. Even with the Order of Radiance—depending on method of choice, some of them could take down a high-level demon, too."

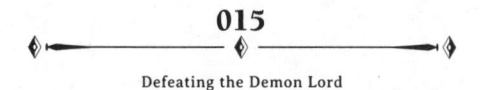

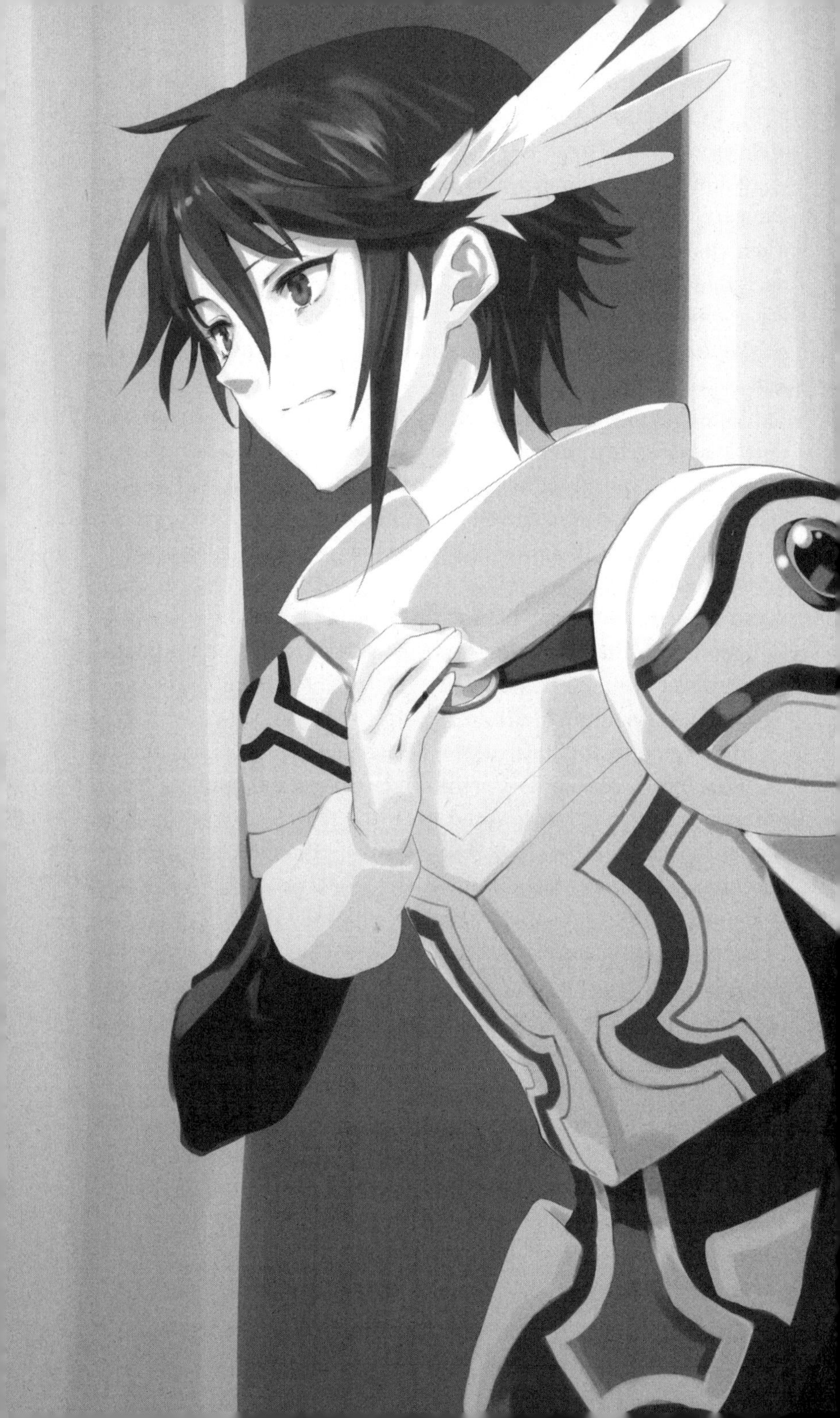

Prologue: A New Strategy

This is hard to believe right off the bat. Heljarl was powerful, much more so than any of the monsters Toudou has fought up until now. Even though they had felt their skills advancing on their multiple-month journey, they were still rendered largely helpless. However, the shining silver knights surrounding Norton didn't flinch.

"And further, Naotsugu Toudou. I have told you before—you have natural talent for battle. In our world, everyone in the Kingdom of Ruxe is jealous of your sword—your natural battle prowess. I personally would take you for my daughter's husband in a heartbeat. Unfortunately—that won't be possible."

"Father?!"

Norton refuses to acknowledge his daughter's gaze and continues. He has the same deep-green eyes as Aria.

"At any rate, you must be tired from your long journey. The entire Kingdom of Ruxe wants to hear your tale. Until then, please take ample respite. If there is anything you require, we shall procure it, within the realm of feasibility. You need not hesitate. Defeating Heljarl is a triumph that warrants no less."

"...Understood. Thank you kindly," Toudou says, her voice slightly deeper than usual.

Accomplishment—yet it's not my own. Respite—yet there's no time for it.

I want to head out to gain levels immediately. Even if that isn't possible, I can't simply lie idle and not do anything. Everything I do is to continue being a hero.

If this was a storybook for the ages, after many trials and tribulations, in the end the hero would defeat the Demon Lord. But this is reality. Such good fortune never strikes twice. Something has to be done before the hero's party suffers a defeat they cannot recover from.

House Rizas resides in a mansion owned by the Kingdom. In one room on the property, Aria is wiping the sweat from her forehead.

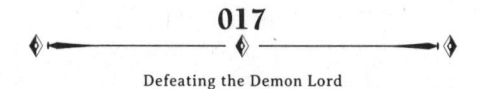

"It's no use, then…?" she says.

"Owww… It hurts…"

At present, Toudou is nothing short of lacking. She lacks an instructor to help her train and level up, and she needs information on the Demon Lord's army to plan her next moves. But what she needs most desperately right now…is new armor.

Toudou groans despite herself. The cause: the binder being tied tightly around her chest.

Her chest keeps growing as she levels up, and after the fierce battle in the water capital, her level has reached the point where she can no longer fit into her armor. The holy armor Fried is a legendary breastplate once worn by the previous Holy Warrior—but it was made to fit a man, and unlike some magical armor, it doesn't have size-altering properties. Although even if it did, there's no way that Toudou could still wear it after this much growth. After all, it remains a secret that Toudou is a girl.

When Aria lets go of the cloth binder she had tied so tightly, Toudou collapses from momentum and falls on her behind.

"There's no point," Aria declares, watching the teary-eyed Holy Warrior sitting on the floor. "Even if you can fit in the armor, you won't be able to fight like this."

Limis, who has been observing this shameful scene from behind, says coldly, "We've got no other choice than to slice them clean off."

"Oh my *God*?!"

"…That seems like a lost cause," Aria replies. "The holy armor Fried isn't particularly sturdy, but it can heal wounds. She wouldn't be able to take it off, and that would cause no end of trouble."

"What the—?!"

Toudou shudders at the thought of her sliced-off breasts growing back inside her armor and being stuck in the holy armor Fried forever. If that happened…she'd probably suffocate to death.

"I never imagined it would come to this, but…we may need to give up on the holy armor," Aria admits. "Even if Nao is able to wear it now…I daresay it's only a matter of time before that changes."

"The overdone sense of justice is a crime."

"She needs to grow in other areas *besides* her chest! Right, Nao?!"

"You're telling me..."

Toudou sighs deeply at Limis's biting comment. Toudou's chest has expanded with every level she's gained, yet Limis's breasts have remained small since the start of their journey. Not that Toudou would say that she wants to trade places, of course—she knows that would just be pouring oil on the fire.

"The holy armor is proof of the Holy Warrior—a hero," she insists.

"......Well, you're able to use the holy sword, so we should be able to get by somehow. Right now, we need a substitute for the holy armor Fried. Ideally, a quality piece of armor that will help conceal your gender—"

"You think there's anything suitable...?"

"I seem to recall a few pieces in the armory that can be adjusted for size... But for the time being, we'll likely need a robe that can hide your body shape. Anything with concealment magic would be best..."

Aria glances at Limis, who is still sulking. Finding a robe with magic properties is House Friedia's domain. Toudou looks to Limis with puppy-dog eyes.

"...I'm sure we'll find something if we look," Limis tells her, sighing deeply. "A magic item that conceals the wearer's identity... That basically narrows it down to things that criminals use, though."

"...Guess there's no solving this one without some kind of sacrifice. We'll just have to manipulate the odds in our favor somehow."

Before long, Toudou will make her public debut and become a beacon of hope for the people. She can't ask for anyone's help here. And if the Church somehow finds out that Toudou can no longer wear the holy armor, she'll be in for a whole world of trouble.

First Report

On the Holy Warrior's Whereabouts and Forthcoming Objectives

After making the rounds to mercenary procurement services and intermediary agencies in the capital, by the time I return to the inn, it is dark. I visited every well-known intermediary that exists in the capital, but in the end, I couldn't find a single individual that met the criteria I'm looking for.

The position of crusader demands more footwork than any other. I'm used to not seeing results even after a full day of roaming around, but not seeing a single ray of hope is mentally trying. That said, loosening my stipulations and adding a new party member that's underpowered would be meaningless. I have money, and I thought I could find at least one reckless desperado, but it appears my outlook was too half-hearted.

Now I'm free for the first time in ages. This is valuable time I can use without Toudou and his party on my mind. I will not waste a single second. Until now on our journey, so many unforeseen circumstances had occurred. I will take this chance to somehow, someway reorientate my framework moving forward.

I return to my room with my papers under my arm. Opening the door, a strong odor of liquor and stale heat envelops my body. A disastrous scene greets me in the living room.

A number of empty bottles of booze clatter at my feet, and dirty dishes are piled everywhere on the large table. There is a bar in the inn, but it appears someone ordered room service.

"......"

Sanya is splayed out across the table; Rabi is in the corner mumbling to herself, eyes cast downward and clutching her knees. I don't see Amelia anywhere, but if she was here, this would have never happened in the first place.

It was indeed I who gave them respite, but this is an absolute lapse in focus. I want to say something, but I resist and instead simply furrow my brow. If Stey did this, I would have given her a piece of my mind, but these two had actually done their jobs. I need to cut them some slack. Approaching Sanya, who looks utterly disheveled, splayed across the table, I grab her silverwolf ear, drooping sadly, and give it a good tug.

"Bwuh?! ???? Wh-what? What do you want?!"

"...Incorrigible. What if I was here to assassinate you?"

"Argh! Don't pull on my ear!" Sanya yells as she tries shaking me off. "Who'd wanna assassinate me anyway? Geez, boss, isn't it rough, going around thinking about stuff like that all the time?"

I thought maybe she was feeling out of sorts, but it appears I was wrong. Her ears are twitching rapidly from shock. She still reeks of booze, but she's at least sober enough to recognize me.

"I was worried that you weren't feeling well. Just be glad I didn't grab your tail."

"My tail?! You were gonna yank my *tail*?! And not just any tail—a werebeast tail. That's—that's messed up..."

"The two of you haven't left this room all day, have you?" I ask with some exasperation. "What a waste of respite..."

Sanya stands up to her full height and responds indignantly, "Werebeasts aren't exactly common here in the capital, y'know. I'm just trying to stay out of sight. My tail and ears aren't purebred silverwolf quality, but they'll still turn some heads. And if that happens, doing my job will be that much harder..."

"......Fair point."

Sanya's not wrong—she and Rabi both would stick out... But

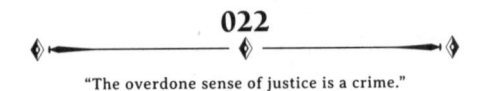

"The overdone sense of justice is a crime."

✟ First Report: On the Holy Warrior's Whereabouts and Forthcoming Objectives

really... Do the two of them plan on staying holed up in here for three full days?

Sanya flicks her slender tail as if shaking off the resentment of having to stay indoors, and she speaks up even louder.

"Rabi's got it bad, too. Word gets out that she's a werebeast, worst-case scenario is she'll be kidnapped. Obviously, we've got recourse for that kind of situation, except it'll be anything but moderate..."

"...You have my apologies. I should've found some way for you to pass the time."

"Darn straight. We can't even exercise in a place like this!"

We are staying in a relatively high-grade inn generally used by merchants. It differs from a mercenary lodging in that there aren't any training rooms. I intended to give them a nice room where they could relax and recover, but it appears I have failed.

"And that's why Rabi is moping?"

"Nah, she's more of a homebody, so this is pretty standard for her..."

I look Rabi over to check on her. Ever since I entered the room, there hasn't been a single indication that she's moved even once. She's wearing her heavy robe, and since her face is turned downward, I can't see her expression. I can hear her muffled murmurs, so I doubt she's sleeping, but it is slightly creepy. We are in no shape to be "homebodies," for God's sake. And this girl is a renowned assassin... I simply can't get my head around it.

Sanya must have been bored out of her skull, and her eyes are now ablaze. She continues talking about things that I don't really need to hear about.

"Oh yeah—she's probably got *that* whole thing going on, too. Y'know, *that*. She's in heat! Wererabbits get it real bad. Haven't been through it myself yet, but apparently wererabbits start really early..."

"......"

023

Defeating the Demon Lord

Rabi stops murmuring. I look toward her slowly and realize that her arms holding her knees are shaking. Still, Sanya won't shut up.

"Chopping off someone's head usually gives her a release, but when she doesn't have an outlet, she tries to stay as still as possible in order to control herself. It might *look* like she's loafing around, but don't get it twisted, boss! Right now, Rabi is in battle with herself. It's incredible, the coping mechanisms wererabbits have for when they're in heat! When Rabi's like that, not even I can touch her. Male, female—she doesn't discriminate."

Well then... Thanks for the note of caution on a rather sensitive issue.

That said, if something doesn't change, we're all in trouble. Judging from her appearance, whether she's in heat or what have you, that means she won't be fit for work until she's...done? We need her again in the future as a divine boon of protection and assassination to cleanly slice off the heads of a few more Demon Lord Army top brass...

"So... When does this 'being in heat' come to an end?" I ask Sanya, keeping my voice low.

She simply laughs at me.

"It *never* ends, boss. I'm willing to bet you have no idea how powerful a wererabbit's carnal urges are. They're in heat all year round. Rabi's half wererabbit, so it's a bit less intense for her, but even she herself doesn't know when it'll let up."

You can't be serious...

I look over instinctively and see Rabi shuddering, trying to overcome the humiliation. If what Sanya says is true, then Rabi won't even have the strength to stop her from talking. And the same goes for fighting, most certainly.

Even though I haven't come close to supplementing our ranks with new members, I'm already being greeted with the discovery of a whole new problem to give me a headache.

"I suppose that means...we got lucky in Cloudburst..."

"?? No, Rabi was in heat the whole time we were there—Aieeee!!"

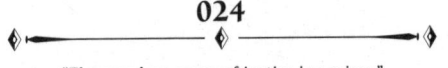

"The overdone sense of justice is a crime."

† First Report: On the Holy Warrior's Whereabouts and Forthcoming Objectives

Sanya cries out and flies into the air, completely keeled over. Without us realizing it, a giant hatchet had been thrown across the room, grazing Sanya's neck before thwacking swiftly into the wall. Rabi stands up uneasily and bores her furious red eyes into us. She's clenching the upper part of her left arm with her right hand, and she looks positively ghastly.

"......A-apologies," she says. "Sanya is...talking nonsense... Please pay it no heed."

"R-right..."

"I can still...do my job. Y-yes, that's right—it's n-no problem at all. This is...how I always am, so...I'm used to it. No need for concern."

"O-okay..."

"......I doubt it will be an issue for you, but, boss...please, not a word to anyone about this. Depending on the situation, I may have no choice but to kill you."

"...Got it."

Is she really okay? If we dispatch her again, isn't there the chance that she'll kill Toudou in a single off moment? Her assassination skills are first-rate. You can never tell if and when she will strike. Taking Toudou's head off would be a piece of cake—he's always unprepared.

I take a moment to clear my mind of ill thoughts and decide to put plans for our strategy on the back burner. Dealing with such a long period of being in heat must make it hard to live. There must be some form of drug that can help control her. I'll try to find it.

"......By the way, what happened to Amelia?"

"...You abandoned her during our vacation, so she's been sulking in bed this whole time," Sanya replies with a shrug as she brushes the spot on her neck that's ever so slightly tinged with blood.

I was obviously right to start looking for new party members right away in the royal capital.

After cleaning up the dishes and liquor bottles in our room, I turn to continue searching for party members who are more dependable.

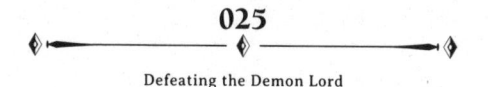

Defeating the Demon Lord

Amelia is stuck sulking in bed, her cheeks puffed out, and Sanya can't stop touching her neck after nearly being beheaded. Then there's Rabi, who's staring at my own neck with bloodred eyes—would anyone look at us and imagine we're a supporting party on a quest to defeat the Demon Lord? I think not. I may have been mistaken in giving everyone respite and stopping their engines from running properly.

"Ares... We're not on the job today. I didn't even say my daily prayers."

I pay no attention to Amelia, who is making statements that are borderline blasphemous, and painstakingly maintain composure while I begin to speak. Yes, we're on break, but of course, I'm going to bring up work at a time like this.

"I finally had some free time on my hands, so I took the opportunity to check out the mercenary intermediary agencies around town. Needless to say, I didn't find a single mercenary that fit my demands—"

"???"

"Uh, boss, remember how you agreed that we'd have today off? I was wondering what you were up to all morning. I know how this goes. If you don't take a break, then we won't be able to, either!"

The three of you certainly weren't struggling to take it easy.

After hitting up the intermediaries and not finding anyone that fits the bill, my next resource is to rely on personal connections. Unfortunately, my connections don't look very useful, but Sanya and Rabi are apprentices of a legendary mercenary. They definitely have a lot of acquaintances. Maybe I can use them to acquire some extremely good personnel at an extremely low rate?

After hearing my spiel, Rabi shifts her gaze my way and says, "There isn't anyone like that, boss. That's not happening."

"What, you're worried that we're not enough?!"

"No, there's...nothing wrong with the two of you per se. We're simply understaffed. I want to cover all our bases."

It's not that I don't have *any* complaints about Sanya and Rabi,

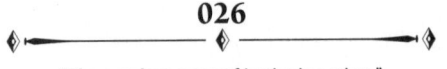

"The overdone sense of justice is a crime."

but there's no use detailing them now. Sanya leans in, and Rabi speaks indifferently.

"Are you suggesting we sell off our compatriots? An accomplished mercenary is capable of mitigating as much risk as humanly possible. Boss, your demands are simply too extreme. Even a sheer desperado has better options for work."

"I fully understand that. I'm looking for people with a death wish. That's what it will take to maintain world peace."

"Yikes, that's a horrible way to put it."

"This is more or less the same method I used to find the two of you. It's not an impossible task," I insist.

Rabi casts her gaze downward and speaks again, this time in the saddest voice I've heard from her to date.

"Well...... That's because you weren't after our master... You were after *us*. I'm pretty sure if you tried hiring him, he would have refused. Our master is an accomplished individual, but he has... more than his fair share of quirks."

"Hmm, I see... In that case, is there anyone else of a similar caliber?"

Pushing through irrationally will draw us back to the light. We will have to reduce costs as much as possible. In the end, we might be able to ensnare someone through the convenient phrase "it will be worth your while," but at any rate, for the time being, if we don't get someone else in our party, we are in trouble.

Rabi's eyes go wide at my question, and she shudders in fear.

"?! A-are you...being serious?"

"......If I wasn't bound by a contract, I'd wanna turn tail right about now. We truly got thrown into the most absurd bunch out there. Granted, I figured that out real quick back in the water capital."

A crusader knows no fear.

Sanya lifts up an empty liquor bottle and stares at it intensely before speaking in a serious tone.

"Our answer's no. No such person exists."

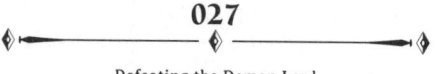

Defeating the Demon Lord

Her voice and face are void of their usual playfulness. All I see before me is a professional mercenary.

"Boss, because you successfully negotiated with our master to hire us—there's a number of folks keeping an eye on you. I'm talking mega-elite mercenaries who don't hang around at the local watering hole looking for regular contract gigs."

"……"

"They're not swayed by large sums of money, and they don't treat their apprentices as disposable. And the one person who takes jokes way too far—that's our master. It's what made him a legend, and he ended up taking half werebeasts like me and Rabi under his wing. If you, boss, really want someone like him for your beyond-dangerous missions…you'll need to show results that'll compel them to help you."

Sanya is spot on, just like Rabi. That said, I don't really care. If worse comes to worst, I don't care if they're totally expendable, I just need to supplement our ranks as soon as humanly possible.

Sanya must be finished with her spiel—she bites down on the empty liquor bottle and looks at me with a narrowed gaze. I can see her razor-sharp silverwolf werebeast fangs.

The mercenaries around town must have heard of our defeat of the sea demon Heljarl. However, if no new members are coming our way regardless, that means that they're not looking to join a group that's accomplished what we have. It signifies simply too much danger—our achievement is seen as fit for heroes. Nobody wants to take on a similar request.

Now that I have a completely accurate understanding of the situation, I look back at my two mercenaries and bark out an order.

"Okay. Sanya, Rabi—talk to Bran and your fellow mercenaries about all the experience you gained working under me and just how much you've grown. Tell them how fantastic of a leader I am and how incredible of a compatriot Amelia is. Spread word of the rare experiences awaiting them—experiences that money cannot buy."

"?! Boss, I…I don't hate it when you cut to the chase, but this feels wrong… Are you asking me to lie?"

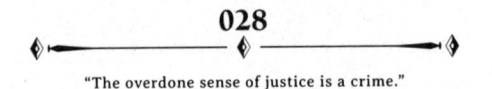

"The overdone sense of justice is a crime."

First Report: On the Holy Warrior's Whereabouts and Forthcoming Objectives

"Listen up, Sanya. Our journey will be exceptionally arduous—but the more people that join us, the higher our survival rate will be. I have an obligation to produce the very best results possible and a responsibility to ensure everyone who joins us comes out alive. Do you understand?"

I choose to sidestep her question. The number of people is an important factor. Sometimes, numbers don't make up for a lack in quality.

Sanya's entire body shudders. Her tail slaps the floor, and she stares up at me.

"No chance. I might look like...this...and I appreciate how tough you are, but I can't help here. I've already talked about the rare experiences this journey provides... I'd really rather you manage with just us for now."

Such meek words. Wait—by rare experiences, does she mean Mermares—?

It seems like trying to squeeze Sanya and Rabi any harder isn't going to work. They're both apprentices of Bran—clearly, they've been taught not to get mixed up in others' shenanigans. That much I can tell, and I guess I need to be content with this.

I look toward Amelia. She's cocked her head to the side, visibly perplexed.

"...Don't you have any mercenary acquaintances, boss?" Rabi asks hesitantly. "I heard that you've worked alongside mercenaries in the past..."

"...Unfortunately, the mercenaries that I know are all on the front lines or six feet under. I sent out letters long ago, but the prospects look thin."

I don't know where she learned about my past, but the mercenaries I'm acquainted with are still on active duty, unlike Bran. They're all participating in the fight against the Demon Lord's army. The front lines are barely managing to keep the army at bay, and even if it was for the Holy Warrior, I can't imagine any of them abandoning their comrades.

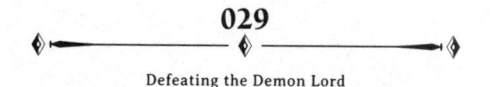

"How about supplementing our ranks from the Church?"

"...Most members of the Church are priests. I don't need any more priests."

I need someone who can supplement what we're currently missing. That means a robust warrior who can support our front line or a mage who isn't a complete blunder. Those are the two types I'm after, but...what can I do? I need to at least try plan B. I already know that I need to have a conversation with them at least once while we're in the capital.

I make my request while not looking at Amelia as much as possible—she's so defenseless, I can hardly believe she's a member of the clergy.

"Amelia. Sorry to bother you during your respite, but I need you to contact someone."

"...And just who might that be?"

"Glacia. I need to speak to her. Bring her here at once."

A number of unexpected circumstances have arisen on our journey supporting the defeat of the Demon Lord, but if pressed to say which is highest on the list, it would have to be the anthropomorphizing of the glacial plant demi dragon. I've slain innumerable demons and seen many forms of outrageous magic, but this was simply outside the realm of the ordinary.

The timing was also terrible, and adding in Toudou's personality, I really had a headache for a while. The fact that the glacial plant is still functioning as a peaceful member of Toudou's party is nothing short of good fortune. (Of course, her good manners are partially thanks to my persuasion.)

All Glacia did was eat at first, which really drained our resources, but after our negotiation in Golem Valley, she's really come into her own in terms of participation. She is of high-level demi dragon blood, and her level of prowess is favorable in comparison with Toudou and company. She stood her own ground in

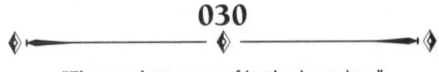

First Report: On the Holy Warrior's Whereabouts and Forthcoming Objectives

the battle against Heljarl, too. I was deeply impressed by her resolve then, and now I see increased potential in her.

I arrive at a bar in the capital popular with mercenaries. As I wait in the back of the joint, which is famous for quantity over quality in their food, a small shadowy figure enters with trepidation, sticking out like a sore thumb.

Her dark-green wavy hair matches her eyes, an uncommon sight in human beings. From looks alone, she seems to be ten years old or so, and among the day-drinking mercenaries here, she's blatantly out of her element.

Mercenaries come in many races, ages, and genders, but a child Glacia's age becoming a mercenary is exceptionally rare. The bar staff, used to seeing rough-and-tumble characters, don't know if she's a customer or a lost kid.

Glacia has come unarmed, leaving her weapon—a war hammer—behind. I check the time, and it's still thirty minutes before our agreed meeting. Crafty little thing... She's definitely learning.

It seems Glacia was planning to wait near the entrance until our meeting, but the moment she sees me, she looks ready to burst into tears. It's been a while since we last met; I can tell she's much more powerful.

Generally, leveling up is a special privilege for humans, but it's not unheard of for other species to level up, too. It's not as effective as with human beings, but they can absorb others' life force and grow in their capabilities. The gap between Toudou and Glacia is still there, although it's gradually closing.

Maybe Glacia thinks that ignoring me has made me upset—she approaches nervously, shaking like a leaf. I can't help but think I put the fear of God in her just a bit too much last time.

When she arrives at my table, she bows her head, her whole body shrinking in size.

"S-sorry I'm...late."

"Why didn't you bring your weapon?"

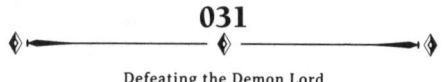

031

Defeating the Demon Lord

"......Huh?"

Mercenaries never go anywhere without their weapons. Those who do are unprepared and seen as soft in the eyes of their compatriots. I'm not a mercenary, but without special reason, my mace never leaves my side.

"You're not late. Glacia, are you...afraid of me?"

Clever girl, Glacia.

I was, after all, expecting her to make a blunder. If she had brought her weapon, I planned on picking on her and intimidating her a little bit, and if she was late—same story, I was going to rake her over the coals.

The only thing holding down the powerful demi dragon Glacia was fear itself. And fear always fades with time. To the extent I don't understand Glacia's psychological makeup, expecting her to be flawless is like asking her to surrender herself to the will of God. I fold my hands and stare deeply into Glacia's eyes.

"You're early, Glacia. Thirty minutes early, that is. What are you doing here already? Didn't you think that might be an annoyance?"

"...?!"

She's dodged all my provocations carefully. Her actions show deep consideration, but I can still smell fear. Making her more afraid than necessary will also prove ineffective, I think. I have no desire to punish her unreasonably.

"I'm only joking. Sit. I don't have any meat skewers for you today. Although we could always order some..."

"Um... O-okay..."

I shrug and smile at Glacia as she takes a seat, but for some reason, she's still shuddering. At this rate, there's no reason to worry about her betraying Toudou for the time being. Dragons are easier to deal with than expected, from what I've heard. And there are dragon warriors that exist in this world, too, I've learned. Whether she's willing or not, my expectations are rising.

"I've come into a bit of money, see. You've been doing a good job of following my instructions lately, so I'm happy to feed you

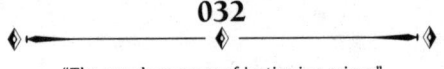

"The overdone sense of justice is a crime."

First Report: On the Holy Warrior's Whereabouts and Forthcoming Objectives

as much as you want today. Order whatever you'd like. We can talk after."

"……"

I hand the menu to the demi dragon turned human girl, who is still blatantly terrified. But her expression doesn't change. Negotiating with her on a full stomach will yield better results, and it's definitely a more effective approach, however...

"At the end of the day, I am an official of the Church. I won't even attack a wicked beast without good reason. It's in your best interest to order something, but whether you decide to eat or not to eat, my treatment will not change."

Glacia finally starts ordering food with shaky hands. Dishes arrive one after the other. Seeing the portions on each massive plate disappear inside her tiny body is nothing short of a magic trick, and everyone is wide-eyed watching Glacia wholeheartedly devote herself to eating.

I observe her studiously. Glacia is definitely a nonhuman. But no one here realizes this.

She has high stamina and physical strength along with her mimicry abilities. Fear tactics work on her, and she's capable of growth. Despite her myriad issues, she could be the perfect solution to how short-staffed we are.

It's a very good thing we didn't eliminate her. This is a blessing of Ahz Gried.

Eventually, Glacia ceases stuffing her mouth after finishing over ten different orders of food. It's hard to believe she made a huge, thick steak disappear down her gullet in mere seconds. The staff, who looked positively worried at first, is staring at Glacia in sheer amazement now. The bill is racking up quickly, but I remain hopeful that the return on investment will be well worth it.

I speak to Glacia again as she quaffs an entire stein of water and exhales.

"All done eating? Let's move on, then. I'll keep it straight to the point. You've done well, Glacia. I need some of your brethren."

Defeating the Demon Lord

"......Huh?"

Glacia's eyes go wide, and she looks up at me in astonishment. She still has sauce around her mouth; that and her dumbfounded stare make her look like just any little girl.

"The more the merrier, but for now, bring me just one of your fellows. Someone like you, who can take on a human form. I don't care which gender, but if possible, a female. Also, don't worry about their level of discipline—I'll take care of that."

This is business. If it helps me save the world, I'll make use of any magical being I can.

§ § §

A water droplet three centimeters in diameter is suspended in the air in front of Toudou as she stands erect and focuses. She stares at the water and tries to move it with her mind. Slowly, the water droplet begins to circle around Toudou, smoothly at first, as if being pushed by the wind, and then gradually with more momentum. After ten minutes, the water droplet is barely visible as it whirs around Toudou with incredible force.

Limis isn't the only one who entered a covenant with an elemental spirit in Cloudburst. Toudou also successfully bonded with a mid-level water spirit, although that hardly compares to Limis's achievement with a high-level one.

Manipulating a water droplet is common training for elementalists practicing water magic. Toudou has convened on actively using the time in the capital and is training in magic at the training room in Limis's childhood home.

Toudou can feel the water spirit she's in a covenant with crying out with joy at the mana flowing through her body alongside a distinct sense of feedback. Maybe—just maybe—this is even more incredible than the first moment she wielded the holy sword Ex.

Since her summoning, because Toudou received the divine blessing of the Three Deities and Eight Spirit Kings, her affinity as

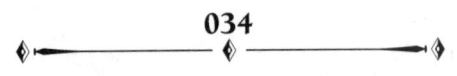

"The overdone sense of justice is a crime."

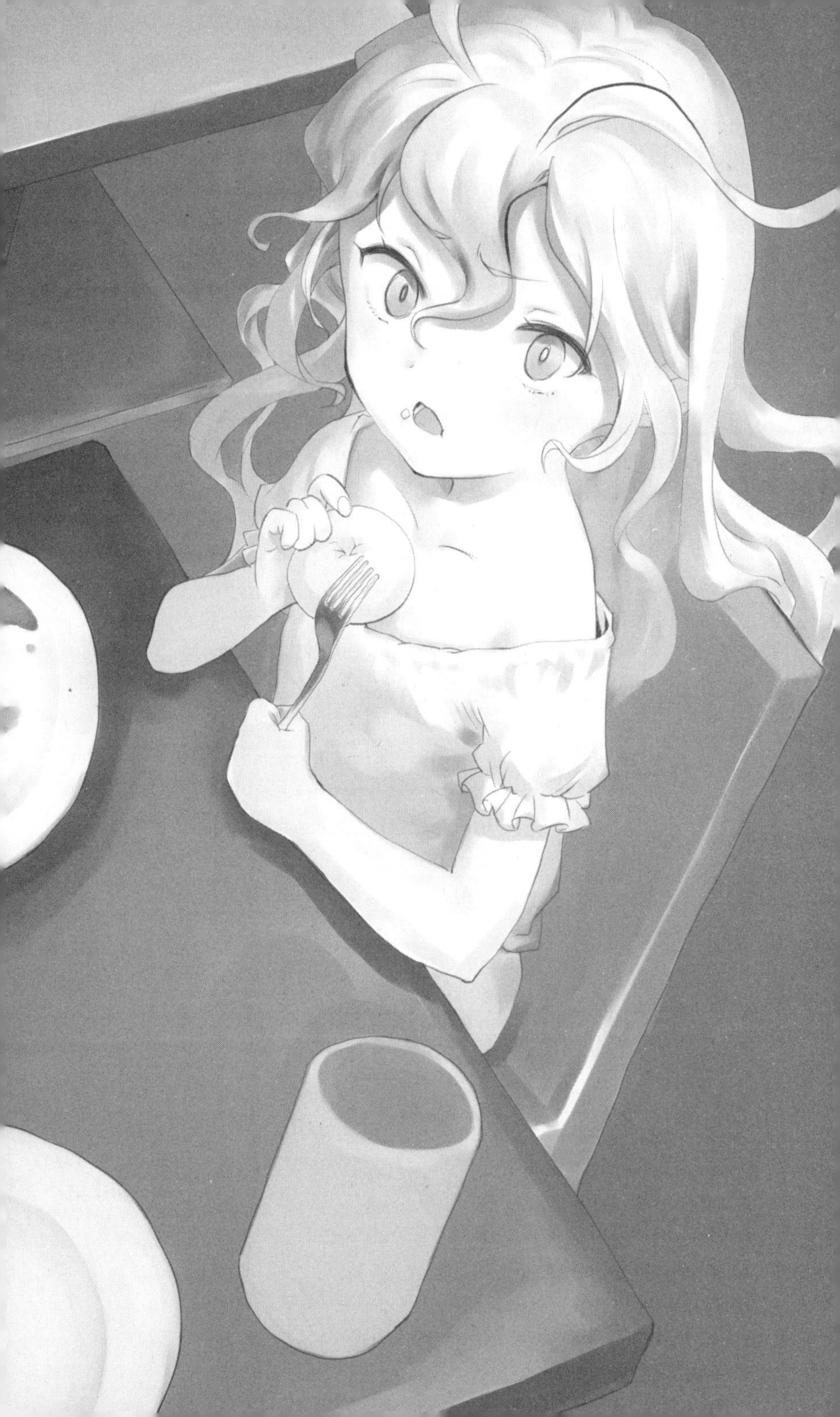

an elementalist has been very high. Without being able to wear the holy armor, and with her shield broken, any battles that come her way in the near future will be quite risky, but if she levels up her magic ability and uses it effectively, she should be able to make up for this fact and make it through her battles.

Toudou focuses her mind, and nearby, Limis yells a sharp command.

"No! Garnet! Stop threatening her!"

"Grrrr... Grrrrrr..."

While Toudou's training is going well, Limis is embroiled in a difficult problem. She's face-to-face with Garnet, the first elemental spirit she contracted with. Although it used to be small enough to fit in the palm of her hand, it's now exploded in growth to be one meter long. Its scales shine with burning flame, and its eyes sparkle like rare gemstones. A short burst of flame erupts from its nostrils, and its mouth is lined with fangs.

"Ugh...," Limis groans, putting a hand to her brow at Garnet's intimidating behavior. "What do I do? These two just don't mesh at all..."

The reason Garnet is all fired up is because of the high-level water spirit cowering and shielding itself behind Limis. After many twists and turns, Limis successfully entered into a covenant with this elemental spirit in Cloudburst. This spirit is supposed to grant massive powers to Limis, but so far, it has failed to wield such power under her command.

"...I guess they're never going to get along. I didn't think Garnet would be so picky," Toudou says.

"Marine seems weaker than Garnet, too..."

Limis's words are tainted with exhaustion as Aquamarine, taking the form of a young girl, shakes its head defiantly on Limis's lap. After entering the covenant, Limis named this spirit Aquamarine to go with Garnet—that much was a success. But afterward, everything was a mess. Really—she should have considered Garnet's attitude since the moment she entered the covenant.

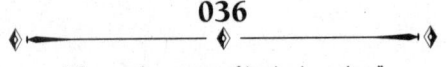

"The overdone sense of justice is a crime."

First Report: On the Holy Warrior's Whereabouts and Forthcoming Objectives

High-level spirits are much more independent than mid- or low-level varieties. Even before her covenant with Aquamarine, Garnet had been throwing a fit and trying to stop it from happening, so there was no reason for things to go well after it was established.

In conception, having this poor of a bond with a contracted spirit would mean that the covenant itself would never have been possible, so this is an exceedingly rare situation. This is a huge misstep by Limis, who was in a huff to get the covenant established in a hurry.

"...It's like Garnet has made up his mind that he hates her."

Limis reaches out to pet Garnet's head, but it twists its neck to avoid her. Limis sighs deeply. An elementalist's prowess hinges entirely on the power of the spirits and mages they work with and the level of chemistry and trust between them, in addition to the chemistry between the different spirits in their servitude. Right now, Limis can't even exercise the same level of power she could before entering a covenant with Aquamarine.

Water and fire are opposing elemental forces. Using the spirit magic possible through borrowing Aquamarine's powers has been interrupted by Garnet, and Garnet's fire magic has been greatly reduced in effectiveness by the presence of Aquamarine, who Garnet hates.

"If this was how things were going to turn out, then I— Oh, forget it."

Limis started to say that she should have rushed to enter a covenant with an elemental spirit other than water, but she quickly went quiet. It wasn't something she could say in front of Garnet, much less Aquamarine, who had entered a covenant with her.

Toudou crouches down next to Aquamarine writhing on Limis's lap and says, "...Marine, can you summon Mermares again? It was thanks to him that we entered a covenant, and if you can get him here, he can get Garnet under control—you do know him, right, Marine?"

"......"

Indeed, Mermares was incredibly strong. Although Garnet was surrounded by water and its powers were reduced then, Mermares quickly fell on Garnet, who was throwing a fit, and got it under control. It was hard to believe that a merman could actually go that wild.

Without Mermares, making a covenant with Aquamarine would have been difficult. Limis and Aria assumed that Mermares wasn't a monster but rather a guardian that had been granted the divine protection of the God of the Sea. And that was why he was so hesitant to help out when they were in a pinch with the high-level spirit. Mermares was far from looking holy or divine, but given the timing of the incident, he had no choice but to duck for cover soon after appearing.

Aquamarine continues shaking her head as Toudou speaks.

"...I guess you can't call on him without being in the ocean. He is a merman, after all..."

"Even if you summon Mermares to calm Garnet down, that isn't going to provide a fundamental solution to our problem."

Everything is happening because of Limis's lack of experience. If her capacity as an elementalist to control Garnet were high enough, then Marine, who she contracted with after the fact, wouldn't have been threatened like this.

Aquamarine has wrapped itself around Limis's leg now, and she scoops it up by the armpit. As a spirit, Aquamarine doesn't have a physical body, and Limis can pick it up easily, even with her thin arms.

With the cold feeling of Aquamarine's skin against hers, Limis says, "It's okay, Marine. Don't worry—we won't make you do anything you don't want to."

Breaking the covenant is possible, but Limis has no such plans at the moment. That much they can avoid.

Garnet must not be pleased at its master's appearance—it belches a massive ball of flame. Because Garnet is her contracted spirit, its flame can't hurt her. Aquamarine, stuck in its master's arms, is frightened but keeps its little eyes fixated on Limis. As

"The overdone sense of justice is a crime."

First Report: On the Holy Warrior's Whereabouts and Forthcoming Objectives

she meets Marine's gaze, a powerful sense of duty wells up within Limis.

"You'll become close soon. I'll coax him into it... Just put up with him a while longer."

It probably won't actually happen soon, but Limis has a few potential ideas in mind.

First, she will raise her own level, allowing her to boost her skills as an elementalist and coax Garnet. Second, she will enter a covenant with another high-level spirit of equal rank and use them as a sort of cushioning.

Hearing Limis's confident reassurance, Aquamarine smiles in relief. Toudou speaks to Limis while she holds Aquamarine tightly, as if consoling the elemental spirit.

"...No matter what, we need to contract with another spirit. Not just you, Limis, but me too."

"You're right..."

The ferocious battle with Heljarl, who held unfathomable power, led to a great shift in the awareness of Toudou and everyone in her party. They need power. Toudou, Limis, and Aria all remain restless about their state of growth.

Limis's eyes suddenly light up when she remembers their compatriot who left that morning looking so sullen.

"...By the way, what was Glacia going out for anyway?"

"Who knows? Apparently, she's got some friend in the royal capital."

"But she's a demi dragon."

"...Glacia's a mystery wrapped in an enigma... She didn't seem to want me to pry, and besides, I trust her. I'm sure she'll let us know if something goes wrong... Oh, hey, speak of the devil—"

Just then, Glacia walks into the training area. Her deep-green wavy hair and tiny body resemble a child, but the hero's party knows the vast, surging power lurking within her.

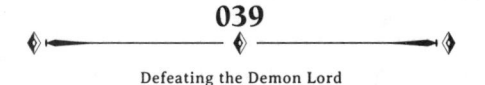

Glacia joined the party through happenstance, but at this point, her battle prowess is reputable. She's as silent as always, but she flew into battle against Heljarl with her physical strength on display. When she wields her giant war hammer, she outclasses anyone else.

She looked depressed when she left alone this morning, but she looks even more downtrodden now. Toudou wonders if something happened to her, but for now, she smiles and waves at the demi dragon girl.

"Welcome back, Glacia. That was quick—did you finish your business?"

Usually, Glacia would probably leave silently or give a simple one- or two-word response. But today, she is different. She looks up with conviction and stares at Toudou with open eyes. Her deep-green irises threaten to swallow Toudou and Limis whole, and she can't find any words. Then finally, Glacia speaks.

"Hey! Toudou, Limis! Glacia's super happy right now! In fact, I'm so full of energy that I wanna take down the Demon Lord ASAP! How 'bout it, Toudou?! C'mon!"

"What the—?!"

Toudou remains frozen in a smile. Glacia's expression doesn't change a bit as she jumps into an impromptu, nimble dance.

§ § §

Seeing my expression upon my return to the inn, Amelia, her usual laid-back self, furrows her brow.

"...It didn't go so well, I take it."

"Glacia, that brat... Apparently, she doesn't have any acquaintances or friends."

I had low expectations from the get-go. Since Glacia morphed into human form, there are a lot of things I don't understand. I confirmed that Glacia doesn't even know why she turned into a human the first time we met, and I surmised that the main cause was not Glacia herself but rather related to Toudou's peculiar trait of having divine protection from Zion Gusion, the God of Love. For

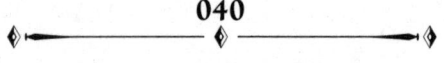

"The overdone sense of justice is a crime."

First Report: On the Holy Warrior's Whereabouts and Forthcoming Objectives

this reason, Glacia not having any dragon friends that can take on human form is well within my realm of assumption.

That said, a monster morphing into human form is a ball of potential—above all, monsters have basic capacities far greater than any human. Their capacity for growth is less than their human counterparts, but since we currently don't even have time for growth, this is the most effective option available.

Above all else, the most exceptional factor is that monsters don't even have avid backers. Unlike Sanya, Rabi, or Amelia, if a monster dies, nobody will come complaining. If necessary, they can be used as a wall, and no matter how many are killed, there will always be more, which makes replenishing the ranks a cinch.

What we need now is to research the mechanism that caused Glacia to morph into a human—and suddenly, at that. Using Toudou to discover evidence by inspection regarding human morphing isn't realistic, but there are others that have Zion's divine protection. If Glacia can get one of her brethren to come our way, I plan on proceeding via trial and error by borrowing the power of divine protection from someone.

However, without any friends or acquaintances, there is no point to my empty threats. I understand that there aren't many glacial plants living in the Great Forest of the Vale, but it would appear that demi dragon glacial plants don't gather in flights; instead, they're animals that demarcate a vast area to live in alone. They are half plant, however, and their method of reproduction differs from other dragons, and they live in isolation...in pure solitude.

Maybe the reason that Glacia, morphed into human form, is so quiet all the time is not because she's just sulky but because her species is simply not very social in conception.

I have no intention of pestering Glacia about this, but at current, our search for new members is back to the drawing board.

"Damn, nothing's working out. Ugh... I need disposable compatriots, ones I don't mind dying."

"...Is that really how you'd define a compatriot?"

I let my real feelings slip, and Amelia looks at me with disgust.

Sanya can't be run into the ground like that due to the nature of her contract, and maybe she knows it, and she's baiting me—she snaps her tail.

At times like this, the numerous encumbrances placed upon me as an official of the Church are particularly regrettable. Without regard to method, there are a number of strategies available to us, but a priest cannot defile the name of the Church—that is, cannot do anything that defies morality.

At the moment, I can't think of anyone that would die for me except Gregorio. I can think of a few that would probably die when we don't need them to... I really need to think of a new option.

"For now, I bargained with Glacia to please communicate more with Toudou's party. She is way too passive. Amelia, can you help with that?"

I originally assigned Glacia to a messenger role. She is to gather information from the other side and give it to us, then implicitly offer our direction to Toudou's party and spark them into action. Lately, Glacia has become more important as a contributor to battle, but she is neglecting her main duties. That's third-rate spy work.

At my question, Amelia bats her large indigo eyes and cocks her head to the side, confused.

"...What exactly do you mean by 'help'?"

"She doesn't seem to know what to talk about with Toudou and his party. I need you to provide her instructions on how to communicate— Oh, by the way, Amelia...... Would you say you have a lot of friends?" I ask her, my expression serious.

"Are you making fun of me?"

I completely forgot. Didn't even consider it. Amelia is actually rather eccentric. She's quite gutsy, sure, but I don't get the sense that she's a particularly gifted communicator.

For some reason, Amelia gives me a very theatric thumbs-up.

"I am a master of simulation. My tricksy wiles will have both men and women like putty in my hands. In just a month's time, a

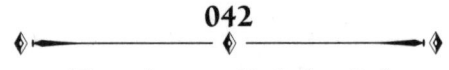

"The overdone sense of justice is a crime."

First Report: On the Holy Warrior's Whereabouts and Forthcoming Objectives

lonely dragon can become the hottest dragon on the block. I have studied numerous books on the subject."

She says this with a glazed look in her eyes and pursed lips. I already know that this woman has a staunch poker face.

This is a real problem… But she's the only one who can facilitate communication with Glacia.

"…My dear Amelia—you're a competent, dependable gal, right?"

I'm grasping at straws by asking her, but she doesn't crack even the faintest of smiles, and she clutches a tight fist to her chest.

"Yes. That's me—your dear Amelia, a competent, dependable gal."

Something about her absurdly overserious expression makes my stomach start to ache. I have about as much faith in her as I would in Stey.

As I fall silent, someone taps me on the shoulder.

"Um, boss, you've got your dear Sanya right behind you—a silver-wolf, the most famously social creature ever…"

This is like…being between a rock and a hard place. What should I do? Can I really trust my compatriots? Relying on one's subordinates is one of the magnanimous tasks of a superior, but can I take responsibility for what happens as a result?

With Amelia in front of me and Sanya behind me, I'm in a quandary. Just then, unable to be left unnoticed, a faint voice falls upon me.

"*Cough, cough*… Boss… If you'd like, perhaps I could keep an eye on things for you?"

Rabi speaks from the corner, her red eyes burning brightly underneath her hood. She looks as haggard as ever.

If I was forced to choose the most diligent, honest one among these three, it would have to be Rabi. That said, if she works too hard and passes out on me, that also invites trouble.

The blessings of Ahz Gried are worth nothing during peak mating season.

Still hacking up a lung, Rabi offers another response in a relatively calm tone.

"*Cough, cough*… Having a task to focus on…will keep me busy."

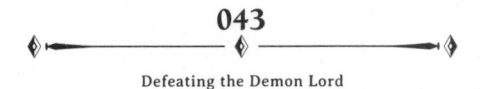

Defeating the Demon Lord

"...Understood. That's a huge help. You'll be Amelia and Sanya's backup. That...shouldn't cause any problems."

Amelia puffs out her cheeks ostentatiously, and Sanya suppresses a laugh.

My mind is made up—I have no other choice but to believe in them. The only thing left is to get Glacia a bit closer inside Toudou and his party's circle. If I can't task her with a job of this level, then how can we call her a compatriot? At any rate...even if she fails, it won't be fatal.

"The ultimate goal is to get Glacia close enough to Toudou that even telling him his faults won't arouse any suspicion."

"Understood. Leave it to me, the beautiful, elegant, sagacious Amelia, your closest confidant and concoctor of inscrutable stratagems."

She has to be taking it over the top on purpose. God, this is infinitely more exhausting than even my chat with Glacia...

Amelia and Sanya immediately gather around the table and start discussing, and Rabi joins them, looking annoyed.

I have separate business to attend to—my arrangements with the Church. I need to ascertain the current state of affairs and prepare our next plan... I have so many things to do, my head already hurts. Oh, and that's right—I need to contact Zolan, who I sent to the Church headquarters, too.

Before moving on to the next order of business, I remember something special that I acquired outside: a potion that controls werebeasts' sexual urges. There are hardly any werebeasts in Ruxe, and this was hard to obtain. Its effects vary between individuals, I'm told, but it's better than nothing at all.

I put the glass bottle containing transparent light-blue liquid in front of Rabi. Her eyes flutter imperceptibly.

"What's this—?"

"A werebeast tranquility potion. It works differently for different beings, but for a half werebeast like yourself, one sip should calm you down for a few days. It might be just temporary piece of mind, but I went out and bought it for you anyway."

"The overdone sense of justice is a crime."

First Report: On the Holy Warrior's Whereabouts and Forthcoming Objectives

"Wow, nice work, boss. That stuff doesn't come cheap, right?"

Sanya whistles, attempting to pull my leg. She's not wrong—it was more expensive than a regular potion—but all solutions require sacrifice. I'm writing this off as an expense, for sure.

Rabi grips the potion in her hand and holds it up, staring with fire in her eyes. Her tiny body shudders.

"......Boss...... You went through...all that trouble...just for me? Thank...you...so...much..."

"Don't worry about it. It's part of your contract."

Considering her contributions during the battle against Heljarl, this isn't nearly enough. I'm expecting even more legendary battle from her moving forward.

Watching over Rabi staring at the potion, Sanya crosses her legs and says, "Good for you, Rabi. I mean, the other day you said those don't work at all, but still."

"......What?"

"Ah-ha-ha, boss, you seriously have a few screws loose. Do you really think that Rabi, who's been through so much, has never tried a potion or two? Like, it's so bad, it even gets in the way of her work."

"...Now that you mention it, you're right. That's my mistake; I should have checked first."

What a waste of money. If I would have just checked, I could have saved it.

"......No, it's fine."

Rabi pulls down her mask and uncaps the potion, bringing it to her lips. She takes the whole bottle down in one swig and wipes her mouth with her sleeve, looking up at me. When she took her mask down, she exposed her skin, which is glowing fire red.

"......This is definitely a tranquility potion. It's working already. Thank you, boss. *Cough, cough!*"

"...Ah, that's good to hear. Don't overdo it, though. Take a break if you don't feel well."

"...Mmm... Okay..."

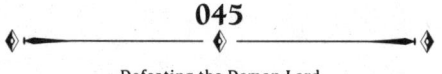

Defeating the Demon Lord

Sympathy is painful business. It's looking more and more likely that there's simply nothing that can be done. Up until now, I've relied on the Holy Warrior getting everything done through brute force, so if that doesn't work again this time, I will be at the end of my rope.

Nothing to do but wait and see, I guess?

I chalk this up to another task on my list and start to think about how to report to the Church.

§ § §

"Toudou, I really think you ought to try harder to level up in earnest. At your current ability, there's no waaay you'll survive what awaits you! Your magic and swordsmanship are so mediocre, it's making all the past Holy Warriors cry. Isn't it embarrassing to need me, Glacia, to protect you? C'mon!"

"……"

"Limis, you're not cutting it. First of all, you don't have enough spirit covenants. And you call yourself an elementalist… I have to stop myself from laughing. It's hilarious. A riot! If you don't have the guts, then you'd better switch places with an actual, accomplished mage!"

"……"

"?! What just happened…?! Limis?! Nao?!"

When Aria comes back from running an errand, she's greeted by Toudou and Limis hugging their knees, eyes glazed over. Glacia is dancing in front of Toudou and Limis, and she twirls to speak to Aria, who is running back and forth in a panic.

"There you are, you sham of a swordfighter!"

§ § §

The Great Church of Ahz Gried lies in the very center of the royal capital. The solemn, massive chalk-white building boasts the

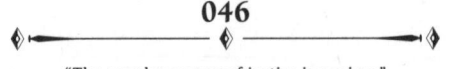

"The overdone sense of justice is a crime."

First Report: On the Holy Warrior's Whereabouts and Forthcoming Objectives

second greatest scale after the Church's headquarters, and as a house of God, this place is constantly filled with many priests.

In a room in the back, I am receiving information from a page. The room, which bears no religious air nor has any windows, features one large desk and many shelves holding innumerable files. A huge map spread out on the desk is marked in various places with Xs.

My mission is to ensure that Toudou can defeat the Demon Lord, but this is something that must be viewed from a bird's-eye perspective. The journey to defeat the Demon Lord also requires cooperation from a multitude of collaborators. Toudou and company's journey is a diligent study in devotion, so publicly announced collaborators are few, but behind the scenes, there are many. Simply eliminating the demons one faces directly is not the same as defeating the Demon Lord. Furthermore, the Demon Lord we're facing in this generation is particularly troublesome.

"...Just what is the Demon Lord's army thinking?"

"In terms of timing, we're currently lined up with the period when the Holy Warrior defeated Felsa."

The marks on the precise map, a treasured item of the Church, indicate the positions of the Demon Lord's army invasion. Until just the other day, the Demon Lord had separated his troops into different corps and was attacking different kingdoms in unison.

In conception, splitting up the army would mean that each unit's battle power would decrease. However, at the foundation of this simultaneous invasion lies the sheer depth of the Demon Lord's army ranks. The Demon Lord Kranos's army is superior in numbers and strength. Each of the diverse, powerful monsters that comprise its ranks have unique specialties, and through different strategic combinations therein that allow shortcomings to be supplemented and advantages to be fully exercised, the army boasts unrivaled power.

Conversely, the human kingdoms can't even come to baseline agreements. After some time, upon finally reaching a framework

Defeating the Demon Lord

for cooperation, they are still being pressed on all sides. The sea was taken, and the overland roads were cut off—textbook military tactics.

However, for some time, the Demon Lord's army, after making such a fierce onslaught, has suddenly completely stopped their invasion. The forces in each region are still being developed, but they aren't engaging in any aggressive attack patterns.

Demons have inherent and powerful aggression toward humans. This goes for those fought against on our journey thus far—the vampire Zarpahn Drago Fahni, fought in the Great Forest of the Vale; Felsa, the steel tiger werebeast, fought in Golem Valley; and the sea demon Heljarl, fought in the sunken temple at the bottom of the ocean. The fact that the human Gregorio had the highest level of aggression thus far remains a mystery—but…there is definitely still something important to discover there.

"…Shit, this is really a pain with every encroaching step."

"I see you're the same as ever, Ares."

The page, who I've worked with on a number of jobs to date and knows me well, looks at me with disdain.

The demons we're facing this time around are different from others—they're too smart. Using magical items is troublesome enough, but the ability to command different monsters with highly individual, egoistic desires at will truly shows the unfathomable nature of Demon Lord Kranos's power.

"Ruxe already has this information, right?"

"Yes. Of course. It's caused quite a stir in each region…"

This behavior is guaranteed to be 80 or 90 percent due to the Holy Warrior. Our opposition absolutely already knows that a hero has been summoned. Does the current stalemate mean that they're thinking about their next course of action? The more I think about it, I realize that this Demon Lord Army is acting calculatedly, like human beings, and it makes me sick.

There is only a single fact I can claim right now—taking down Heljarl was a good omen. And defeating him before the Demon Lord

"The overdone sense of justice is a crime."

First Report: On the Holy Warrior's Whereabouts and Forthcoming Objectives

could give him an accurate awareness of the Holy Warrior's identity was also good fortune. Despite his strength, the sea demon Heljarl, who had closed off the oceans, was comparably more important than any of the others in the Demon Lord's inner circle. This fact will absolutely matter down the road.

However, the next time we face off against an upper-level demon, it won't go down as well as it did against Heljarl.

"If you see any suspicious movement, please let me know at once."

"Understood."

I need a method to ascertain the Demon Lord Army's movements. I want spies on the inside. And I need to finalize a plan to increase Toudou's levels. I'm curious about the result of the analysis performed on the magical item we obtained from Heljarl, and I can't let up on searching for new compatriots.

Regarding armaments, I have a moment to consider this further. Toudou's armaments at current are first-rate, but his shield has been destroyed, and his other equipment isn't completely optimized.

Is it too much to ask for a powerful group of female spies with vast financial resources and powerful armaments to come forth to cooperate with us willingly...? And...increasing my own level certainly comes last in order of importance.

I leave the room and walk along the hallway outside. Perhaps due to the situation of our current era, the Church is filled to the brim with people. It would be fantastic if God could defeat the Demon Lord for us, but unfortunately, according to the teachings of Ahz Gried, only believers have the power to restore order to the universe.

Just then, the page, who walks beside me, speaks again, suddenly remembering something.

"By the way, did you hear? The Mad Eater has a new apprentice."

"......I'm aware."

"Of course you are—I would expect no less. Apparently, this apprentice is going to take the next crusader exam."

"?! *Cough, cough!*"

The page's eyes go wide in surprise as I suddenly erupt in a cough.

"Huff... Phew... Don't worry, I'm fine."

Unbelievable. This apprentice can be only one person—Spica. This is simply too soon. The exam to become a crusader includes restrictions that are mitigated by a portion of the holy doctrine, and it is very difficult. It's a completely different world from the Holy Warrior test that Toudou took (and failed).

The chances of Spica passing the exam after less than a year under Gregorio's tutelage are slim to none. Not to mention, I can't imagine Gregorio allowing someone with such fragmented competence to take the exam in the first place.

"......I suppose anything can happen in this day and age."

Spica becoming Gregorio's apprentice is a total gamble to begin with. He's anticipating her growth, but it's also terrifying—at any rate, why the hell is he making her into a crusader? This is a total change in direction.

There is a lot more I want to say... But really, under the blessings of Ahz Gried, I'm sure it will all work out. Just as I put all the responsibility on God, the magic communication device I forgot I'm wearing on my ear vibrates.

The connection cuts out for a moment before the call starts up—I can hear Amelia's distraught voice in my head.

"Ares, we're in trouble! It's Toudou... He's become a hermit!"

???? ...Where on earth did that come from?

I rush back to the inn where my party members have gathered.

Sanya is smiling uncomfortably, and Rabi's gaze tells me that she's still feeling unwell. Amelia's expression hasn't changed at all, predictably. After examining all three of their appearances, I take a deep breath.

Whenever I think I can't control my emotions, I take a deep breath. It's a technique I use to keep things running smoothly.

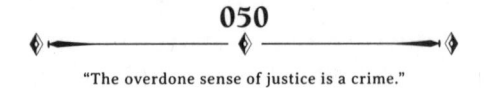

"The overdone sense of justice is a crime."

✟ First Report: On the Holy Warrior's Whereabouts and Forthcoming Objectives

When Amelia first told me the news, I was shocked, but I told myself, *It's okay, he's just...holed up inside somewhere. No big deal, he's just...staying inside...*

"What happened?"

"We used Glacia to light a fire under Toudou, but then he totally shut himself in," Amelia replies. "He won't leave his room."

What did they make Glacia say? For the past six months, I've made new plans, again and again, without fail. I've searched for new party members, instigated special training for them, helped them level up...all so that Toudou can defeat the Demon Lord.

I can't have him falling to pieces now. However, knowing Toudou's disposition, I'm not really worried about that happening. If he was going to snap, he would have a long time ago. What the hell does that mean, anyway? "*Light a fire*" under him? He "*totally shut himself in*"...?

"Ah-ha-ha-ha-ha... N-no worries, boss. We were just teasing him a bit... I mean, yeah, he just needs some time for reflection, y'know?" says Sanya. Her ears are flat against her head, and her face is twitching as she spins her best revisionist tale. "I think it works out, actually, that he's so complacent now. Y-yeah... If he cracks from a little thing like this, then he's of no use anyway."

"I'm sorry, boss... I've been so distracted...... I couldn't stop them." Rabi's head is swaying back and forth.

I look around at my competent, dependable compatriots.

"Are you really asking me to tell our higher-ups that you three have broken the will of the Holy Warrior?"

Toudou dying on our watch would be one thing, but if we manage to leave him with deep psychological damage, I can't imagine how the Church would react... I've been taking such special care to make sure this sort of thing doesn't happen... And in the span of just a few hours—just what the hell did they make Glacia say? I told her to make sure to point out Toudou's faults without causing total chaos!

"Get in contact with Glacia and make sure Toudou gets back on his feet! Before his party gets summoned to the castle!"

The royal capital is an important client for the Church. The stronger the Holy Warrior is, the greater the influence the Church will have on Ruxe. They have no interest in authority, but with great influence, their web of interference will expand, and the cards in their hand will increase. Before Toudou can become a true hero who can defeat upper-echelon demons, he must first at least become an elegant palanquin for the Church. We cannot afford a misstep of this banal nature!

"Um... Are we supposed to get him back to his old self? How?" Amelia asks me.

"Boss, sorry, but that just ain't happening. We really had Glacia rip into him, and the fact that he's in such shock shows that it's already sunk in."

Are...you...for real? Just what in the name of all heavens did they have Glacia say?

And, Toudou! Don't put so much stock into the words of some demi dragon girl who only joined your party halfway through your quest!

"Kill him with compliments! I don't care, it doesn't matter if it's lies, but you will make him feel better!"

As I desperately bark orders, Amelia and Sanya exchange glances.

§ § §

Just exactly what am I doing...? Glacia wonders silently, clutching her growling stomach as she stares at the ceiling. Nobody is inside Limis's private room. Glacia's companion, who she spent the last half year eating and sleeping alongside, isn't showing any signs of coming out from the room she's holed herself up in.

Glacia is a dragon. Her life expectancy is vastly longer compared with that of humans, and she doesn't understand human sensibilities. She can understand human language, but the core of her existence is fundamentally different. For this reason, she doesn't

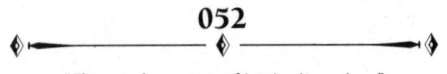

"The overdone sense of justice is a crime."

First Report: On the Holy Warrior's Whereabouts and Forthcoming Objectives

understand why Toudou has been shocked into not wanting to come out from her room. She doesn't really even care.

The most important thing for Glacia right now is not angering the truly terrifying human. That's all. In other words, this means that she needs to obey the orders of the human who can immediately make the other girl come flying at her head on command.

"You need to, you know...cheer her up, console her. Like, 'I was lying before,' or 'Toudou, you're so cool' or 'Toudou, you're doing such a great job.' Anything is fine."

These instructions are so much more unspecific than what Glacia had heard at first. She turns toward the door of Toudou's room. It's been over a day since she hasn't come out. Even without being asked to, it was high time somebody checked up on her. Glacia is hungry... She considers how to cheer Toudou up lackadaisically before opening the door.

It wasn't locked. Glacia slowly peers around inside. There's a big bed, a bookshelf, and a dresser. And then—in the middle of the room, there's a door...and Glacia is sure it wasn't here when she previously visited.

Glacia can hear her skin turning pale. Toudou's other party members, who've been instructed to cheer her up, too, are nowhere to be found, not even a shadow.

Glacia rushes around the room in a huff, trying to find Toudou and the others. She looks under the low bed and checks in the closet. Nothing. No one. But she hasn't left the room. There aren't any windows. And there's nowhere to hide. But she's not here.

One of Glacia's roles is standing watch. Until now, she's taken extreme care in this task. This is a failure. If anyone finds out, she has no idea what the terrifying human will do to her.

Should she run? The thought enters her mind for a moment but tries to escape; the terrifying human will sift through every blade of grass to find her and enact unimaginable torture upon her, she's sure.

That's right—in order to maintain the credibility of her own

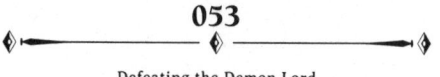

053

Defeating the Demon Lord

words. That man, who sheds neither blood nor tears, doesn't even care just how loyal Glacia has been. She can't have him as an enemy, not now.

Glacia goes limp, and she sits on the bed. Her mouth is dry as a desert. A slightly annoying girl's voice reverberates in her head, but now isn't the time for that. How can she get Toudou back...? She needs to report to Ares as soon as possible, but if she can only say she didn't find anyone, she might be accused of killing Toudou and the others.

Just then, Glacia notices a note that's been left on the bed. She picks it up with a trembling hand.

I'm off for some secret personal training. Don't worry about me. If you get hungry, ask the maid for food.

"What's the matter? Glacia? Did something happen?"

Glacia punches the soft bed with her small fist.

§ § §

"What a nightmare..."

"...At the very least, Toudou is nowhere within my range of detection."

Hearing Glacia's report and the result of Amelia's detection attempt, my stomach hurts for the first time in a while, and I use a holy technique to feel better.

If Toudou is going to shut himself in, I want him to stay put. I can't have him going off on selfish tantrums. And if he is, he needs to at least announce his intentions to the Church. I never thought he was so mentally weak that lighting him up a single time would cause him to fall recluse... And supposedly recovering so quickly also remains a riddle.

Losing track of Toudou is a nightmare. Not only that, but taking extra time to realize this fact further compounds the nightmarish nature of our situation. Turns out what I thought was a horrible dream was just the beginning.

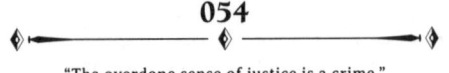

"The overdone sense of justice is a crime."

First Report: On the Holy Warrior's Whereabouts and Forthcoming Objectives

The room is behind a secret passage. It has no windows, and if someone left from the door, even that infernal dragon girl would have noticed for certain.

Above all else, there was a note left in the bedroom. The chances he was kidnapped are low. Toudou has disappeared from Limis's residence. The Friedia estate is filled to the brim with talented elementalists. In terms of security, it's borderline flawless.

"Get in touch with the Church. Tell them: 'Toudou has disappeared under the pretext of personal training. Find out if anyone has seen him,'" I say to Amelia. "In secrecy, of course."

"Understood."

Only a small faction of the Church and upper-echelon individuals of the Kingdom of Ruxe know of the Holy Warrior's summoning. This can't become a major incident.

"I need to see the scene. There must be a mechanism somewhere."

Relax—first I must relax. People don't just disappear without reason. The fact that a letter was left behind saying he's off for some "personal training" means that Toudou left of his own free will.

I want to investigate the area, but Limis's bedroom is in the deep reaches of the Friedia estate. The Friedia family doesn't know that the Church is monitoring the Holy Warrior, and an investigation will not be a simple matter. If the Church's monitoring is exposed, this would sow seeds of mistrust and also be equivalent to the Church announcing that they don't actually believe in the Holy Warrior. These are matters that far exceed my own personal scope of responsibility. The decision to announce the truth or not will be made by my superiors.

Or perhaps we could use Glacia to let them know that Toudou's gone missing? Toudou going missing within the Friedia estate is a major incident, from the family's perspective. What a total mess...

As I pace back and forth in our room, Sanya pipes up.

"Hmm... Should I sneak in? If anything, I could just claim I'm a friend of the family and probably get through."

055

Defeating the Demon Lord

"There is no chance they'll let a completely unknown person into their estate on those grounds."

What's more, currently the Holy Warrior is accompanying Limis. If they let in Sanya, the Friedia family's security is vastly weaker than I ever imagined. And Sanya's half werebeast to boot.

Rabi coughs briefly and speaks, eyes blazing red.

"Boss, maybe I should go...?"

"......Hmm. Well..."

In all common sense, Rabi infiltrating the premises is impossible. She's extremely accomplished, but let's face it—brass tacks, she's a murderous assassin rabbit. There is only one possible option left I can think of.

Just thinking about it makes my head split with pain and my stomach churn. Nonetheless, I must play the cards I'm dealt. Although this is all a result of Glacia's mental assault on Toudou, he still deserves to be raked over the coals for acting with selfish impunity. What exactly does he intend to do if the king of Ruxe calls upon him while he's on his apprenticeship?

I stop in the corner of the room and breathe deeply. Holding my stomach, I assume a flawless, prepared mentality and boot up my magical transmission device.

"This is Ares Crown. Please connect me to Stephenne... Yes, that's right, that Stephenne. Yes, the former operator who was fired and is now under house arrest. Not a mistake. Yes, I'm perfectly sane. No, well, of course I understand. I didn't want to get involved with her again, either. That's enough—connect me through to her!"

"Who...is he talking to?"

Sanya is astonished. I've never been admonished like that by an operator. But at this point, we'll all go to the grave together. I'll make Toudou regret ever selfishly taking up that personal training.

Stephenne Veronide, a junior nun under Amelia, is high level, possesses great holy energy, and is trained in the magic arts. But

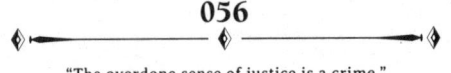

056

"The overdone sense of justice is a crime."

☦ First Report: On the Holy Warrior's Whereabouts and Forthcoming Objectives

all those assets come with a massive caveat: She's a complete ditz with unmatched incompetence.

She caused us a heap of trouble in Golem Valley, and I finally got rid of her entirely. To think a day would come where I'm asking her for help... Why the hell does God feel the need to put me through such trials?!

"At last... At last, at long last, you need my powers once again."

"Enough. Just get over here. You have five minutes."

"I underwent training. I'm stronger now. By my estimate...approximately one hundred and fifty percent stronger in terms of battle prowess. I, like, totally think I'll be helpful to you."

...Now I'm really worried that Toudou and his party are going to bite the dust.

"Enough. Stey, do exactly as I say. You are still under house arrest, but you couldn't resist the urge to go outside, and after slipping out, you found yourself in the Kingdom of Ruxe. This isn't someone else's idea. It's mine and mine alone. You got that? Say it back to me."

"But, Ares... There's just one problem. It turns out...I've already tried escaping a bunch of times, and now there are five guards standing watch—"

"I don't care. That's completely on you and your selfish nature. I don't care what it takes."

I already know that Stey has been picked up and is currently being held at the Church headquarters. Aside from one critical flaw, she's almost perfectly capable. Just like Amelia, her grades at school were at the top of her class. What has this world come to?

Above all else, she is perfectly suited for the current task at hand. Stey previously studied elementalism at the Friedia estate, and she's on good terms with the family. As a bonus, she's the daughter of a cardinal. Truly, what is this world coming to?

Before actually starting our conversation, I planned on using a soft touch to effectively butter her up, but the second I heard her

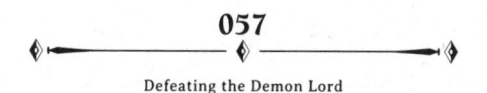

Defeating the Demon Lord

voice, I remembered everything that happened a few months ago and treated her gruffly.

It takes five hours minimum to reach Ruxe from the Church headquarters. In Stey's case, she'll have pursuers on her heels, so it will take longer. There's the wait for a response from the Church's top brass, the wait for Stey, and the mental preparations I'll need for Stey's arrival—if Toudou returns by that point, I'll just dismiss Stey. But let's not get ahead of ourselves.

Thirty minutes have passed since I gave my convoluted order. Calculating backward to when Toudou disappeared, I infer a number of locations that Toudou could actually be planning to use for his apprenticeship. In that moment, my field of vision becomes distorted, and a massive impact rushes through the air around me.

The glass window in our room shatters in an instant, and Sanya yelps curtly before hiding behind the bed. I stand up immediately and hoist my mace in my right hand, staring intently into the center of the room.

"......"

"Mmph... Ugh... Ouch... Ugh... Oof... A-Ares?!"

Standing on top of the desk and chairs now shattered to smithereens, a girl appears instantaneously, almost magically, and lifts her head to greet me with joy.

God has granted powers to a being completely unworthy of them. Stephenne Veronide has erupted into our room, and I instinctively swing my mace up toward her, just barely stopping myself from hitting her, and instead punch her in the face with my left fist.

Stey cries out in a strange voice and falls to the ground. I address her seriously, saying, "Stey... My God... Did you actually learn transportation magic...?"

"Urghhh... Is that really all you have to say to me right now?"

Holding her head in her hands, Stey looks up at me with tears in her eyes. Teleportation is one of the most secret magic arts. It's not something that should be used on a whim or to look cool.

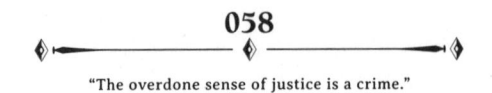

"The overdone sense of justice is a crime."

First Report: On the Holy Warrior's Whereabouts and Forthcoming Objectives

A number of high-level mages can use it, but I haven't seen a regular human use it in a while. If Stey has learned this skill in the short time since we separated, she's nothing short of a bonafide genius. Maybe she's a demon in disguise?

Actually, if she's using teleportation, that means she's into a whole new field of elemental spells compared with what she was using previously...

"Wha—? Who's that? Did you call for her, boss? Hold up... That magic she just used—!"

"......Boss, you have truly incredible connections. But...I really think you should...take the location into account next time... *Cough, cough.*"

The two mercenaries I bought with the money from selling Stey are taken aback. Honestly, I'd like to agree with their perspective.

But if I praise Stey now, she'll get stuck-up. I need to make sure to discipline her harshly, or I'll never be able to use her to my full advantage. She's just that kind of girl. Not to mention, she isn't the least bit timid regarding her capabilities—even more than Toudou, she has an iron will.

I force myself to sit down on the bed calmly and cross my legs. Stey clasps her hands together and grins.

"Yes...! I did it! Finally, I did it! It was worth studying so hard! Teleportation—you can totally call me a sorceress now, don't you think?"

Actually, this could be the youngest person I've ever seen learn teleportation. If she wasn't such a ditz, she might legitimately qualify as a sorceress.

"Hey, Stey. Have you seen what you've done to this room?! Do you seriously need to be told to use the door?"

"Huh? Huhhh? Umm... Well...... You gave me this summons totally out of the blue, and I just...did everything I could to get here, y'know?"

My heart goes out to Stey's monitors. If I was in their shoes, I

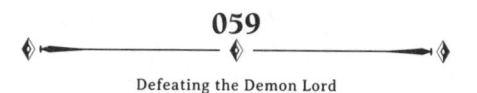

Defeating the Demon Lord

would quit on the spot. I'll have to contact them later. And I'll suggest they put her in a room that will prevent her from teleporting.

I didn't bring her here to make nice. The sole reason that I summoned Stey in the first place is because I didn't have anywhere else to turn. She's nothing more than Limis's friend who's gifted with magic. I'm fighting fire with fire.

I grab Stey by the chin. She looks like she wants a compliment. Instead, I give her forceful orders.

"Stey, you are going to investigate Limis's room in the Friedia residence. *This instant.* Got that?"

"Th-this instant?!"

Stey's eyes go wide and her shoulders shudder at my menacing stance, but she quickly starts fawning and smiles sheepishly.

"Heh-heh... Gee, I remember how this feels. It's like I'm back to work or something? Okay, I'll do my best!"

Acting bashful now? What a piece of work. She's gotten stronger, not only physically, but mentally. Sheesh. And she was already a handful before. Just what sort of training made her even stronger...? Toudou needs a slice of that pie.

I feel defeated for the first time in a while, putting up as little of a fight as possible to bark a brief command:

"...Go!"

"Hmm? Boss, whatcha eating?"

"Stomach medicine. Takes my mind off things somehow."

"......R-right. I don't need any myself, y'know."

Half dejectedly, I pop stomach medicine pills into my mouth and chew them. We are monitoring Stey's circumstances from a removed location near the Friedia estate. I was already informed of her successful entry through her report via communication magic.

Goddammit, can she do anything now?

"Listen up, don't you dare mess around in there. I'm not kidding; this is not a damn joke. You are a friend of Limis's, and you're just there to visit her. Don't say anything else, nothing unnecessary, got it?"

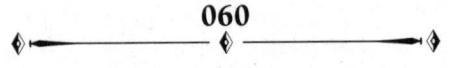

"The overdone sense of justice is a crime."

First Report: On the Holy Warrior's Whereabouts and Forthcoming Objectives

"Yes, I understand. I tooootally understand. It's fine. I am Limis's good friend after all! Heh-heh... Ares, just pretend like you're watching me, all powered up, from the poop deck of a shit ship."

Poop deck of a shit ship... She must be trying to make a joke, or perhaps she's just trying to keep the atmosphere lively. I know it's totally irrational, but I'm still about to blow my top.

This is not good. Irrational behavior is unacceptable. A true leader must always remain tolerant. I need to exercise self-control.

"If you're that worried about it, you shouldn't have asked for her..."

Sanya's comment is spot on. It might be too late, but I am becoming hasty. Perhaps my anger toward Toudou has piled up too much. I need to be more tolerant...

I rattle out more of the stomach medicine into my hand from the bottle and stuff my cheeks. An acrid taste and peculiar aroma fill my mouth, but if this will keep me distracted, I'll chalk it up to a win.

"*Cough, cough...* Boss, you'll ruin your health...," Rabi warns me, sounding concerned.

She's always out of sorts, and here she is worrying about me. Do I look that rough?

"?! Ares, I got a free pass! I'm home free! The guards all let me in without question! Did you see that? They just let me right in! Heh-heh... It's been a long time since I visited Limis's house, but I guess everyone here remembers me... I'm so happy..."

No, they're just shying away from getting involved in guaranteed trouble—damn, Stey, you're invincible!

"'Kaaay, I'm going in now. Oh! Glacia! It's been so long. Wait, why are you running away?!"

"...Don't worry about that. Hurry up and investigate the area. If you notice anything, no matter how trivial it might seem, make sure to tell me."

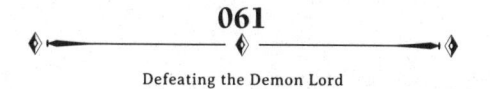

"I get it already! I'm not the same girl you once knew, Ares! Papa's been praising me lately, too, saying that I rarely stumble now, and I've grown so much—"

"I don't care—just do your job! Keep your head on a swivel! Don't touch anything carelessly no matter what happens!"

"Yessir. Pardon the intrusion! Oh-ho? What is this...?"

Stey still doesn't know how to read the tension in the air. But it looks like she's found something. Glacia couldn't get to the point no matter how many times I asked her. She's a worthless dragon after all. Lower on the hierarchy than Stey? That's rough...

I can hear Stey talking, her interest clearly piqued.

"It's...a door. This goes to one of the secrets of Limis's house—the training room. I've only heard the rumors..."

"Training room." This is my first time hearing of one at Limis's home, but in magic-user families with established lineage, having a training space created in another dimension through high-level magic is a common story. It seems that as Glacia said, Toudou perhaps hasn't actually left the room.

We should be able to avoid the worst possible outcome at this point, and I sigh in relief. Sending in Stey was worth the risk. She can be useful at times... If it was just a training room we were looking for, maybe we wouldn't even need to send her—

"They say Mr. Friedia trained here or that, like, generations of House Friedia have to do all their training in this space. A-and also, the magic here is supposedly super dangerous— Eep?!"

"Huh?! What happened? Hey, what's going on? Stey?! What do you mean dangerous—?"

My connection with Stey cuts out suddenly. I hurriedly call out again, but there's no reply. The line is completely dead. The connection was perfectly stable until just now. Even if the line drops, it usually connects again instantly.

Meanwhile, I feel a faint memory lingering after the last thing Stey said. It was probably just a premonition, but likely spot-on. Stephenne Veronide is just that kind of girl.

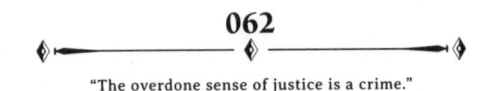

062

"The overdone sense of justice is a crime."

First Report: On the Holy Warrior's Whereabouts and Forthcoming Objectives

"What happened?!"

I empty the remainder of the stomach medicine bottle into my mouth and chew before replying, "......She probably just fell down."

Stey tripped and entered the training room. I'm too annoyed to even feel sad.

I think I've seen all I need for now. When Amelia gets back, we need to take care of this.

I call on the Church for additional information. In a stroke of good luck, the Friedia training room is well known in the Church's circle, and I'm able to collect some information on it quickly.

Amelia looks perplexed. "Ares... Is it true that you called on Stey while I was away on your orders?"

"She's a mage who's close with the Friedia family—it was a necessary response. I'll take any complaints you may have, but I have no intention of debating this decision."

Sometimes being dealt an absurd hand calls for a ridiculous play. And Amelia is my subordinate, meaning I have the right to make all decisions and take responsibility for them.

Amelia furrows her brow at my reply and says, "...Very well. I see you're fine with proceeding as you please, without ever consulting me. Ares, you inhuman brute!"

"...That's not a complaint. And Stey is your junior!"

Calling me an inhuman brute just for sending for her junior... Although—maybe she's not wrong. Maybe I *am* a brute?

Sanya is dangling her legs off her chair and waiting for her next orders.

"This...is fortuitous," I say with gusto.

"That's never actually been true every other time you've said it."

"Yeah, you tell him, Amelia!"

"I am no longer accepting complaint tickets. Listen up!"

This is good fortune. An absolute boon!

It's not good to be overly pessimistic when taking on arduous tasks. Toudou's hermitage was way too sudden, and I really wish he would have let us know first, but it's not exactly the worst thing in the world.

"According to information we've acquired, this training room Stey mentioned was built by the very first head of the Friedia family. Its purpose is for elementalists to gain real-life experience and temper their skills. For Toudou, this isn't even a difficult ordeal, really."

"Huh? What does that mean?"

Sanya's eyes flash wide as I speak. Werebeasts have incredible physical aptitude, but on the other hand, their resistance to magic is quite low. Sanya is a silverwolf werebeast, so she has more magic resistance than some, but it's still not her strongest point.

Although Rabi's species of werebeast is very frail and vulnerable, Rabi herself is a stone-cold decapitation machine for some reason.

"So elementalists are getting real-life training and honing their skills," she says softly. "That means...they're facing off against spirits... Right, boss?"

"...You're right. Rabi, you're always on point."

An elementalist's true strength is determined by the magic they use—and the decision to adopt or reject necessary spells. Employing a great number of spirits, elementalists need to command attack, support, and healing magic respectively, making a vast number of choices during battle.

An elementalist's power is directly determined by how they respond to the different monsters and situations they are faced with. For example, entering a covenant with a powerful spirit is worthless if their aptitude is low to begin with, and conversely, even if an elementalist can only contract with low-level spirits, if they are able to select from extremely high-level spells, they can potentially become an archmage.

House Friedia is beloved among elemental spirits. When contracting with high-level spirits, it stands to reason that their

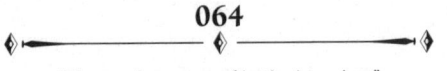

"The overdone sense of justice is a crime."

First Report: On the Holy Warrior's Whereabouts and Forthcoming Objectives

pedigree determines they are well trained in fully employing the powers of any spirit they are in a covenant with.

"Fighting against spirits requires a particular preciseness when making situational decisions... If House Friedia indeed created this training room......then this would be a natural assumption... Isn't that right, boss?"

"Yes, that's correct."

The progenitor of House Friedia created a training room using the spirit they were in a covenant with. According to information held by the Church, training rooms are inhabited by a number of diverse spirits, allowing trainees to learn under live combat practice.

I'm not sure exactly what kind of spirits might be found within, but I doubt they feature high-level spirits. If the enemies are spirits, that's a perfect fit for Toudou. That said, it is straying a bit from the true intent of a training room.

"? I get that Toudou's's going up against elemental spirits," says Sanya, "but why aren't those a problem for him?"

"!! That's because—" Amelia begins, but then Rabi speaks over her, with her tiny voice and ruby-red eyes staring up at me intently.

"It's his holy sword and armor, boss. I confirmed it with my own two eyes. They both have a vast amount of holy energy imbued within. The holy armor Fried reduces damage from all types of magic, and the holy sword Ex can cut through beings without physical form. Toudou is still untrained, but with that equipment... True, most elemental spirits would be a breeze for him."

Rabi must be twitching her ears—her hood is jostling slightly.

It's an incredible observation from such little information. Amelia looks at Rabi in shock, like she's been beat at her own game.

Don't get competitive now.

"A-plus answer, Rabi," I tell her. "I'll reward you with a carrot later."

"It was a simple subject, but...thank you, boss."

I was kidding about the carrot, but she must be happy about the compliment. Her eyes, the only part of her I can really see, soften slightly.

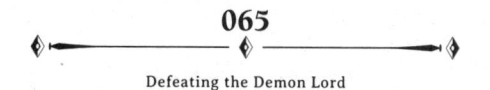

"Toudou's shield is broken, so I'm a bit worried, but I'm sure he'll be fine. With the holy armor, the chances he is severely wounded are low."

The holy armor Fried is a sacred armament that has both vast physical and magical damage-negation properties. According to information held by the Church, the armor protects all four limbs, of course, but it also reduces damage to areas of the body not directly covered, too. This is also a reason behind Toudou not receiving any major damage thus far on our journey.

In conception, the quality of an armament generally matches the wearer, but having superior equipment is one of Toudou and company's greatest strengths.

We've faced so many top-tier foes so far that I've nearly forgotten, but Toudou has the armaments of a true hero.

At any rate, his goal in the training room is to hone his elemental magic; his swordplay is beside the point. As for why he went into that training area in the first place, Toudou and Limis haven't yet entered covenants with spirits from every elemental affiliation, nor have they even met the minimum requirements to begin such training. Will it still benefit them?

We've sent Stey in, and even if we ignore their progress from now, they should be back before long. If they manage to clear the training room and Toudou's confidence gets a boost, that will be killing two birds with one stone.

"Amelia, there should be a gate in Limis's room. Can you use that to find out what Toudou and his party are up to?"

It's a major long shot. Amelia's detection magic is based on a similar principle to sonar, allowing her to probe a single area in question. However, despite the fact that my expectations are zero, Amelia looks to be pondering deeply at my query.

"That would be impossible with regular detection magic. However...if I try really hard—"

"Try your very best."

"In order to use my special form of detection magic, I need a

"The overdone sense of justice is a crime."

First Report: On the Holy Warrior's Whereabouts and Forthcoming Objectives

strand of hair from the target and plenty of motivation. Right now, I have neither."

I can't tell if she's being serious or completely facetious. Magic using a strand of hair... Does she intend to put a curse on Toudou? This is too bizarre... But there's no time to waste trying to solve Amelia's mysteriousness. Moving right along.

"...Amelia, talk with Sanya and draft some compliments for Glacia to give Toudou when he and his party return. I'll check them over."

"Oh... Are you serious?"

"Yeah, why just me and Amelia? What about Rabi?"

These two really ripped into Toudou, and now they want to rope Rabi into their scheme... Do they even have souls? Maybe the most inhuman one among us isn't Stey but rather one of my benevolent colleagues?

I scowl at Amelia and Sanya, who begrudgingly comply.

I really hope that Toudou has his confidence back when he returns...

Toudou is the Holy Warrior. He is the one the God of Order determined to have the qualities of a hero. He's faced many problems along the way but managed to successfully overcome each one. Deep down, I haven't written him off.

This I know: If he puts his mind to it, he can do anything. He tends to take things too far...but I'm sure it'll all work out this time, somehow.

Just then, I notice that Rabi is curled up atop her bed and staring at me.

"What's the matter? You just rest for a bit. All you need to focus on is getting your head back in the game."

Rabi is my ace in the hole. Her flaws run deep, but she's nonetheless the one who beheaded Heljarl. I'll only be able to use her once or twice more for assassinations. Or maybe not at all—killing Heljarl was such a master stroke. I should resign myself to returning her to Bran.

Rabi is sharp as a tack, but if this funk of hers keeps up, then she won't be of any use going forward. And then there's Stey, who would normally be considered top-class based on her abilities alone... Seriously, what is this world coming to?

"Umm... Boss, thank you for being so considerate. And also... I..." Rabi's glance falls to the floor, a rare occasion, and she fidgets with her fingers nervously before saying, with conviction, "That reward—my carrot... Umm... When can I...have it?"

"...That was a joke."

"......Oh. A joke."

Rabi's shoulders droop heavily, and she casts her gaze further downward. The Rabi I first met would have used more caution, but maybe she's come to trust me? Does she really want a carrot? If it actually motivates her, I have no problem with buying her one, but—

Assuming an air of importance, I continue, "...Indeed, you do deserve a reward, though. Hmm... For your next great achievement, I'll buy you something else."

"I understand."

Rabi nods meekly and clenches her fists. Sanya comes largely free of charge as long as I give her the occasional training session, and these girls are really worth their bang for the buck. I will definitely keep half werebeasts on my radar when searching for additional party members.

While I wait for Toudou's return with bated breath, later that evening I am told that he's returned from the training room, badly injured and barely escaping with his life.

This is truly beyond the pale.

I take stock of the current circumstances, contacting the Church to dispatch a first-rate priest who will be able to heal Toudou's wounds. I offer Creio an explanation peppered with excuses. Given the situation, I can't be acting cocksure.

I have been mentally prepared to do damage control after a

"The overdone sense of justice is a crime."

First Report: On the Holy Warrior's Whereabouts and Forthcoming Objectives

defeat someday, but Toudou's loss is shocking in nearly every way possible. I have been gauging Naotsugu Toudou, the Holy Warrior, in terms of total power at a closer distance than anyone else. There are some individuals within the royal capital and the Church that are evaluating Toudou's power excessively, but I am not the same. In the same breath, his abilities are commensurate with those of a hero, often causing stark amazement.

With the holy armor and holy sword, there is no good reason that Toudou should have failed the training. I can't find any good reason that he would have lost, even now. I fail to adequately gather my thoughts and make orders for the information to be concealed.

Toudou's name is not yet well-known, and I can't afford a pockmark on his face from a mere training incident using a magical item. In the time I spend mitigating circumstances, the sun has set for the day.

I catch up with Amelia, who has been running crazy in every direction, too.

"Is Stey back yet?"

"No...not yet. She hasn't responded."

"Shit, what the hell is going on...?"

Everything is completely unexpected. Has the Friedia family been overcome by demonic powers and forced to plot an attack on Toudou? I'm having delusional visions of such scenarios playing out. That's just how shocking Toudou's defeat really is.

"H-hey, chill out, boss. Stuff like this happens from time to time."

"Does that mean I have to put up with it? Things have been going *so well* up until now!"

Come to think of it, everything might have been going a bit *too* well, but we have had our share of tribulations. We've overcome each instance of trouble, and Toudou and the others have grown, and I have matured, too. How could we bungle up this badly when I look away for one second!

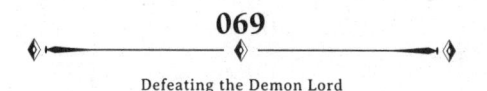

Toudou facing defeat is certainly not good, but Stey not coming back is perhaps even worse. Stey is the daughter of a cardinal. I thought it wouldn't be a big deal when I sent her in, but if she up and dies on me, I'll be in a world of trouble... Could we cover this up quickly and quietly? The fact that we're facing an ocean of pain regardless of whether she lives or dies has me nearly at my wit's end.

As I grind my teeth in deep thought, Rabi looks up at me with her bloodred eyes and says quietly, "Boss, forgive my presumptuousness... But we should first of all be thankful that Toudou has come back alive. Please calm down... If necessary, I'll even let you...t-touch my...ears."

Rabi takes down her hood and sticks out her flattened ears. I manage to restore some manner of calm. Rabi's right; I should first and foremost be happy that Toudou didn't die. We've avoided the worst-case scenario. As long as he's alive, we can still recover from any other situation thrown at us. That is a small consolation amid tragedy.

If the leader becomes overwhelmed, nothing that needs to get done ever will. I cough curtly and narrow my eyes.

"You are correct indeed. Toudou is currently recuperating. When he's completely healed, we'll move forward with a detailed investigation of what went wrong and how to move forward. Amelia, I need you to prepare to extract information from Toudou when the time comes."

"Understood. I will make appropriate arrangements."

"Boss, what should I do?"

"...Sit still and stay out of the damn way. You are combat personnel. We don't need you right now."

Sanya is not a member of the Church. For this reason, right now she's limited in her capacity to do much of anything. I turn my gaze from Sanya, who is pursing her lips in dissatisfaction, to Rabi, who is sitting perfectly still, her ears still sticking out.

"Rabi, I'm sorry for forcing you into telling an awkward joke. It appears I've been lacking in composure."

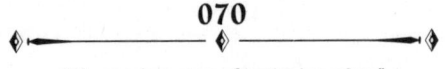

"The overdone sense of justice is a crime."

First Report: On the Holy Warrior's Whereabouts and Forthcoming Objectives

"...It wasn't a joke, though... *Cough, cough*... If there's anything I can do for you, I will." Rabi puts her hood back up.

Not a joke, eh...? Do wererabbit ears have some sort of sedative effect?

In all seriousness, just how could Toudou have lost? Toudou isn't used to battling elemental spirits, but he had Limis by his side. Just what were they missing? Levels? Knowledge? Experience? My response will depend on what went wrong. Is training at the Friedia household simply that arduous...?

In a moment's time, a sharp pain erupts in my stomach. I can feel a presence approaching, and the door to our room flies open with force. I reach for my stomach medicine bottle, which I've just refilled.

"Ares! It is I, Stephenne Veronide, back from the void!"

"...Y-you're rather peppy today..."

She could've let us believe that she was dead for a little while longer...

Amelia, Sanya, and Rabi are staring in utter disbelief at Stey, who's all bright-eyed and bushy-tailed. Her appearance hasn't changed one bit since she left initially. If anything, her eyes are even brighter now.

Stey takes a few steps toward me and trips with gusto on nothing at all, falling to the ground... At this point, I want to demand compensation for mental and physical damages from Cardinal Veronide himself.

Stey picks herself up amid the empty stares and silence and sticks out her ample chest pointlessly, beaming.

"Ares, you owe me a compliment! I cleared the training room without any problem at all! The number one divine spirit even praised me! Wow, I'm amazing!"

"......"

"Heh-heh-heh... I also acquired a new power! This will allow me to be even more useful!"

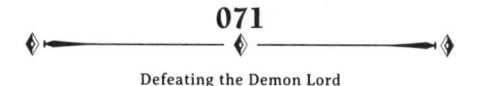

The intent of this exercise...has become completely lost. This isn't right. I sent her in after Toudou to check up on and protect him, not to clear the training room on her own and acquire new skills.

I scarf down more stomach medicine. I feel like murdering monsters to excess. Narrowing my eyes, I give orders to my comrades—the ones who I can depend on and who are waiting quietly.

"Ugh. Somebody make her shut up. I'm headed outside the city to go berserk on the first monster I can find."

"Wha—?! Ares! Me too! I'm coming along!"

At this point, she has to be purposefully testing the limit of my patience.

§ § §

When it rains it pours, and it's currently raining every calamity feasible. The training room that the House Friedia founder created was in itself a form of discipline assigned to humanity from the divine spirits, and a significant number of people are said to have lost their lives within. Nonetheless, when Toudou actually visits that world, it is beyond anything she ever imagined.

The training room behind the door is really more of a crucible—located inside a massive tower, distinctively a part of the spirit world.

The tower is rife with mazelike corridors filled with spirits from every elemental affiliation, taking every possible shape, that fall upon Toudou and attack her. A wind dragon slashes forward with an invisible blade while a giant earth serpent spews forth a cloud of poisonous gas. These life-forms, called spirit beasts, are created through collaboration among multiple spirits of different elemental affiliations and are a world apart from any of the monsters that Toudou has fought thus far.

Physical attacks are largely worthless here, and even Aria's magic blade hardly does any damage. All the attacks wielded by spirits are high-powered magic damage attacks, giving them increased range and area of effect.

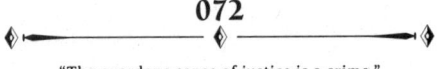

"The overdone sense of justice is a crime."

First Report: On the Holy Warrior's Whereabouts and Forthcoming Objectives

This place is a definitive training space for elementalists. Armor, shields, and swords hold little value, and in order to oppose the spirits encroaching upon them here, they must use their own contracted spirits for defense and counterattacks.

Nonetheless, Toudou's weapons and armor are exceptionally strong. Aria's armor has high resistance against magic damage, too, and Toudou's holy sword Ex can slice through spirit beasts without physical form as if they were normal beasts of flesh and bone. Both of Limis's contracted spirits are high-level, and to an extent, they can rip through the spirit enemies with little concern for elemental affiliation.

However, this fact ends up delaying Toudou and Limis's decision to retreat. As they climb higher up the tower, more powerful spirits begin appearing, and on the very top floor, it's said that a spirit awaits that the Friedia family progenitor, who created this crucible, contracted himself.

Toudou, Limis, and Aria have reached their breaking point. The tower's mazelike structure is riddled with blind spots, and fending off ambushes from spirits is even more mentally demanding than it is physically. It's much like their battles against hordes of undead in Yutith's Tomb, except these enemies are simply on another level. Furthermore—in the narrow corridors, their attacks with large areas of effect are nearly impossible to dodge, even if they can see them coming.

There are holy techniques that can boost magic resistance, but Toudou can't use them yet. She didn't have any need for them thus far, and for this reason, she has delayed learning them. What's more, she didn't need them because of her holy armor, but right now, she can't wear it.

The injuries lacing Toudou's body are giving her more of a shock than actual pain. Toudou hasn't received any major damage on her journey. The only major injuries she sustained were during the party's battles against Gregorio and Heljarl.

At this point, Toudou doesn't even have it in her to join in the attack. The bloodied Holy Warrior has used enough holy techniques to fully deplete her holy energy for the first time in a while, and she's not able to heal quickly enough. Against these countless elemental spirits, Limis, too, is soon drained of her magical energy. Aria tries to cover the group and open a way forward, but even the party member with the most stamina remaining is rendered powerless.

Toudou, Limis, and Aria all lose consciousness—the next thing they realize, they're sleeping in separate beds. Enveloped in the sensation of floating up through deep water, the first thing Toudou sees when she regains consciousness is a high ceiling. She rebukes her body, heavy as lead, and tries to get up, only to be wracked with pain. Toudou furrows her brow deeply.

"I... Oh......"

Toudou recalls the scene she saw just moments before losing consciousness and gasps in fear. She has been involved in many dangerous battles thus far, but being summarily defeated and falling unconscious is a first for her. Heljarl was leagues more powerful than Toudou, but she had nonetheless fought him one-on-one; this life-and-death battle against numerous powerful spirit beasts and unrelenting magic attacks was different.

However—why is she still alive? Toudou's world is brimming with fantastical elements, but it's not a video game. She can't simply re-spawn at a save point after losing a battle.

All three of them should have been annihilated. Limis was out of magical energy, and Toudou was covered in blood. Aria was just as bloodied the last time Toudou saw her, and they were so far from the exit. She can scarcely imagine what kind of miracle must have occurred.

Toudou peers around quietly. She's in Limis's room, which she remembers. Aria is lying down next to Toudou, her hands and feet also wrapped in bandages. Toudou can tell she's breathing based on the rising and falling of her chest.

Just as Toudou starts getting out of bed to find out what's going on, the door opens—nice timing.

"The overdone sense of justice is a crime."

First Report: On the Holy Warrior's Whereabouts and Forthcoming Objectives

"Limis! Thank goodness..."

"Nao... You're finally awake."

Limis enters the room alongside Glacia, who looks a bit disgruntled. Limis sighs deeply and sits down on the bed.

"How are your injuries? Someone from the Church came and cast a healing spell on you... You know you almost died, right?"

"Oh... Yeah. I'm still in a little pain, but otherwise, I'm okay."

"Aria had the most severe injuries. She was fighting on the front line until the very end—but don't worry; it looks like she's out of the woods now."

Toudou is deeply relieved and puts a hand to her chest. Aria's level is lower than Toudou's. All that armor kept her better protected than Toudou, but what good does that armor do against a maelstrom of magic attacks?

Limis smiles weakly and explains further.

"After you and Aria lost consciousness, I used White Flag—I can only use that when everyone else has been knocked out... I'm so lucky the spirits listened to me. They got us out of there and back to my room, where Glacia was waiting. She took one look at us, all on death's door, and went and got help."

"I see... And then..."

In a real battle, they would have been dead, no question. Toudou finally realizes the gravity of the situation, and a cold shiver runs up her spine.

No, not just in a real battle—if Limis hadn't used White Flag in time, they would have all perished.

"Glacia...thank you," says Toudou.

"......"

Glacia wordlessly averts her gaze. Maybe she's embarrassed; it's impossible to tell from her expression.

That was a close one. Toudou hadn't intended to take the experience lightly, but at this point, she can't deny she'd treated it as a simple training exercise. Claiming that she got ahead of herself won't cut it.

Limis suddenly hangs her head. The tips of her long, golden hair brush the bed.

"I'd heard the training was tough, but I had no idea it was like that... I'm so sorry. This is all my fault."

"...No, it's on me... I took the elemental spirits too lightly."

Toudou is under the divine protection of the Three Deities and Eight Spirit Kings. That means her magic resistances are far greater than a human being who doesn't have the blessing. And that must be why Toudou assumed that she'd be fine, even though she wasn't wearing armor. She'd been wearing armor since the start of their journey, and she stopped giving it second thought. The reason that she's avoided grave injury thus far is certainly largely due to her armor's strength, she realizes now. The sheer power of her holy sword Ex is undeniable. If Toudou stood at the front of her party with the holy armor equipped, she could cut through and forge a path forward, making life easier for everyone. Reducing the overall damage the party takes also allows her to conserve healing spells, meaning she can get in more attacks or moves otherwise.

As she racks her brain, Toudou holds her head and sighs so deeply, her soul nearly escapes her body. However, these idle ruminations are all but meaningless now—Toudou has tested her armaments to just before their maximum limit.

This most recent battle has presented Toudou with so many new challenges. She realizes her blatant lack of proficiency as the Holy Warrior, and the importance of contracting spirits of all elemental affiliations is impressed upon her gravely. Above all else, she realizes that she cannot be overconfident in the resistances granted to her solely by divine protection. She needs to move forward with choosing a new set of armor post-haste.

Limis's head hangs limply as she bites her lip. Of course, Aria has new challenges to face, too.

Nonetheless—right now, they are all simply happy to still be alive. They will live to fight another day.

Sapped of strength, Toudou collapses onto the bed. The soft

"The overdone sense of justice is a crime."

impact sends a small jolt of pain through her body. She can't help but smile at the pain. It's proof that she's still alive.

That moment, a shrill voice interrupts the scene.

"Toudou! Limis! Good afternooooon!"

"......?"

Am I hearing things...?

Toudou sits up again and looks at Limis, but she's simply looking back at Toudou, equally perplexed. They've both heard this voice before; its speaker has no business being in this room. That girl parted ways with their group back in Golem Valley.

Maybe I hit my head earlier?

As Toudou taps the side of her head, the door to the room is flung wide open. Thrown into confusion, Toudou's thought process comes to a jarring halt.

The girl with dark hair and eyes, who doesn't belong here, beams with a smile and cries out loudly in the faces of Toudou and Limis, frozen stiff.

"Heal delivery service! Per Are— Um, I mean a real person's request, and I'm here to treat you with a healing spell! Aaand... Oh, right! I'm here to listen to your story! Why'd you fail the training so badly? Even I made it through that! Also, did you wear your armor, like you're supposed to?!"

Toudou falls back onto the bed and closes her eyes, choosing to pretend that nothing has just happened.

§ § §

"Ares! I asked them what happened, just like you ordered me to!"

"Oh. Go on then, tell me already."

Stey's expression doesn't shift one iota despite my sullen response. Her resolve remains upper echelon.

God must really love Stey. And even the omniscient, omnipotent God can't cure her of her ditzy nature. Or wait... Maybe her ditzy recklessness is how she balances the scales with her incredible aptitude?

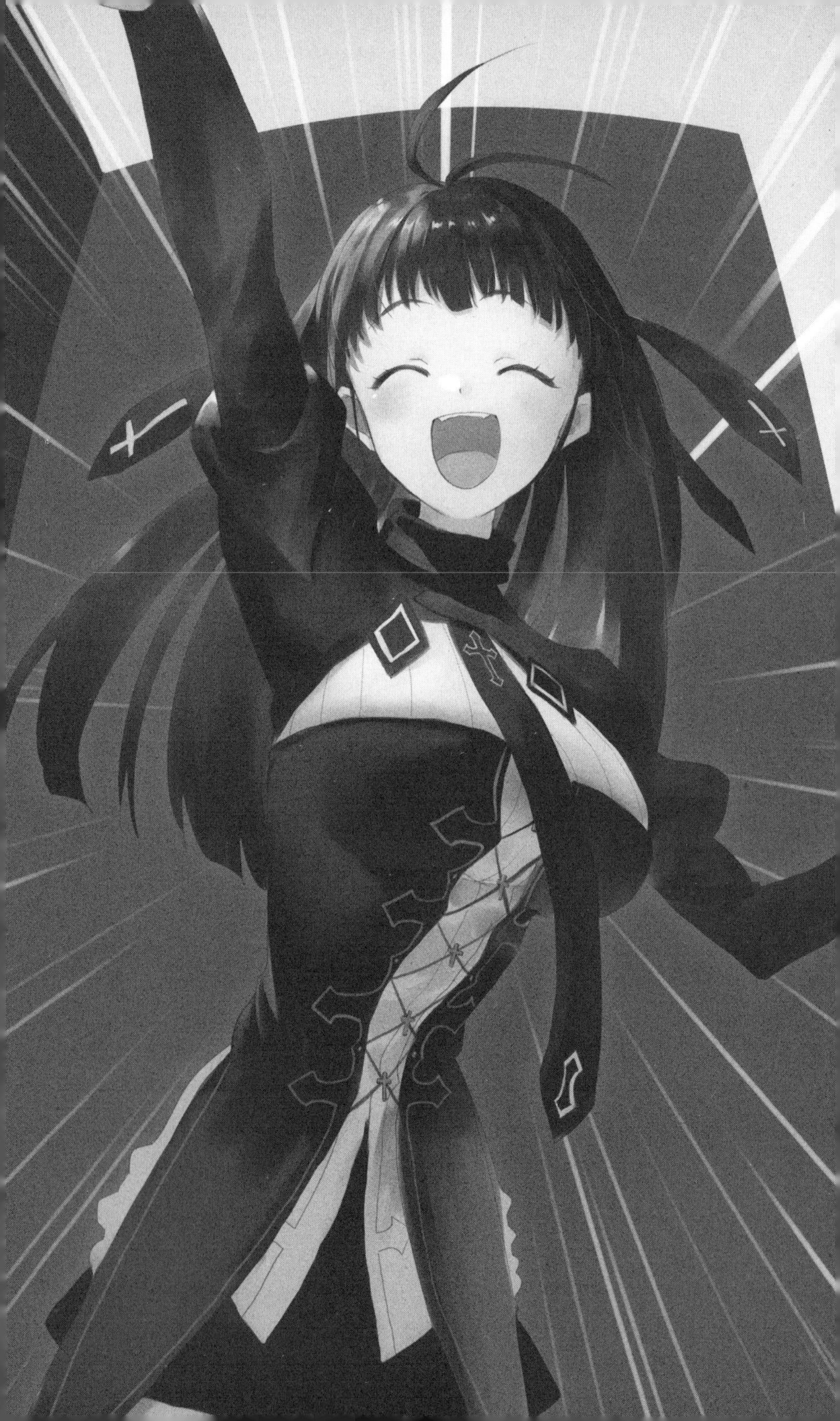

First Report: On the Holy Warrior's Whereabouts and Forthcoming Objectives

Stey is beaming in everyone's faces—I really can't figure out how she gets so much satisfaction out of life—and fills me in.

"Turns out Toudou *wasn't* wearing his armor! Ares, you were right all along!"

"......And surely you asked him why...yes?"

Stey's report is par for the course, but the way she says it really grinds my gears. I manage to keep my anger in check when I press her for further details, and now her smile is even bigger.

"Of course I did! Toudou has decided to undergo a total makeover, so he can't wear the holy armor Fried anymore!"

What the hell is she talking about...?

Second Report
On Acquiring Legendary Equipment and Fortifying Battle Power

The day has nearly ended, and the city is flooded with bright magic lights. It's very rare to see magic that illuminates an area with colorful light without using flame, but it is used on occasion, including festivals. There are even mages that specialize in light, but making light dance for an extended period of time requires a considerable amount of effort. Naturally, this also incurs costs, and for this reason, it remains a rare spectacle.

Here, however, the streets are flooded with magical light on a daily basis. The hustle and bustle in this city rivals that of the royal capital, and even Amelia, who's usually cool as a cucumber, looks positively dumbstruck. She's holding a rope attached to someone's neck, and that someone—Stey—is positively starry-eyed. The temperature is fairly low, but thanks to the body heat of the throngs of people coming and going, despite the late hour, it's hot enough to make you break a sweat.

A three days' carriage ride from Ruxe, this place has many different names: the city that never sleeps. The city of night and light. Vice city. And lastly…casino central.

This city of night and light, Lymuth, is the only city known for its casino in all of the Kingdom of Ruxe. Adventurers and mercenaries love to gamble, as do a number of priests. Even wearing their priest's robes, they hardly stick out at all. According to talk around the Kingdom, Lymuth is a regular on lists of "top three cities you have to visit at least once."

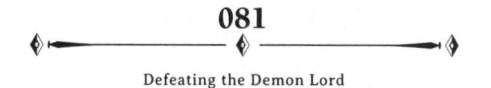

"The Demon Lord's invasion may be at a standstill, but these crowds are really quite something," Amelia comments.

"It doesn't make a difference," I reply. "Even if the invasion was going full force, Lymuth would be just as lively up to the moment the hordes broke through."

The security here, a city rife with desire, is top class even among the rest of the Kingdom. As a servant of the God of Order, I have my own thoughts about this place, but the Church recognizes that this city has come into existence this way. In fact, Lymuth also features an exceptionally decadent church—unlike any other—built very close to the casino.

I wouldn't typically step foot in a place like this, especially while I'm helping to defeat the Demon Lord. Yet, deeply ashamed as I am to be here, I've come for one thing in particular...

I look to Sanya, whose eyes are positively glittering, and the other members of the party, who are reeling from the heat.

"Okay," I tell them, "I'm going to explain our motive here again. According to the Church, one of the prizes at this casino is a powerful defensive armament—summetal armor—that has been used on many battlefields. Legendary armor. It's already been appraised and vetted. Given Toudou's makeover, we absolutely need to acquire this item."

My stomach aches painfully. This is truly a fool's errand. I have no idea why legendary armor is being put up as the prize at a casino, nor do I understand Toudou's so-called makeover whatsoever.

Furthermore, Toudou now claims he'll be wearing a "cloak of infinite darkness" that has anti-detection properties, something he came into possession at the Friedia estate. In what world does a hero wear that sort of thing?! For fuck's sake!

There are few defensive armaments that can truly replace the holy armor Fried. If we don't find something here...

Sanya is staring at the giant casino bathed in magic light, her eyes agleam and her voice shaking.

"Y'know, boss, I really like this side of you."

"The overdone sense of justice is a crime."

✟ Second Report: On Acquiring Legendary Equipment and Fortifying Battle Power

"Cut it out. I know you just want to have fun at the casino. But listen well—this isn't time for fun and games. Got it?"

In order to acquire the armor, we need to collect a vast number of casino coins and exchange them. I tried my hand at devising a way to acquire the prize alone, but it isn't possible. This place is privately managed, and my authority has no effect here. Buying a bunch of coins to exchange for the prize with cash is also not feasible. The coins at this casino come in two types: those purchased with cash and those acquired from winning bets. And prizes can only be obtained in exchange for the latter.

A number of other rare weapons and armaments aside from the summetal armor are on display at the casino, but winning bets is the only way to acquire them, and at this point, nobody has managed to win enough.

Letting rare weapons and armaments simply lie idly in times like these is the root of every evil, the pinnacle of corruption, and a great loss for humanity.

"By the way," I start, "I have terrible luck. I've never won a bet without cheating, and this casino has strict anti-cheating countermeasures in place."

"...Yeah, and the bet you won to acquire our services was a real con, too."

"*Cough, cough.* Boss, please let me handle this. Leave it...all up to me."

Rabi's face is beet red due to the heat enveloping us. She's wearing her heavy robe and a mask, but many eyes are still falling upon her, and she looks ready to faint. If any of these drunk gamblers make a pass at her, I won't be able to defend them when heads start to roll. Rabi just needs to lie low.

"We've secured enough funds, but there's no wiggle room in our budget. Not a single person has ever won this item—no famous mega-rich types, mercenaries, or otherwise. Do you hear me? We absolutely must obtain it."

Stey salutes me—a pitiful sight as she's still leashed up.

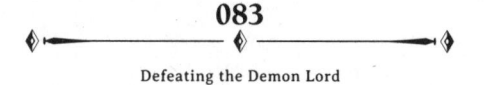

"I'll get it done, Ares. I've been banned from three different casinos!"

"......I've never depended more on you than I have today, Stey. I don't care if you get banned from this casino, too, but we have to get our hands on that armor somehow."

This is not fun and games. Our actions here will directly affect the future of Toudou's journey. I tried complaining about Toudou's "makeover," but it was useless. Creio ordered me to support the hero. Goddammit!

I channel all my energy into barking out an order.

"Amelia, Stey, Sanya. I don't care how much money you use—it is absolutely imperative that you obtain that armor. Just don't cause a scene. Rabi, you're on standby in the hotel."

"Hell yeahhhh!!"

"......Understood. Thank you, boss."

Sanya roars with joy for reasons beyond me; Rabi coughs repeatedly, looking unsteady on her feet.

"What will you do, Ares?" Amelia asks me, eyes blinking.

"I'll be identifying the kind of heresy this casino's owner is up to."

This isn't fun and games for me, either. I'll wrap this up in no time. They'd better think twice about underestimating this crusader.

Crusaders are granted vast authority in defending the world from powers of darkness, but there is a procedure in terms of confirming the existence of heresy. It's easy in the face of demons. In the majority of kingdoms in our world, killing a human being without reason will lead to charges of murder.

The authority of the Church of Ahz Gried is also deeply rooted in nearly every kingdom. As evidenced by the fact that Gregorio is still walking freely, almost anything can be covered up, but taking the most peaceful route is always optimal.

I'm used to it at this point, but I still can't forgive and forget. Why must I be tasked with laying down the law on not only demons, but also human beings?

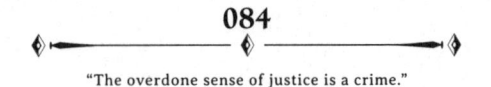

"The overdone sense of justice is a crime."

✞ Second Report: On Acquiring Legendary Equipment and Fortifying Battle Power

My subject this time around has money. And in the vast majority of cases, money is connected to power. What's more, if even a portion of that money is trickling down to the Church as donations, I'll have a real pain in the ass on my hands.

The church in Lymuth is not far from the casino. Even a few hundred meters away, the massive structure is easy to spot, and I stare with eyes wide as saucers. It's a veritable chalk-white palace. The steeple is fitted with a bell, and it's beautiful even compared to the dignified grand church of the royal capital. Invoking their ire will be well worth it.

It's already midnight, but the church of Lymuth is still well lit. Just inside its massive open door, a number of people that were obviously absorbed in gambling until just moments before are gathered. They must be here to make a plea with God.

Praying to the God of Order, Ahz Gried, will not cure bad luck, which I have demonstrated myself, but there's no reason for me to confront any of these gamblers. I push my way past the throng and show my left earring—proof I'm a man of the cloth—and am led through. Crusaders are given ranks for times exactly like this.

I'm guided to the very back of the church where a stocky priest is waiting. He is of large build, but he's more wide than tall, and he has a distinct double chin. Nonetheless, the way he stands gives off a slight air of solemnity, and as the pastor of this church, his appearance is fitting. His white robe is adorned with gold threads and is clearly very expensive. The man views the earring on my left ear warily and ostentatiously furrows his brow.

I ignore him and look around the room. The pastor's quarters are rustic in comparison to the church's opulent facade. However, looking carefully, I can see that no expense has been spared in the details. The wooden desk is a gorgeous item, clearly crafted from high-grade timber, and the liquor bottles quietly adorning a glass shelf would probably cause my eyes to pop out of my head if I knew their cost.

I thank the nun who guided me here and step forward, putting my hand to my chest before bowing.

"Pardon me for visiting you so late. I am Ares Crown."

"...Brother Ares, welcome. I am Teo Lonabardi, the pastor here at the church of Lymuth. A fellow priest visiting at this hour—I've never once seen such a thing during my tenure in this city."

"The pleasure is all mine, Brother Teo. This is my first time in Lymuth, and it's full of surprises. Incredibly, although it's well into the night, the streets remain very crowded. I had heard the rumors, but—"

"Yes, that's just the sort of place Lymuth is, though I scarcely believe it's unique in that regard. Now then, what business have you?"

He hasn't made it directly clear on his face, but it seems that Brother Teo doesn't want me overstaying my welcome. Nor should he—as far as the head of the Lymuth chuch is concerned, any high-level priest who visits is an enemy. And I am indeed his enemy.

I focus my mind and shrug visibly. "I don't intend to stay long. I'll cut right to the chase. Do you know who runs the casino in this city?"

"Well...of course. It's Petor Derholm, the wealthiest person in Lymuth. Some call him the casino king. There isn't a soul in this city who doesn't know him."

"And he gives you sizable donations, yes?"

"...Yes. We are fortunate in that he is a man of deep faith. And those donations are perfectly legal. It's no grounds for interrogation at such a late hour," Teo replies curtly, momentarily furrowing his brow.

He obviously has the confidence to evade any further questions, too. Or perhaps, without any enemies in the city, he's become arrogant. Teo must be acquainted with Petor. Money, authority, and the Church are infinitely related through ties that can't be cut. If I keep prodding with this fact in mind, I should be able to fulfill my objective peacefully.

I raise my left hand and point to the black ring on my ring finger—the symbol of a crusader. Teo looks suspicious.

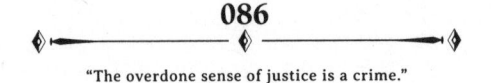

"The overdone sense of justice is a crime."

Second Report: On Acquiring Legendary Equipment and Fortifying Battle Power

"I am a crusader," I tell him. "There is concern of heresy regarding Petor. I'm asking for your cooperation, Brother Teo."

"A crusader...? What foolishness... Petor is an innocent man. What evidence do you have of his heresy—?"

Teo doesn't show any signs of being flustered yet. Crusaders are the Church's black ops. Our ranks are kept hidden from the public, but how clueless must a fellow priest be if he's never heard of the Out Crusade?

I approach the blissfully ignorant priest and look down at him. I smile but make sure to show a slight tinge of hostility. His expression changes; he must realize what's happening.

"Listen up, Teo Lonabardi. *I* will decide if the man is innocent. If you want to prove his innocence, then you must cooperate with my demands. It would be foolish to resist. Everyone who's resisted so far has regretted it."

Anyone profoundly wealthy ought to have heard of the crusaders. If this Petor is smart enough, this should all be over quickly.

I haven't the slightest clue why famous weapons and armor are prizes at the casino. These items show their true potential in the hands of a skilled user. I might understand the logic if we weren't currently under attack by the Demon Lord's army, but treating these valuables like mere baubles gives an insanely false sense of security.

How dare they use real items! Offer works of art or something made of precious metals instead!

"Th-this is tyranny! You can't possibly be allowed to do this!" Teo yells, spraying spittle, his face beet red. He's visibly sweating.

"True, I hear that a lot. But I *am* allowed to do this. You see, I *have the authority* to convict you *without a shred of evidence*. And disposing of a member of the Church will be a snap."

This right I have allows me to quickly execute any demon posing as a human on sight. It's not technically legal, but that doesn't matter. What do laws matter when dispatching the legions of darkness?

087

Defeating the Demon Lord

Just whose permission do I need to do this? God's.

I sit on the wooden desk and stare Teo down. I've taken it easy on him, but even after feeling my over-level-90-pressure, he still has the guts to defy me. A man of the cloth indeed.

"I assumed you wouldn't cooperate from the get-go," I tell him. "However, I'd really rather not kill you. Brother Teo—God wants the summetal armor. Do you understand?"

"?! Th-th-that's the casino's crown jewel! There's no chance! Many famous mercenaries have tried to barter for its purchase, but Petor has firmly rejected them all!"

I already know this. If it was easy to obtain, I wouldn't have come this far. I will squeeze as much as I have to out of these people. I will make them acquiesce. The fact I haven't truly laid into Teo yet proves that I'm at least more benevolent than Gregorio.

"Again, Brother Teo. I am demanding that you make this happen. Or do you wish to be implicated in heresy?"

"He—he has countless people protecting him! Your threats will not work on him!"

"I will be the judge of that—"

It's true that Petor's guards are around the same level as frontline mercenaries. I heard the handful of leaders he paid a pretty penny to hire are even over level 80. That's unheard of in a place like this, and they could prove difficult in battle. But this isn't a battlefield. I have a vast number of options available to me.

Killing someone so high level would be a waste—I relax my face and lighten the pressure. I get down off the desk and brush off my robes, lowering my tone to continue:

"—although... Yes, I see. Thank you for your cooperation."

"...Wha—?!"

Teo is wide-eyed; I remain utterly solemn.

"Your testimony has made it clear, Brother Teo—Petor is a heretic. He is absolutely a pawn of the Demon Lord Kranos."

"?! What? No, that's not—"

"Hoarding top-class weapons and armaments in a casino inhibits

"The overdone sense of justice is a crime."

Second Report: On Acquiring Legendary Equipment and Fortifying Battle Power

humanity's military strength—a truly spiteful strategy. Without your testimony, I never would have realized it. Truth be told, I was only intending to make a monetary offer for the summetal armor... But in the name of the God of Order, I will seize all his assets and wring any information I can out of him. You are Lymuth's savior."

A ruthless hand to play, by all accounts. I don't hesitate to stamp out anyone who gets in my way, but executing Petor without hard proof would have too much impact. That said, I'm not counting it out if it becomes necessary.

Teo's face turns distinctly blue. He must have caught my drift. If Petor is determined a heretic by the Church and has all his assets seized, the pastor, Teo, will bear the full brunt of the accusation.

The casino is Lymuth's lifeline. Without Petor, the city will face great repercussions. Not to mention he has many cohorts; retaliation will certainly be on the table. I highly doubt Teo will be able to protect himself.

"O-okay, I understand." Teo scratches his head feverishly, his voice shaking. "I'll cooperate! I doubt it will work, but I'll bring the matter to him. If you could please...have mercy on me."

"Listen, Brother Teo," I urge him. "I have *absolutely zero interest* in you. To be blunt, I have no interest in Petor, either. I will use whatever means necessary to reach my goal. In order to quell the hordes of darkness, I will sacrifice however many precious lives it takes, though it pains me deeply."

Don't worry—I'll keep quiet about the fact that this is all for the sake of Toudou's "makeover." That is my version of compassion.

"Therefore, I expect you to answer my demands faithfully. Don't think that you can escape the grasp of a crusader."

§ § §

Amelia Nohman isn't very fond of particularly loud or glitzy places. Peering up at the building covered in magic lights flickering, she feels like she's having some sort of weird dream.

When Ares ordered her to obtain this summetal armor, Amelia balked, whereas normally, she would have shown any aptitude necessary for the task, regardless of whether she thought she could actually tackle it.

"Wowww... It's been so long since I stopped by a casino! The atmosphere! The spectacle!"

"So even priests visit casinos... Well, it's been a while for me, too."

The only reason Amelia hasn't turned white as a sheet yet is because of Stephenne and Sanya. Although the casino has Amelia feeling timid, when Stephenne and Sanya look up at the same building, their expressions don't change at all. If anything, Stephenne looks just like a kid in a toy store, and Sanya is trying to play it cool on the outside, but she's actively hiding her excitement.

Hopefully they haven't forgotten that this is part of our journey to defeat the Demon Lord..., Amelia thinks.

It makes enough sense in Sanya's case—mercenaries from all walks of life and all epochs have a tried-and-true reputation for loving alcohol and gambling. But Stephenne is supposed to be a member of the clergy, someone blessed with a far superior home and upbringing than Amelia—raised like a princess, really. So why does a casino have her so giddy?

The only thing Amelia can understand is that the party is in a predicament. Stephenne has seen a number of tasty morsels whisked away right before her eyes. Amelia has confidence that she's being useful in the background, but as everyone's subordinate, Stephenne's every act and thought have been exceptional. She's been dragged around to numerous locations and seen her fair share of trouble, but in the end, she's accomplished the rare feat of actually making the party money. Amelia can't hope to successfully imitate her.

For this reason, if Stephenne once again plays an active role in their success at the casino, Amelia will barely have a leg to stand on. This is a do-or-die situation; Amelia can't sit and talk about how the atmosphere turns her off. She has to help control the other two and obtain the summetal armor. And if possible, they should acquire

"The overdone sense of justice is a crime."

Second Report: On Acquiring Legendary Equipment and Fortifying Battle Power

other weapons and armaments up for grabs as prizes, too. Then and only then will Amelia seal her fate as Ares's irreplaceable right-hand woman.

"So what sorts of things do they have at a casino?" Amelia asks.

"Whaaat? You've never been to a casino before? Welllll..."

Stephenne sounds annoyed as she begins explaining. Amelia had a sour look on her face at first, but as she hears Stephenne talk more, she can't help her eyes going wide. It appears that Amelia was working with outdated information. There are more games that can be played at modern casinos than she imagined. Card games and roulette are the standards, but the plethora of games invented during this dark era also include slot machines, devised through feats of the newest magical engineering, and abominations that allow players to put two captured monsters against each other in battle to bet on which will win.

Lymuth is also called vice city. Observing closely, there are a number of people with pallid complexions hulking in the shadows of the glitzy neon signs. Some of them probably lost their entire fortune to gambling.

The Church is tightfisted. Even for the most important assignment of supporting the Holy Warrior, they don't provide much in terms of budget. They are largely responsible.

Just then, Amelia asks Stephenne, who looks ready to barge into the casino at any moment, "By the way, Stey... I'd just like to check something: What games are you best at?"

"...Huh?"

Stephenne's eyes grow wide. She puts her finger to her lips, looking perplexed and shaking her head.

"I'm not bad at any casino games, actually."

"...Pardon?" Amelia furrows her brow. "No, you see...... With all the various games out there, you must at least have your strengths and weaknesses—"

Stephenne giggles bashfully. "Hee-hee-hee... But, like, I've never lost, even once? Gambling is what I'm best at."

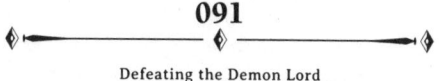

Defeating the Demon Lord

"Oh, c'mon, Stey...," says Sanya.

"Hee-hee-hee-hee..."

"Ah-ha-ha-ha-ha..."

Sanya and Stephenne both laugh. Sanya likely thinks that Stephenne is joking—but Amelia, who's worked with Stey for so long, knows the truth: This girl is legit.

Stey has all the dignity and presence of a champion. Come to think of it, Ares can see through Stephenne's devices easily. Perhaps to replace the important things she's lost as a person, she's acquired particular strengths in other areas?

"Just leave this to me! I'll make sure our time here is smooth sinking!"

This won't end well..., Amelia thinks, concerned. But Stephenne remains completely indifferent to her as she struts up to the casino with full confidence. Sanya rushes to follow her and so does Amelia—she doesn't have much choice.

No choice whatsoever. They need to use whatever method has the highest winning odds. The most important thing isn't that Amelia actively contributes but rather that she meets Ares's demands to a T.

Just as Stephenne is about to enter the casino, she trips over her legs and falls to the ground magnificently. Thanks to Ares's training, her ditzy, klutzy nature has supposedly gotten better over time, but only in terms of relative systematic error, it seems.

"Whoa... You okay, Stey?!"

A number of eyes fall on Stey. Sanya, still largely unfamiliar with such a spectacle, rushes over to her. She takes Stey, who is holding her nose with tears in her eyes, by the hand and helps her up. The next moment, a hand rests on her slender shoulder. It's the hand of a hard-faced man wearing a well-tailored black suit, and a number of others in the same black garb follow behind.

Sanya's expression turns volatile for a moment, and she quickly turns suspicious. The suited men are not ruffians. They're from the casino management—security agents ready to pounce when something goes wrong at the establishment.

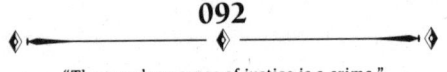

"The overdone sense of justice is a crime."

Second Report: On Acquiring Legendary Equipment and Fortifying Battle Power

The atmosphere around them quickly shifts due to the bizarre scene unfolding. Then one of the suits speaks with affected courtesy to Stephenne, who's staring blankly.

"Stephenne Veronide. You are indeed Stephenne Veronide, yes? I hate to tell you this before you've even entered, but please stay out of this casino."

"?!"

Stey's eyes instinctively go wide. She has no idea what's going on, but the suited man's expression is profoundly grave.

"What?! Wh-why, though?!" she shrieks. "I've never even been in this casino before! How do you know my name?!"

The security detail narrows his eyes at Stephenne's frantic plea, draws a bundle of papers from his jacket, and thrusts one sheet toward her. It shows a photo of Stephenne from a number of years back. The man delivers his verdict quietly.

"Stephenne. It's not a problem that you win too much—the problem is that you don't lose."

He's disgusted, but not angry. Stephenne falls, crumpled in a heap.

The party won't be able to depend on Stephenne after all. She's been snuffed out before even starting to gamble, and now she's been completely marked. Just how much havoc does one have to raise to be treated this way?

This really was smooth sinking. Amelia looks up at the suits with tears in her eyes and pats Stephenne, who's resisting futilely, on the shoulder. She speaks to her in a voice far more considerate than she was really intending.

"Stey, don't worry—Sanya and I will take care of your opposition."

§ § §

I highly doubt Stey will come through for us...

I've been waiting fifteen minutes at the location that Brother Teo provided for our meeting. My eyes instinctively widen when I spot the hard-faced men who appear in the middle of the street with its magical neon lights.

These men are capable. Petor Derholm, Lymuth's top dog, has many guards, and these are among the highest ranking. There are only six of them, but their immense life force is proof of their vast experience. Considering the aura they impose, their levels must be...around 70, I'd venture. Easily higher than Toudou. Their sleek black suits look like designer wear, but they're actually slash-proof and bulletproof—weaker than a full suit of armor, but given these guards' high level, they won't have any problems in a place like this.

There isn't a mage among them; mages don't make for proper guards. And although perhaps a given, there aren't any priests, either.

This sextet specializes in close-quarter combat due to their high physical prowess stemming from their powerful life force.

Meanwhile, there's only one of me...but really, if this is all I'm up against, I'm sure I'll manage.

One of the men, with pale-blond hair and pierced ears, sharply glares around him before looking toward me.

"You—you must be the priest that Brother Teo spoke of."

He lurches his whole body forward in an attempt to intimidate me. His physique is robust and well built, however—he's gotten soft. Levels raised through accumulated life force never decrease, but that doesn't mean that there isn't potential to become weaker. What does increase with life force accumulation is one's *lower limit*. Indulging in excess creates excess flesh, and going a long time without battle makes a person get rusty. Toudou is definitely stronger than this. He should be. Probably.

This man isn't concealing his animosity—or rather, his imposing nature toward someone supposedly weaker than him—as I introduce myself with an outstretched hand.

"Yes, I'm Ares Crown. The pleasure is mine."

The man smells faintly of alcohol. His lips tremble, and the corners of his mouth turn up a bit before he sticks his hand out roughly.

"The overdone sense of justice is a crime."

Second Report: On Acquiring Legendary Equipment and Fortifying Battle Power

I take his hand in mine, and before he can shake it, I squeeze with all my might.

"Gehhh?!"

Flesh crumpling and bones breaking. The smell of blood. Body heat. A shriek. A sharp intake of breath. I am a priest. I don't have that much faith in my strength, and I wouldn't even compare to warriors of a similar level, but with twenty levels between us—now that's a different story.

The man writhes in pain and tries to pull his hand away, but this handshake isn't over yet.

He loses all composure from the sudden agony, and then another man cries out, "Y-you bastard—!"

"You just tried to crush my hand, didn't you?" I tell him.

I'm not here to compromise. Nor do I intend for a carefully reconciled agreement that will allow us to see eye to eye. I am no master of tactful expression. I don't have time for that. I've already made a declaration of war through Brother Teo.

The blond man yanks his hand back. The flesh of his hand, still connected to mine, creaks and groans audibly. But I don't let go. He can heal his wounds later—I intend to make him forfeit his hand, one bit at a time.

"Wh-what do you think you're doing—?"

"You've really lost your touch. You're nothing but a pack of cowards who turned tail from the battlefield."

"?!"

I am a rational man. All humans have rights, and even during this turbulent era, those rights are more or less protected.

Being strong and capable doesn't obligate someone to fight. Level 70 is upper echelon; nobody reaches that number without skill and good fortune. That's easily within the top 1 percent of humanity in terms of level. Given the times we're in, there's no doubt in my mind that these guards have all seen combat.

But now, as security detail for the so-called casino king, they're pressuring everyday people. They think they can simply crush my hand—a hand belonging to a loyal servant of the God of Order—and that alone is proof of their impiety.

But I don't mind. They're free to believe in whatever they like. I don't intend to quibble with these men over this.

"Do you really think you're as strong as you were in your heyday?" I ask.

This is simply a matter of business. His hand still in my grasp, I grab the man, now on the verge of collapse, by the face.

I narrow my gaze and focus my energy. Feeling my high-level pressure, the rest of the security detail stiffens.

"Even after gorging yourself on life force, a limited resource, to level up, you're now interfering with God's will—what incredible gumption. Given your strength, you'd at least make a decent partition over on the front lines."

"Y-you— Are you back from the front lines yourself?!"

A suit toward the very back, clearly with the highest life force, looks at me, slack-jawed.

Even now, storied veteran mercenaries and knights are fighting to suppress the Demon Lord's invasion day and night. The front lines are facing massive manpower shortages. The battlefield is in constant flux, and the casualty rate remains extremely high. Very few return home alive. I was there as a part of my assignment, and although my service was brief, I'll never forget how fetid the air was on that battlefield.

I've heard tales of those who fled combat, although they must be very few in number. Anyone with the guts to fight on that battlefield has to have exceptional willpower. If someone managed to reach level 70 only to flee battle, why would they flaunt their might in a place like this?

Performance. That's the most necessary thing. We need to support the Holy Warrior, and not a second too soon. I can't help but smile.

"I'm quite fortunate in general. Fortunate enough to be able to take out the trash and make a negotiation all in the same breath."

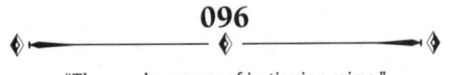

"The overdone sense of justice is a crime."

Second Report: On Acquiring Legendary Equipment and Fortifying Battle Power

"G-grrahhhh—!"

One of the suited men takes out a knife and slices at me. His steps are fluid, and he doesn't hesitate in attacking.

But he's too slow. Still gripping the other suit's hand, I take a few steps back and evade the flurry of blows. Felsa, the steel tiger werebeast we fought in Golem Valley, was orders of magnitude faster than this. Even compared with Sanya, who's probably a few levels below the suit, they are obviously weak.

Focus your bloodlust. Don't scream, don't moan, don't be scared. Enemies always attack with the intention of taking your life. It's kill or be killed—have I forgotten this most basic lesson that even a greenhorn mercenary knows? Deterioration of the senses is truly terrifying.

I whirl the blond man around to face my attackers, letting the knives, kicks, and punches glance off him as a human shield. He won't die if I immediately heal him with holy techniques. It doesn't take long before my opponents completely lose their will to fight.

Drunks surrounding us at a distance have now picked up on the brawl. The fact that mercenaries aren't called upon us proves that guards I'm up against have been used as substitutes for city guards for quite some time.

I fend off several attacks with my human shield, and by the grace of God, he is unscathed as I cast him aside. I stare down at the men, now battered and bruised.

"Tell Petor, your master, to get me that armor this instant. Understood? The only reason I haven't taken you out myself is because it would be highly illogical—and inefficient."

Controlling vain, stubborn cowards who've fled the battlefield is my forte.

I'm sure Petor has more goons at his disposal—and there's a good chance he's got mercenaries of a vastly higher level, too.

At any rate, I've done everything I can for now. Petor should be willing to hear me out.

"It's not that I can't take you out, it's that I won't. Not yet, at least. Ahz Gried is telling me to do it, but I happen to be more charitable than my lord."

I sigh deeply and give a stern reminder to the pathetic little lambs cowering before me.

Twenty or thirty minutes have passed since I warded off the mercenaries. I am now guided along by a new group of mercenaries to a palatial estate on the outskirts of Lymuth.

This casino king—surely, he's loathed by some. The many security guards at his estate corroborate this, along with the high-level watchdogs that have undergone special training and are also on the loose.

Upon entering a gate guarded by a high-level gatekeeper, I'm received by a black-suited steward. He's a middle-aged man with an air of fake politeness, but his every movement is calculated and refined, and he doesn't present a single opening. Clearly another security detail.

Walking through the estate grounds, I can sense a multitude of high-level individuals scattered throughout. I don't detect any now, but there are probably traps set here, too. A typical estate for someone involved in crooked business.

"You've disabled all your traps..."

"...Well, yes—we have a dear priest in our midst. It's only natural," the steward says, to my surprise.

Sly dog... This is certainly unexpected. That said, it appears that roughing up those mercenaries has paid dividends. I highly doubt that I'd be receiving such a placid welcome otherwise.

"I came prepared to fight to the death, you know."

"...Surely you jest. We have no such intentions ourselves."

"My mistake. It's a fight to the death in terms of peaceful persuasion. Negotiation is closely related to a duel, no? *Especially* for you."

"......"

The steward falls silent. I gather that I've made an error.

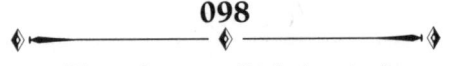

"The overdone sense of justice is a crime."

Second Report: On Acquiring Legendary Equipment and Fortifying Battle Power

I've threatened him a bit too much. Those I'm up against aren't the type to fight back harder the more they're attacked. I'm willing to do whatever it takes to complete my mission, but everyone has their breaking point.

You still need to justify your means to an end even if you're getting there by brute force. If only I could exploit some sort of weakness here...

As I ponder my options, we arrive at a drawing room. Despite his casino king moniker, the decor and fixtures are quite modest. Looks aren't everything, I suppose.

After being kept waiting a few minutes, Petor finally appears.

The ruler of Lymuth is a man of slender build. He wears a gray suit similar to his guards, and although he appears to be gentle, an unsettling light flickers behind his eyes. This man isn't one to be messed with; he's distinctly more violent than the average merchant. That's my impression. He is definitely the real deal. A mere puppet pulling the strings could never appear this genuine.

As Petor enters the room, he gives orders to the men following him.

"No guards needed. That is an affront to our guest. Wait outside."

"But... Yes, understood."

The guards look toward me with piercing glances before exiting the room.

How shrewd... He really doesn't want to give me a reason to thrash him, huh?

Petor Derholm, the casino king. His life force indicates he's over level 50, but he must have used money to raise his level. Nothing about him indicates that he has any experience in battle.

What a pain. Thrashing an ordinary citizen...breaks my heart.

"A pleasure to meet you. I'm Ares Crown. I believe you've heard from Brother Teo, but I have something to ask of you, hence why I'm here. The fate of humanity lies in the balance. It would be my distinct pleasure if you were willing to cooperate."

"Goodness...how polite. First of all, I must apologize for my subordinates' behavior. They can be a rough-and-tumble bunch... Mr. Crown, I am Petor Derholm. I manage a number of casinos here in Lymuth. The Church and I are quite friendly with one another, and I hope to get along with you, too—if possible."

I stand up and extend my hand. Petor smiles, and as if he knows how I crushed one of his mercenaries' hands, he immediately clasps my hand with significant force.

Taking a simple approach is the trick to keeping things running smoothly. I don't need to think about this man's authority or the trouble I could get myself into if I go overboard. If I'm going to get strung up by my heels, I'll worry about it when the time comes.

I will do everything in my power to achieve my current goal. We crusaders merely execute orders—taking responsibility is not in our job description.

I explain why I've come without delving into the details. Petor already knows who I am, given his position. After hearing what I have to say, he nods solemnly and gets right to the heart of the matter.

"Of course, I intend to cooperate with you. However, simply handing the summetal armor over to you would be difficult. That is the crown jewel of my casino. A number of reputable mercenaries and nobles have approached me to purchase it, but I've refused every one of them. Cutting a deal for a casino prize with cash is rather cheap, wouldn't you say?"

"I certainly would."

"The reason there are two types of coins at my casino—play coins and payout coins—is to prevent such transactions. It's quite a hassle, but it keeps things fair. Casinos must always remain fair. Don't you agree?"

"I couldn't possibly argue with that."

"...I'm so glad you understand, Mr. Crown."

Fairness, eh. And from what gift horse's mouth?

The summetal armor has always been the casino's crown jewel. In our current situation, where the fight against the Demon

"The overdone sense of justice is a crime."

† Second Report: On Acquiring Legendary Equipment and Fortifying Battle Power

Lord has arrived at an earnest crescendo, this armor renowned from many different legends has more value than any cash sum. Merchants must also be after it, in addition to mercenaries and nobles. True fairness would dictate that someone already acquired it long ago. The other valuable armaments available as prizes have all been switched out multiple times, but the crown jewel has remained. This means that something is keeping it in place.

I take a sip of the tea provided and narrow my eyes, glowering at Petor.

"That's why I'm asking you to bend the rules. That armor belongs to you, Petor, meaning that you must certainly be willing to listen to reason. Am I mistaken?"

"...I have certain policies in place."

"Oh, I'm sure you do."

"......"

After having spoken so eloquently, Petor now falls silent. He's... gauging the situation.

Crusaders are of ill repute, largely because of the Mad Eater. But Petor is a businessman. He'll certainly want to avoid a confrontation with the Church of Ahz Gried, which boasts the greatest power and influence in the world.

Petor remains silent for some time, and as if embodying a forfeiture, he throws both hands in the air.

"No mere cash sum can replace this item. However... Yes, indeed. Never mind the mercenaries and nobles. If the Church claims that they need it so badly...then I may be able to find a solution, depending on the conditions."

The summetal armor is no doubt the perfect prize to attract customers. But it's also the proper kind of equipment for the Holy Warrior, while for Petor, it's nothing more than a money grab.

Petor inhales deeply and stares directly into my eyes.

"Mr. Crown. I've heard tales of the crusaders who lay waste to all enemies of humanity. If you lend me a hand...I'll willingly gift you the armor."

I breathe deeply and bluntly refuse:

"That's impossible."

"...I'm sorry. Did I mishear you? I swear that you just said 'impossible.'"

"It's not happening. I'm too busy. I can't assist you."

Wasting even more time when I've been in a huge rush to acquire the armor would be a complete reversal of priorities. I have no idea when Toudou will do something drastic, and further, I can't predict when the Demon Lord Kranos and his troops will make their next move.

I sigh deeply and speak again to Petor, who's now dumbfounded.

"It's a donation, Petor. Donate it. I'm here for charitable donations."

"What...did you say?!"

"Selling the armor for cash might cause issues, but if you donate it to the Church in the name of defeating the Demon Lord, the criticism from your patrons will be minimal. Your casino's reputation will go up. Petor, it's a donation. Understood? You *will* donate that armor. It's absolutely necessary in the fight against darkness. I'll send a thank-you letter."

§ § §

Ridiculous... What is he thinking? Is this man truly a priest?

Petor Derholm, Lymuth's long-held ruler, scowls at this visitor he could not refuse. He can't stop his face from twitching. The Church that worships the God of Order, Ahz Gried, has the greatest number of followers among all the religious organizations throughout humanity. Even the smallest village has a Church of Ahz Gried, as proof of their sheer scale.

The foundation of this faith are the miracles of God—magical prayers—called holy techniques. Magic exists in a number of forms, but none of them can match the holy techniques, which can have exceptional versatility and can conjure powerful miracles so quickly.

"The overdone sense of justice is a crime."

✝ Second Report: On Acquiring Legendary Equipment and Fortifying Battle Power

Most humans that become wounded or adversely affected by disease don't purchase medicine—they run straight to the Church. The Church uses miracles to cure wounds, dispel curses, and perform level-up rituals. Since time immemorial, the Church has been at the core of human existence.

Part of what attracts people is how the power of the miracles themselves is proportionate to faith.

The Church of Ahz Gried's priests must be exceptionally faithful to its creed. They are required to lead a clean and pure existence, abhorring sin and saving the weak, standing up against all that is evil. And while their powers increase with greater levels of faith, conversely, if they engage in behavior that goes against their creed, they will eventually lose their power completely.

While there are such priests who have completely fallen from grace, there aren't any offenders that can somehow still perform powerful miracles.

Petor has heard rumors of the crusaders: members of the Out Crusade, the Church's sole organization devoted to destruction. The silver-haired man in front of him is the real deal, no doubt about it. His priestly earring and the black ring on his finger—a symbol of his agency of divine punishment—truthfully make it even more evident, considering how Petor's guards were thrashed without any chance of rebuttal. This man can use the holy arts—that much is certain.

Petor was unable to shut him up through a display of force. No one in Lymuth would defy Petor, but if he injured a priest who commands powerful miracles, nobody would come to his aid, either. Even the mercenaries that he painstakingly recruited would demand that he void their contracts. Over 90 percent of the healers who accompany mercenaries are from the Church, after all.

The summetal armor is the casino's crown jewel. Petor has never considered giving it up even once, but this man he's now up against is especially troublesome. The Church doesn't have the authority to confiscate the armor, but if Petor mucks this up, there's no telling what the rumor mill might say about him. The companies that helped establish the casino would likely pull out in unison, and Petor would be left with all the blame.

This is why he has to concede. The crusaders wield great authority, and they supposedly answer to the orders of the Church's cardinals and no one else. If Petor could get this silver-haired crusader indebted to him, then he could be convinced to forfeit the armor. But instead—

"A donation……? Wh-what a peculiar request, good priest. Are you asking that I simply hand over this legendary armament, which I procured completely through my own funds?"

Not even Brother Teo in all his avarice said such a thing. Petor has already given a great number of donations. He is an extremely valued contributor to the Church.

Petor sounds like he's on edge, while Ares Crown's eyes remain as placid as the surface of a clear, quiet lake.

"Well, that's one way to put it…but yes. It would be much nicer to see the armor actually put to use instead of on display in the casino."

"…This is tyranny. The Church has fallen onto hard times indeed if it's now demanding donations from its pious lambs!" Petor yells in comdemnation.

Just outside the room are scores of Petor's high-level guards, all of whom are well versed in violence, but Ares's brow doesn't flinch an iota.

"Yes, indeed. Oh, we'll return the armor to you when we're done using it. If it's still in one piece, of course."

"That is…out of the question. You dare call this a negotiation?! I…am a businessman—a benevolent merchant! Are you asking me, of all people, to shoulder this kind of loss?!"

"Precisely. You *do* realize that I'm with the Church?"

"That's not the sort of organization the Church is!"

How—just how? How can this man remain so completely composed and unflappable?!

"The overdone sense of justice is a crime."

Second Report: On Acquiring Legendary Equipment and Fortifying Battle Power

Unbelievable. Petor's initial anger was an act, but he nonetheless can't fathom how someone could be this thick-headed, even after all his dealings with shrewd merchants over the years.

"No, that is *exactly* the organization we are," says Ares. "And doing whatever it takes to accomplish the Church's goals is my job."

A bead of cold sweat drips from Petor's forehead. A foolish thought enters his mind—is the church that this man speaks of not the Church of Ahz Gried after all?

Ares sighs deeply. "Truth be told, you are the one at fault, Petor. You and your casino. I am no devil. I'm simply here to acquire the armor through legitimate means."

"A-are you, now? In other words, good priest...do you mean to say that m-my casino doesn't offer a legitimate means of obtaining this armor? That we are a dishonest business?"

"That's right."

Petor sees an opportunity. He slams both hands on the desk in front of him in desperation. His whole body shudders as he glowers at Ares Crown. This is a perfectly natural display as far as Petor is concerned. He then grits his teeth.

"This is a disgrace! Utter contempt! I won't stand for this, not even from a priest with a prestigious church!"

It's certainly true that obtaining the armor through legitimate means is difficult. But Petor isn't doing anything illicit—it's just that the odds of obtaining the summetal armor are about as good as ten miracles occurring in succession.

All the dealers employed at his casino are old aces, and even the newest slot machines are designed to cleanly rid customers of their every last dime. That's not to say that no one ever wins big at the casino, however.

Petor continues his apoplectic charade, his eyelid twitching as he tells Ares, "I have no intention of opposing the Church—but given all that you've told me, simply conceding would rob me of my dignity! Why don't we have us a contest?"

"Contest...?" Ares looks suspicious.

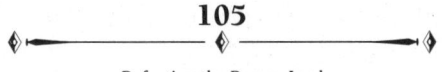

Petor proceeds to speak rapid-fire. "Yes, that's right. My casino has never seen an incident of fraud. I'll provide you with chips—and you'll play the games."

"Hmph. But it's impossible to win at your casino. I'd hardly call that a fair contest."

Indeed, there is nothing fair about the casino. It's simply a place for entertainment. As far as management is concerned, it's all about transactions.

But Petor doesn't mention any of this. He cracks a smile.

"Au contraire, Mr. Crown. You insulted my casino. Now you must take responsibility for your words."

Petor is both a businessman and a gambler. However, he's never participated in a contest like this one.

"If, by chance, you can't win even once, and you lose any means of acquiring more chips...then I will accept that my casino is fraudulent and gift you the summetal armor or whatever it is you want!"

Absurd. How can a casino that's impossible to win at come to symbolize Lymuth itself?

Gambling is all about percentages. Card games, roulettes, and slots are all predicated on this. And that's why Petor has refused entry to anyone with excellent good luck who might come in and run the house.

Petor smiles as he proposes a contest that cannot be won. Ares, meanwhile, doesn't bat an eye.

"Sure, why not?" he replies. "I should own up to my accusations, at the very least."

§ § §

"Ngh..."

"Don't worry, Amelia, I know you've got tons of strengths! You have so much going for you! You can do it!"

Stephenne is encouraging Amelia, whose shoulders are shaking

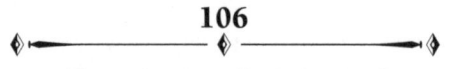

"The overdone sense of justice is a crime."

⁜ Second Report: On Acquiring Legendary Equipment and Fortifying Battle Power

intensely. The security detail who's keeping an eye on Stephenne is watching Amelia, completely unsure of what to think.

Amelia's mountain of chips has been whittled down to a paltry number in the span of just a few hours. She received some coins that are granted for winning, but she isn't anywhere close to her goal. Her funds have plummeted, too; this is utter defeat in every sense of the word.

"N-not yet. I still need time... Oh, I could just pawn my cross—"

Amelia's cross is silver. It's a symbol of her faith, but if she needs to sell it to complete the mission Ares has given her, those are the breaks. She cannot afford to fail. Amelia hasn't been able to contribute as of late, and this is the last straw for her.

As Amelia stands up, Stephenne clenches a fist and cheers, "I-I'm sure of it! You're gonna win the next time, no doubt about it! Let's go get that money right now!"

"...You're not going to stop me, I see."

I might as well pawn off Stey, Amelia thinks as she returns to her senses. She then notices that a crowd has gathered in the center of the casino.

Perhaps someone's winning big? It's not a particularly raucous crowd, though—in fact, they're all exceptionally quiet, waiting with bated breath. What's going on...?

§ § §

Cardinal Creio Amen falls silent for a moment after I bring him up to speed. He then speaks with disdain.

"Is that so...? You really went overboard, Ares. Petor is a formidable figure."

"But he's not our enemy. I don't mean that I'm stronger than him, but rather that he's not against us."

My current mission is to support Toudou. Our enemies should remain the Demon Lord Kranos and his minions only. No matter how high my level, I am still just a single man. I don't have the time to waste on one corrupt figure.

Petor is shrewd and powerful, with treacherous aspirations, but he's not likely receiving guidance from the Demon Lord. He is the ruler of Lymuth, the city of casinos. That much is blatantly clear. If he's exposed as a traitor, he'll be put to death, guaranteed. If we are going to investigate someone, it should be an individual who's not so obviously shady. Even a corrupt figure doesn't pose a real problem if they don't have any ties to the Demon Lord.

Atop the desk is a large bottle filled to the brim with silver liquid. Stey's eyes are shining while Amelia sits holding her knees. Sanya seems fed up with the both of them.

All three of them decided to take on the casino through a different route, but the fruit of their efforts has been less than desirable. It would appear they've lost the majority of the money I entrusted to them, but that was inevitable. I didn't think they had a chance to begin with. It's Stey, after all.

"Boss, are you serious...? Is that ploy even possible? Did you swindle them?"

"I did no such thing."

"Whoa......"

Sanya's expression is stiff as a board. Petor's little competition was over before it started, and I won. There isn't any reason I should win at gambling—especially if the casino is working in favor of the bookmakers. For this reason, I will keep busy without depending on luck. If I'm going to win at gambling, I absolutely need a way to cheat.

But when it comes to turning a loss into victory, I'm unrivaled. Petor must have never imagined that I would keep losing without even trying, but his face was clearly contorted. That said, he couldn't find a cheat that didn't exist, and even if I didn't win his little competition, I didn't have any intention of leaving without the armor anyway.

"Wow, Ares! We make a great team, you and me!"

"The overdone sense of justice is a crime."

† **Second Report: On Acquiring Legendary Equipment and Fortifying Battle Power**

"Watch it or you're dead."

Stey was banned from the casino before she even set foot in it, and I shut her up quickly. Then I turn my gaze back to the bottle on the desk. This bottle is the spoils of war, our trophy for victory—

"This…is the proverbially infamous summetal armor, huh? It's…liquid."

In the past, a great number of heroes have employed this legendary armor, very different from the holy armor, while traversing the battlefield. There are other magical armaments that look absolutely meaningless at first glance, but I have never seen a piece of armor that looks so completely disparate from the typical shape of armor.

One theory claims that the summetal armor has vastly greater physical robustness than the holy armor Fried. Conversely, the holy armor Fried has greater magic resistance, but at any rate, this armor isn't exactly the best option for Toudou. The holy armor Fried is much more suitable for the Holy Warrior…but this will suffice.

If Toudou doesn't like this new armor, either… Maybe he should just die.

"…Petor… That dog… He didn't dupe us, did he?"

I can't imagine that Petor would have disguised the armor, after threatening us so menacingly… But how do you even equip this…? I ponder for a moment and look toward Stey.

"Right— Stey, you try it on."

"?! Um, what?! *Me*?!"

Having two mercenaries is a gift. I can't lose Amelia, who can support administrative tasks related to the Church. My sudden order makes Stey flinch at first, but the second I open the bottle, she sticks her finger in without hesitating.

…*This girl knows no fear.*

"W-wow! Wowww! It's…cold? Eek?!"

The summetal armor inside the bottle begins to writhe, emitting a magical light. Stey cries out. Sanya takes a step back, and Amelia gasps.

Defeating the Demon Lord

The summetal armor can be equipped by a warrior of any body type, I've heard. The reason for this has become abundantly clear.

The liquid starts creeping up Stey's finger. It proceeds to wrap around her arms, neck, shoulders, back, and chest before heading for her lower body. Stey's eyes are darting back and forth frantically. *I guess the summetal armor can be equipped over a robe.*

"Wh-wha—? What the? This feels so weird! It's squeezing me—!"

I hear a quiet *clank*. All that's left in the bottle is a single medal etched with a crescent moon. I hold up the bottle, examining it closely. *This probably removes the armor, somehow.*

"Wow! It's so light! It's kinda tight, but it's almost the same as clothes!"

Stey jumps up and down. Her foot slips, and she crashes to the floor. Just as she's about to smack her head, a piece of the armor extends to envelop her head. A thunderous crash of metal resounds.

"Holy moly!" Stey yells from the ground in amazement. "Not a scratch! That didn't hurt at all! I want this!"

Not a chance in hell.

The holy armor Fried has the capacity to reduce damage to an extent through a shield that was automatically deployed for the wearer. The summetal armor seems to actually physically reduce damage. It's a simple difference but…very significant. Wearing this armor over the top of the holy armor Fried would provide maximum strength.

Sanya sighs shortly and says in amazement, "It's, like, what should I say…? Boss… This armor is something special."

She's right… This armor is exceptionally valuable, and certainly worthy of its legend. The only problem is the way it makes the wearer look. Stey's body is covered in the silver armor, and her massive breasts are outlined to perfection as she sticks them out with force.

"Wow! Look at this! It supports my breasts, so I don't even need a bra! I want this!"

The summetal armor is closer to a bodysuit than anything. It

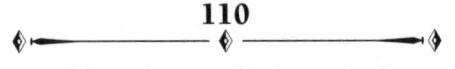

"The overdone sense of justice is a crime."

✝ **Second Report: On Acquiring Legendary Equipment and Fortifying Battle Power**

puts Stey's curves on full display—her breasts, arms, waist, and rear. She claimed that it was constricting her earlier, but that's apparently exactly what it's supposed to do. Even worn over her robe, it shows every curve of her body. How best to describe this...?

"...It's totally salacious," Rabi says quietly, speaking for everyone present. Her red eyes peeking out from the hood of her robe are peering at Stey.

Stey, still enjoying the fresh sensation and looking absolutely on cloud nine, squeezes her breasts with gusto and lifts them.

"Look, Ares! My boobs are so *hard*!"

And you call yourself a woman of the Church?!

"......I could do that, too, if I wore it," Amelia says quietly by my side.

"...The real issue is whether Toudou will like it."

This equipment puts the wearer's curves on blatant display. Depending on gender and personality, it could put off some people majorly. I imagine that Amelia would ultimately refuse. I would think it's necessary to put world peace before personal embarrassment, myself...

"Check it out, Ares—even inside of my skirt is all silver! I'm not embarrassed at all!"

This woman of the cloth raises the hem of her holy robe, which is wrapped in metal and turned silver. I would like to have a word with Cardinal Veronide, who raised her. Have some shame!

I give up on snapping back at her and make up my mind to move on, hefting my mace by my side.

"Let's test its strength for the record. After that, we'll gauge appropriate timing and send it to Toudou via the Church."

Aria will understand the true value of this armor. I won't let Toudou complain. And I won't let him wear that cloak of infinite darkness, that's for damn sure. The Holy Warrior can't simply be strong. A hero has the obligation to look like a hero to everyone around them.

"The way it shows every curve...... This could be a major problem," Amelia says ominously.

Defeating the Demon Lord

But why? Is Toudou embarrassed? Why would he be? What kind of hero does he think he is?!

"Oh, by the way: I need you to divide up and stay on guard. If something goes wrong, you need to apprehend Petor. The casino itself isn't evil, but if they get in my way, we won't have any choice. This—is the will of God."

"...Boss...that's exactly the kinda thing a villain would say."

I finish my message, and Sanya is looking at me with a stiff brow.

Petor is a capable man. The casino is an effective source of decompression. If possible, I want to leave the casino alone, but defeating the Demon Lord comes before everything. If they get in our way, we have no choice but to stomp them out. That is simply the nature of my job.

After obtaining the legendary armor in vice city, we are immediately set on our next objective—returning to the royal capital, where Toudou and company await. We have been slow on our feet due to Toudou's time spent withdrawing away from us, but before long, the capital will be ready for action, too.

As a result of inspecting the summetal armor by getting Stey to try it on, we've discovered it's even more powerful than rumors claimed. Its automatic defenses respond to attacks to one's blind spots, and once the wearer masters the armor, it can expand at will to protect allies.

It's effective against both blunt and slash attacks; even when I punched Stey with middling force, she was simply knocked backward. The armor is liquid, so it doesn't get damaged—certainly worthy of its legendary status. So its only flaw is that it can't be worn over other armor?

Putting on the summetal armor over a robe isn't an issue, but it doesn't seem to react unless it's in direct physical contact with a living being.

No matter. This will more than do the trick—it's a warrior's armament. This was well worth all the trouble we went through.

"The overdone sense of justice is a crime."

✟ **Second Report: On Acquiring Legendary Equipment and Fortifying Battle Power**

Arriving at Ruxe, we head to the Church to entrust the armor to them. Stey took a shine to the piece and now looks dejected.

"It was so fun... I really want one, too."

"If only it could prevent you from falling down when you trip, too."

"......!!"

Just stop. Don't look at me like I've actually come up with a brilliant idea. That was obvious sarcasm.

At any rate, Stey was able to control the armor with ease, but will Toudou really be able to as well? Stey has surprisingly high capabilities in strange ways, so I'm worried. Sheesh, maybe Stey should just defeat the Demon Lord for us.

"Come to think of it...if I ask Papa, then maybe..."

Stey keeps mumbling and grumbling to herself, but her father is the man who he is, and I don't think she's completely joking. Her father, Cardinal Sylvester Veronide, is a man of legend. A former business magnate, he now has the Church's authority in the palm of his hands, and his influence cannot be questioned. He's such a blind, doting parent, that he even had Stey, obviously unfit for a woman of the cloth, made into a nun, too.

I'd give Stey back to him in a heartbeat if he could supply summetal armor for all of us.

A few days after returning to the royal capital, the day has finally come.

"Ares, I have an update on Ruxe's next action: They plan to debut the Holy Warrior to the public," a stony-faced Amelia tells me.

"Hmm...... At last."

This comes as no surprise to me; I'd been thinking it was about time for Toudou's debut.

The Holy Warrior's existence has been kept a secret for a long time. Even among the Church, only a small fraction of upper-level individuals know, and the same goes for the Kingdom of Ruxe. This was all in the name of preventing information leaks.

The Holy Warrior has massive latent potential, but at the

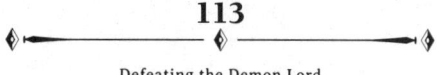

moment of summoning, their level is paltry. The demon army knows this, too, and if they become aware of the Holy Warrior's existence, they will attack in a frenzied struggle to the death.

We've already encountered a number of the Demon Lord's vanguard on our journey to support the Holy Warrior. Toudou would have been guaranteed to lose to each one of them if he was by himself.

Nonetheless, we have reached a breaking point, it seems. A number of kingdoms allied with Ruxe have been leveled, and even for Ruxe, the battle against the Demon Lord's army has pushed them to the brink in a brutish standoff. Humanity is not strong enough to fight with all hope nearly lost.

However, conversely—with hope, humanity can rise to fight again. Even those nearly lost to despair, forced into battle with their backs against the wall—they will find the energy to fight again if they learn the truth of the Holy Warrior's summoning. On the heels of our brilliant victory against the sea demon Heljarl, right now is perfect timing.

"How will it be announced?"

"A massive parade. The Hero's Procession of Light of ancient legend. This much is certain."

Amelia is visibly shocked. "Isn't that...exceptionally risky?"

"Yes, very much so. However, there isn't another choice. There is no choice when it comes to holding the procession. The sacred scripture holds that: 'When the hero is summoned by the God of Order from another world to ours, we must proceed by their side, bathed in light.' Even if the Kingdom tried to reject it, the cardinals and Church elites wouldn't allow this. It's all part of the hero-summoning ritual."

There is no avoiding this path. Because of its necessity, it must be completed, regardless of the risk.

"We must make sure to prepare for the possibility of attack."

"The parade will be held within the Kingdom of Ruxe, no? Could there...possibly be insurgents?"

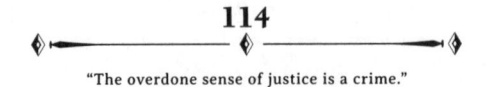

"The overdone sense of justice is a crime."

Second Report: On Acquiring Legendary Equipment and Fortifying Battle Power

"Yes, absolutely, there are. The Demon Lord Kranos is like none other before him."

I won't go as far to say there are traitors in our midst, but the Demon Lord's hand nearly extends that far. He already has magical items that can detect the blessing of Ahz Gried handed out among his elites. He must already have spies mixed into human cities as well.

Eventually, Toudou must stand before all of humanity. To stand in front of them and guide them. To become the leader of the forces of humanity and become their spiritual pillar of support.

This is the destiny of the Holy Warrior. And the holy light of procession must follow their summoning, falling to illuminate their footsteps immediately behind them.

Personally, I think it's premature to debut Toudou to the public. Even with Toudou's face, name, and very existence hidden, we have faced dire trials and tribulations. Toudou's level has not risen as expected. Limis and Aria are still too weak. Even when it comes down to it, putting Glacia in front as a wall to protect us will be grossly inadequate. Above all else, the hero's party still lacks a priest.

The dice have already been cast. I can offer all the admonition I want, but the decision isn't up to me. Just then, I hear Sanya's voice from outside the door.

"Boss, you got a visitor."

"Hm? Who is it?"

"A nun. I'm letting her in."

A nun... Maybe a message from the Church? If they've been sent directly, it's probably another complication coming our way? They've been nothing short of endless...

I pause my thoughts for a moment and approach the door. When I open it, I see a nun with ash-gray hair standing before me.

A pitiful but sweet face; her eyes are also ash-gray, and her long hair is tied back.

Her clothing is—black. I can't tell what her physique is like, as it's hidden beneath the jet-black robe. She's carrying a massive cross on her back.

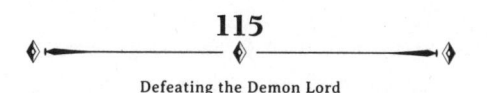

The nun smiles from ear to ear when we meet. She speaks in a calmer and more collected voice than I remember.

"Mr. Ares... It's been so long...!"

"?! You...... It can't be... Spica?"

Spica is the orphan girl we first met in Yutith's Tomb during our plan to get Toudou over his fear of the undead. It hasn't been that long since we left her in Purif, but the difference is like night and day. She was once thin from malnourishment, but she's not nearly as baby-faced as before. The girl looks at least two or three years older now.

I heard that she was training to become a crusader under Gregorio—but as I'm lost for words, Spica smiles at me and opens both arms, flying toward me in what's nearly a body check.

"Yes, it's me. It's an honor to see you again."

"!!"

From an outside perspective, this would be the loving embrace of long-lost compatriots. But I saw it: the lacquer-black dagger concealed in her right hand, now fleshier yet still slender.

I leap back and grab that hand with my own while I swiftly reach my left hand into her chest pocket, removing another dagger. Her robe flutters, and I can see a number of daggers nestled inside.

Spica...has gone bad.

Spica, the orphan who Amelia chose based solely on her looks, proceeds to scream, "Only impostors die!"

Gah! Now I know why Gregorio attacks everyone he meets!

Nevertheless, Spica has nothing on me in terms of reach—she's still a child. I grab her by the head, aggressively slamming her into the wall.

I then bind Spica with rope and tie her to a chair. Amelia tells me I'm going overboard, but Spica just tried to kill me. No matter how cautious I am, it won't be enough.

Her level is still low, I've surmised, but judging from her ambush, I can tell she's been tainted by Gregorio's blood. I was

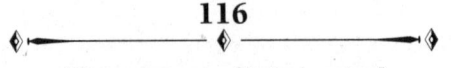

"The overdone sense of justice is a crime."

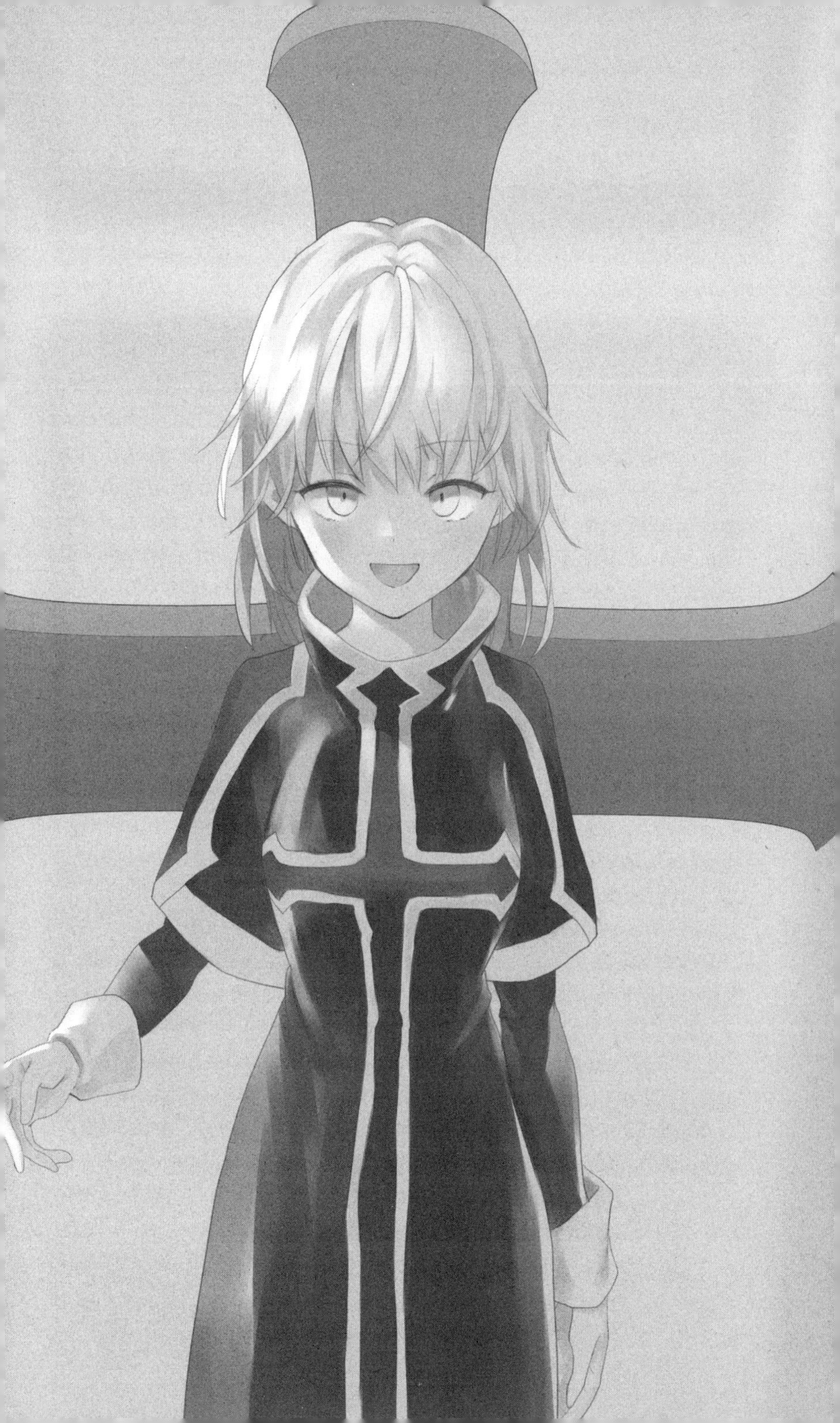

concerned Spica wouldn't be able to withstand the hardcore training when we first gave her over to him, but I never imagined she'd be tainted in the same way... Spica took up apprenticeship under Gregorio to acquire enough strength to join Toudou's party, but—could he now sic her on Toudou? This is bad... I have no idea how it will play out.

Sanya sniffs the massive cross on Spica's back and furrows her brow.

"Boss, look, this cross—it's a hunk of iron. And it smells like blood."

"It's both a weapon and passive means of strength training. Two birds with one stone...although it's certainly sacrilegious."

Priests aren't typically allowed to carry bladed weapons. The exceptions are crusaders, allowed through special circumstances, and holy knights that can circumvent the religious paradox by wielding a special weapon, the crossblade. The fact that Spica wields a dagger shows how exceptional she is.

A priest who can wield bladed weapons and holy techniques is a force to be reckoned with. That said, priests don't usually need to be good attackers. I'm strictly looking for a pure support role...

Spica comes to after losing consciousness. I cast a healing spell on her and held back in the first place, so her wounds won't cause a problem. She bats her eyes and confirms her surroundings for a moment before looking at me and smiling.

"It's been so long, Mr. Ares."

"Don't even try to struggle," I warn her as her bound arms squirm. "Buffs can be cast on materials made from animal products. Your robe is specially made, and you won't be able to dispel it."

Spica's eyes go wide. She...really has gotten stronger.

The quickest way to take down a member of the hordes of darkness is to make them second guess themselves and go in for a sudden kill. That said, no matter how well this is explained verbally, it's generally impossible to assault someone that you know. Generally.

"Um... Please untie me. I am here by the will of God. My master...has sent me for further training."

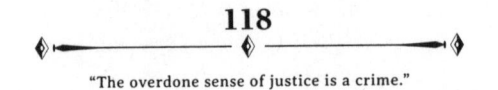

"The overdone sense of justice is a crime."

Second Report: On Acquiring Legendary Equipment and Fortifying Battle Power

She's truly...a thespian. Because I know what she was like before, I imagine she'll have even more influence on Toudou now. I need to flip this into a positive. Depending on how I use her, it could lead to Toudou...completely revolutionizing his mentality?

"I'll let you go, but first, let me tell you something."

I sigh deeply and look down at the greatly changed Spica, glowering at her as I assert, "There's a problem with you determining just who is real and who isn't. Remember this—you can't be an impostor if you're dead. If you die—you're the real deal. Demons are almost always stronger, after all."

Spica's ash-gray eyes are as wide as the full moon.

I remain cautious as I listen to Spica's tale. Just as I'd expected, after we parted ways with her, Spica was subjected to hellish training by Gregorio, including ample real-life battle scenarios in the mix.

"Whoa... I had no idea the Out Crusade did that kinda stuff! Holy crap..."

"*Cough, cough...* I was also subjected to a similar experience, but the scale was completely different. For mercenaries, any death means that ill repute will soon follow... *Cough.*"

Sanya and Rabi are both disgusted. They would be further hurt by the Church's report, but it's likely true that the Church takes advantage of more fresh blood than they do mercenaries. The Church has infinite ways of gathering flocks of people, after all...

Spica is tensing up her whole body and looking at me with trepidation. Her appearance is a vivid reminder of how she looked when we first met, but the way she casts her gaze is completely different. It seems like now she's constantly probing for weak points... She's really become accomplished.

"My master, Gregorio, told me that all I needed was the finishing touches. He said that if I visited you, I could gain experience through innumerable powerful hordes of darkness attacking."

"Ares... I think she's a lost cause, don't you?"

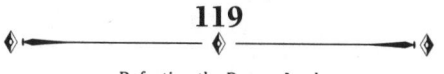

A biting comment from Amelia, the one who originally brought Spica into the fold—she has some nerve saying that now.

"Spica has you to thank for bringing her down this path... I think we should try adding her to Toudou's party."

"Wha—?! Are you sure that's a good idea?"

Amelia looks at me, questioning my sanity, but...she's not the one that our party needs. We need a warrior who can easily become a sacrificial pawn or an administrative assistant that can take on the burden of managing paperwork. I don't need a hot-blooded priest. If it was just Gregorio, I could simply take advantage of him and leave him in the dust, but I can't simply assign Spica random crazy work.

In any case, we have enough attack power between Sanya and Rabi alone. No matter how arduous Spica's training was, it was only a year or less, and she doesn't even hold a candle to Sanya and Rabi, who both trained under a famous mercenary. I really don't even need Spica or Stey.

It's pretty dubious whether she'll actually have good chemistry as a member of the hero's party, but this is a process of trial and error. If she fails, we'll pull her out.

Spica pipes up suddenly, as if remembering something.

"A moment please, Mr. Ares. As an ardent follower of the God of Order, I...have every intention of heeding your commands. But aren't you forgetting one very important thing?"

"Am I? Spit it out, then."

Spica glances pitifully at the others in the room: Sanya, Rabi—who still looks unwell—Amelia, and Stey.

"The ranks...within the party," Spica replies sheepishly.

"You can't just say whatever you like as long as you're tactful about it—you realize that, right?"

The old Spica would never talk like this. Just how am I supposed to determine this party's ranks anyway?

"It's battle you're forgetting," she adds. "The God of Order's judgment is absolute. If he wills you to win, then you cannot lose."

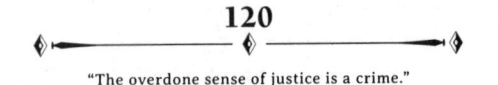

"The overdone sense of justice is a crime."

Second Report: On Acquiring Legendary Equipment and Fortifying Battle Power

I have a bone to pick with Gregorio. Yet at the same time, I'd rather not get involved with him again.

From what I can see, Spica has vastly increased her real battle experience. There's still a palpable difference in level, but someone like Amelia might lose easily to her.

Perhaps due to her silverwolf instincts, Sanya—who once approached me with a plan to compete for rank in the party—is glaring menacingly.

"Sanya. Take her for a spin. And let me know how she performs when you're done. If you lose to Spica, you're officially below her in rank."

§ § §

Spica Royle has a realization under a beam of sunlight that feels like God's jubilation manifest. Yesterday, she took innumerable blows during the competition to determine rank, but thanks to divine protection, she isn't experiencing any pain or exhaustion.

In the room assigned to her, Spica performs her daily morning prayers. She has learned so much. The Out Crusade third order Gregorio taught her many different things—from fundamental doctrine to battle tactics, how to maintain her mental state, and the "friends" affiliated with the Church. It was a full repertoire.

For the past six months, the training she was assigned by her master was so severe that training she had taken part in with Toudou and company seemed like mere child's play. At first, she was nearly in tears complaining due to the harsh training, but by now, she's learned to accept everything.

Spica's piety has been refined during battle with the inexhaustible hordes of darkness. God only provides training that allows His servants to break through to the next level. Defeating the Demon Lord Kranos is a lethal mission, but being tasked with it is a matter of sheer honor, and quite simply, the greater the trials and tribulations faced, the better.

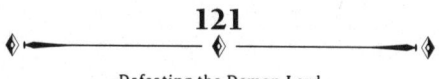

In other words, this implicates Ares as the greatest servant of God, one who has been tasked with the greatest of hardships, who will exercise the force of the Holy Warrior, the strongest human being known to man.

Knowing the hardship that awaits her, Spica is terrified, but at the same time, she cannot contain her excitement. After preparing for her journey, she returns to the living room, where Ares is waiting with a scowl.

Even though Spica is fully prepared this time, Ares questions her true intentions, just like he did in Purif.

"You are completely sure of this, yes?"

"Yes. I will fulfill my position to the fullest. I have completed all preliminary exercises."

"She'll be fine, boss. There's something definitely different with this one."

Sanya had really shown her stuff in the competition for rank, but she is clearly annoyed as she speaks. Sanya is tough as nails. She's definitely the type of party member that Ares would choose. She's despondent at having lost, but having an even tougher comrade is a blessing.

Crusaders are truly cut from another cloth. They maintain immaculate faith while taking on the responsibility of saving people. Spica is immeasurably more powerful than before. Just how strong has Toudou become?

Inhaling deeply, Spica takes a first step into the life that was once her former dream.

§ § §

"Mmph... Just what the hell am I doing?"

A feeble voice unbefitting of a hero. After failing the training in the House Friedia training room, Toudou has been confined to Aria's home. She's allowed to walk the gardens of the estate, and they've been providing anything necessary when she asks for it,

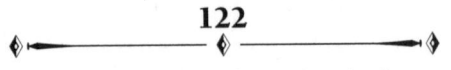

"The overdone sense of justice is a crime."

Second Report: On Acquiring Legendary Equipment and Fortifying Battle Power

but she's not allowed to leave the grounds to hunt monsters. She protested, but when it was pointed out again how she was defeated in training, she didn't have any recourse.

Without any other option, Toudou brandishes her sword in the spacious training room on the estate grounds, attacked by restlessness. She had never even gripped a sword before being summoned, but now it functions like an extension of her limbs. The radiance of the holy sword is the beaming light of the wielder's will.

Toudou and her party are growing. They have increased their levels and gained experience, getting slowly yet certainly stronger, step-by-step. Toudou knows this. And yet...

As she swings her shining sword downward, Toudou sighs deeply.

"...Can I really become strong enough just by refining my swordsmanship?" she grumbles despite herself.

"Of course you can... However, the quickest way to increase strength is raising your level," Aria replies with a brief sigh, her sword still in hand. "The same goes for any profession. If two people with different amounts of life force come face-to-face, this world will always give preference to the higher one. That's why our attacks barely worked on Heljarl, even when we had him outnumbered. It's just like how a top-class thief can run up walls because their life force is high enough to eclipse the laws of physics."

Aria's expression remains solemn as she speaks. Toudou has heard this great principle of the world many times since being summoned.

For this reason, Toudou must level up. As the tip of Aria's blade stops on a dime, Toudou can distinctly feel her refined swordsmanship and lengthy devotion to her craft, but her life force still surpasses even this.

"...And now, in our world, the one with the greatest amount of life force is...the Demon Lord Kranos."

A single being with enough life force to outmatch thousands of warriors. The blessing of the God of Evil. Aberrant demons have gathered under a colossal force of darkness, morphing into a malfeasance that this world simply cannot contend with.

Defeating the Demon Lord

Right when Toudou was summoned, she was provided with both explanations and apologies. She was told that the might of a hero was needed to save our world. Our world is at its wit's end, to the point where we need to borrow power from a human from another world. Everything must coalesce in order to defeat the Demon Lord: effort, talent, experience, levels—and divine protection, which is something that only a handful of people can obtain in our world.

Toudou recalls what she was told earlier and frowns.

"But wait... Isn't it simply too early to let the hero's presence become known?"

Toudou isn't capable enough to call herself a hero just yet. The Kingdom of Ruxe is the one that has ordered the hero's whereabouts be covered up until she becomes truly capable, while remaining on the lookout for demon attacks. Norton Rizas told Toudou that defeating Heljarl was a direct result of Toudou's actions. Nonetheless, it doesn't change the fact that Toudou has still yet to unearth her true potential. If anything, Toudou has just badly lost in her trial with the spirits.

Why did it have to be at this certain juncture? Toudou sighs again, and Aria speaks to her listlessly.

"That's because...we are truly at our wit's end, I believe."

"...I guess we've just been kept out of the loop, huh...?"

Until now, Toudou has journeyed throughout the Kingdom of Ruxe and devoted herself to training. The only time she left the Kingdom was when they traveled to Cloudburst. But wherever they went, Toudou never saw the level of disaster that she first envisioned.

This isn't an indication that the Demon Lord's invasion is far weaker than Toudou had imagined. Rather, it should be assumed that Toudou and company have actually been traveling to relatively safe places. Toudou has seen many individuals far stronger than her on this journey. However, the Demon Lord Army that Kranos commands comprises a foe that cannot be contended with in her current state—and with Toudou at the vanguard, she wouldn't be able to accomplish anything whatsoever.

"The overdone sense of justice is a crime."

Second Report: On Acquiring Legendary Equipment and Fortifying Battle Power

She could fight alongside someone else, but that is not the role that is demanded of Toudou.

She isn't convinced it's the right move, but she has no recourse to deny Ruxe's demands. Aria and Limis also have their own positions to consider.

When Toudou was summoned, she really thought she'd be able to benefit others through her power this time. She was convinced that she'd be able to save the world. For the chosen hero, she thought it was a certainty (thinking back on it), and she had an almost unfounded confidence. However, now—she has lost it.

How can she protect people without showing them her faintheartedness? Can she really defeat the Demon Lord? Can she become truly strong?

The holy sword she's wielded for so long doesn't have a single chip or blemish, and it silently reflects Toudou's dismal expression.

In that moment, Toudou realizes something, holding her sword up with a steely gaze.

...Wait...what? The holy sword Ex... Did it always look like this?

The polished silver-blue sword is imbued with pure light and created by God, its blade as light as a feather, capable of slaying any demon that stands against it. Toudou was legitimately stunned the first time the blade, gleaming with cool light, was handed to her—it was as beautiful as a museum exhibit. Just staring at it gave her a sense of reality regarding the fact that she was actually chosen as the Holy Warrior.

It's been so long since she actually stared into the blade, but this isn't just a coincidence. There is no mistake. An unknown, bizarre chill runs up Toudou's spine as she whispers in shock.

"Is the light...getting dimmer?"

"...What?"

It's not possible. The holy sword Ex is a weapon of legend—it can slash through innumerable foes, the true mark of a hero.

It will be fine; it will all be okay. This is all a figment of my imagination. It was probably like this all along.

Toudou grips the hilt fiercely and swings the blade as her body desires. Silver-blue arcs trace through the air from the high-speed chain attack she wasn't previously able to pull off.

In conception, the holy sword Ex can only be wielded by a hero. The fact that Toudou can still wield it is proof that she is the Holy Warrior. That said—her blade was useless against Heljarl.

As this fact races through her mind, Toudou grits her teeth.

"Crap—!!"

"Wh-what's the matter, Nao?"

When the Kingdom of Ruxe bestowed the holy sword Ex upon Toudou, they told her that it was a holy sword capable of shredding through all of creation. That it was a holy sword that previous Holy Warriors had used to dispel many hordes of darkness and to destroy the Demon Lord to bring salvation to our world.

The sword's light has dimmed. Toudou doesn't know why, but she knows that it can't be a good sign. She can't afford...to simply not realize this. Nor can the Kingdom, the Church—or her comrades.

It's okay—now's not the time. The holy sword has still recognized Toudou. And Aria and company haven't realized it's getting weaker.

Toudou's hands are dripping with sweat. Is her ragged, labored breathing simply from swinging the sword? She puts the holy sword back in its scabbard. Aria had been watching her sword dance from afar, but now she runs over with worry on her face.

"Are you okay, Nao? You're blue in the face—"

"Yes, yes, I'm okay. I just thought... I really need to try harder, that's all."

What should she do? How can Toudou return light to the blade?

Wait—is the fact that she can no longer wear the holy armor Fried also just a coincidence?

Until now, Toudou had been convinced that there wasn't anything she could do about it, but this fact now rises again in the back of her mind. The holy sword has lost its light. The holy armor is no longer wearable. If there is some connection between these two facts, it must mean—

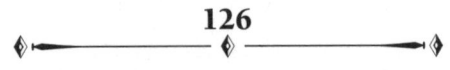

"The overdone sense of justice is a crime."

At that moment, a servant runs toward Aria, greeting Toudou with a bow before speaking to Aria with a stern face.

"Miss Aria. There is a young lady here, a nun who calls herself Spica Royle, who says she would like to speak with you. What shall I do?"

§ § §

I chase any thoughts of Spica from my mind for the time being and ask Amelia to take care of consolidating our military assets. The events of Toudou's time will demand fierce battle, and pushing through that with half-baked warpower will prove difficult.

Making the Holy Warrior's presence known is akin to exposing his location. The Demon Lord they're up against is a cunning beast. If the Demon Lord's army ascertains Toudou's whereabouts, they will almost certainly attack. While the army's movements have been shockingly quiet since the defeat of Heljarl, it must be considered that they have been planning this entire time to destroy the Holy Warrior with every fiber of their being.

However, in the same breath, this means that Kranos is particularly aware of the Holy Warrior's presence. If humanity can use the hero's existence to their best advantage, there is a chance they can stop their enemy's attack without ever entering battle.

Just then, Sanya yelps out from her position lying on the couch, where she's not offering any form of contribution to the current duties at hand.

"Oh yeah, boss. I have a great idea! Worthy of a bonus!"

"……"

"If you're worried, you should give the Holy Warrior a body double! That way, even if they get attacked it won't matter, and plus, you could easily snuff out a traitor. Whaddaya think?"

"No chance."

It's not even worth considering.

Sanya, who had been feeling good about herself, rouses from the sofa in shock.

"Whaaat? Why not? Don't tell me that you, of all people, are gonna claim it's unethical."

"Of course I'm not."

"Totally. That's a relief... So why not, then?"

......*What exactly do you mean by 'that's a relief'?*

Rabi is once again huddled in a corner staring at me. Stey is frantically poring over a mountain of books that Amelia dumped on her.

I breathe a small sigh and ask, "What would you think, Sanya, if you heard that the Holy Warrior used a body double?"

"Hmm......? I mean... It'd be kinda pathetic."

"That's why we're not going to use one."

It would be feasible if no one knew, but if word got out, no excuse would cut it. For this reason, neither myself nor any of the cardinals considered a body double even once from the beginning. If we ever did consider it, there wouldn't be any reason to ever show the Holy Warrior's face.

"Um, but...isn't that better than Toudou dying? His level's still low, and no matter how strong his divine protection is, he's not invincible. He's got stronger divine protection than Rabi does, but she could still take him out no sweat. And her protection's just from some native god."

"?! ......It's a pretty evil God, to boot," Rabi says quietly with a cough.

She did call this deity the God of Beheading—one that only lops off heads. A god of removing heads from necks. Native gods have particularly niche blessings, but they're unrivaled within that specific niche.

I know full well that Toudou isn't invincible. Nonetheless, using him to defeat the Demon Lord remains our quickest, best option.

Sanya crosses her arms and looks highly vexed.

"Y'know, I've been thinking about this a lot... Compared to all the legends...isn't Toudou, like, super weak? I mean, he does have some aptitude—but the Holy Warrior's supposed to be the hero that

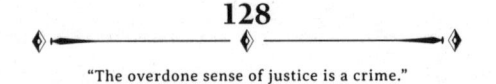

128

"The overdone sense of justice is a crime."

✝ **Second Report: On Acquiring Legendary Equipment and Fortifying Battle Power**

comes through in humanity's most dire time of need, right? Cleaving through mountains with their blade and splitting the heavens with their magic and all that. Someone with no equal in this world. It might just be folk legend—but I honestly can't see Toudou getting to that point, no matter how much he levels up."

I must say, my evaluation of Sanya has quietly risen. I should expect as much from the disciple of a legendary mercenary after all.

Sanya... She's sharp. Dangerously sharp. I can't have her saying anything more.

I narrow my eyes and stare at her meaningfully. She shudders and looks at me with trepidation.

"Sanya, do you know the phrase, 'Out of the mouth comes evil?'"

"?! What?! Was it something I said?!"

"Sanya, this is an order: Never say that again. I don't want to kill my own allies."

"C'mon, boss, you wouldn't execute me for slandering the Holy Warrior, right?! Besides, if anyone should get the guillotine, it's you."

What is she talking about? It appears that...adding more smart asses to our side is going to cause further problems.

Nonetheless, I need to make good use of her. Sanya kicks her legs on the couch and puffs up her cheeks. Her actions are playful, but her eyes are placid. At this rate, she'll never again say anything like she just did.

"Sanya, if you don't have any other tasks on the docket, I'll put you on guard duty. If you have the time for such errant thoughts, then you need to toughen up. You'll get fat lounging on that sofa."

"...Aye-aye, sir. I won't get fat. Silverwolves don't."

Sanya leaps lithely off the sofa and bursts out of the room, her ears twitching visibly.

§ § §

"Sister Spica, never giving up thinking is paramount. In the past, my friend Ares said, 'Everything has a reason.' Heh... He was so

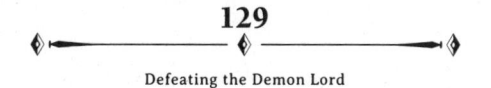

right. Nothing happens without reason. For the Church to be fixated by this allegory, and for my friend, Ares Crown, to be selected as First Order—comes with nothing short of certain reason."*

Spica's master, Gregorio Legins, is a religious fanatic beyond denial, no matter how hard he may try to keep up other appearances. The teacher's thinking is simple while also being extraordinarily pliable. His mind runs at a quick clip, being able to easily chew and separate the sour from the sweet. Spica was able to quickly recognize after just spending some time with him that her master didn't get this way simply through fanaticism.

"My friend Ares is strong. He has far greater power than any of the other stewards of the faith. But if pressed to give one reason for his strength—it would easily be his sagacious mind. And not in terms of deep scholarly learning—I believe that he has truly superior powers of perception."

Gregorio is never one to shy away from conversation, but when talking about Ares, he always becomes more loquacious than usual and more severe. The underlying emotions are envy and jealousy.

"His perception is keen, and he's humble. I was so shocked. Even before he was discovered by the cardinal—when he was even younger than you are now—he already grasped the 'secret to power.' And for this reason—I believe that Ares was bestowed with the great responsibility of defeating the Demon Lord."

It is the night before departure in a dimly lit room. The pale, somber candlelight illuminates Spica's cross. Her master told her that it was a parting gift. She is unsure of the true motive behind his words, but she realizes that they are very important.

"I will only say this once, Sister Spica. This is of utmost importance. There is a certain reason for everything. The reason the Holy Warrior is powerful—is not only because the holy hero has particular capabilities."

Spica's master's eyes are narrowed pleasantly, but the brute force of his words spoken in a hushed tone make him sound like a monster.

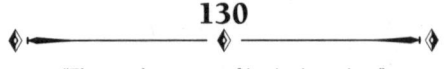

"The overdone sense of justice is a crime."

Second Report: On Acquiring Legendary Equipment and Fortifying Battle Power

* * *

"Toudou... It's been such a long time."

"Spica! Your outfit—"

The Holy Warrior, Naotsugu Toudou, looks the same as ever—a well-kept appearance and unwavering, powerful eyes.

In the past, Spica had nothing to her name. Forget the reasons—the only reason she found the courage to move forward is because of the girl in front of her, without a doubt. She had nearly forgotten when involved in her recent training, but now, meeting Toudou again, she is awash with emotion.

She thanks God for her life and the chance to meet Toudou again. Spica remains inexperienced and unskilled, but she is markedly different from her previous self. She now has the guidance of God, and she can use holy techniques. Recently, she's even acquired experience with most common battle situations.

She has received a single order from Ares: Support the Holy Warrior as closely as possible. She's not simply responsible for participating to add battle prowess, but she will also communicate the Church's intentions and adjust the party's movements accordingly—a very important role to play while guiding them to defeat the Demon Lord.

Spica is much stronger than ever before, but whether she can fulfill her responsibilities properly now depends on her divine protection. Her hand becomes itchy from the fear, tension, exhilaration, and homesickness that rack her, and she puts her hand inside her robe, on her chest.

"Did you already finish your apprenticeship with Gregorio?"

"No, I'm actually still in training... But I'm able to use holy techniques now. Look, I have proof..."

Spica shows off the earring she's wearing, a symbol of her mid-level priesthood. Her master can only use exorcism techniques, but as a priest, Spica can use whatever holy techniques are necessary.

Limis looks at Toudou, eyes wide as saucers. "Nao, she's totally eclipsed you..."

Defeating the Demon Lord

"Wow, rude... I can use them, too, you know. I mean, I haven't taken any tests yet—but really, Spica, it's been ages. I'm so happy to see you again."

Toudou steps toward Spica with a beaming, jubilant smile. Spica's eyes well up instantly.

And then—once Spica creates an opening, she seizes that opportunity to attack Toudou.

"Ah...!"

Her attack is partly instinctive. Spica takes several cross-shaped daggers from her breast pocket and lets them fly. Gregorio always told her to never let her guard down. He ambushed her on umpteen occasions. Ares ordered her not to attack Toudou, but old habits die hard.

If Toudou dies, she's a complete fake. Nothing anyone says to the contrary will convince Spica otherwise.

All three of the throwing knives that Spica released in a single motion slice through the air with a shrill hiss and sink directly into Toudou's abdomen.

"?!?!?!?! Huh? Wha—?"

Toudou's eyes go wide with shock. Her face instantly contorts in pain, and she hunches over.

Spica, meanwhile, is equally surprised.

"?! I'm s-so sorry," she says. "It was an accident—I d-didn't mean any harm— Um, I'll heal you!"

Limis and Aria cry out and hold up Toudou as she crumples to the floor.

"Huh? Wha—? What did you just—? Nao?!"

"Nao!!"

"B-but she just left herself wide open—it's not like she'll die or anything!"

Spica knows how to pick her targets. It's been ages since she's actually landed a hit. Besides, how could someone as inexperienced as Spica manage to ambush the Holy Warrior and injure her...? Unfathomable.

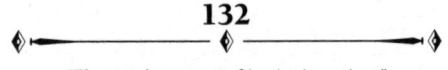

"The overdone sense of justice is a crime."

"Guh... I'm...dying..."

Spica casts aside the trillion things running through her head and hurriedly lays Toudou on the floor. She then pulls one dagger from Toudou's stomach without a second thought and casts a healing spell on her. Spica is constantly battered and bruised, so this is the holy technique she's most skilled with.

The effects are immediate. Toudou's wound begins healing the moment the dagger is removed, and there's hardly any blood.

"Toudou?! Why aren't you wearing your armor?! Life is a constant battlefield! You have no idea when the legions of darkness will appear—"

"?! Spica, enough! Nao's dying here!"

No—she won't die.

Spica pulls out the second dagger and shrieks, "If she dies, she's an impostor!"

§ § §

"What? She...attacked Toudou?!"

"It was a conditioned response, we're told," Amelia replies. "Should we force her to leave? Fortunately, Toudou has already been healed..."

I look to the sky. Attacking the Holy Warrior is simply inexcusable. I ordered Spica not to actually lay into him, but it would appear that she's been tainted by Gregorio to a far greater extent than I imagined.

At any rate, we're short on manpower and time. Toudou wasn't actually killed, so we should be able to recover from this.

"...If he will recover, there's still hope. If Spica looks to continue to be a problem, then call her off."

"*Cough, cough.* I think we already have a mountain of problems, boss."

"Rabi, when is your incessant period of being in heat coming to an end? That's another problem."

"Hmph..."

Rabi's face turns beet red and she clutches her knees. She's telling me about our myriad problems, but I've known about them since day one.

Just then, Stey, who was speaking with the Church through communication magic, stands up and immediately trips like she was born to. As I look down and stare into her eyes silently, she turns her face up toward me and reports, as if nothing awkward happened.

"Ares! We have a problem! It's about increasing guard numbers for the parade—our application...was denied. There weren't enough people, so they said no."

"Ask your father."

"Wha...?"

"Ask. Your. Father. I am well aware of the manpower shortage."

Other than crusaders, the Church's military is limited to holy knights and monks, and that has always been paltry. Creio is the leader of the Church's military branch, but he's not free to do whatever he wants.

Further, there are only five cardinals that substantively run the Church's operations. Creio Amen and Sylvester Veronide comprise two of these cardinals. Since two of the five are our compatriots, most big asks can be pushed through.

I stoop down near Stey, who's still on the ground batting her eyes, and grip her by the cheeks.

"Stey. If anyone, you can do it. You can do anything you put your mind to. I'm depending on you. You got it, Stey? Ask. Your. Father. You can do that, right?"

"Y-yesh. I can do zhat."

"That's right. Now sit up. Don't stand. Got it? I don't have the will to respond the next time you crumple in a heap."

Stop doing extra. Skillfully and accurately complete what I tell you to. Stey's role right now is exclusively that of a prisoner.

I give an order to Stey's elemental spirit, who can't be seen but is always close by.

"The overdone sense of justice is a crime."

✝ **Second Report: On Acquiring Legendary Equipment and Fortifying Battle Power**

"Cacao. Please supervise this worthless woman of the cloth."

"Um... Ares, please don't give Cacao weird instructions. Ouch! Cacao?! Don't kick me... Oww! Ares! Make it s-stop!"

"Kick her more. Make her work her ass off."

"N-nooo..."

Cacao is certainly showing promise. Too bad it's invisible. I want to appoint it as my direct underling. It would be a huge relief for Stey to simply be able to move about normally...

As I sigh, I catch a glimpse of Amelia, who's been on a call with Spica. She's visibly shocked. Our eyes meet, but she quickly turns away from me. This would certainly indicate that more bad news has come our way.

I prompt her to spill it with another glance, and Amelia scrunches up her face, clearly having a hard time finding the words, and finally speaks with fear in her voice.

"Ares. About Toudou—according to Spica, he's no longer able to put on his armor."

"What?! The holy armor Fried doesn't fit? What happened?"

"Yes... It appears...he's physically outgrown it."

He outgrew it...... True, Toudou is at the right age for a growth spurt. Did he get taller? If he can't wear the armor any longer, there must have been a huge change in his physique. I should have thought of this earlier and been prepared for this contingency.

Although it's not something that needs to be hidden, it seems that Stey is simply not trusted.

"Spica is...um...asking if Toudou can be thinned down to fit in the armor somehow."

"Tell her to stop immediately."

Even a storied mercenary wouldn't force their body to fit into a certain piece of equipment. And just what part of Toudou do they think they can whittle down? His...legs? That would be a true impediment to his aptitude in battle.

However, I'm slightly relieved. If the situation entails not simply a makeover or image change, then it was worth our while to

135

Defeating the Demon Lord

spend so much energy obtaining the summetal armor. Fortunately, body size doesn't matter when it comes to that armor. We're starting to hit a lucky streak.

"However... Well... Is that really possible? For the holy armor to no longer fit?"

"Hmm... Well, if it's no longer the right size, Toudou isn't going to be able to wear it. The holy armor Fried does not have size-adjustment capacity, from what I know."

"Yet...the holy armor Fried is a symbol of the Holy Warrior, is it not?"

As a priest, Amelia's doubts are wholly justified. According to legend, the hero wore the holy armor Fried and wielded the holy sword Ex to drive back darkness. But the order is reversed.

"It has an exaggerated title, but the holy armor Fried is just strong armor that the hero once wore in the ancient past—"

The holy armor received this appellation *after* the hero used it. Only those with the divine protection of Ahz Gried can equip it, and they have been few and far between. Technically, anyone can wear it so long as they meet the requirements.

Anyone who equips the holy armor Fried would be considered a hero. That certainly deems it special armor, but just because Toudou can no longer fit in it, that doesn't mean he isn't the Holy Warrior.

By definition, the Holy Warrior is the person selected and fortified via the hero summoning ritual. Strictly speaking, the hero summoning isn't a miraculous occasion that calls upon a hero, but rather a miracle that forges a hero from someone who is properly qualified for the role.

Amelia's eyes grow wide. Rabi pushes her face into her knees and is covering her ears; probably a display of her intention to ignore any information that she doesn't need to hear. As far as Sanya goes, I want to boil the grime from under my fingernails and make her drink it.

"Tell Spica not to worry about it. The summetal armor works

Second Report: On Acquiring Legendary Equipment and Fortifying Battle Power

on all sizes, so if anything, this is a stroke of good fortune. And if possible, make sure the moron who got ambushed knows that life is a constant battlefield."

"Understood," Amelia replies. "Does this also mean that the holy sword Ex is not proof of the Holy Warrior?"

"...Size doesn't matter for swords, now does it? If Toudou can't use his sword anymore, he's beyond hope."

Ex is an extremely standard longsword. Just how much would Toudou's physique have to change for it to no longer suit him? Is this an issue of muscle mass? Did he suddenly beef up and grow twice in size?

Despite all the things I said, the holy armor Fried has been used by every Holy Warrior since the first generation. There hasn't been a single Holy Warrior that hasn't been able to wear it. It shouldn't be a problem, but this will have to be reported to Creio.

The sword is much more important. With the brilliant flash of its blade, the Holy Warrior's power is on full display. Even if he can't wear the holy armor Fried, even if his level is still very low—none of this poses a real problem.

Just as with the holy armor, it's not a given that the Holy Warrior will be able to wield the holy sword. At the same time, they absolutely must use it. The Church has made it so. That sword is a symbol of the source of the hero's power—the Holy Warrior's Creed.

Not a moment later, the magical communication device attached to my ear vibrates. As I pick up the call, I hear the same voice as always, calm and solemn, to the point of making me angry.

"Ares, we're in a tough spot. Information that the Holy Warrior failed his training has been leaked. At this rate, distrust will run rampant. This Holy Warrior is a bit too modest. Do you hear what I'm saying? We need more drama. Do you get it? We need a spectacle fit only for a Holy Warrior. Crushing Heljarl is an accomplishment from the distant past at this point, understood?"

Creio's voice remains tranquil, but the powerful emotion lying under the surface isn't lost on me. After digesting his words,

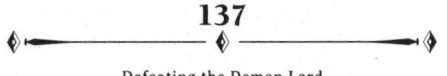

I understand exactly what he means and reply, "...What's the scenario?"

As if whispering, bestowing an oracle upon a lost lamb, the cardinal speaks.

"That is what you will provide. Tell me whatever you need."

"...Time."

"That we do not have. We are in this pickle together, Ex Deus!"

The call cuts out as soon as Creio gives his curt, one-sided answer. I stare blankly around the room, silent.

Stey quietly turns her gaze away from mine, and Amelia obviously turns away, too. Rabi continues to hold her hands over her ears. Sanya has gone outside and is yet to return. I can see my own pallid, stiff expression in the polished window glass.

Okay now, how to approach this...? I've taken on a number of different assignments in my time, but creating a theatrical spectacle is a first.

At present, excluding a few exceptions, the only people who know about the hero's existence are upper-level individuals from the Kingdom and the Church. That means that distrust of the Holy Warrior could naturally only spread among the aristocracy. It will take something explicit to dispel this sentiment.

A distrusting eye cast from the aristocracy would certainly influence our activities moving forward. I have to deal with this before rumors start to spread. In that case—my best chance will be smack in the middle of the parade to reveal Toudou to the world, won't it?

"We'll host the production to establish Toudou's status as the Holy Warrior in the middle of the parade. All our experience handling Toudou's movements from the shadows will play in perfectly... This is certainly good fortune."

"So you're going for it, eh? I don't think you were really in control the whole time, personally."

"I really thought that the Church was, like, y'know, a more honest organization."

"The overdone sense of justice is a crime."

Second Report: On Acquiring Legendary Equipment and Fortifying Battle Power

Sanya has returned and offers her thoughts with an odd look on her face after hearing my idea. Yes, the Church is honest... The average believer is an honest person. However, there are moments in our world where that is simply not enough. The only reason assignments like this fall into my lap is because crusaders somehow end up being a one-stop problem-solving shop. There's nobody here that can save me.

According to legend, whenever the Holy Warrior falls into tribulations, the heavens have always been on their side. The Holy Warrior has a grave responsibility to bear. That said, we can't control it, and we certainly wouldn't be keen to bet on it, either.

However, this current strategy...will almost certainly require a sacrificial lamb. Getting a powerful performance out of the Holy Warrior will require real tragedy.

I glance toward Sanya and Rabi. I would like to keep our inner circle, including them and Stey as well, uninvolved in this strategy, but it can't really be avoided. I don't have the leeway to be persnickety regarding who's in on it.

All of a sudden, Sanya snaps her fingers loudly.

"Oh yeah, I have a great idea. What if you equipped the merman armor and went buck wild in the middle of the city? And then the Holy Warrior can lay you out flat! I think that'd make for a real spectacle."

"That actually is a great idea."

"Wha—?!"

Sanya's eyes are wide as saucers. What's with the expression? If they're actually good ideas, I'm up for hearing as many as possible. I don't care how it gets done. The only thing that matters is completing our mission.

"Sanya, I want you to bear most of the responsibility."

"What?! Um, n-no, no, thank you."

Sanya answers immediately and crosses her arms in an X to say, "no way." How dare she have the gall to ask someone else to do something she's opposed to!

139

Defeating the Demon Lord

I cough briefly and continue. This isn't time for fun and games.

"All jokes aside, the merman armor is out of the question. Mermen don't live on land."

"Oh... Yeah, that's a good point..."

Above all else, a merman going up against the Holy Warrior is too much of a hard sell. No matter how much of a ruckus the merman raises, taking him down isn't really going to raise the Holy Warrior's stock estimation. We only have one chance to pull off this dramatic performance.

The heart of the matter is that unless we do something about Toudou's weak-minded attitude lately, we won't reach any fundamental conclusions at all.

"Ares, leave the performance up to me!"

"......"

Stey has her hand raised, but I completely ignore her. There aren't any jobs left that she could handle. What we really need is a powerful enemy. A powerful foe, tragedy—and most obviously, witnesses.

Yet as a follower of the God of Order, I cannot allow for casualties to occur. It would be one thing if someone passes away without our intention, but putting together a plan that assumes people will die from the get-go is completely out of the question. The larger issue is that Toudou's level is still so low, and anything that he could accomplish could also easily be accomplished by Ruxe's knights. Thinking about it even briefly, I realize how challenging this really is.

"...Rabi, Sanya. Begin gathering information on powerful monsters in our vicinity."

"You can't really be considering luring them in, can you, boss?"

Rabi's ruby-colored eyes open wide, peering my way.

"I'll consider that after the fact. Conditions could change, and our proposed script might become...unnecessary, after all."

Finding something that only the hero can accomplish comes with certain limits. The hero's unique capabilities entail that strong

"The overdone sense of justice is a crime."

Second Report: On Acquiring Legendary Equipment and Fortifying Battle Power

defenses provided through the divine protection of the God of Evil will quickly crumble, but finding someone with the divine protection of the God of Evil is just as uncommon as someone with the divine protection of the God of Order.

In this regard, Zarpahn, who we fought during our first adventure in the Great Forest of the Vale, was definitely a rare breed.

"Boss, that's called terrorism, y'know."

"Sabotage is your specialty, isn't it?"

"...Just what exactly do you think of us...?"

We have to make it happen or bring it to us. How can we create tragedy? And what sort of performance can we stage that will limit sacrifice to a bare minimum while also amply expressing the Holy Warrior's unique capabilities? No matter how high our level, considering these large-scale factors with only five people (three, really, if you count Stey as a negative), it's fairly obvious that we simply don't have the manpower.

Sanya sighs deeply. "Sheesh, boss, you're such a workaholic. You don't even have the Church's support—if I were you, I'd have thrown in the towel already."

"This is business. And it's not accurate to say I don't have the Church's support."

The fact that I can work without obstacles is thanks to the Church's support. A high-level priest can't work without some form of barrier around them. Creio has done everything possible to break all of them down, and beyond that, I am his best-kept agent.

"I need to collect my thoughts. Begin gathering information. Otherwise, if you have a good idea, let me hear it. I'll dole out bonuses if you do."

"...Next time a carrot won't be enough, boss," Rabi says poutily, casting a sharp glance my way before standing up.

"Fine by me. Whatever bonus you want, I'll give it you—His Eminence will, that is."

We're in this pickle together, that's for certain.

Just then, I hear a cold voice:

Defeating the Demon Lord

"Still clutching at the Church's pursestrings as always, eh, Ares?"

Both rife with calculated coldness and warmth, this solemn voice has captivated the hearts of countless believers.

Amelia and Stey are staring, transfixed. Sanya and Rabi look toward the door. I instinctively click my tongue.

"I've told you time and again to not dole out compensation without approval," the voice adds. "Who do you think balances the accounts?"

The door opens slowly. A number of knights in full-body silver armor enter before guiding a man inside. His white robe emanates holy light, and he is tall and well built, while his eyes appear transcendent.

However, above all else—the aura surrounding his being is simply different. Even a layman would notice—it's a peculiar aura that defies simple explanation through adjectives.

This man has obviously been almost too imbued in a place of holy sacrament. Sanya and Rabi's faces change color. They've clearly ascertained his identity.

One of the five cardinals of the Church of Ahz Gried—His Eminence Cardinal Creio Amen. An agent of God himself, capable of purifying even the deepest stain of sin.

I immediately feel a bad omen. For this man, who gives orders at the Church headquarters, to directly show his face here is a rare occasion indeed. I forget the numerous doubts in my mind and stand, narrowing my eyes to glare at him.

"Well, well, well... I certainly didn't expect to see you here... Did the lost little lamb bring us a welcome gift? I would prefer cash, personally."

"?! Ares?!" Amelia uncharacteristically blurts out in haste. But Creio doesn't pay any mind to irreverence.

The knights that preceded Creio are holy knights—special troops that can use holy techniques. This holy squadron exists to protect the Church, and as they're tasked with escorting the likes of

"The overdone sense of justice is a crime."

Second Report: On Acquiring Legendary Equipment and Fortifying Battle Power

Creio and other officials, showing off their authority is one of their central roles.

None of the holy knights move a muscle at my insolent remarks. Instead of emotion, the only thing I can read from them is an absolute allegiance to give their orders precedence. But...really, why are they here?

Generally, a cardinal leaves the Church headquarters only for important events. And it's far too soon for Toudou's debut. My face remains in a scowl.

"Boss... Should we leave the room?" Rabi asks me hesitantly.

"No, stay here. I've already spoken about you."

Everyone knows that Toudou is the Holy Warrior, so at this point, there isn't anything to hide. Creio peers into my eyes like he's trying to see into my soul, then he finally speaks in a hushed tone.

"Why so grim, Ex Deus? I simply came to pay you a visit. I just happened to be passing by."

"Sorry, but save your sermon for next time. Get to the issue at hand; I still have a litany of responsibilities to take care of."

I can't stand moving forward like a slug. Creio is my superior, and I, his subordinate, but there is no good reason that a cardinal would go out of his way to see me. And meeting me with the others present is good cause for a cardinal's rank to plummet.

Creio tenses his shoulders and takes a step back to create space. I remain staring with wide-open eyes, and the cardinal speaks again, now ceremoniously.

"Very well, Ares. Today, I have brought reinforcements. To put it in your words, I guess they are something like a welcome gift. The Church doesn't have any surplus of manpower, but...you seemed in dire need. That is correct, yes?"

"What?"

Just what the hell does this mean? Of course, I want reinforcements, but that doesn't explain why Creio is here.

As if guided by Creio's voice, the door opens again. A single knight walks into the room. They're wearing lacquer-black armor emblazoned with a golden cross scale, a completely different outfit from the rest of the holy knights.

They have a shield hoisted on their back and a crossblade on their belt. Their entire head is covered by a helm, obscuring their face.

Above all else, my eyes are directly drawn to their height. Full-body armor is generally very heavy and made to wear by individuals of large stature. However, this knight is just about as tall as I am, even with their helm.

Amelia is dumbfounded. Sanya's and Rabi's eyes are as wide open as humanly possible, and they're frozen stiff. Their expressions have shifted to look even more precipitous than when they ascertained Creio's identity, but I can't fault them for it.

There are a number of emblems for the Church of Ahz Gried—and only three people who can use the strongest holy techniques known. The Holy Warrior summoned through holy sacrament is one, and the Saint is another.

This knight is another such emblem, the Church's pride and joy: the eternal captain of the holy knight order of the Church of Ahz Gried. A knight that lives infinite lives as an immortal through divine protection. A living legend.

The legend has been told in innumerable myths, and even if you don't know of the Saint, or haven't heard of the Holy Warrior, there isn't a chance you haven't heard of this knight.

Furthermore—this knight is a member of the Out Crusade as a second order crusader. I can finally envision the blueprint that Creio has laid out. Yet I am still far from happy.

I see stars for a moment. Of course, I've been wanting reinforcements for quite some time, but this is simply too heavy. I understand why Creio, one of the Church's top elites, would bring this knight to us directly. It's a sign of *respect*. Observance toward someone who has devoted so much time to the Church.

This is absolutely not my place to speak, but I instinctively do so anyway.

"The overdone sense of justice is a crime."

Second Report: On Acquiring Legendary Equipment and Fortifying Battle Power

"Are you looking for a place to die, Sister General?"

The knight shrouded in black remains silent, staring at me.

"The leader of the holy knight order has to be someone exceptionally famous. You've been alive since time immemorial, and the demons you've slain extend back for millennia. You're...a living legend."

Sanya must be nervous as she speaks to the knight in black timidly. After Creio entrusted the Sister General and an accompanying knight to me, he sure left in a hurry. That curmudgeonly dog, all he does is heap nuisance upon me during our communications. Now that we meet in person, he's left even more bothersome responsibility in his ill wake.

Just as Sanya said, this knight is the greatest miracle that the Church is endowed with. Eons ago, the God of Order, Ahz Gried bestowed three great powers onto humanity in order to fight against the legions of darkness, who boasted such formidable, horrible might.

The Holy Warrior. The Saint. And—a holy knight.

"The lacquer-black armor is proof that it's stained with the blood of felled hordes of darkness. 'And God said, ye of humble faith, I have heard your prayers and bestow you with strength. Your body will never rot through my divine protection, and only when you have altogether eliminated the forces of darkness shall eternal peace return to our world. Only you can represent God, only you can protect the people—Grace Godicent Trinity.' You've been alive since the age of the gods, so there's no way that you're a human being."

Grace offers no reply to Sanya's rude assumption. Instead, the knight accompanying Grace speaks for her. Across generations, one individual from the ranks of the holy knight order is selected to be her attendant; in exchange for her powers, Grace is unable to speak.

The accompanying knight is a girl in her mid-teens. Her hair shines a bold silver-blue, reminding me of the blade of the holy sword Ex, and she has well-set features, although still appearing

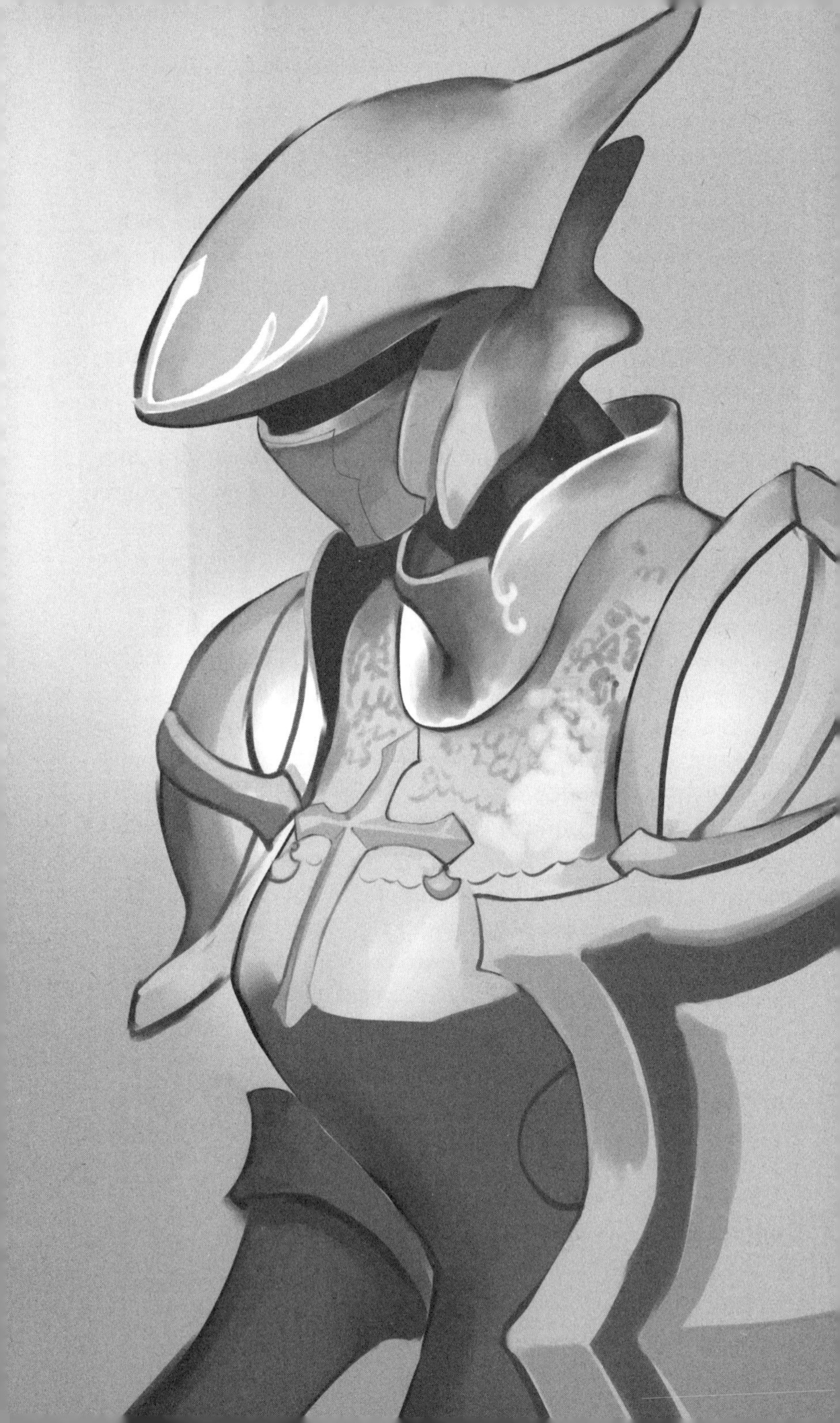

young. However, despite her age, she stands with a powerful, refined presence.

I can't grasp her level without a thorough analysis, but it can't be any less than 50. Her brow twitches noticeably at Sanya's comment, but she gives a quick, icy retort.

"Indeed, Captain Grace is not a human, but a vehicle of God. In order to abstain from impurity to the greatest extent possible, she does not speak. As unworthy as I am, please allow me, Eve Lucrao, to speak on her behalf."

"So she's always in that armor? Maybe it's...empty inside?"

Eve's brow twitches again at Sanya's rudeness. It looks like she's still working on her poker face.

"Sanya. Silence. And it's obvious, but of course she dwells within the armor. The God of Order only bestows his power upon human beings."

That said, this is a problem. Grace is altogether too famous and hard to work into my strategy. I mean, come on—even Stey, who's always loud and annoying, has fallen completely silent. The lacquer-black armor emblazoned with the golden cross is famous, and Grace can't remove the armor that she received from God.

Nonetheless, acting exactly according to Creio's intent offends me gravely. I have a notion as to why he brought her here—and I will inevitably have to fall in step meekly. The fact that Creio didn't say anything specific means that his mind was filled with some form of regret or grief. That's why he left how to use Grace completely up to me.

Amelia, who's been silent so far, suddenly whispers, "Ares, have you seen the person inside Grace's suit of armor?"

"Yes... But I'm not telling you a thing."

The Sister General's actual face is a secret among secrets within the Church. Even for crusaders, very few have actually witnessed it.

Amelia remains steadily silent for a while before asking, in a tiny voice, "...Was she beautiful?"

"Amelia, sometimes I really struggle to understand your thought process."

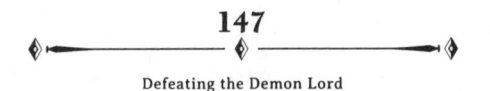

I'm begging you to take this more seriously.
Eve looks up at me and speaks with the least emotion possible.

"Mr. Ares Crown. According to orders from His Eminence, Grace Godicent Trinity will leave her position in the holy knight order temporarily for three months, alongside myself, Eve Lucrao, to be at your command. We have heard of your decree from God. While it doesn't apply to Captain Grace, I am young and inexperienced, but please command me to do your bidding until I break."

"We appreciate your efforts, Eve Lucrao. For the record, did you leave your last will and testament behind?"

"Of course...I have. To the extent that I am a part of the holy knight order, and for as long as I live—"

I don't think that Eve fully understands the position I occupy. I can sense strong tension in her voice. For a priest, I am quite young. Without really considering Grace, I am at least a whole zodiac cycle, or twelve years, younger than any other high-level priest. My youth has worked against me at times. She might be thinking that I am some great, magnanimous man.

Okay now—no matter how legendary these knights may be, they're still new to our squad. Thinking about what lies ahead, how I handle this first interaction will prove paramount. I look at Grace and speak softly.

"Well then—that's good. For the moment we need to ascertain your level of strength."

"?!"

Eve's eyes grow wide as she assumes I'm doubting the power of a true legend. However, Grace doesn't move a muscle. I'm actually aiming to find out how useful Eve will be to us; I'm not so concerned about Grace.

"Sanya, you're up. We'll start with Eve."

"Awww, me again?! Just my luck..."

Sanya is wagging her tail, unable to hide the enthusiasm in her voice. The girl is obsessed with battle... But her skills are perfect for gauging a person's combat abilities.

"The overdone sense of justice is a crime."

Second Report: On Acquiring Legendary Equipment and Fortifying Battle Power

"I never thought the day would come when I'd be facing off against a knight of legend... Heh-heh..."

I said Eve would go first; didn't she hear me? As I sigh, Eve speaks out, clearly miffed.

"Sir Ares, forgive my presumptuousness, but I must say: It is utterly impudent to test Sister General Grace, who has fought for millennia to protect humanity—?!"

Yet Eve is interrupted by the Sister General herself. Standing up, she stretches her arms out in front of Eve, standing straight as an arrow. Her posture is unmistakably that of someone who has stood on a battlefield for so long, and expansive holy energy resonates distinctly from her body wrapped in full plate armor.

Until now, before the Sister General arrived, I was the number one crusader around. Eve must not be used to being cut off—she looks perplexed and embarrassed but soon looks directly at me.

"Very well, then... Sir Ares, you will bear full witness to the power of the holy knight order. Let's begin with me."

The holy knights are a special infantry class that hold both the attack and defense powers of a knight combined with the healing and buffing capabilities of a priest. Clad in armor from head to foot with massive shields, wielding maces and crossblades, their solid defenses and healing abilities liken them to guardian deities. The Church hosts a procession of the holy knight order regularly, and innumerable viewers have watched, their hearts leaping with joy.

It's easy to think they have the best of both worlds, but the holy knights are quick to become half-baked. If one requires the attack power and defenses of a knight and the healing and buffs of a priest, then they simply need to find one of each. Holy knights themselves are quite rare, and among the different mercenaries that fight on the front lines, they're often considered nothing more than colorful baubles.

Sanya and Rabi are light and nimble, and there's a reason that these two female mercenaries don't wear heavy armor. In the long run, it's generally far more effective for them to prioritize offense over defense and go straight for the kill in the face of demons and monsters, regardless of the colossal physical strength these beasts may boast. Come to think of it, neither Gregorio nor Spica wear heavy armor, too...

In a remote corner of the royal capital, at a private training area, the sharp clash of metal against metal can be heard.

"Hot damn, I heard that holy knights are hard as nails, but it's really true!"

"...Impudence!"

As Sanya attacks with blinding speed, Eve, in full heavy armor, blocks her skillfully.

Most holy knights choose a mace as their main weapon, but Eve is holding only a massive crossblade as long as she is tall and a shield. The violent clash of metal on metal resounds again. Seeing Eve block attacks from Sanya, who is certainly many levels above her, and not lose her balance whatsoever, I can tell Eve is a proficient warrior. That said, it's also very obvious who has the greater advantage.

Eve being able to wield a weapon that even a large man would have trouble swinging around is only because she's cast a holy technique to buff herself. Eve has buffs and healing through holy techniques and powerful defense through her heavy armor. These factors are only truly put on display when a number of holy knights are gathered together. For better or worse, they are not suited for battles focused strictly on the offensive.

In the time that Sanya can get off ten attacks, Eve is only capable of swinging her crossblade once. Sanya's mixing in feints, too, and doesn't have any problem seeing through Eve's attacks and avoiding them. Eve also deflects a kick with her shield, blocks Sanya's knife with her crossblade, and takes one poke to the body but comes away unharmed—a very close match, indeed.

In actual battle, Sanya would come out on top. Sanya doesn't

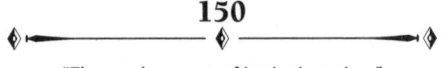

"The overdone sense of justice is a crime."

Second Report: On Acquiring Legendary Equipment and Fortifying Battle Power

have a buff cast on her right now. On the battlefield, I would have buffed her, and with a buff, she doesn't have any competition. This is the holy knights' greatest weakness.

Holy knights are trained to be effective on their own as well, but on the battlefield, there isn't any reason for a single knight to take the full brunt of an attack.

"Okay, it's about time to fight for real!"

"Grr...!"

Sanya cries out, clearly having fun, and steps up her speed. Her legs fly lithely, and she is in complete control of her body without making a sound. The tempestuous fury and powerful waves of attack that she commands through her supple muscles simply outmatch any human that she comes across. In a flash, Eve's gaze fails to pick up on Sanya's location, and a kick from Sanya lands directly on the back of Eve's head.

Eve, without any protection on the back of her head, crumples to the ground from the attack. It's certainly impressive that she doesn't lose hold of her shield or crossblade. She quickly stands up and goes on the defensive, but her brain must have been rocked, and she can't find her balance.

Knights are weak to attacks from behind. The inner ear is a particularly tough spot to strengthen with buffs. This should be good enough.

"We have a winner. No objections?" I ask.

"...No—none here," Eve answers, clearly vexed. Fortunately, she doesn't put up a fight. This wasn't a real battlefield, and if it was, I can only assume she would've played a different hand.

"No need to get so down. Your prowess is far greater than I expected. You have talent."

"......"

"Woohoo! That's one victory for me!"

Sanya twirls gleefully. She got to show off several techniques she learned from Bran.

Quit it with the twirling!

Besides, it's no surprise that she eked out a win against a holy knight, someone who specializes in defense. Grace, who had been keeping quiet next to me, takes a step forward. Her suit of armor makes a loud metal *clang*, and the sheer force of each step she takes is not normal. I couldn't say she moves quickly, even if trying to compliment, but the gravity she moves with has clearly been fostered over millennia.

Sanya looks profoundly serious for a moment before quickly cracking a smile. I can see her wild instincts flickering deep in her eyes.

"Time for the second round. Immortal knight, prove your legend! My master had his own legend, too!"

Grace doesn't respond; instead, she slowly brings out her sword and shield, brandishing them in Sanya's face.

My entire field of vision is awash in white, and the sound of a massive explosion erupts through the training grounds. When the light finally dissipates, the victor is revealed.

"……"

Rabi gulps audibly, her face white as a sheet. The training grounds have been racked with a massive fissure and crater, with Sanya crumpled in a heap at the bottom, looking like a spent dishrag.

Grace has only attacked a single time, and observing the result, she doesn't even flinch. Nor has she moved an inch from the location where she first stood and brandished her armaments. She looks like a sculpture.

"We have a victor," I declare.

Grace finally lowers her blade, and Eve runs over to her.

"Marvelous work—Captain Grace."

"Eve, heal Sanya."

The light that erupted from Grace's blade was the power of God manifest. Her blade tore through the earth with a single attack, and her massive shield didn't budge even receiving the full brunt of

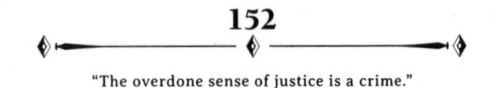

"The overdone sense of justice is a crime."

✣ Second Report: On Acquiring Legendary Equipment and Fortifying Battle Power

Sanya's attack. The training area has been absolutely obliterated. We're going to have to pay a restoration fee.

"This is...the power of the immortal knight."

"Truly incredible... I had heard the rumors, but..."

Amelia and Stey gasp for breath as they stare into the aftermath of destruction. Yet they're wrong—they are both probably just blown away at the power Grace displayed. However, there's a different reason Rabi's face has gone white as a sheet. She can't pull the wool over my eyes.

I put my hand on Rabi's shoulder as she trembles with fear. Her body convulses as she looks up at me with her red eyes.

"Boss... Are you...going to kill me?" she asks me nearly in a whisper.

Just what do they, all of them, think I am?

Rabi looks like she's about to get her head lopped off at any second, but I grab her by the wrist and smile. Did she realize the Church's secret, something no one should pick up on?

"Rabi—I don't hate a good observer."

§ § §

When Sanya comes to, she realizes she had been laid to rest on a bed. The first sensation she experiences is pain. She screws up her face at the dull pain throughout her whole body and shakes her head in an attempt to assuage the strong sense of dizziness.

"Mmph... Ugh... Huff..."

"! Sanya, are you okay?"

Rabi is waiting on a chair nearby, and she rushes over to Sanya. They both share the same master and have nursed each other back to health after losing consciousness a long time ago.

"Do you remember what happened?"

"Uh... Yeah, and I'm still in shock... I knew she was the stuff of legend, but still..."

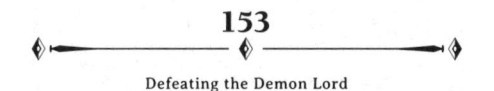

Sanya furrows her brow and scratches a minor burn mark on her arm.

Sanya is half werebeast. Although she appears mostly human, her silverwolf blood is most prevalent in her physical strength. The distinction visible in her outward appearance is her ears and tail, but the strength of her bones and muscles isn't even comparable to humans.

Holy knights are a rare breed. Sanya had never fought one before, although that doesn't explain why she lost this skirmish. In a real battle, Sanya would be dead. Still, this result is unexpected. She'd rushed at her opponent from behind, putting her speed—her greatest asset—on full display, but the legendary knight chose to—

Sanya clicks her tongue and smashes a balled fist into her other empty palm.

"It was a counter. And a shield bash at that. I can't believe she came at me with her giant shield—that seriously came out of nowhere."

Not to mention, the knight didn't even move an inch. The burn mark on Sanya's arm is a result of the holy technique Grace used. The timing of Grace's counter was impeccable, in retrospect. She easily reacts to an ambush on her blind spot at the hands of Sanya Chatre and the speed that only she can generate. It was like getting crushed by a wall.

This is the exact point a holy knight suited for specializing in defense should arrive at—she isn't suited for making a direct attack, but even when taking one herself, her full-body armor meant she was barely left with a scratch. But to think that she wouldn't even let Sanya get off a single sword slash...

Rabi blinks at Sanya and asks, with trepidation, "What...else?"

"What else...?"

Sanya doesn't understand the question and cocks her head to the side. The sheer pressure that emanated from Grace's body as she stood solid as an impenetrable fortress, not budging an inch upon receiving Sanya's attack—her deft shield deflection showed every sign of her training throughout the ages.

"The overdone sense of justice is a crime."

Her retort was many levels more subdued than Sanya ever imagined, but it was fitting for a knight of legend.

"...That's really it. Did I miss something?"

"Okay. It's just... If you bragged to master about this, he would be so jealous. There are very few mercenaries who've actually battled hand to hand with a bonafide legend."

Sanya really wants to win next time, but if her opponent is going to have lived since time immemorial, then of course her life force will be on an unprecedented level. The individual boasting the strongest life force in Sanya's experience is either her master or Ares, but they both have an average life expectancy to deal with.

Is there anyone that could go up against that monstrosity and win?

Rather—why didn't the Church deploy the holy knights to defeat the Demon Lord? Sanya furrows her brow as this doubt enters her mind. Just then, Rabi pitches forward and puts her face close to Sanya's.

Those timid features; those ruby-red eyes. Sanya is speechless.

"Sanya," Rabi says, lowering her voice, "that knight is the Church's secret—their secret final weapon. I don't know what the boss is making of all this, though……"

She then falls silent for quite some time.

Rabi is from a species of runts. Sanya is leagues stronger. Aside from her divine protection, Rabi is in only slightly higher standing than Sanya because her timidness is directly linked to her proficiency as a mercenary. Even now, a sense of fear that cannot be quelled lingers in her quiet eyes.

Secret. Final. Weapon. Sanya waits stiffly for her companion to speak again.

"...I-in other words...," Rabi says with uncharacteristic reluctance, "o-our current mission may be just a b-bit more dangerous than usual."

"...What? C'mon, I know that perfectly well by now."

Sanya is staring wide-eyed at Rabi, who averts her gaze.

Her soft voice, now barely a whisper, makes it sound as if she's talking to herself.

"The Church...will do anything it takes. The boss is vulnerable, but he'll see things through every step of the way. Be careful—you heard nothing, saw nothing, and said nothing... Otherwise..."

Sanya watches in disbelief as her close friend leaves the room, still blathering quietly.

Did she hear some particularly bad news?

§ § §

"I-I'm here, boss...," comes a frightened voice following a knock at the door.

"In. Now."

Grace and I are the only ones in the room. I gave everyone else random tasks to get them out of my hair. The immortal knight has been staring at me reproachfully for some time; she must be trying to tell me not to do anything drastic. I completely ignore her.

Grace is strong—but she still needs a collaborator. An accomplice who is quick-witted, audacious, and a little timid.

The doorknob turns, and Rabi enters the room. I can't help but stare in amazement. She's done a complete about-face from her usual heavy robe. She's wearing a loose-fitting camisole that could be loungewear, showing her slender arms and legs. Her skin, transparent enough that her veins are visible, is on full display. Only her face is flushed bright red. Moreover, she's wearing a black blindfold. Her rabbit ears are lying flat.

"Why are you dressed like that?"

"*Cough*... I caught a cold... And for some reason...I can't see... anything."

"......"

"As presumptuous as this may seem...I think I might inconvenience you like this. So, um...... May I leave? I can't see anything, and I can barely hear."

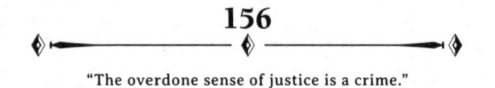

"The overdone sense of justice is a crime."

Second Report: On Acquiring Legendary Equipment and Fortifying Battle Power

Rabi trips and bangs her head against the wall.

"What about your tongue?" I ask her as she crumples to the floor.

"...I don't have one."

What an outrageous lie. Of course you have your tongue.

Rabi always keeps a weapon concealed inside her heavy robe, but in this skimpy outfit, she can't hide a thing. Then I remember something, and I turn to confirm it with Rabi, who's now sweating bullets.

"Come to think of it, I've heard some wererabbits can use their ears to slay their foes."

"?! Well...... Yes...... But, boss—my ears are so...short. Look, look!"

If Amelia or Stey did something like this, it would be nothing more than a joke, but Rabi is a stoic mercenary. So is she trying to avoid me by goofing off and changing the subject? An interesting tactic... I won't let her have her way.

Her skimpy outfit must be meant to show that she isn't armed. As she stands up, Rabi's ears twitch noticeably. Even a blindfolded wererabbit's hearing is good enough to easily ascertain what's going on around them.

I approach Rabi and scoop her up off the floor. She cries out and squirms.

"Gyah! B-boss! What are you...? N-no, don't be so rough—"

"...You're quite warm... I guess that's your normal body temperature."

"S-stop, r-right now! This is a violation of my contract! It's sexual harassment! This is...not what I signed up for! I—I quit! I'm quitting this mission! I'll...tell Amelia everything!"

"I thought you didn't have a tongue?"

"......"

Rabi stops writhing, but her heart is still racing, and her face is even more red. I return to my chair with her still in my arms and put her on my lap so she can't escape. Acquiescing, Rabi goes limp and rolls over onto her back.

Defeating the Demon Lord

"F-fine, I understand," she says shakily. "D-do whatever you want with me. So please...I beg of you. Please...just let Sanya—"

"You won't get any sympathy from me, Rabi. No matter what antics you pull, I know it's all a sham—I've seen more than my fair share of buffoonery ever since I took on this assignment. And I've since learned a few things."

Animals demonstrate submission by showing their bellies. I put my hand on her stomach, and Rabi cries out again, writhing. Her ears are twitching like mad, but she can't cut my head off if she's lying down.

I look up at Grace; she's been standing there, immovable as a statue.

"Sister General, I recently visited Golem Valley for the first time in ages. Madam Carina was well. Her faith in God remains as strong as ever."

"......"

"Time just flies by, doesn't it? Gregorio is training his disciple while I've been tasked with defeating the Demon Lord. And you—you remain the Church's last line of defense."

The Sister General doesn't say anything. I wordlessly apply slight pressure to Rabi's stomach with my hand.

"Gyah!"

"Rabi, I have a question. Tell me—why didn't the Church summon Grace as the Holy Warrior instead of Toudou?"

"...I...don't...know..."

Rabi's face turns even more red. Granted, it's always red. Now she's visibly terrified. But I know how to tame beasts. I want to keep my hands as clean as possible—but I don't have a choice here.

I fill my hand with light and begin rubbing Rabi's stomach gently. She convulses repeatedly, but I refuse to let her go.

"Gyah—?! Wha—?!?!"

"I'm not going to torture you. You're not in pain, right? Some things are more terrifying than pain, though."

Holy techniques are founded in the power of healing. With

"The overdone sense of justice is a crime."

Second Report: On Acquiring Legendary Equipment and Fortifying Battle Power

healing comes pleasure. And powerful pleasure can drive a person mad. Some incorrigible priests in the past devised ways to use powerful light to seize people's hearts and minds.

As it goes against holy doctrine, there are very few left who use it now, but depending on how it's done, it can be very effective in negotiation.

Rabi is Bran's disciple. She might be able to resist pain, but she can't possibly resist this.

I trace my fingertips along her stomach over her clothes. Her flesh feels soft. Her body heat rises as a yelp escapes her, and her breath comes ragged. She smells sweet. Rabi twitches and convulses repeatedly. Her blindfold is already soaking wet with tears. Once I give her a good dose of treatment, I finally stop.

"Resistance is futile, Rabi. Say it. I already know what you've realized."

"...Ungh..."

There's no use hiding things or playing dumb. I'm *the one who hired* you. *I'll get you to cooperate, even if by force.*

This wouldn't work on Sanya; she's too tough. Rabi is a fearsome assassin, but Sanya, who's vastly superior in terms of physical strength, isn't so easily subdued. Plus, there's the problem of Sanya's disposition. Collaborators need to have tight lips, after all.

Rabi cries out like her heart is going to explode. Using this forbidden technique on a werebeast in heat is a little too effective, it seems.

I wait for Rabi to settle down, no longer touching her abdomen. She continues gasping and retching for a while, and the second she finally calms, I put my hand back on her stomach. She shudders again and covers her face with her hands.

"Gyah... Ahhh, ahhh... O-okay... I—I...understand..."

"Good girl, Rabi. I don't hate a keen observer, you know."

Unfortunately for her, any battle tactics involving Grace require cooperators who really know the facts. Rabi keeps panting for a little longer, but suddenly, she speaks in a voice so low that I have to prick my ears just to hear her.

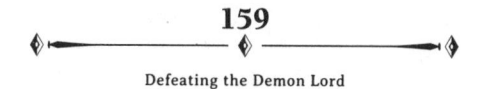

"This is...j-just my imagination, perhaps, but—I think Grace is...*old.*"

No member of the faith would believe this. Grace, the undying knight, alive since time immemorial, has been predestined by God to lead an eternal life spent in battle. For her to grow old—that would defy the holy creed.

The immortal knight. The knight of time immemorial. The silent knight. The true holy knight. Grace Godicent Trinity.

She doesn't say anything but nods ever so imperceptibly and turns to Rabi.

"What makes you think that?" I ask Rabi.

"Sh-she didn't...use...her sword...is why. The way...she moves... It's like...an elderly person."

I doubt the sword is the only thing that gave her away. Holy techniques are not omnipotent powers. Even with buffs, old age will take its toll and slow a person down. Observing Grace's every movement, it could be ascertained that she's trying to keep her physical activity to a minimum. According to legend, Grace is a keen swordfighter who sweeps through the battlefield with unprecedented speed to mow down the hordes of darkness.

Her full body armor is what prevents her from sitting down, because once she sits down, she can't get back up quickly. The reason she subdued Sanya with a counter move was to avoid any strenuous movement.

"Why did you try to hide this realization?" I say to Rabi.

"Mmph... B-because—gyah!"

Of course, she's right. If word gets out that the immortal knight will die, then humanity is doomed. At the very least, the entire global power structure would instantly be redrawn. That's just how colossal an entity Grace is. And now, when we're being attacked by the Demon Lord—the timing couldn't be any worse. That's why the Church hasn't been able to mobilize her in the fight against the Demon Lord.

I imagine Rabi hid this realization because she thought it would

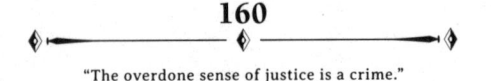

Second Report: On Acquiring Legendary Equipment and Fortifying Battle Power

be considered religious heresy. But she's really losing her cool. I won't dispose of her; whether she realizes it or not, Grace will die.

This is an undeniable fact. The only variable is whether Grace will die of old age or on the battlefield, whether it'll be slow or quick. That's why Creio brought her to us—so that she can live and die on the battlefield, her long-cherished desire, and so that we can make the most effective use of this living legend.

For example: If Grace dies and Toudou is able to vanquish the demons that felled her, the Holy Warrior's reknown will eclipse even the immortal knight. That said—I won't let Grace's end be just *any* death.

"Grace, how many years do you have left to live?" I ask.

Rabi squirms and pushes her ears into my knees as hard as she can. She clearly doesn't want to hear any more. Grace has remained absolutely silent up until now but finally looks my way. Her helm is sealed tight; I can't see inside, even in the slightest. A faint, weak voice, like a whisper emerges from the helm:

"Three."

Rabi's body stiffens for a moment. She must have heard that. Those keen senses ought to be a problem sometimes.

Nonetheless, Grace isn't dead yet. But even in the best-case scenario, I have to believe that she has only three years left and no more.

At any rate, we have little time left before she can no longer fight. This is my last chance to use her as an ace in the hole.

Just as I wonder what to do next, I'm struck by a sudden revelation.

I'd been agonizing over the spectacle of Toudou's debut, but this...*this* we can potentially use.

"I see... We won't need to kill any demons to increase his renown."

I raise my head to gaze at Grace, who's fallen silent again. My mouth twists into a grin.

"Good news, Grace. It looks like you'll be able to experience something new, even at your advanced age. Have you ever nurtured another human being?"

Third Report
On Utilizing an Ancient Legend

In a room prepared for Toudou at the Rizas estate, Toudou and company are being made to kneel before a girl far younger than them. It's Spica, and she's rebuking the party while toying with a dagger created in the shape of the cross scale.

"Toudou, get your act together! The reason your holy techniques aren't improving more is because you skip your prayers every morning! You'll never defeat the Demon Lord with that attitude!"

"S-Spica... Did something happen to you?"

It's quite clear that Toudou's techniques aren't even close to Spica's expectations as a full-fledged priest. Of course, Toudou is aware of her lack of improvement, and she, alongside Aria and the others, is unable to hide her bewilderment.

The agitation that coursed across Toudou's face immediately after being stabbed is nowhere to be seen now. Her wound has already been healed, and because she realizes Spica hadn't done this out of malice, she has no intention of dredging up the issue again. That said, in the past few months, almost too much has changed.

Limis and Aria feel the same way.

"...This is definitely Gregorio's influence," Limis says with a scowl.

"It's faith, Limis—I have deepened my faith!"

"......Yet Nao is the only one of us who uses holy techniques,"

Defeating the Demon Lord

Aria adds, putting her hands on her knees and straightening up. "Why include me and Limis in this...?"

Her expression is severe as she casually betrays Toudou. At first, Toudou thought Aria was a serious warrior, but she apparently got Aria to really open up.

Spica, meanwhile, remains as blunt as ever.

"Yes, that's right, Aria! You see, the God of Order, Ahz Gried, watches over all, regardless of whether they can use holy techniques. You two ladies have been tasked with the holy decree of defeating the Demon Lord, so don't you dare forsake your God! Defeating the Demon Lord is still a far-off fantasy for you all, for certain!"

"...I come from a family of magic users," says Limis. "We just pretend like we're followers of the God of Order, but we're actually more believers in the spirit realm—"

"That's not an issue. Ahz Gried is magnanimous and would never be concerned over such trivial matters."

While being scolded by Spica in her trademark high-pitched voice, Toudou can't help but feel unable to endure much more. That said, Spica studied under Gregorio for Toudou's sake, and Spica has returned noticeably more powerful. Toudou, on the other hand, is losing even the light of her holy blade, and she's on the verge of being utterly feckless. What can she possibly say in response?

Or rather—this is an exceptional opportunity. If Toudou can renew her faith, there's a chance she will be bestowed anew with divine protection.

Toudou focuses all her energy, committed to turning over a new leaf.

"Toudou," says Spica. "Regarding your breasts outgrowing the holy armor: That growth is excess flesh of the spirit!"

"?! Excuse me?!"

"Because you don't pray to God and live humbly, the flesh of your spirit has shifted to your bosom, rendering you unable to wear

"The overdone sense of justice is a crime."

Third Report: On Utilizing an Ancient Legend

the holy armor! This is most shameful! It's all an admonition from God."

"????"

"The vast majority of believers are thin. Limis—you, too, must learn from their example!"

"?! Huh?! Wh-what does that even mean?!"

"Look at Aria! Not only has her spirit's excess flesh shifted to her bosom, but so too has her magical power—and now she doesn't have any magical power left."

"......"

Limis and Aria are frozen stiff after getting caught in Spica's castigation crossfire. Aria's lack of magical power is a particularly touchy subject. She doesn't remember telling Spica about that—when did she find out?

Toudou's party members look at Spica as if she's lost her mind, but she refuses to hold off.

"My master says that demons are depravity given physical form, yet humanity has triumphed against them! He also said that it doesn't matter if the faithless perish, but I feel differently. Have no fear—on my life, I will turn you into a commendable Holy Warrior! I was shocked when you didn't dodge my dagger; if my master had attacked you when you had your guard down, you would be dead."

"If I'd been up against Gregorio, I *wouldn't* have let my guard down."

Toudou had left herself wide open only because it was Spica who attacked her. Limis and Aria were certainly in the same boat.

Just then, Spica's expression darkens. She lowers her voice.

"Toudou, I have yet to meet one, but...the most powerful demons can turn into humans. Most demons prefer attacking head-on to flaunt their strength, but a craven few will occasionally shape-shift into people's acquaintances."

So maybe this isn't Spica, but actually a demon that shape-shifted into her?

The thought crosses Toudou's mind for a moment, but Spica looks so serious; Toudou isn't about to rip into her and say as much. She quells the emotions surging within her and steers the conversation back on track.

"Okay then... What do you think I should do, Spica? I'm already taking some intensive training, for what it's worth..."

Toudou isn't simply loafing around. Right now, though, she's forbidden from going outside to fight any monsters.

Spica puts her hands on her hips and peers at Toudou.

"From my perspective, what you lack most is...composure."

"C-composure...?"

"Yes, that's right. If you have faith, then your mind will not stray no matter what life throws at you. This is the most fundamental of all concepts!"

Spica's words are slightly overbearing, but to Toudou's ears, they are exceptionally painful. On Toudou's adventure so far, she has been manipulated to no end. It was almost like God was testing her. Alongside Spica in Yutith's Tomb, Toudou showed a particularly shameful side of herself, but even in other locations, if she were asked if she remained calm and composed, she would have no choice but to shake her head vigorously.

Even now—she is unsure of herself. Is she really the right person for the holy sword? And as if further exposing her uncertainty, the light of the holy sword Ex has started to go dull.

Limis scowls at Spica and quickly objects.

"But *you* were shaking like a leaf when you stabbed Nao."

"......I'm still...inexperienced."

...Come to think of it, Spica realizes, *Gregorio once said something very similar.*

Spica coughs quietly, regaining her composure, and adds, "Okay now, it's time for you all to meditate and pray to God. Meditation is the foundation of the truth behind holy techniques. You will never be able to use them without a solid foundation."

"Medi...tation...?"

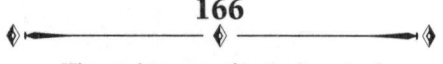

Third Report: On Utilizing an Ancient Legend

Toudou feels like she's been tricked. After being made to kneel and getting totally unloaded on by Spica, she was convinced that her training would be even more punishing. Besides, Toudou already practices meditation regularly. It's the most basic of basics.

Toudou's strength is waning with every passing moment.

"We'll begin with a half day," Spica says, her expression serious. "You must remain entirely focused."

"?! Half...a day?!" Todou exclaims incredulously.

Spica sounds as if she's explaining something perfectly logical to a complete dolt.

"This training has a storied heritage. Fasting while devoting your mind and body to praying to God will see your faith increase substantially. Aria and Limis will do the same, of course."

Toudou, meanwhile, falls speechless at this unexpected development in her training.

"...And what will you do the whole time, Spica?" Limis asks, looking perturbed.

"I will be attacking you all, obviously."

"What the—?!" Limis shrieks.

Spica's expression doesn't change. With the tip of her finger that resembles a small whitefish, she traces a line along her knife and looks toward Toudou and company as if appraising them.

"'True faith cannot exist without suffering. Our souls are laid bare in the moments before death,' my master said. Another individual devised this highly effective training method, which Master Gregorio then honed. Don't worry—I'll heal all your wounds."

"Wh-wh-what?!"

Just who the hell devised such a twisted training method?! Toudou wonders. *They must be a demon themselves!*

"Okay, so is this how it's going to work?" says Limis. "You'll keep attacking us and we just pray the whole time?"

Straightforward, but hellish. Rough on the body and mind in equal measure.

Spica looks pained at Limis's objection.

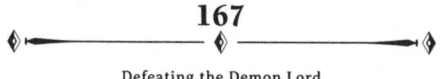

"Fear not... This training is also very difficult for the attacker!" she exclaims. "Your body will be wounded, Toudou, but so too will my soul!"

Toudou already had an inkling, but this world's religion is far more...*aggressive* than anything in the world she came from.

Spica produces a number of knives from her breast pocket in succession. Toudou heard that priests aren't supposed to wield bladed weapons, but the blades Spica carefully removes from their scabbards are razor sharp—they don't look like ritual implements.

"The knowledge I acquire of the human body by observing your wounds and by subsequently healing them will increase my holy energy. And by facing death, the three of you will reach even greater heights. O Ahz Gried, please bestow your divine protection upon Toudou and her party and keep them safe from death."

So we might die? ... Wait—this can't be happening. We'll never hear the end of it if we get beaten to a pulp in the Rizas estate.

Just as Toudou is about to protest, the door to the room opens.

"Enough!"

Spica turns toward the sudden voice like a bowstring pulled taut. Toudou and the others quickly go on the defensive. But the Holy Warrior stares dumbfounded when she sees who has made an appearance.

The new arrival is wearing traveler garb that keeps exposure to a minimum. Her white skin looks like it might slough off, and her eyes are bloodred. However, this time she's not wearing a thick hood, and her flattened ears growing from her head are completely visible.

She holds a staff in her hand that has never been seen until now.

"Rabi... Is that you...?"

There's no mistaking her: The girl before them is indeed Rabi, the monster researcher who fought alongside the party in the battle against Heljarl.

This beautiful girl has remained a mystery ever since she claimed she was chasing after Mermares. She was also the one who decapitated Heljarl.

"The overdone sense of justice is a crime."

✝ Third Report: On Utilizing an Ancient Legend

The party separated from Rabi in Cloudburst. What in the world is she doing in a place like this now? What's more, they are all inside the Rizas estate. No matter what the circumstances, there isn't any world where she could just walk in here without permission.

Rabi looks past the hero's party, all staring aghast. Her eyes fall on Spica, who is oddly quiet. The traveling monster researcher then speaks, shocking everyone.

"That's enough, Spica! You have gone too far. You...are *fired*. Per a heedless request to play the classic role of 'sage who provides the occasional well-timed counsel,' I—the traveling monster researcher Rabi, now under the cardinals' direct orders—will be taking over things from here."

§ § §

During his battle against the sea demon Heljarl, Holy Warrior Naotsugu Toudou came face-to-face with his own deficiencies and struggled to overcome them. The hero had much yet to learn, and thus the Church, which had at last united with humanity, sent him a new armament and a mighty ally by the graces of God.

This legendary enchanted defensive armament, used in innumerable battles with storied warriors, was lying dormant at a casino. However, the armament's owner—a man known as the casino king—was compelled by Toudou's righteous heart to offer him this summetal armor.

His new ally was an emblem of the Church, another guardian of humanity. Long ago, when humankind could not yet defend itself, this woman of the cloth appeared like a bolt out of the blue, taking up her sword to save the world and rescue humanity from extinction.

This knight had divine protection and was granted immortality as a reward for dedicating her entire livelihood to battle. She is none other than the Sister General—the strongest teacher imaginable.

The Sister General has continued to fight for longer than any other being, and the immense experience and prayers she has gained as a result will now serve to awaken new powers in the Holy Warrior, who has yet to fully manifest the capabilities bestowed upon him by God!

Equipped with the teachings of the holy knight who has devoted her entire existence to the world, along with this powerful enchanted armor, no foe stands a chance against the Holy Warrior.

To battle! Slay your enemies, Holy Warrior, protector of all humanity!

The fate of the entire world rests on your shoulders! Focus not on the minutiae, nor on the methods you devise!

Fight, Naotsugu Toudou! Humanity's dawn draws near!

"—and that's basically how we'll approach it."

The people listening to the synopsis I went through great pains to concoct decide to chime in.

"...Boss, you really never learn, do you?"

"...Ares, did your brain melt in your skull?"

Sanya's question is incredulous; Amelia's is completely deadpan.

I spent so much time and effort on this scenario, and their remarks are uncalled for. Particularly Amelia's. I mean...I'm her boss.

Stey, who's blinking repeatedly, is the least comprehending person here.

"Huh? Um, Ares... What about my part?"

You are...cashable goods... If an appraiser shows up, I intend on selling you off. The sooner, the better.

Grace has reached her limit. She can probably still command a first-rate level of prowess, but I cannot allow her to fight on the front lines. That said, using her to create a spectacle will be easy. Having Toudou kill a foe that fells Grace on the battlefield will effectively and easily promote Toudou's strength. However, there is a risk involved that I cannot ignore.

Grace hasn't been visibly in action lately, but she remains a source of hope for humanity. Using her up on Toudou is a total waste and would also go against my principles. Even if Toudou is

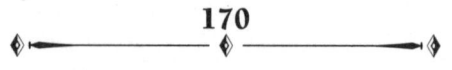

"The overdone sense of justice is a crime."

Third Report: On Utilizing an Ancient Legend

able to provisionally defeat the Demon Lord, Grace's existence will become a definite problem.

In comparison, having Grace tutor Toudou and company is the perfect solution. This will allow Toudou to become stronger, and deploying someone who's as big of a deal as Grace will definitely show the aristocrats in Ruxe that the Church is taking this seriously. Further, if Toudou becomes known as the disciple of the immortal knight among the populace, they will never doubt his strength. As a bonus, through this plan, we might also be able to straighten out Spica, who has grown altogether too much, thanks to that goddamn trickster Gregorio.

As I put my hand to my forehead, Sanya speaks again.

"Crazy that Rabi's on board. And she of all people gets to play the sage...... What did you do?"

"The issue has been resolved."

"...Huh. Well, Rabi didn't say anything, so that's all fine and dandy, I guess."

Sanya nods, not sounding fully convinced.

I should've taken care of that horny rabbit by force from the beginning.

Coincidentally, Rabi is the perfect mentor. Toudou's party knows how capable she is from the battle against Heljarl, and what's more, no epic hero's tale is complete without the appearance of several mysterious characters. Could a sage figure like Rabi possibly show up in our hero's tale under this particular set of circumstances...? Admittedly, it sounds pretty dubious.

"Hey! Hey! Ares, what about my part in this?"

Somebody. Please sew the trap shut on her, this indomitable and uncouth character.

"Amelia, please request that the Church prepare to spread the word of what I've detailed thus far across the land."

"Hmm... And what will you do if Toudou never actually matures?"

"Toudou's growth is not a concern at the moment. Listen up—what we need right now is solidarity."

Our current plan is aimed more at the upper echelon of Ruxe, as opposed to the commoners. Through this strategy, we should be able to assuage some suspicion regarding the Holy Warrior. Once the deepest ranks of the Kingdom have been racked with doubt, it will be too late, no matter how flustered we become. Nonetheless, our ranks aren't showing any sense of urgency. We need to become a single unit, and quickly!

"I think my feelings about the Church are going to change...," says Rabi. "Actually, they already have, I'm pretty sure."

"If you let anything slip, you're dead."

"?! W-wow, what a token threat... Ha-ha, ha-ha... D-don't look so serious."

Rabi is really lacking when it comes to these things. Sanya has already taken on some of the responsibility, but she's prone to slipping up and leaking important information.

In that moment, Amelia claps her hands, as if suddenly remembering something.

"If that's the case, then why don't you find another hero with the divine protection of Ahz Gried to mold into your Holy Warrior?"

"...And just where can I find someone with divine protection to tailor accordingly?"

One of the reasons that the Church's hero-summoning ritual is so top-secret is because there are truly very few beings that have the divine protection of Ahz Gried. Further, warriors so gifted they have a chance of defeating the Demon Lord are even more rare, and combining such a warrior with the divine protection of Ahz Gried? You might as well say they don't exist whatsoever, and those few who may be qualified are almost always already kept by other kingdoms.

Calling upon an apt hero who doesn't have immediate family would be terrifyingly convenient, but that would also amount to an inhumane ritual.

The God of Order is wary to so quickly hand out their divine protection, after all... They are also known to choose individuals indiscriminately. The fact that those with divine protection inside

"The overdone sense of justice is a crime."

Third Report: On Utilizing an Ancient Legend

the Church are so few is proof of this, and it seems that the God of Order doesn't actually prefer the most pious believers. Or perhaps they aren't the type to feed fish that have already been reeled in? Just...perish from my sight already.

Stey blinks repeatedly, looking puzzled. She pulls a typically ditzy move, putting both hands in the air and jumping up and down, shouting, "Ares! Ares! Actually, I can— Mmph?!"

Remaining silent, I physically pinch her lips shut. Amelia and Sanya can't believe their eyes.

Just what did Stey think she was going to say? I take a deep breath before giving orders. I remain calm, but I can't help my voice from lowering.

"Don't make me say something you don't want to hear. Until the appraiser shows up, gag her, tie her up, and lie her down."

"...Aye-aye, sir."

Sanya moves snappily to gag Stey and bind her hands and feet. Stey emits muffled gripes through the gag with tears in her eyes, but really, I should be the one doing the complaining. I cough once curtly and take control of the situation again.

Okay now, Holy Warrior. The table is set. You will become stronger, whether you want to or not.

Grace Godicent Trinity—show us the merits of your timelessness!

§ § §

The second she sees the figure standing before her, a powerful shock like a bolt of lightning rocks Toudou's entire body to the core.

The knight is covered from head to toe in lacquer-black armor. The look is exaggerated, but Toudou has already seen many knights dressed in full body armor since coming to this world. Wurtz, the half-giant priest she met in Golem Valley, boasted an even more majestic appearance.

That said, in comparison, the knight before her now is even more incredible. They are almost difficult to describe, but if forced to put it into words, it's like their body is tasked with carrying the authority of God. The female knight following alongside emanates a very powerful life force herself, but next to the knight in black, it's almost like she doesn't exist at all.

All of Toudou's compatriots are at a loss for words, too. Aria whispers, as if dreaming, "Her name is...Grace?! Impossible. The Church sent their strongest holy knight?!"

Rabi, who had brought both knights, coughs and opens her hands palms-up exaggeratedly toward Toudou.

"*Ahem*... Toudou, the Church has determined that you are now strong enough to be worthy of receiving her instruction. And once you have inherited her power and supplication, the true Holy Warrior bloodline that lies dormant inside you will awaken!"

"What...did you say?! The Holy Warrior...*bloodline*?!"

Toudou is thrown for a loop. Her heart pounds in her chest, and she feels great power surging through her body...which quickly fades.

".........Umm... I'm Japanese, for the record."

"...My boss insisted that we not sweat the details—another one of his heedless requests! This is your training! You *will* embrace it! God decrees it! The righteous bloodline does not run through your veins—it is your soul itself! This was written in the stars the very moment you were born!"

"Huh?! Uh... Okay."

Many, many doubts flood Toudou's mind, but her distinct lack in power is undeniable. If she is going to be afforded a chance to receive instruction from the strongest holy knight in existence, then she cannot feasibly complain.

Just as she is coming to accept the situation, Spica, who hasn't said a word, steps forward.

"W-wait a second! Toudou, you must receive God's instruction alongside me! It is preposterous to think you will get stronger from such basic training! There is no meaning to studying without pain; these are the words of my master. These are also the words of your superior, Rabi!"

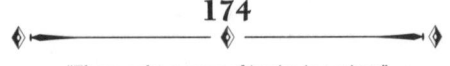

"The overdone sense of justice is a crime."

Third Report: On Utilizing an Ancient Legend

Rabi has remained mostly silent, but now she shudders and speaks coldly, refusing to give Toudou a chance to agree or disagree.

"...Said superior is a brute, and there isn't any good reason to abide by his words."

§ § §

"The Church sent the immortal knight to provide guidance to the Holy Warrior... They're really taking desperate measures now."

Ruxe, the royal capital—inside the castle at the center of the city, the Kingdom's top aristocrats are gathered around a circular table. The rustic and unadorned room doesn't fit the exterior of the chalk-white castle. The room also lacks decoration, save for the number of different weapons that are hung on the walls. Of course, this doesn't indicate that the castle's interior was always this modest. It was once famous for being gaudy and dazzling, but everything changed when Demon Lord Kranos came on the scene.

Several other kingdoms have already been demolished. All the treasure adorning the castle's interior was removed and replaced with armaments. The Kingdom of Ruxe has not been attacked yet, but this is simply a matter of good fortune.

The Holy Warrior is the Kingdom's ace in the hole. Their summoning requires significant compensation, and the individual is chosen entirely at random. According to the Church, this hero is a mirror image of the summoner's faith. If the summoning fails, humanity will lose all trust in the Kingdom of Ruxe. Ruxe was at their wit's end, to the point where they had to depend on the summoning ritual.

For now, only the Kingdom's upper-echelon cadre knows about the Holy Warrior—partly because such knowledge can attract demons, but also, if the hero summoning fails, the Kingdom will still have options.

At present, opinions of the Holy Warrior are mixed. He is certainly qualified for the role. However, the hero isn't without his issues: He banished his party's priest and is vehemently opposed to working with men. His defeat of Heljarl, who had been nigh untouchable, was indeed a great victory, but the Holy Warrior has since failed his training even with the help of his magic items from House Friedia. His level, too, is much lower than anticipated.

Nonetheless, word of the hero's arrival will spread. Defeating Heljarl has only accelerated this process. The Holy Warrior's debut should be at the behest of the Kingdom who can then provide further assistance more easily and openly.

Until just the other day, Ruxe's concerns had far outweighed their hopes. The aristocrats knowledgable of the Holy Warrior's summoning understand history well, and they have their own doubts about the Holy Warrior's capabilities.

That said—the room where they've currently gathered is full of enthusiasm.

"So the Church was similarly concerned about the Holy Warrior's slow growth."

News of the immortal knight's deployment has turned any and all doubts on their head. Nobody expected this. If the Holy Warrior is the Kingdom's ace in the hole, then the immortal knight is the Church's equivalent.

She is an undying saint who has forged many a legend on countless battlefields. The supreme holy knight who willingly sacrificed her very soul in order to save humanity. A guardian of the people, she has wielded a blade, magic, or even the power of God to drive out the scourge of darkness.

Though hardly anyone has ever actually seen her, everyone alive knows her legend. What's more—the legend is not simply something of the past. Even some within Ruxe's army have witnessed her ungodly might with their own eyes. No one has heard much about her for a long time, but the fact that the Church has dispatched Grace now means that they are committed to taking a stance that closely aligns them with the Kingdom moving forward.

"The people will also be relieved to learn that Grace is fighting alongside the Holy Warrior."

"The overdone sense of justice is a crime."

Third Report: On Utilizing an Ancient Legend

Grace is the strongest of all knights. However, she is not active on the vanguard. According to the Church's official doctrine, Grace is an embodiment of God's might, and relying on God's might can lead to corruption. Therefore, Grace must be careful not to use her powers recklessly. Nonetheless, her direct support of the Holy Warrior will bring comfort to those who spend their nights in fear of a demon attack.

Just then, Norton Rizas, who sent his own beloved daughter to join the Holy Warrior's party, furrows his brow and speaks solemnly.

"But Grace has never focused her efforts on guiding another person... Surely His Eminence knows this, yet he's still acting rashly. Perhaps he's considerably more confident than we realize?"

"There is nothing to be concerned about," says one male aristocrat. "Grace has been alive since before Ruxe was founded, so I daresay she has instructed a number of people—perhaps dozens—even if it's not quite common knowledge. We should be focused on what happens after the Holy Warrior reaches his full potential."

"Hmph..." Norton Rizas grunts lightly.

The Church has a conservative side. No one anticipated Grace's recruitment because it involves considerable risk.

In the event that Grace's training fails, both she and the Holy Warrior will have their reputations affected.

Fostering a person's growth is a difficult task, and Norton Rizas, commander of the Kingdom's army, knows this best. Grace may be a living legend, but he doesn't have faith that she will succeed—because above all else, she cannot speak.

It's unlikely that His Eminence Creio Amen came up with this plan. Whoever did come up with it had no idea how it would turn out, nor are they concerned with how it gets done—this person has to be a bonafide gambler.

§ § §

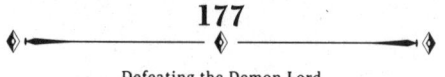

Our strategy, hereby named Operation Legend of Old, has commenced. Up until now, I created plans that eliminated risk to the extent possible. However, the success of our current strategy will certainly require a healthy dose of good luck.

Grace is my associate, but I still don't fully understand just how powerful she is. Furthermore, I can't predict Toudou's movements. That said, at the end of the day, all we can do is work for the best result possible. If we fail—the legend will die.

"A routine update: Spica is in a bad mood. Her master had some words for her, and now she's snapping at Grace."

"Talk her down somehow. Grace is the real deal. Even if we can't boost Toudou's level, we can raise his technical skill. You must get him in shape before the grand reveal! Ten times! He needs to be at least ten times stronger!"

"Ares, we've received a complaint from an upper-level member of the Church regarding the use of the immortal knight—"

"Tell them to direct all complaints to Creio!!"

"Boss, there aren't any mythical beasts around here that are huge and grandiose, much less weak!"

"What did you say? Are you prepared to become a merman yourself, Sanya?!"

"?! O-okay, I'll take another look!"

"Ares, I made you some tea— Oops!"

"Sanya! Go drop Stey off in the mountains while you're at it!"

Stey spills the tea everywhere, and I grab her by the scruff of her neck, pushing her toward Sanya, who looks at me, reviled. Stey, who would just use teleportation magic to return even when dumped in the mountains, looks just like a cursed doll.

Right now, we don't have any time for frivolous concerns. We have to formulate a plan to deal with the next wave of the Demon Lord Army's forces. For them, the Demon Lord is enemy number one, who they must deal with right away. As long as the Demon Lord Army has a magic item that allows them to ascertain the Holy Warrior's level of divine protection, the next time they attack, it will be with pinpoint precision. The capital has robust defenses, but there are demons that can disguise themselves as humans, too. It's

"The overdone sense of justice is a crime."

Third Report: On Utilizing an Ancient Legend

not realistic to stop every last rat that tries to make its way inside the city.

I look toward Stey, who is writhing and trying to escape from Sanya's grasp, while on the verge of being completely cornered into her inevitable horrid fate. Hmm... Maybe we could try Operation Fake Holy Warrior? No... That could damage the *real* Holy Warrior's reputation.

"...Tch. Quelling the demons preemptively or avoiding them just isn't a realistic approach. Perhaps we need to engage the enemy directly."

Demon Lord Kranos's stronghold is in the realm of demons. If worse came to worst, I wouldn't be able to breach such a location, given my lack of divine protection.

Until now, Toudou has always had protection by his side, but before long, we really need him to be strong enough to fight on his own.

§ § §

Legendary mercenary Bran Chatre always told Rabi how quick-witted she was.

Rabi's capabilities on the battlefield are like walking a tightrope. No matter how much divine protection she has, a wererabbit's physical prowess is very low—an insurmountable handicap. When fighting on the vanguard alongside her strong brethren disciple Sanya, their difference is clear, and Rabi needs to constantly remain aware of her surroundings. If she doesn't take down attackers in a single blow, she's as good as dead. Remaining prepared in this regard has turned Rabi into the stone-cold assassin she is today.

Rabi's greatest weapons are her keen ears and well-developed observational skills. However, in the current moment, those strengths have backfired.

This job is beyond dangerous—Rabi realizes that knowing too much will directly lead to bodily harm, but she has lived this way for as long as she can remember, and she can't simply stop her cerebral impulses now.

It has been some time since she received the request and has worked alongside the others. Sanya is always carefree and hasn't caught on at all, but when calmly considering the request they've been given, Rabi knows it's been absolute chaos since the beginning. The Church's proposal of aiding the Holy Warrior from the shadows is wholly contradictory to the very nature of the legend.

The Holy Warrior and the immortal knight are clandestine beings, formidable secrets that the holy church devoted to the worship of the God of Order, Ahz Gried—the largest religious organization in this world—has continually kept under wraps.

Even Rabi, who scoured innumerable texts and obtained as much knowledge as possible, has never heard an inkling of Grace possibly growing old. And what's more—she's pretty sure that fact isn't the crux of the secret, either.

Rabi's boss fully intends to get her even more deeply entrenched. He'll use Rabi's natural disposition to turn the tables on her—and if she finds out something that she wasn't supposed to know, she'll be snuffed out or else be made into a slave with a chain around her neck who will work for the Church for the rest of her existence.

Bran surely needs a pawn under his control, one that has razor-sharp wit and understands the situation accurately and who is totally faithful, never threatening to betray him. The reason that Rabi was chosen over Amelia or Stephenne as his subject is because they don't seem faithful enough to keep secrets and aren't timid enough to never even think of letting one slip.

Rabi is meek to a fault. Even though she understands the harrowing fate that likely awaits her, she can do nothing to escape.

"How are things going with Toudou?" Rabi asks Grace.

A chance encounter of legends. After the slight grievance with Spica, Rabi and Grace are in a different room.

Grace hasn't shown a single sign of being rattled by Toudou, much less Spica's display of riotous behavior. She remains standing

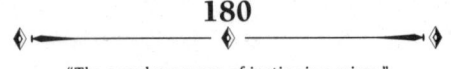

"The overdone sense of justice is a crime."

Third Report: On Utilizing an Ancient Legend

royally. Her aloof appearance is perfectly fitting for a hero, but it's not really necessary right now.

Grace turns her head slowly and looks toward Rabi. However, she doesn't even feign to speak. Instead, her accompanying knight standing with an abstruse expression, Eve Lucrao, speaks gravely.

"If I may—because Captain Grace cannot engage in conversation, I will speak on her behalf. Judging from what she has seen up close—quite frankly, Toudou's supplication toward God is lacking."

"Please continue."

"The God of Order favors Toudou, yet Toudou himself does not fully believe in God. This is why Toudou cannot fully command his own power. His natural capacity allowed him to fight reasonably well, but in his former world, it seems that not enough importance was placed on faith. Spica, an apprentice of the Mad Eater, is on the extreme end of the spectrum—but Ex Deus's concerns, and His Eminence's request for Grace's support, are completely valid."

Contrary to her appellation of Holy Warrior, Naotsugu Toudou's holy energy is very low, a fact that Rabi has gradually realized. Holy energy is different from a warrior's level in that it cannot be so simply raised. Levels can be raised just by hunting monsters. Magic power can be raised by casting spells. However, holy energy does not increase simply by using holy techniques.

Boosting holy energy requires supplication. Just as priests are able to realize miracles slowly through daily devotion to prayer, tempering holy energy takes time. The reason that Ares hasn't formulated any plan to raise Toudou's holy energy thus far is likely because he couldn't find any way to do it quickly and effectively. Furthermore, since holy energy is difficult to correlate with combat strength (Ares is a distinct exception to this rule), it makes sense to prioritize adding an expert priest to the hero's party instead of boosting Toudou's holy energy.

"Attempting to foster holy energy is not pointless. The divine protection of Ahz Gried implies a vast amount of power bestowed, but that power also depends on the target's total holy energy. If

Toudou can increase his holy energy and receive power from Ahz Gried, he will become more powerful than imaginable compared to now. This is our current outlook."

But just why did Ahz Gried bestow divine protection on someone of such little faith?

Rabi shakes her head to dispel the abrupt thought.

"Our boss has commanded us to instill within Toudou a distinction as not just a mercenary but as the Holy Warrior—no matter what it takes," she tells Eve. "If Toudou can wield the divine protection of Ahz Gried in an even greater capacity, that would be ideal."

But that's extremely difficult. If getting Toudou to become significantly stronger was so easy, it would have been done ages ago. The support they've been giving Toudou from the shadows has really just been an exercise in buying time. Ares worked to give Toudou different achievements, but achievements without actually improving competency will lead to certain failure. Rabi convinced herself it was all related to the budget allotted from the beginning, but now it's clear that Ares was stewing with impatience the entire time.

"The issue lies in the method. Raising holy energy requires time, as we all know. For an individual that's come from a different world, this is only exacerbated. And we are short on time."

Many humans in this world have received the blessings of Ahz Gried since childhood yet still cannot use holy techniques. Coming from a different world and being ordered to believe in another God sounds like a high hurdle from Rabi's perspective. If it was a divine revelation from God, that would be a different story, but from what Rabi knows, that's not even true...

Eve falls silent for a time at Rabi's words before speaking again gravely.

"Attaining faith through easy means is an unspeakable phrase for a holy knight—but we are under a special set of circumstances. We propose invoking the special ritual of the Thirteen Rites of Phimas."

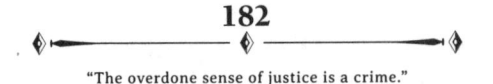

"The overdone sense of justice is a crime."

✝ Third Report: On Utilizing an Ancient Legend

§ § §

"This concludes our report," Rabi says. "We're told that Grace will abide by your decision, boss—but do you know anything about the Thirteen Rites of Phimas? I had never heard of it myself."

I recross my legs and frown.

"The Thirteen Rites of Phimas... It's an ancient ritual. That said, Grace definitely came up with something outside the box."

She's focused on something completely different. I was hoping Grace would work Toudou like a horse and temper his strengths, somehow exciting him for the cause and increasing his faith, but the Thirteen Rites of Phimas could be an even better strategy.

Rabi purses her lips tightly and waits for me to speak. After collecting my thoughts, I finally explain, "The Thirteen Rites of Phimas refers to thirteen different disciplines once taken on by Saint Phimas to temper holy energy. Phimas was able to deepen his faith through these rites—and eventually acquired a technique to raise the dead, it's said."

"Raise the dead...?! Is that...even possible? I...had no idea—"

"The ritual became obsolete a very long time ago. Amelia and Stey, you've probably only just heard the name, right?"

Raising the dead is the ne plus ultra of holy techniques. It overturns death—something unavoidable—necessitating a vast amount of holy energy, and even in the long history of the Church, wielders of this technique can be counted on a single hand. For this reason, Phimas was a priest of incredible ability and faith.

Saint Phimas is long gone, but the impact he left on the Church remains immense. And above all else—despite his great influence, there is a reason that the name Saint Phimas is now largely unknown.

"Wh-why did it become obsolete?" Rabi asks hesitantly.

"Well, because it's ineffective."

".........Huh?"

Rabi blinks in disbelief, and for good reason.

"Rather than being ineffective per se, individuals who lost the holy energy required started to appear one after another. Since then, the Thirteen Rites of Phimas became a very dark taboo within the Church, and the very name Phimas was covered up."

"Wow..."

Rabi looks astounded. Phimas was, of course, incredible enough to be canonized as a saint. However, because of this fact, his method of discipline simply didn't get through to other priests of lesser faith.

Human beings all have certain aptitudes, and Phimas had a heart of faith since well before he engaged in this discipline—an absolute heart of faith that may have grasped the miracle of raising the dead, even without such discipline.

The fact that neither Creio nor I landed on this ritual as an option is of no surprise. It has been many years since anyone that can actually conduct the ritual has existed within the Church, and if the Holy Warrior loses their holy energy, there isn't any reason to even consider it.

"...Should we reject Eve's suggestion?"

"No... Let's do it."

"?!"

The Thirteen Rites of Phimas, which robbed so many priests of their holy energy and shook the Church to the core, remain under circumstances that are difficult to explain within the Church. However, this fact provides added value for actually pursuing them. First, I'll need to report to Creio and get his help persuading the Church elites, who will most certainly oppose the idea. If the ritual succeeds, the Holy Warrior will gain an exceptional amount of power and what's more—

I stop to compose my thoughts. The more I do, the more I realize that, given our circumstances, this must be the best possible option. Goddammit, Grace, you're certainly an adept warrior—but I had no idea you were capable of coming up with superior strategy, too.

"The overdone sense of justice is a crime."

Third Report: On Utilizing an Ancient Legend

It will work...! This strategy has to work! With one small revision, that is.

An unforced smile spreads across my face. I fold my hands and speak to Rabi, who's clutching her chest while awaiting my words.

"However, thirteen is too many. The entire Thirteen Rites of Phimas would take five years to complete, at minimum. We don't have that much time. We don't need all of them to be effective anyway. Let's say two... No, three—three will suffice."

§ § §

The immortal knight: an absolute servant of God; the legendary knight sworn to protect humankind for eternity, blessed with powers of immortality and fated to battle forevermore. Their existence is common knowledge among most humans in this world.

In Toudou's previous world, this knight would be a famous mythical character. But this world is different: It has gods that provide divine protection, meaning that the immortal knight's existence actually makes sense.

There is no way to understand why the Church of Ahz Gried decided to play their ace in the hole now after so much time. That said, if they claim it will help further temper Toudou's capabilities, then that's exactly what she needs. At the very least, it is vastly preferable to having Toudou learn from Spica, who has changed drastically ever since accepting tutelage under Gregorio.

Toudou waits with bated breath for Eve to speak, and her eyes go wide at what she's told.

"Three...ultra rites of Phimas...?" Toudou says.

"......Yes—that's...correct..."

Eve may have her own concerns—she looks extremely uncomfortable.

Toudou was given a rudimentary education upon arriving in this world, but she's never heard the name Phimas. Aria and Limis, on the other hand, appear to recognize it.

Limis folds her arms and whispers, doubtful, "Phimas... I've heard that name. I don't know a whole lot, but I believe he was a saint—I think he devised a formidable method of ascetic training."

"Is......is that so? You're quite a learned girl—very few believers even know his name...," Eve says, her expression stiff for some reason.

Aria puts her hand to her chin and furrows her brow. "Me and Limis come from aristocratic families...which means we have a certain degree of knowledge about these things. And yet... I could've sworn that Saint Phimas came up with far more than just three rites—"

"Well, sure, but Phimas's ascetic training was a grueling process that took at least several years," says Limis. "I remember reading in a book once that it was too harsh on a number of devotees, many of whom ended up taking their own lives."

Years of grueling training...? It's not completely absurd, but they definitely don't have such leisure currently.

Toudou looks to Spica, who still hasn't reacted, even after what Eve said. She looks like she wants to speak, but she's folded her hands behind herself and pursed her lips. It's almost like some power is keeping her silent.

Grace remains standing solemnly, as always. Eve continues, now forcing her voice into a hush.

"Nothing—is impossible in the realm of the unknown. The three ultra rites of Phi—Phimas......are a recent development—a new discipline for a new era...!"

"Wha—?! A new...training method?"

"Surely there is a problem with arbitrarily modifying a practice that a saint developed, yes?" Aria asks.

"......Th-the—foundations...remain the same. There—aren't any problems—at all."

...She doesn't sound too convinced.

Just as Toudou was starting to really worry about Eve's temperament, which seems somehow off, or maligned, Rabi—who had been

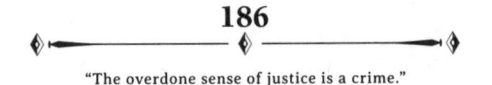

Third Report: On Utilizing an Ancient Legend

completely silent—offers her own insight. Her tone is the polar opposite of Eve's, somehow filled with a vast level of confidence.

"No problems. None whatsoever. The most powerful brute priest has extracted the core elements from the training Phimas came up with and rearranged it to be manageable in a shorter time frame! It's received a cardinal's approval, and a number of other priests have already personally experienced the results. The number of rites has decreased, but the grueling nature of the training has become more severe."

"I...see...," says Toudou. "So it's even more intense."

"Yes—Rabi is—exactly right," Eve agrees, shaking like a leaf.

Making a training that already forced some participants to take their own lives even more grueling—just what does it entail? Nonetheless, no matter how severe the training, there isn't an option to avoid it now. If it allows Toudou to acquire the power necessary to defeat the Demon Lord, and to once again make the holy sword Ex shine brightly—there isn't reason for even a moment's hesitation.

Rabi and Eve both nod deeply while looking distraught, and they look toward the holy knight of legend.

"...Understood. Of course I'll do it. But...what exactly am I doing?" Toudou asks hesitantly, swallowing a lump in her throat.

"Okay," Rabi begins, her expression severe. "First—you will eat until your stomach nearly ruptures and pray within a waterfall in a massive caldera, all while confronting true darkness."

"......Huh? S-say what now????"

Toudou briefly thinks she misheard, but next to her, Aria and Limis are similarly dumbfounded.

Eat until your stomach ruptures... Why, though?

Toudou asks Rabi to clarify, and she merely repeats herself, without flinching her brow in the slightest.

"This is the first of the three ultra rites of Phimas—eating until your stomach nearly ruptures and praying within a waterfall in a massive caldera, all while confronting true darkness. Don't worry. Everything is ready for you."

§ § §

Eve Lucrao does not approve of the abridged Thirteen Rites of Phimas.

The full Thirteen Rites are as follows:

- Receiving instruction from an oracle
- Acquiring a relic
- Prayer upon eliminating impurities
- Prayer within a source of fire
- Prayer within water's end
- Reaching the apex of light
- Saving one hundred thousand people
- Establishing a covenant with a sacred beast
- Receiving instruction from ten high priests
- Spiritual discipline of the inner self
- Confronting true darkness
- Encountering God

The final rite is revealed only when these twelve are fulfilled. They usually take five years minimum, or up to ten years in some cases. They are not meant to be exercised in an emergency.

Amelia and Stey are both deadbeats, and Grace is a storied warrior who's already tasted the bitter swill of our world, but Eve is a pious believer. Even with Rabi here, leaving everything in Eve's hands would be entirely premature. If my suspicions are correct, Creio sent her and Grace to us partially as an education for Eve.

She's a holy knight raised in absolute purity; her faith isn't so easily swayed.

"We'll consolidate the prayer-centric rites, get them all done at once," I tell Eve. "We need to take a flexible approach."

"You...you call yourself a priest?! Prayer is the most important aspect of the Church of Ahz Gried... The Thirteen Rites of Phimas demand prayer in every situation imaginable. Prayer within fire,

Third Report: On Utilizing an Ancient Legend

symbolizing genesis—and from within water, meaning conflict—further, the rites require one month of fasting wherein the practicioner prays after eliminating any and all impurities—before finally arriving at the apex of light. Just how do you expect to consolidate all these rites?!"

Of course a square like her wouldn't understand this... True, you need religious devotion to attain a high level of holy energy, but there's no going back if we fail to defeat the Demon Lord.

Simply put, the Thirteen Rites of Phimas are actually a very popular method of ascetic training for pushing a person to their limits until they reach divine providence. The rites themselves are so rigorous that very few have actually completed them, but breaking a person's spirit is what really matters. We don't have enough time for all thirteen rites; Toudou only has until his public debut to get this done. I'm sure God will understand.

"We're not starving Toudou. We can't have him losing that much muscle. If anything... Hmm, if anything, he needs to eat more, *lots* more. And mostly protein!"

"...???"

There are other methods of pushing a person to their limits. Being forced into grueling training with your gut bursting would be even rougher than going in hungry, and then eliminating impurities— That's right: There's no point in trying to eliminate impurities through starvation.

In fact, conquering the self when stuffed to the brim with filth is what makes a true believer!

"Prayer within a source of fire... So, a volcano. And 'water's end' is a waterfall...so we'll have him meditate under a waterfall in a caldera. Prayer within a waterfall caldera while stuffed to the gills with food. This easily combines three rites into one."

"A-are you—out of your mind—?!"

"Eve, Ares is serious. Seriously off his rocker."

Just whose side are you on, Amelia...? And no, I'm not out of my mind. This is an exceptionally effective training method that remains in accordance with legend. Not to mention, Phimas is such a minor religious figure; we'll definitely be able to dodge any flack.

As I bore my serious gaze rife with pressure into Eve, she speaks, pained.

"B-but... All right. Does a caldera—that also has a waterfall... even exist? Phimas—traveled all across the world as he offered up prayers."

"Good point... No, wait—one of the Thirteen Rites involves fighting against darkness, right?"

"Yes, that's...because Phimas was both a priest and a monk, from what I've heard. Surrounded by true darkness, he used prayer as his only weapon to fight against demonic forces and keep them at bay..."

Once again, this proves that Phimas was a real gung-ho moron. It's no surprise that so many who followed his teachings ended up dead.

We can't have Toudou dying on us during these rites. Providing him with a successful experience is the goal—that, and making sure he comes out of Phimas's ascetic training victorious, is our priority.

I grip Eve by the shoulder and stare straight into her eyes.

"Keep Toudou blindfolded during the rites. A thick blindfold, one that won't let in even a sliver of light. That takes care of confronting true darkness. Look, we don't need an actual caldera or a waterfall, either. Now we have four rites combined into one—that's two birds with one stone."

"?! So—you are asking me to lie—?!"

"No one is lying. You'll create a caldera and waterfall for us. Eve Lucrao—this is an order. You are under orders by His Eminence Creio Amen to obey me. That means my orders are as good as his. So do as I say."

Priests serving the God of Order cannot lie, according to doctrine. For this reason, an absurd plan like this one requires discretion. Do we really have the luxury of griping about it? I am doing everything in my power to get Toudou to the next level.

"The overdone sense of justice is a crime."

Third Report: On Utilizing an Ancient Legend

"Got it, Grace?"

"……"

Grace responds with silence. But silence is the same as approval where she's concerned. Eve slouches her shoulders, clearly ready to acquiesce. Okay, now we have Rabi here, too, and we can start moving this plan forward somehow.

I'll make a call and get Spica to keep her mouth shut. She's been imbued with all sorts of nonsense by Gregorio, who's even more of a piece of work than I am, but that means she'll be pliable. Stey, dumb and ditzy as ever, comes up with her eyes sparkling and taps me on the shoulder.

"Ares, Ares! Is there anything that I can do to help?"

You are simply too gullible, too pliable. This is not the time to get all excited! This is not a fun game for you to play!

Next, I need to prepare the God that Toudou will encounter, alongside the people that he will save.

"This is absolutely ridiculous, don't you think?" Amelia asks me.

"Hmm... Well, it makes a lot more sense than wearing a merman costume and exploring the ocean floor."

"...When you put it like that, I can't possibly respond."

Amelia averts her gaze. It was my idea in the first place; is she mocking me? In fairness, that whole Mermares fiasco was truly inane...

At any rate, we're now focused on Operation Phimas. Our strategy, taking the saint's namesake, is now moving forward full steam. The most important part of this plan is just how well we can manipulate the system with Toudou and the others. From time to time, holy energy can also increase or decrease simply due to personal illusion. This is the reason Gregorio, who adheres to a fanatical credo, has been able to remain ageless, and also why some priests known for their piety have suddenly lost all their powers.

Faith should be deepened through daily supplication and

experience, but for the task at hand, we simply don't have time. Although we can perhaps deceive others through words, we cannot deceive ourselves that way. Our biggest bottleneck is the fact that a transcendental God that can bestow certain powers didn't seem to exist in Toudou's world. I can't even begin to imagine such a world; whatever deity ruled it must have been very hands off.

Toudou needs to get past these cultural differences and develop a belief in God.

The most difficult aspect of the Thirteen Rites of Phimas is saving one hundred thousand people. The word "saving" is used, but what Phimas actually did was heal injured people using holy techniques; at any rate, this will take time. Regardless of the fact that he has Ahz Gried's divine protection, given Toudou's current powers, it would take him a number of years.

The next most difficult aspect is the instruction from ten high priests, which is also bound to take an inordinate amount of time. A high priest is capable of wielding high-level holy techniques, and they must be a minimum level of 50. Priests have a hard time leveling up to begin with, so getting them to this threshhold is very difficult.

Cultivating holy energy requires planting the seeds for a heart of faith, and for Toudou, who doesn't even have a solid heart of faith himself, this task could more or less be deemed impossible.

If Toudou does manage to clear these two rites, no matter how much of a blockhead he may be, he will have ascertained holy energy on par with a high-level priest. Then, after clearing them, he will be met with a chance to encounter God. Tackling this rite head-on is a very tall mountain to climb.

It goes without saying that those who have successfully confronted the God of Order—who is of such grandeur that they can bestow divine protection—are few and far between throughout history. Toudou has the divine protection of the Three Deities and Eight Spirit Kings, and he might pull it off somehow, but gods... for the most part...are exceptionally fickle. Phimas was able to

"The overdone sense of justice is a crime."

successfully encounter God, but so many other high-level priests with similar hearts of faith failed.

Phimas, you bastard... Did you only create these rites because you managed to execute them yourself?

Just thinking about these rites is a dedicated assignment, but I do feel fortunate that the task we must carry out is laid out directly in front of us.

"Let's start with what we know we can accomplish. Even at the longest, we can't afford to spend a whole month, considering the timing of Toudou's public debut."

"Hey, Ares, isn't there anything li'l ol' me can do to help?"

Quit it with the cutesy act. Stey's hands are outstretched as she smiles without a single iota of nervousness on her face. I grab her by the cheek and pull, boring my gaze into her.

"Don't you dare do anything over the top. Your major role here is to ask your father to pull the troops away from the parade. Got it?"

"Y-yes...yessir!"

This is a do-or-die situation. Keeping close watch on the parade and the surrounding area, and tempering Toudou's capability—if we can succeed in both, our lives will become a lot easier.

Stey starts traipsing whimsically out of the room, and she trips and falls once flat on her face before leaving like nothing happened. As I watch her go, Amelia turns to me, her cheeks puffed up ostentatiously, before asking, "... So...isn't there anything li'l ol' me can do to help?"

"......"

There are too many things. All arrangements, for starters. Amelia can use communication magic, meaning her tasks span every last arrangement that needs to be made—communicating with the Church and checking regularly on developments on Toudou's side. From managing budgets to whatever the hell else needs doing, it's all up to Amelia, the one girl that I can really trust to get things done. It's just like I've been saying all along!

As I fire a silent look toward her, Amelia—most capable Amelia—hurriedly averts her gaze.

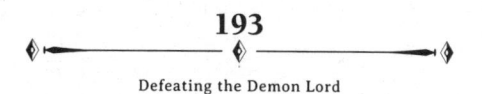

"B-by...by the way...," she begins. "What about the covenant with the sacred beast? Acquiring a relic should be easy enough if we simply procure one from an applicable source, but sacred beasts are not so easily found, right?"

"True, you're not wrong..."

The Church certifies all sacred beasts, which refers to unsullied beasts that have both sagacity and a heart of faith. Establishing a covenant with one is no simple task, even with the Church's support, and Toudou being recognized by the beast will also take time.

For the task at hand, we don't have time to establish a covenant properly. A sacred beast is a powerful ally to have, but they aren't strictly required. Of course, if we could have found a chance to establish a covenant with one along our journey, that would have been incredible—this is something I'm well aware of.

"We'll use Glacia as a sacred beast."

"?! Th-that's...certainly a tall order, isn't it? She can't even use holy techniques—"

"What does it matter? Toudou will learn holy techniques, and we have Spica, too, so it's fine. Using a dragon that took on the form of a human girl in the place where our adventure all started—it'll make the perfect spectacle, don't you think?"

"...Hmm... Almost *too* perfect..."

It will be fine. When trying to get points across to the commoners or the aristocrats, the more basic and easier to understand, the better. The only problem is that the Church doesn't consider glacial plants as sacred beasts... But Glacia is assuming a human form. As long as we give Creio the lowdown and he approves, no one will doubt us.

"Get me a magic potion that'll change the color of her hair. We'll have Glacia drink it at precisely the right time. Make sure her hair turns stark white."

"...As white as yours, then?" Amelia asks.

What kind of reaction is she trying to get out of me?

Our plan is set. Rabi, Sanya, and even Stey—everyone is going

"The overdone sense of justice is a crime."

Third Report: On Utilizing an Ancient Legend

in full tilt. Limis and Aria also need to have their powers boosted, but for now, we must focus on Toudou.

It's time to commence a new order of business.

§ § §

Rabi—erstwhile traveling monster researcher and now envoy to the Church—makes an announcement without so much as batting an eye:

"It is time to officially commence the training."

"W-wait...! Am I really expected to undergo this training with my stomach nearly bursting?!"

"...Toudou, the God of Order decrees that you put on more weight."

"...B-but I'm too stuffed..."

The table in front of Toudou is crammed with plates, and the majority of them are piled with meat; mountains of fried salami, thick steaks...even the huge bowl of soup that would take both arms to carry and colorful salad in front of her are filled with meat. Just looking at this spread is enough to make the stomach groan.

Aria is a huge eater compared to Toudou, but even she can't believe the volume before her. It's obviously way too much for just one person. A pitcher filled to the brim with milk is provided for Toudou's beverage, and the intention to make sure she is completely nourished, no matter what the cost, is apparent.

Toudou has taken part in a number of different trainings since coming to this world, but this one is definitely a first. Limis has a small appetite to begin with, and she's full just watching, too. As Toudou continues to be dumbstruck by the sheer volume, Rabi speaks to her bluntly.

"All of it... You will polish off every last plate."

"?! You can't be serious!"

Toudou had vaguely assumed as much, but being told so point blank is a massive shock. Her eyes grow wide, and her body stiffens up.

"N-Nao...... You can do this," Limis whispers.

Toudou's compatriots, who have conquered in battle against many strong foes alongside her, can now barely manage to look her in the eyes. This battle against food might be more of a nuisance than any monster they've encountered. Rabi, who's not a particular ally in this fight, pipes up to offer support.

"...The God of Order decrees that Limis and Aria also need some extra meat on their bones."

"?! Us too?! What do we have to do with this?!"

Aria looks desperate. This is an inordinate amount of food even for her. But can she really claim this doesn't have anything to do with her...?

Limis looks like she's been sucker punched from behind as she gazes around the room in a huff.

"W-wait! What about Glacia? She's part of this, too, right?"

"Yeah! If we had Glacia with us..."

Glacia is easily the biggest eater in the whole party. Compared to her, even Aria's appetite looks minor. Glacia's black hole of a stomach caused the group trouble a number of times along their journey, but just to imagine it could come in useful at some point—

Where is Glacia, anyway? She was with us this morning...

Toudou is looking around frantically as Rabi sighs shortly, putting her pointer finger to her forehead before saying, "Glacia...has been excused for a physical evaluation by the Church. There is the possibility of a certain power lying dormant within her—at any rate, she may appear again once this rite is finished. This food is for the three of you. You will stuff yourselves with this nouriushment until your stomachs are threatening to rupture."

"Geh—! W-well... Um... How about Spica? Oh yeah—she got called away by the Church, too..."

An escape route is not presenting itself. At this rate, the first terrifying rite will lead to certain vomiting.

"...It's pretty obvious that we can't force down this amount of food... Besides... I, um... If I get any bigger, I won't be able to wear my armor..."

196

"The overdone sense of justice is a crime."

Third Report: On Utilizing an Ancient Legend

Toudou is complaining before even taking a single bite, and Rabi coughs quietly before speaking again.

"Fret not. We have a new set of armor for you. And...this isn't an amount of food you can't force down—it's an amount you *will* force down. Toudou, this rite will be the crucible in which you learn to exercise your own life force."

§ § §

Life force. All living beings have it, and in this world, it directly indicates one's level of power. Rabi and others from this world absorb other being's life force upon killing them, allowing them to level up and become even stronger. That said, occasionally it's misunderstood: the true essence of absorbing life force isn't to enhance physical strength.

This is understood slowly through real-life experience in battle, but a higher level of life force means that the user will "be given preference." One's level must be raised considerably in order for this effect to be noticeable, but the difference between understanding this fact or remaining ignorant of it has a massive impact in the long run. Finally, living organisms that reach high-level status are given preference in accordance with the laws of physics.

Inevitably, human beings with extravagant amounts of life force will be given preference in regard to the yoke they're tied to—their lifespan—as well. Just like the immortal knight of legend, the Sister General.

The Holy Warrior is crestfallen as she sits in front of the full-course meal that the Church has provided.

"Hngh... I c-can't take any more..."

Toudou and company have done their best, but only one-third of the plates have been emptied. Aria is blue in the face, and Limis looks like she's going to vomit as she turns her face away.

Getting enough nutrition is very important. A vast amount of energy is consumed on the battlefield, and nutrition is necessary to create a muscular physique. The Holy Warriors until today have included many men of delicate features, but there aren't any negative repercussions to a well-developed physical presence. That said, of course, Naotsugu Toudou isn't even a man.

Rabi cracks the whip in her hand against the table and delivers an assertion, a decree. She states that they must all have confidence in order for the apprehension in their hearts to disappear. She also details how her brute of a boss will tear her in half if they don't suck it up.

"Don't say you can't take any more—you must force it down! I've already told you, judging solely from your gap in life force, this is practically nothing! If you are given preference, this amount will be easily digested, and you'll be able to store just that much more energy. At that point—you'll be able to fight for days on end without any food or water."

"…If that's true, Rabi then you should prove it by example."

"…No, *you* are the one who must become stronger."

"Ngh…"

Destruction and rebirth. Toudou is not a human of this astral plane. For this reason, she must continue to break down common knowledge.

Life force and an iron will are required to be given preference in this world. If you presume something isn't possible, it never will be. It's likely that the Thirteen Rites of Phimas included such brutal training so that he could destroy his own idea of common sense.

The three ultra rites that Ares came up with are a total mess, but in a sense, they are solid in terms of reason. They would be intolerable for anyone participating but are still better than being forced to face off against Demon Lord Army elites in a swimsuit. That said, everything is proving quite difficult for Sanya in particular…

Aria traces her fingers along her stomach, now fully bloated. "D-did Grace really face this exact same training?" she asks, clearly in pain.

"Of course she did. Grace could consume ten times this much

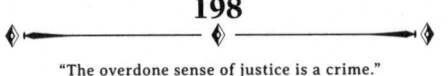

food without even batting an eye." At this point, Rabi is making things up as she goes.

"...What a monster." Limis shudders.

If Limis has the capacity to crack jokes, she can definitely still eat more. It'll take a bit longer before Eve gets the caldera and waterfall ready. Rabi re-grips the whip in her hand and turns on the overbearing boss attitude.

"Keep eating while offering up prayer and hope until this food becomes your flesh and blood—next you three will be blasted by fire while a waterfall rushes down upon you! If you can't resist through your life force, you will die."

"...This is your idea...of prayer?"

"Keep your eyes forward, on the prize! You are the Holy Warrior! This is divine providence!"

The girls cannot be restored to normalcy. Making a shorter path to increased strength requires casting something else aside.

Toudou grabs her fork with restored conviction and starts shoveling piles of meat into her mouth with abandon. Aria and Limis also start falling on the plates of meat again, like zombies. Leadership is affecting them positively, in this case. At this rate, they might be able to attain preference over the food in front of them before too long. However, attaining preference through life force alone is quite difficult.

This is the first step of all first steps. Establishing preference over food, which has no consciousness, is one thing, but establishing it in the face of a demon with innately high life force since birth is a whole new level of difficulty. When two living beings come face-to-face and their life forces collide, the baseline of their life forces shift to become relative. Without an extremely high level, the human being in this equation will be taken advantage of.

In order to push back against this, Toudou and company must become familiar with exercising their life forces. The training they're currently undergoing—pushing themselves to the brink of death—will allow their survival instincts to catalyze their life force to protect their bodies. What they're experiencing is something similar to the human fight-or-flight response.

...Did Ares maybe get stronger this way—?

Just when Toudou was considering the idea, Eve and Grace enter the room, looking exhausted. Their preparations are complete. Toudou and company have just put down their forks. They've eaten enough for the time being.

Rabi takes the blindfolds out of her pocket and stares at Toudou with a wicked smile, the corners of her mouth upturned ever so slightly.

The three ultra rites of Phimas—no, of Ares—shall now begin.

§ § §

"I've heard all the details from Amelia. You're pulling the most ridiculous stunts, as usual."

"Faith is fostered over long periods of time. Acquiring it in a shortened time frame requires stirring the pot. The ends justify the means. If the Holy Warrior acquires more power, we should be satisfied. Isn't that right, Creio?"

Even as Creio admonishes me, I'm formulating a plan. The dice have already been cast.

The best method for carrying out an over-the-top plan is to purposefully not ask your superior for their opinion. Manipulating the system with faith as the backbone of our plan isn't something that Creio could ever approve of, given his position, but an arrow drawn from the quiver and launched cannot be put back.

In all honesty, the three ultra rites of Phimas are quite a feat of strength. The official Thirteen Rites had the potential to wipe Toudou out, but the rites I've devised could theoretically lead to an abasement of the Church's authority.

Nonetheless, my duty is to enable Toudou to defeat the Demon Lord. The Church's quibbling over faith is none of my concern.

"...Hmph... When put that way, yes, everything is the guidance of

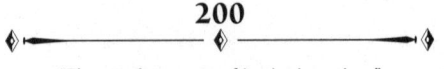

"The overdone sense of justice is a crime."

God, I suppose. We must remain prepared. And...did you manage to come up with a name for this plan? That's always been your greatest shortcoming, Ares."

I hang up the call without saying anything more. By "remain prepared," Creio certainly meant conjuring a proper excuse for the moment when the three ultra rites of Phimas are cast into the light. If the training Toudou undertakes is exposed as a hastily condensed version of the actual rites, we'll all face a litany of trouble. In order to avoid this, we'll need to infiltrate the Church's inner circle with a proper, convincing excuse beforehand.

I am perfectly capable of putting faith second in order to complete our mission, but Creio is almost always stuck in his realist ways.

Our plan was a last-minute pinch hit, but it's actually coming along nicely. Rabi, Grace, and company will guide Toudou while Sanya acts to procure necessary items and implements. Amelia is in charge as liaison with the Church through communication magic, and Stey will leverage her father's authority to acquire necessary funds. Members of the Church and Ruxe will work to ascertain the Demon Lord Army's movements. I've pushed Spica as far away as possible to make sure she doesn't say anything unnecessary. I will oversee the entire affair, and in the end, if Toudou comes out with more strength than now, everything should be perfect.

Just then, Rabi returns for a regular report. She clearly left the actual training site in Eve's and Grace's hands.

"Everything going well?"

"Right. It's not going well, boss. Toudou is still alive, of course, but he's having a rough time. I believe he'll more or less harness his life force—but whether he'll acquire true faith remains extremely dubious. Objectively speaking, boss, this training you devised looks incredibly...strange."

"He'll acquire that faith one way or another when he fulfills the last rite: encountering God."

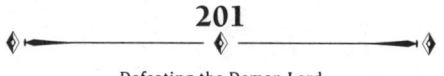

In all honesty—as long as Toudou learns how to exercise his life force, he can still grow. Holy energy isn't an absolute must. What we need right now most urgently isn't holy energy for Toudou but rather an outward-facing level of persuasive power that will turn the Church elites.

Of course, a boost to Toudou's faith at the same time would be even better...

Rabi sighs briefly and stares up at me.

"Never mind receiving instruction from an oracle—what do you intend to do about saving one hundred thousand people and receiving instruction from ten high priests?"

The three ultra rites of Phimas are just for appearances' sake. Toudou doesn't need to accomplish all thirteen original rites, but it does need to look like he did. I've already taken this into consideration, of course.

"We'll get ten individuals who are each worth ten thousand people."

"What?"

"All ten of them will be saved by Toudou, and when they become high priests, we'll take care of both stipulations at once."

"...???"

One hundred thousand people is simply too many. Phimas couldn't possibly have counted every last person he saved, anyway...

The relic can be acquired through Grace and given to Toudou, and for the sacred beast, we'll paint Glacia white. For spiritual discipline of the inner self... Well... That will come later. Our biggest concern right now is whether we can pull all this off before the parade.

Rabi was silent for a while but now pipes up again with trepidation.

"...Boss, is there a chance you've been completely broken by work?"

"Play it cool, Rabi. You need to convince Toudou that everything you tell him is accurate—obvious, even. Your level is much higher than his; if you put your mind to it, you can pull this off. Show him exactly how to wield his life force."

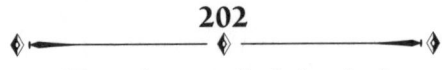

"The overdone sense of justice is a crime."

Third Report: On Utilizing an Ancient Legend

"...Yessir! Erm, boss."

What we really need now is a procedure, a flow. We're using honorable, distinguished methods to enact honorable, distinguished rituals, and as a result, we will absolutely acquire honorable, distinguished power. That's all there is to it.

"Ares, it's ready."

At that moment, the door opens wide. Glacia enters the room with Amelia holding her hand and pulling her in. Except Glacia's hair isn't the usual green shade—it's now white as the driven snow. As I furrow my brow and observe, Glacia shudders, and she shows an expression of fear. I step closer to her and take her long, wavy hair in my hand. Perhaps because she was formerly a glacial dragon, her hair is cool to the touch and heavy. The color is perfectly natural on her—it's not white from old age, and something about it feels magical.

"Do you like it, Ares?" Amelia asks. "We used a magic concoction from the Church's stockpile."

"The color is spot-on, but she looks too raggedy. I want her in something that screams 'sacred beast' from a mere glance. We can't change who she is, so we need to make up for it with her appearance. Get her a robe embroidered with golden thread. She'll be in Toudou's party for a long time; her armaments should be adequately powerful, too. Work with Stey to throw something together. Cardinal Veronide is a former merchant, so he ought to have a few ideas."

"...Boss, I really respect how you always manage to take advantage of every option available."

Don't even start!

Glacia's face is worn with fear, anxiety, and impudence. I grip her by the cheeks and pull, just a bit. Her eyes fill with tears, and I can feel her muscles tense.

At this rate, I suppose I don't need to worry about her betraying us. If she did, and came for our heads while we were lulled to sleep, nobody would be laughing.

"Amelia, you're on acting coach duty. You must imbue Glacia with the presence of a sacred beast."

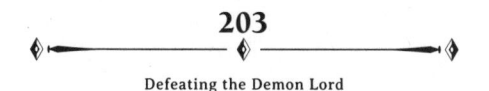

"...Aren't you taking advantage of my convenience just a bit too much?"

"I have faith in you, most talented Amelia."

"...Yessir."

Amelia's eyes are lifeless, and she looks toward Rabi, who also has dead eyes, for confirmation. The two of them take dead-eyed Glacia and leave the room.

Okay—will this strategy prove to be a powerful boon or a wicked stroke of bad luck?

I sigh deeply and take out a mask that I haven't used since we were in the Great Forest of the Vale.

No matter what happens, to overcome the predicament we're in, we'll have to navigate umpteen iterations of the impossible.

§ § §

Toudou's consciousness is flickering. Her breathing is ragged, and she feels like she might vomit at any second. The reason for this is quite obviously the vast amount of food that she forced into her body and down her esophagus just a while earlier.

Her field of vision is wrapped in a deep black, and nary a sliver of light is seeping in. Her arms have been forced behind her back, and she is in handcuffs. She can hear the pained cries of her compatriots all around her, and her heart is laden with tribulations.

Unbelievable... Toudou can't fathom that she was actually forced to eat until her stomach threatened to burst, and now, that she's blindfolded...

What's more, she knew this was going to be absurd training, but Toudou clearly took "eating until her stomach nearly bursts" far too lightly.

The fact that she hasn't vomited yet is a sheer miracle. Is this a result of her taking advantage of her life force? If she were forced into rigorous physical exercise right now, she would absolutely vomit. The only stroke of luck is that she doesn't think she'll be

Third Report: On Utilizing an Ancient Legend

forced to do so until the next rite begins... The next rite is getting blasted by a waterfall in a caldera... Ascetic training under a waterfall.

Toudou is led handcuffed, still blindfolded, into a horse-drawn carriage. Immediately after, her body is rocked by the carriage lurching and shaking fiercely.

Toudou's stomach is sticking out like a balloon after having force-fed herself to the limit. She's in so much pain she can't even think straight. She is absolutely committed to not vomiting. This is the only thing that Toudou can think about right now. If she vomits, her pride as the Holy Warrior will be smashed to smithereens.

"Ungh... Blech... I'm gonna puke—"

"Ngh... Ugh..."

Limis's and Aria's pained cries are on par with Toudou's. Regarding where they're being taken, they weren't told a specific location. It would appear that the church has a secret training ground, but can a caldera and a waterfall both truly exist in the same location?

After mitigating her pain through prayer while being rocked back and forth by the ride, the horse-drawn carriage finally comes to a stop after a few minutes.

"Here we are," Rabi announces.

Holding her stomach and gasping for breath, Toudou asks, "Unghecch... Huh...? A-aren't we...still in the...capital?"

"...No need for further questions," Rabi replies indifferently. "By the grace of the God of Order, Ahz Gried, anything is possible."

"D-does 'anything'...include...a caldera?"

"......It does!"

"No way... I've never...heard of...such a thing..."

Limis and Toudou clearly feel the same way about the situation. Rabi sounds exceptionally sure of herself, but no matter what world they are living in, and despite the most powerful nature of the almighty God they are following, making a caldera from nothing just isn't normal.

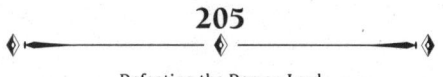

However, their messenger is an envoy from the Church. Followers of Ahz Gried are reported to never lie. Rabi isn't exactly a priest, but nor is she a bald-faced liar.

Toudou hears a heavy metal *clang* of a bolt being opened. Her blindfold still blocks any shred of light from entering her vision—something that would've normally caused her great anxiety if she wasn't stuffed to the gills.

A door opens with an audible *creak*, and then—a powerful blast of heat and thunderous noise rocks Toudou's entire being. For a brief instant, the air is knocked from Toudou's lungs, and even the pain in her stomach disappears. The deafening sound rocks Toudou like a massive slap, and her whole body instantly becomes soaking wet, as if she swam in the ocean. The sound was unmistakably the rush of a waterfall, crashing down against a voluminous body of water.

That means... This heat... Can it be...?

"We have arrived. This is the training ground that serves as the true foundation of the three ultra rites of Phimas. Unfortunately, because you will be fighting against darkness, we cannot remove your blindfold—but you understand, right? You can see it, yes, in your mind's eye? The waterfall blasting your body and the roiling caldera of lava!!"

Eve has been waiting at the site for them. "...Y-yes," she says. "I can see it—in my mind's eye."

There isn't any way a caldera could be so close... But there is the precedent of the magic item that allows the user to teleport to a training site that Toudou used at the Friedia home. Toudou can't personally see it in her mind's eye, however; that's far too advanced for her—

"A cal...dera...?"

"Yes, a caldera."

"I-it...doesn't smell bad, though."

"...That's just the type of caldera it is."

"...Y-yes, that's—exactly the type—of caldera—this is."

The door shuts behind them with a heavy *thud*. Fresh air ceases

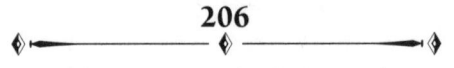

"The overdone sense of justice is a crime."

Third Report: On Utilizing an Ancient Legend

to enter the room, and the effective temperature inside instantly soars. Toudou's entire body starts oozing globs of sweat. The heat and humidity are nearly unbearable—a veritable sauna.

Toudou didn't exactly feel great to begin with, and this is the worst. The food she forced down just earlier is now nearly at her throat. Regardless, Rabi clearly doesn't have any intention of showing Toudou, who is being attacked by misery on all sides, even a shred of mercy.

For the record, Toudou remains the Holy Warrior who will save the world. Despite the fact that Rabi looks sweet and lovable, apparently, she's an old-school medieval slave driver at heart.

"Beginning now, Toudou, you will be blasted by a red-hot waterfall while standing in a pool of lava. A human of meager faith would melt in mere seconds. But if you continue praying fervently, you will escape unscathed."

"?! Buh?! What?? You're joking—I was told about the waterfall, but not about any roiling lava!"

"If you clear your mind of mundane thoughts, the fire will be pleasantly cool. Continue to pray while being pushed to the utmost limit, and when you reach the border of life and death, you will learn of the true darkness in your own heart. When you overcome it, you will become one step closer to walking with God."

This is preposterous beyond belief. Toudou knows that she's become significantly stronger with time, but this is not something that can be withstood just through prayer. Or do people in this world simply swim in lava without dying on the regular?

Right now, Toudou can't see the faces of her compatriots who have helped her through every tight situation they've encountered on their journey. An inexplicable, loathsome anxiety racks her being. While lost in the darkness, Toudou won't know up from down or left from right. At that moment, Rabi softly rests her hand on Toudou's shoulder.

"Safe travels, Holy Warrior," she says, her voice unreasonably gentle.

She then shoves Toudou, and the thick, roiling lava envelops the Holy Warrior's entire body.

§ § §

"Gngggghh...?! So...hot... Aargh...!"

"Owww—it burns...!"

"What the—?!"

The room is faintly lit. Against the ferocious thunder of water crashing, short, stifled cries reverberate. This is one of the three ultra rites of Phimas—the rite of supplication. This training intends to temper the Holy Warrior's foundation, their holy energy, by never forgetting prayer to their God, no matter the circumstances. However, as a knight of the glorious holy knight order—one selected for their talent as the right-hand woman of the knight of legend—watches the scene before her, she can only see it as a grand farce.

An impromptu pool prepared in haste has been filled with a special heated slime. The "waterfall" cascading incessantly into the pool is simply hot water, and even an average person could handle it without severe difficulty.

Within the Church of Ahz Gried, there is a remarkably special division—those tasked with fighting against the forces of darkness, called crusaders. For these members of the Church, fallacy that would never be accepted for normal followers of the God of Order is allowed. This, however, is extremely unlike any Church-affiliated training she's seen thus far.

The Holy Warrior is doing everything she can to withstand the hot water cascading upon her like a waterfall. Heat whirls around her entire being. Her face and extremities are swollen red from the extreme temperature, and her expression is contorted in pain.

However, this is not all a result of her prayer. The slime pool that Eve reluctantly sourced per Ares's demand wouldn't cause any severe physical damage without a prolonged exposure to such a temperature.

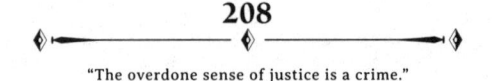

"The overdone sense of justice is a crime."

Third Report: On Utilizing an Ancient Legend

It's thick and gooey, which is similar to lava, in a way? And then there's the waterfall of scalding hot water. If Eve was the one undergoing this ascetic training, her expression wouldn't have changed one bit.

Rabi Chatre, who Eve has been assigned to work alongside, is supporting the Holy Warrior in a tone so monotonous, it sounds like she's reading from a script.

"That's great, Toudou! Your prayers are wonderful. You're really holding your own against that lava."

"Ngh... So hot... But...I can handle it... Also, um...is this...actually lava?"

"What else could it possibly be?!"

The special blindfold used on Toudou is made for Church rites, and it doesn't let in a single strand of light. Directly confronting darkness means coming face-to-face with one's own soul. Even knowing this, seeing Toudou and the others blindfolded and standing in this pool makes Eve chortle. No matter how much presence of faith one manages to obtain, resisting actual lava is no small feat. Anyone would melt instantly.

Eve shoots a quick glance at her superior, Grace, who stands solemnly next to her. Is this really going to suffice? Doesn't this blatantly violate their creed? Seeing Eve, clearly highly invested in the situation, Grace turns her head slightly to the side.

...There isn't anything that can be done.

Falling in line under Ares Crown is an order from Cardinal Creio, and subordination is not permitted. As long as this is true, Grace, who is under his direct control, is assumed to be in agreement as well, and Eve, who is a pious follower of her God, must also fall in line.

Eve's lack of experience must be to blame for why she's so dreadfully uncomfortable during these rites.

"...Pray as hard as you can! Cast aside worldly desires and embrace your faith in God!"

"Mmph...!"

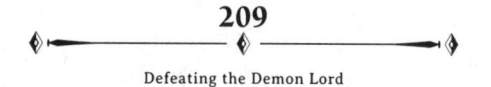

The Holy Warrior grits her teeth at Eve's deprecating, desperate rebuke.

At the end of the day, does this training have any real meaning, despite Ares's claim that the prayer-related rites would all be consolidated? To be honest, substituting fasting for stuffing oneself to the gills is entirely problematic to begin with, but this rite can scatter the suffering across too many factors, and Toudou can't focus on each of them properly. At current, the Holy Warrior has no way to experience the true terror of darkness. She's far too busy with all five of her senses.

And if the rites of prayer have been ameliorated (are they really better?) like this, then how the rest of the rites will turn out is a cause for tremendous anxiety.

The Holy Warrior, Limis, and Aria are all bloodred in the face. This isn't the result of sheer pain but simply exposure to hot water. The slime pool and red-hot waterfall would be nothing more than a pretty damn hot bath to any individual of even moderate level.

This is absolutely not what Eve had in mind when proposing the Thirteen Rites of Phimas... Inconsolable emotion wells up in her chest.

Suddenly, Rabi calls out, "Please continue to pray just like that for a while. Without ceasing—at the end of your training, you all will be recognized by the great God of Order and receive his divine protection and power, that much is certain!"

"G-go...God?"

"You're just making stuff up!"

"Guh... I've never heard the God of Order making anyone do something like this!"

"Silence! You know nothing! Besides, it's not like I'm here because I want to be!"

Rabi herself doesn't know the next thing about the God of Order. And she really let her true feelings slip there at the end.

She starts waving toward the back of the room occasionally and walking forward. Eve follows, holding her breath so that the hero's party doesn't notice her while they undergo their training.

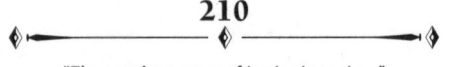

210

"The overdone sense of justice is a crime."

Third Report: On Utilizing an Ancient Legend

§ § §

A mercenary serves a totally different function than a knight. A knight is predicated on loyalty, while a mercenary is nothing more than a piece on the board. Mercenaries have no need for loyalty. For example, no matter how moronic the order, the only thing expected of a mercenary is the capacity to execute without fail, like a machine. Of course, a mercenary needs a proper head on their shoulders, but any superfluous reservations will only serve to shorten their lifespan.

The current task at hand requires far more intelligence than strength. In terms of ease of use as a mercenary, Sanya is far easier to employ than Rabi, but she also lacks observational skills. The current order from her superior is to guide Toudou to become even more deserving of the title Holy Warrior. For this quite peculiar task, Rabi, who values silence, is obviously more suitable.

Eve opens her eyes wide and reacts as expected.

"What?! Just what does—that mean, precisely?"

"Hush. Toudou and the others will notice us."

Rabi puts a finger to her lips, and Eve quickly lowers her voice.

"B-but... That is s-simply a ridiculous—proposal, don't you think...? We are already participating in deception, but to lower the temperature of the hot water slowly—as they continue to pray... Unfathomable."

Of course, it's beyond absurd. The entire point of this training is for Toudou to become stronger, but they're already putting the cart before the horse. That said, Rabi's employer isn't the Church—it's Ares. As a boss, he would never make meaningless demands.

"......My boss believes that mental state greatly influences physical condition."

"To a certain extent, maybe, yes."

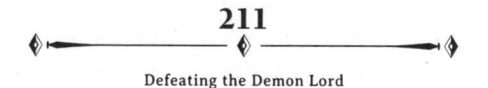

"...Toudou is under the God of Order's divine protection. In our battle against demonic forces, we have an extremely powerful source of backup... My boss doesn't doubt Toudou's strength, even for a moment. Right now, our main priorities are healing Toudou's fatigued mind and acquiring the trust of the boorish, uncivilized aristocrats of Ruxe, according to him."

It's all about results. Above everything else, all they need is to produce results. In the off chance that Eve gets skittish and runs for the hills, the responsibility will lie with Rabi, who's been given direct control. In response to Rabi's words, which were intended to win over the holy knight, Eve bites her lip in frustration.

"...If that is Ex Deus's intention...then I shall prepare accordingly."

Eve leaves the room in haste. The building the Church prepared for the training rites was a rush construction job. They filled a pool with special slime, and from above, borrowing the power of mages, they made a waterfall of hot water a reality. With the lights turned off, heat has filled the interior of the room, but without a blindfold over Toudou's eyes, getting her to believe this is an honorable, distinguished training ground would have been impossible.

Eve's direct supervisor, Grace Godicent Trinity, has not flinched one single iota at the current state of affairs. Just what is she thinking? Her expression is hidden by the lacquer-black helmet covering her face. But even if she wasn't wearing a helmet, her expression could still be completely blank underneath. Species of beings deemed to live for such a long time often have their emotions gradually worn down to next to nothing over the span of their lives.

Continuing to fight since ancient mythological time immemorial until the modern era—this epic feat simply can't be accomplished while remaining fully sane. If Rabi was in the same position, she would have turned away in disgust and run away forever.

"Lady Grace. If you have anything to say...I will happily convey it to my boss. You are able to communicate through writing, yes?"

Rabi and Sanya's boss, who put them in this foul situation, has clearly acknowledged Grace's superior position. Taking a denizen of ancient legend and asking them to participate in rites that undermine sacred doctrine...that seriously takes nerves of steel.

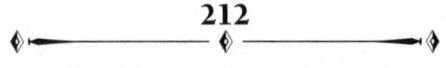

"The overdone sense of justice is a crime."

Third Report: On Utilizing an Ancient Legend

Rabi's proposal to Grace was only half-baked. Grace remains silent for some time before shaking her head to the side and trudging out of the room with heavy steps.

§ § §

While communicating with the Church and the Kingdom, I continue to guide our plan along with care. It's been a number of days since the three ultra rites of Phimas have commenced. It's a miracle, but the situation is proceeding smoothly. Thanks to borrowing the talents of the knight of legend, we are receiving top-notch evaluation from the aristocrats. Distrust in the Holy Warrior has been largely assuaged. In this case in particular, this is the result of trust that the Church has built over the years—authority, as it's called.

Our first order of business is to raise the name value of the Holy Warrior. Their name embodies hope and will also become the supporting pillar for all of humanity. However, conversely, a hero whose name has become known will not be forgiven in defeat; a hero who is known can never return to their former self. The Holy Warrior precisely embodies the concept of a double-edged sword.

As the night falls into deep darkness, Sanya, who I have given a number of tasks, returns. Sanya's role includes surveying and procurement of items, alongside speaking with mercenary acquaintances to seek their cooperation. Perhaps due to the singularly physical nature of the duties she's taken on, the exhaustion on her face is palpable.

"I'm back... I talked to a bunch of people. There's about ten on standby. It's a good part-time gig for most. It was an easy sell once I told them the Church would be offering a stipend."

"Nice work. What about things with the aristocrats?"

"...No way I could do that by myself. By the way, it's only a rumor, but apparently, a bunch of these aristocrats are real hard asses. Sign of the times, I guess... Still, I doubt any of them would get involved with demonic forces."

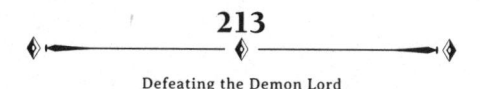

Sanya shrugs and grabs a glass of water off the table in front of her, downing it in one go. Wiping her mouth with her sleeve, she sighs shortly.

"I mean, betraying humanity for demonkind isn't even a profitable deal. The entire Kingdom would be destroyed, and then what are the aristocrats gonna do? History will tell you that much."

"...Yeah, you're right."

Demons look down upon humanity. Even if someone betrayed the Kingdom and collaborated with the Demon Lord to destroy our world, they'd be left all alone, without a single backer. Talk about all pain, no gain. There have been examples in history of those who betrayed humans to successfully participate in the Demon Lord's malfeasance, but they were instantly slaughtered, alongside their entire family and kin. These past Demon Lords in question were likely not very intelligent. There isn't any question that this betrayal has effectively precluded the Demon Lord's invasion in our current age. What's more, because the demonic forces know of this history, they are unlikely to approach humanity to make any sort of deal.

I furrow my brow deeply.

"...That said, the party in question could lead the demonic forces in without ever knowing their true identity."

"...Well, I guess...that could be true, but..."

The Demon Lord's army can employ innumerable forms of mimicry, and some demons have the capacity to transform into humans. The Kingdom is vigilantly aware of this fact, but even without using mimicry, there are demons that simply look human to begin with, and there is also ample possibility of species in the Demon Lord's underling's ranks that don't necessarily look like enemies to the general public, like Rabi and Sanya.

Further, even if they don't directly betray humanity, there will always be someone who leaks information. Trying to investigate every last possibility would prove endless and futile, but in terms of just during the parade, for a few short hours, we should be able to stay on top of it.

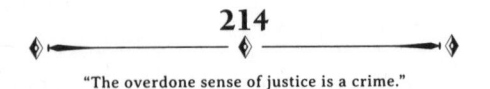

"The overdone sense of justice is a crime."

Third Report: On Utilizing an Ancient Legend

"If the Demon Lord Kranos is an intelligent being, he will attempt to infiltrate the parade behind our backs by sending insurgents. We will monitor all access points to the city. If you notice anyone that seems out of place, make sure it's reported immediately."

From Kranos's perspective, Heljarl's death must have been unexpected... The chances of someone under the Demon Lord's control already infiltrating the capital are low. On the other hand, if a lower-ranked monster has snuck in as a human being without causing a huge ruckus, we could be in for a world of trouble. There are always exceptions to the rule—for example, a demon that has been a part of human society for a long time.

Security at the parade is founded on the prestige of the Church and the Kingdom. They won't deploy soldiers in formation because it's bad optics, but the greatest extent of precaution possible will be rolled out across the capital. The Demon Lord Army directly attacking the parade in great numbers will not be possible. An assassination attempt in smaller numbers could be, however. Or perhaps I'm just reading a bit too far into things...

I take a moment to reassess my train of thought.

"We don't necessarily need to remove them immediately. If the Holy Warrior can suppress an outside enemy at the same time, their grand reveal will be of immaculate acclaim."

"...Boss, are you truly a man of the cloth?"

If the parade is attacked and Toudou can repel the enemy, it would be the greatest display of a hero's strength possible. We fully plan on making Toudou's newfound strength through Grace's instruction as widely known as possible, but having him involved in a sensational incident would make things even more convenient.

That said, bringing in a monster from our end, which we considered initially, would certainly be in poor taste. We have gone to great lengths to bring out Grace and restore trust in the Church, so we don't need to go overboard. In the off chance that this was outed as part of the Church's playbook, we'd be in a heap of trouble.

We need to aim for the greatest risk-reward outcome possible.

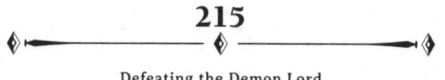

"Hmm... Okay then. Sanya, I have your next task. Devise an attack against the Holy Warrior and covertly recruit the participants."

"...Are you serious?"

"Don't misunderstand. They won't actually attack Toudou. We just need them to agree to cooperate."

The Demon Lord Kranos is likely smarter than we realize. Even if he is assumed to attack the parade, we need contingency plans.

Sanya is looking at me coldly, and I grip her by the shoulder, peering deep into her eyes, searching for something. Sanya is a proud and capable warrior of silverwolf werebeast lineage. The Demon Lord has many worshippers among werebeast species, but I can trust Sanya.

"When one of Kranos's underlings infiltrates, they will attempt to contact others with influence in the antihero crowd. If you think you can lead them on, you are to do so, and if that seems tricky, you will get rid of them beforehand."

"...Gehhh... Just hearing you say that, my ass is already in pain. I've been employed by many different people thus far, but even the most coldhearted among them never made such an outrageous order. Just who do you think I am?"

Sanya is talking tough right now, but her silverwolf instincts will guide her to obey her boss. As long as they have your trust, these werebeasts are exceptionally faithful. Yet under the service of the Demon Lord, they would be far more troublesome than she's ever been.

While she is definitely complaining, Sanya doesn't show any sign of trembling in fear like Rabi.

"Don't think that supporting the Holy Warrior in defeating the Demon Lord is just some average request. Go. Now. If something happens, I'll send backup."

"Yes, boss. Pretty unreal, we're worked to the bone without a second to spare... What happens if I create a group to attack our hero, but the Demon Lord's inferior never approaches us to make contact?"

"The overdone sense of justice is a crime."

Third Report: On Utilizing an Ancient Legend

I furrow my brow in response. "Didn't I tell you to get rid of them?"

With only minimal instigation, anyone who would join a group planning to attack the Holy Warrior, an individual personally summoned by the Church, would only become a nuisance if left alive. As often happens, minute details like these will eventually pile up and make or break the final outcome.

Sanya shudders from head to toe. "......Boss, you're less of a pontificate and more like a leader of organized crime."

My order must have resonated with her, because Sanya then breaks into a smile.

Pontificate, mob boss—they're really one in the same here. We are definitive enemies of Demon Lord Kranos. I'm trying my damndest to make Toudou into a proper Holy Warrior, so as far as Kranos is concerned, I truly am a leader of organized crime.

§ § §

Just how long has this confinement lasted?

A windowless, shutoff room. The only sounds come from the sole prisoner. He's to the point of losing his sanity. His strength is at bare minimum; if he were injured in his current state, he wouldn't be able to regenerate on his own.

At first, he summoned every last mote of strength and intelligence to escape the shackles that bind him, but it was impossible. The specially made shackles have sealed away his strength, preventing him from so much as conjuring a spell. He was already weakened after his defeat in battle. Even an undying demon cannot manifest their powers without sustenance.

After such a long time without the faintest inkling of someone coming to check on him, he realized that the head of the family didn't intend to simply castigate or kill him, but rather keep him locked up interminably. His powers are bound, and he cannot escape, nor does he have any means of sustaining himself.

Left alone to weaken and rot, being forced to stare his reality dead in the eyes—this is a hell that could only be conjured by another vampire. They are a special species of demons in this world who possess supernatural powers. Among them, some who have existed since antiquity are well known as particularly resented enemies of the Church of Ahz Gried.

Fahni—it's neither a first nor a second name, but rather a single word representative of a vampire in the truest sense. These ferociously powerful vampires of old had never once joined forces with any Demon Lords, so when word got out that one such vampire was working with the Demon Lord Kranos, that led many to believe that these ancient beings were at last on the decline—yet their power has not waned one iota.

Zarpahn Drago Fahni may have exhausted much of his power during the battle in the Great Forest of the Vale, but he stands in the evil gods' favor and has killed more people than anyone else. The Demon Lord Kranos took a particular shine to him, even among the many members of the Fahni bloodline. But now, to think that he was so easily captured…

He closes his eyes, and the only thing that enters his mind's eye is his battle against the Holy Warrior. Zarpahn was ill prepared back then. His powers were also not at full capacity. When they meet again, oh yes—then he will be ready.

Zarpahn continues suppressing the urge to scream, swallowing his roiling emotions. He uses the last of his withered powers to maintain consciousness as it threatens to fade. He must avoid consuming any more energy. If the Fahni vampires wanted to kill Zarpahn, they would have most certainly already done it. They're no fools; no Fahni would do something like this just to push Zarpahn's buttons.

Just how many times has it been? he asks himself, his breath ragged. Then his ears suddenly start ringing.

"Zarpahn. Zarpahn Drago Fahni."

A distant, disinterested female voice echoes in his head. Zarpahn is momentarily convinced he's lost his mind, but that is not the case.

"The overdone sense of justice is a crime."

Third Report: On Utilizing an Ancient Legend

A chill runs through his entire body. This sudden impulse, strong enough to bring him to his knees, is proof positive that this voice comes from the source of the blood running through his veins, the source of his power.

Fahni, the storied Vampire Lord, speaks without any regard for the position Zarpahn is in.

"Orders from Kranos: You have one last chance—one last opportunity to kill the Holy Warrior."

"An...oppor...tunity...?"

"So you are still lucid... I despise ineptitude, but I despise you even more. It's as if I'm looking at the person I once was long ago."

At last—the time is ripe. Time for revenge. Zarpahn's strength, on the verge of withering away for good, just barely returns. The shackles that hold him down shatter and break away, allowing the magical power that had been forced into nonexistence to once again well within him.

Zarpahn rubs his limbs, then licks his parched lips. Familial hatred. What absolute perfection. Zarpahn can't help but respect his Fahni kin, yet he abhors them so. Someday, somehow, he will overcome the urge to kill.

Zarpahn will tear his vampiric progenitor limb from limb and force them to kneel before him. Yet he will need the Demon Lord's help to see it happen.

To make the true lord of all vampires—one who fought and survived longer than any other—submit to Zarpahn, he will need—

"The Holy Warrior will take part in a grand reveal in Ruxe. That is where you will strike. This time, with everything you've got."

The voice disappears after saying everything it had to say. Silence again falls over the room.

Fahni didn't mention what will happen to Zarpahn if he fails in his mission. There's no need; the consequences are that clear.

Zarpahn, of course, intends to put every ounce of his being into this newfound opportunity, without needing to be told so. As much as he loathes Fahni, the Holy Warrior is even more loathsome.

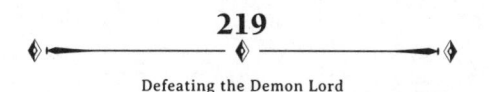

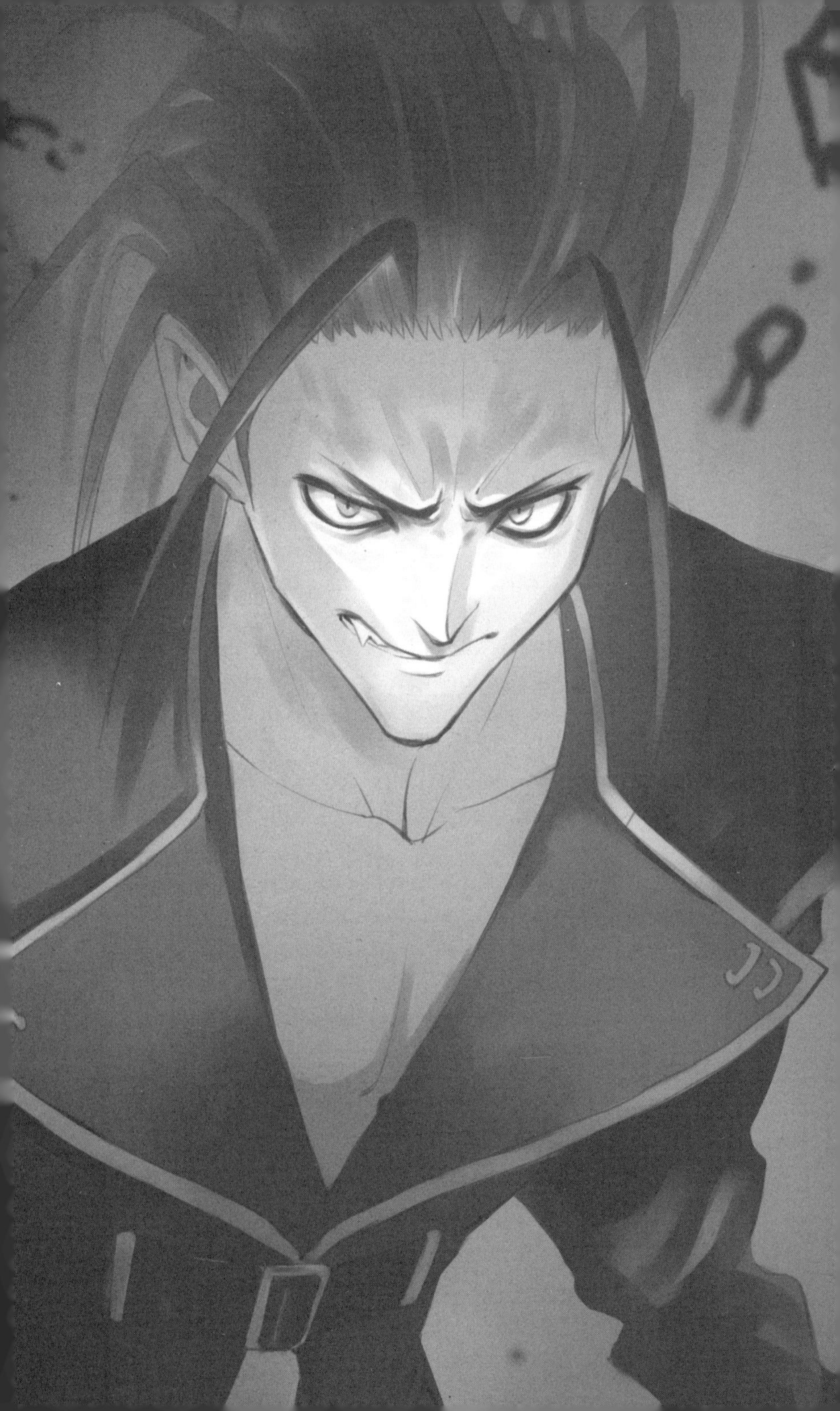

Third Report: On Utilizing an Ancient Legend

Being trifled with by the freshly summoned Holy Warrior who was merely slaying monsters in the Great Forest of the Vale to level up... It's the failure of a lifetime.

His time has come. Zarpahn will turn the Holy Warrior's parade into a masquerade of bloody mayhem, and by borrowing the power of the Demon Lord's army, kill Fahni. Then Zarpahn will become lord. Through the divine protection and favor of Lucief Arept, God of Darkness, Zarpahn Drago Fahni will accomplish this goal.

Zarpahn laughs deeply, with gusto, and conjures an incantation through the magical powers that have just been freely restored to him.

The entire room warps into a frenetic haze. All that remains is darkness.

Fourth Report

On Encountering God

Toudou overcame the climax of pain and suffering on day three. On day four, her concentration increased even further, and it felt like the waterfall of hot water was emanating a certain spiritual presence.

The most terrifying aspect is Toudou's level of concentration. While stimulated on all sides by innumerable different sensations, most people would not be able to maintain focus. Yet due to level of life force, there is a sense of superiority that is dependent on force of will. In this sense, the Holy Warrior is nothing more than a ball of potential power.

One week has passed since the rite of supplication commenced—one part of the three ultra rites of Phimas. When Eve enters the locked room to ascertain the situation, she whispers, astonished, "It can't be... This is absurd...!"

"...Did something unexpected happen?"

"......Toudou's holy energy—it's rising. Visibly. I can—see it."

"...Huh? Are you joking?"

At Eve's unexpected proclamation, Rabi's eyes are wide as saucers. For a moment, she assumes it's a joke. Yet hearing Eve's tone, and realizing how hard it was for her to actually say it, Rabi realizes she's being serious.

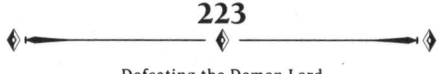

The ascetic training that Rabi and company have assigned to Toudou is certainly meant to raise her to a level far beyond any priest. That said, not a single one among them actually believed it would have a positive effect. According to Ares, the originator of the idea, it wouldn't work.

For a person of strong faith, the current result is hard to digest. Eve looks like she just woke from a horrible nightmare and speaks again, frantically trying to control her breathing.

"Can this really be the guidance—of God...?"

"...The perfect example of truth coming from falsehood."

Rabi bores her gaze into the door. Her refined auditory perception can discern the hiss of steam rising in the room alongside the hot water crashing to the ground. She can also hear Toudou and the others gritting their teeth. Does Toudou really believe that lava is the source of fire? The blindfold has worked perfectly. She is now barely conscious. There is a high chance that she believes everything is very real.

At any rate, Toudou's holy energy actually rising is an unforeseen silver lining. The goal of the three ultra rites of Phimas isn't to directly increase Toudou's strength, but the stronger she can become, the fewer tasks that Rabi and company will have to take on in the future.

"Toudou appears to be maintaining ample concentration. We might be ready to advance to the next level. Ares Crown has expressed his desire for all three rites to be completed as quickly as possible, after all."

Eve doesn't even feign to hide her frustration. Her words are rife with irony. They are trying to compress what would normally take over ten years into a single month's time... Completing the training quickly isn't even a point of discussion.

The three ultra rites of Phimas are broken into three stages: supplication, alms, and accession. Supplication boosts faith, the rite of alms establishes virtue, and the rite of accession sublimates human character to be closer to God.

The rite of supplication has effectively concluded. Next is the rite of alms. Prayer through the rite of supplication took one week,

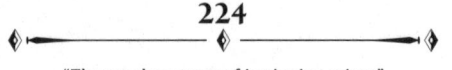

"The overdone sense of justice is a crime."

Fourth Report: On Encountering God

meaning they have three weeks left. Rabi doesn't know what the next rite will entail—because Ares hasn't even decided yet. It will be utterly incoherent and banal, that much she is sure of...

In that moment, an inexplicable sense of malaise suddenly racks Rabi. She twitches her ears and looks all around her. This sensation—yes, it's very similar to what she felt when she realized that Grace is indeed aging...

Rabi's master, the famous mercenary Bran Chatre, never opposed the Church of Ahz Gried. He is one of many who lay claim to innumerable followers of the God of Order throughout this world, expanding beyond the borders of individual kingdoms. Judging from her boss, Ares, and his level of strength, she had an inkling thus far, but it turns out that the Church of Ahz Gried is somehow just different from other religious organizations.

Rabi has confidence in her own strength, but she can't even compare with the Church, which very likely possesses more battle prowess than an entire kingdom. She is very fortunate to have ever met Ares. That helped her realize that she must never oppose the Church. As long as she continues to display her usefulness and doesn't act to betray, Rabi's safety will remain guaranteed for the near future.

"?! What?! Are you—serious?!"

"God saves those who are at risk of being lost."

Eve's expression only becomes more rigid as the conversation goes on, while Ares nonchalantly shrugs.

The rite of alms that Ares concocted is another level of insanity, even compared to the now completed rite of supplication. Ares's wicked gaze belies his status as priest once again. The order coming from him, a corrupt priest that simply defies description, is wholly sacrilegious. It's truly remarkable that the God of Order has even vested power in a man like this to begin with. Although she doesn't hate Ares, Rabi can't help but feel this way, so how deeply shocked must Eve be?

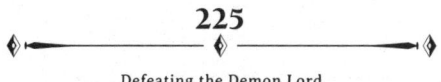

Rabi takes on Ares's deep stare, and her short tail twitches reflexively.

"...Um, yes, if you say so, boss," she replies hurriedly. "That said, I can't guarantee the result. The rite of supplication had meaning in terms of boosting holy energy, but the next rite you've proposed, boss, is quite frankly reckless."

"Our only requirement is finishing this ascetic training as quickly as possible. Do it."

Boss... Eve's expression is getting darker the longer she looks at you.

Although also true of the last rite, this next order is really just grandstanding. The process is given far more consideration than the end result. The Holy Warrior embodies the hope of humanity, but if she turns out to be nothing more than a papier-mâché tiger, the world will be doomed.

"...Understood."

"You're so obedient."

"Well, it's not my life at stake. Plus...I've already made up my mind about you, boss."

Ares nods in satisfaction and snaps his fingers. Ten men and women of all ages enter the room from the back. They are skinny and gaunt, and their shabby appearances make them look like beggars at first glance, but looking closely, it's apparent that every one of them has a powerful light dwelling in their eyes. They're suppressing it, but they're all concealing significant amounts of life force.

"These are the people Sanya recruited, the objects of salvation. Saving one of them is the same as saving ten thousand people. They're like bonus characters."

"Heh-heh... We're pros at gettin' saved."

"The Mercenary Guild of Losers... These guys will take on literally any job you give 'em. You really dug deep for this one, boss."

The Losers are quite famous among mercenary companies. The mercenary crew is full of banned and taboo individuals, and they

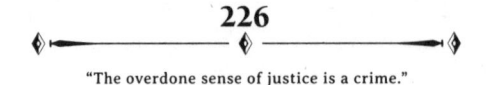

226

"The overdone sense of justice is a crime."

Fourth Report: On Encountering God

don't only offer services in battle; they are a useful outfit that will do absolutely anything asked. Normally, an individual's skills and résumé would be questioned when entering a mercenary guild, but the Losers don't even care. Their average level is pretty low, but in terms of sheer number of members, they are proud to be top class.

"Yeah, and also, they've got a knack for priesthood. Sure, they're useless right now, but with a little salvation, they'll become high priests in short order. Perfect, right?"

"We might not look like it, but we're a shrewd bunch... Heh-heh... By the way, what's the name of your God again?" says a stooped old man. He licks his dry lips with a long tongue and smiles.

Toudou is a total sucker if she's willing to believe that these people are high priests. Individuals who don't even know the name of Ahz Gried have no business being here, and their personalities seem horrible, too.

Eve turns away from the man and starts spasming. A battle between His Eminence's order to follow Ares's demands and her own faith is roiling inside her...

Sheesh, the boss is getting seriously desperate.

Ares turns to Grace, who hasn't even flinched despite the absurdity of the order.

"Grace, use them to their highest potential. You get it, right?"

"Boss, you truly do not know fear..."

His status as upper-echelon crusader aside, it's unbelievable that a priest would take a certified legend and mold it to his own devices.

The color of Eve's face has changed, but Grace simply nods curtly, without any sign of fear. The silent legend and her emotional subordinate. And Rabi, who must somehow control it all immaculately. The road ahead is riddled with grim prospects.

The strategy employed in the water capital was far better. The current plan needs to be laid to rest as soon as possible. As Rabi sighs, one of the Losers—a man—speaks up without even stating his name.

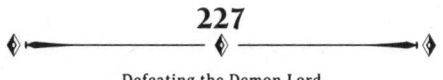

"Mr. Ares, sir, there's a bit of a problem. Not the whole high priest thing, it's just that not a one of us knows how to use holy techniques. How's this gonna work?"

"I'll be assisting you in secret from the shadows."

"……Man, oh man. Well, that's just perfect!"

"I'm sure you know this already, but I'll explain one last time: We won't be tightfisted when it comes time to pay you. So do exactly as you're told."

"…Y-yessir, we're very much aware. That is our sworn duty—!"

Ares might as well have been laying eyes on an enemy—his razor-sharp gaze screams that he doesn't trust a single one of them. The old, bedraggled Loser draws back a little.

When Ares darts his glance toward the door, the Losers get his drift and start filing out of the room quickly. Ares claps his hands together and looks around at Rabi and company before speaking with with utmost seriousness.

"Now begins your duties. Grace, take these people with you and guide Toudou in their salvation. He's saving ten thousand souls through ten people, so one hundred thousand people total. After they achieve salvation, they'll be anointed high priests, thus accomplishing the 'receiving instruction from ten high priests' rite. Once Toudou is successful, you can gift him the summetal armor as a relic. That's four rites down: receiving instruction from an oracle, acquiring a relic, saving one hundred thousand people, and receiving instruction from ten high priests."

It's hard to say so when Ares looks so confident in his decree, but this is truly absurd. He thinks he can just string the numbers together at his whim.

Granted, I'll still do what he asks…

Eve speaks nervously in place of the silent knight Grace.

"………B-by the way, just how much—time do you think—we shall be granted?"

"We've already used up one week. We need to save time for extenuating circumstances. Get it done in five days."

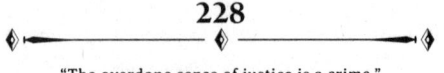

"The overdone sense of justice is a crime."

Fourth Report: On Encountering God

"……"

The color is quickly draining from Eve's face.

Bit by bit, this devout believer's faith in training the Holy Warrior is being whittled away... When all is said and done, will Eve still consider herself a woman of the cloth?

Ares might have pushed her over the edge—Eve is now glowering at him, her mind clearly made up. Just when she opens her mouth to speak, Grace steps forward silently between her and Ares.

"?! Captain Grace?!" Eve cries.

"……"

Grace and Ares exchange glances for a mere few seconds. What implicit understanding did they reach? Grace quickly nods and leaves the room. Eve rushes to follow her.

Ares's proposal was deemed worthy of being immediately followed. A chill runs up Rabi's spine.

I knew it... There's something going on here. Something that I haven't quite realized yet, and something that I am probably not supposed to know—a secret. It must be a taboo hidden by the Church that's far more secret than Grace's old age.

Ares stares Rabi in the face. His eyes are probing, trying to determine something, and Rabi's heart feels like it's frozen solid. She reflexively bites her lip.

"...W-well then, I have things to prepare—please stand by for good news, boss... And, well, it's totally unimportant, but because I am timid, yet so very, very faithful...I don't think there's any reason for you to look at me that way."

Rabi manages to look somehow disgusted and states her case. Ares looks disappointed and simply gives her an order.

"...Go, Rabi. I have high expectations of you."

§ § §

Noise. Pain. Heat. Impact. Toudou's ascetic training is nothing short of being tossed around by a raging current.

The agony in her lower body from overeating has been overwritten by a swelling, seething heat, and that heat was quickly overwritten by the pain of the red-hot water endlessly crashing down on her. During her training, the raging, torrential deluge of pain is beyond what Toudou was actually able to comprehend, and while her consciousness teeters on the edge, the only thing that is allowed of her is prayer.

Toudou's consciousness forfeited long ago. One would hesitate to call this the realm of self-effacement. It is simply unfathomable that she hasn't already died. Even in this world, where a God resides, when it's time for people to die, they simply perish, from what Toudou knows... At any rate, Toudou lived for an entire week without a single recollection of her own actions or knowledge of her whereabouts.

Now she awakens in a room that the Church has prepared for her.

The wallpaper and floor are both stark white, and three beds line the room. A large table includes three chairs. Bare-minimum home appliances are included, but there aren't any windows. The room is somehow oppressive, just like every room that Toudou and company have stayed in during their ascetic training.

Here, she is forced to eat until her stomach nearly bursts before being dragged away to the training location—an endless cycle lately.

Toudou is already near her limit. Aria and Limis are being forced to train with Toudou everyday, too, and the exhaustion is palpable on their faces. Toudou is the same, and although she's not gravely injured, her eyes are completely dead.

Toudou is working under the pretext of tempering her holy energy, and it would seem that she's actually succeeding in doing so, but as for Aria and Limis, they're really only biting the bullet and facing the repercussions.

"...Aria, Limis, are you guys okay?"

"...Yes, I'm fine."

"...What exactly is the point of all this training...?"

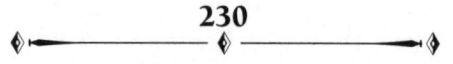

230

"The overdone sense of justice is a crime."

Fourth Report: On Encountering God

Just how long are they going to be subjected to this litany? Limis was whining a lot at the beginning, but she's already given up entirely. When conditions become truly deplorable, human beings stop being able to even produce tears.

It's true that the agony of being overly full and the heat they're experiencing are far less severe than when this all started, but it's pretty hard for them to believe they're actually getting stronger. At least taking off their blindfolds would let them actually feel something, but they aren't allowed.

According to their regular schedule, it's about time for Rabi to come around. They'll have breakfast, which is increasing in volume every day—forcing the volume down is the beginning of their training regimen.

Toudou closes her eyes and begins to prepare for the day. Focusing her consciousness, she forces her stomach into a state of emptiness. Recently, she's realized that managing life force is largely centered around the dimension of assumption. Perhaps something similar to the hypnosis she knew from her previous life?

Fatal disparity threatens to present itself when a certain phenomenon becomes distorted, but mental concentration is one of Toudou's strong suits. Looking next to her, she sees that Aria and Limis are also sitting with their hands on their knees, focusing their mental synapses to razor-sharp levels.

Just then, there's a knock at the door. It creaks open alongside the sound of Rabi's quiet, gentle voice. Seeing her face, Toudou's eyes go wide, and Limis and Aria have the same expression on their faces.

Rabi looks serious, as always, but something is decidedly different about her. Above all else, the smell of food that she is always pushing on them right away is nowhere to be found. Toudou swallows a lump in her throat. Rabi inhales and exhales deeply before rattling off what she has to say in one breath.

"I have received adjudication from Grace that determines you have offered enough prayer to proceed to the next rite. Starting today, you will move on from the rite of supplication to the next step."

"...What? We're...done?"

This unexpected decree doesn't fill Toudou with joy but rather trepidation. She blinks repeatedly, and Rabi speaks again clearly.

"Yes. You are finished. You, Toudou, must now certainly be self-aware of your increase in holy energy."

"...Well, I guess... Um, but...isn't this a bit too sudden?"

Rabi's right—the agony has dwindled, and their holy energy has surged. But their understanding of self-awareness is still very thin. Toudou only has the memory of being manipulated and thrown around like a rag doll. Aria and Limis are also looking at Rabi with cold, dead eyes.

"I can sense your internal condition. However, please relax. Because of course, the next step...is way worse than everything you experienced until yesterday."

"?! Wha—?!" Toudou shrieks.

"It gets 'way worse'...?" Aria murmurs, verbalizing Toudou's feelings.

What form of ascetic rite could possibly be more absurd than being forced to pray continuously in a pool of lava while being blasted from above by red-hot water...?

Toudou can't stop her expression from stiffening. Rabi furrows her brow at Toudou before speaking toward the door. A number of men and women wrapped in shoddy robes of all ages, shapes, and sizes enter the room in succession. At a glance, they look to be regular citizens, but the sparkle in their eyes indicates that these aren't just ordinary people.

As always, Rabi states the next mission succinctly.

"These are people who have received their fate from God. It's anticipated that saving just one of them will indicate the equivalent salvation of ten thousand people. Toudou, you will save every last one of them."

"One becomes ten thousand... What the—?"

232

"The overdone sense of justice is a crime."

Fourth Report: On Encountering God

Toudou instinctively repeats Rabi, who remains solemn as stone, nary an eyebrow twitching. However, observing closely, Toudou can see that the light in Rabi's eyes is starting to sink heavily. Yes—just like Toudou, Aria, and Limis.

Now begins the second rite, which from a different perspective is even more terrifying.

§ § §

Sanya races around the entire capital, using her legs and mind, alongside old connections, in order to acquire what's needed. Obeying the leader of the pack is in a silverwolf's blood. The capacity to think is also necessary, but a mind for insubordination is not.

Sanya has strong human roots, and she doesn't have fur, but her competitive spirit forces all the hair on her body to stand on end. To prioritize the benefit of the entire group, the leader of the pack must be coldhearted at times.

Ares Crown is supreme in every sense of the word. Supremely out of his mind. As a mentor, he's problematic, but as leader of the pack in action, he's a man of unparalleled talent. Sanya, alongside Rabi—who evaluates others from her own perspective—is also simply following the orders given to her, no matter how ridiculous they are. She definitely has a special kind of aptitude.

This is a dangerous assignment. Anyone who would join a unit poised to defeat the Holy Warrior is a degenerate beyond reconciliation. Managing such a crew is a tall order, and one mistake could cause them to turn and attack her. Nonetheless, the assignment is worth taking on.

Ares's proclamations are so exorbitant, sometimes Sanya doubts her own ears, but she likes it that way. It lets her in on all sorts of interesting moments. She gets to fight tough enemies. A sharp, stinging sensation has grasped Sanya by the heart, and it's not letting up. If he demanded that she offer up her life, she would, Sanya thinks—that's how great of a pack leader Ares is.

The Kingdom of Ruxe is proud to be a kingdom on the greatest scale humanity has ever known. Nonetheless, with great brilliance comes shadowed darkness. To the extent that the army of Ruxe is mobilized against the Demon Lord's army, criminals have already increased in the Kingdom. Sanya wore a thick hood and hid her face as she gathered more members. There is a fine line between those who can and cannot become mercenaries. As she ran throughout the royal capital, Sanya quickly found enough people to join up.

Most of them have hatred for the Kingdom. Some of them don't even understand why they'd attack the Holy Warrior. Others are simply in it for a payout. And then even others are probably joining up while being contracted out by another employer. In total—they number over fifty. That's quite the impressive result, given how hard Sanya worked to go unnoticed by the Kingdom.

Sanya rented out a bar on the outskirts of the city and gathered everyone in a single place. The joint reeks of drunkenness and roils with fetid heat. Sanya can feel the innumerable gazes trying to pierce her body through her thick robe. She hasn't shown her face, but her gender has likely been made out from her voice and scent. A silverwolf's nose can discern every emotion possible from scent alone: doubt, inferiority, contempt. Here, there are only human scents.

This isn't enough, not even close. Sanya will keep her net up until she catches more. Her boss wants her to fulfill her task to the greatest extent possible. Now Sanya speaks, adjusting the timbre and tone of her voice accordingly.

"I am grateful for you gathering here. However, this simply isn't enough. We're here for a certain reason, and I will aim for perfection."

"...But what of the Holy Warrior's public debut? I have heard the rumors that they've been summoned—but where did you hear about this debut?"

A man with a sharp gaze speaks up in a low, threatening voice. The majority of the members gathered here are only of average

"The overdone sense of justice is a crime."

Fourth Report: On Encountering God

skill, third-rate, really—but a number of professional assassins are also in the mix. They're clearly only here thanks to funds from shadowy contributors.

What's more, rumors of the Holy Warrior's summoning have leaked to the outside world, just as Sanya expected. You can't stop the gossip train, as they say. Sanya had been working under the assumption that only the Church's inner circle and elite aristocrats knew of the summoning, but it's been reported that the Holy Warrior trained at Ruxe Royal Castle, and some have even said to have brought them food. A smile cracks over Sanya's face as she speaks again.

"...It simply means that there are some excellent folks among us who are unsympathetic to the miracle of the Church, the Holy Warrior's very existence. Someone who can throw out an immense sum without thinking twice. You don't need to demand any more information than that. None of you want to die too soon, right?"

"...If your information is certain, I have no further complaints."

The sum that Sanya proposed to each of these miscreants to get them here would be enough for the average citizen to live humbly for the rest of their life. And now—she's dealing with that number times one hundred. If she plans on killing off every last one of them anyway, she figures she should go for broke, which will give her the upper hand.

Sanya loves being prepared to get her hands dirty for her boss's sake. If Ares is planning to have the Holy Warrior put on an incredible display of acting, then Sanya will put on a show of equal measure. She crosses her legs and laughs again, now with sheer disdain.

"If we're committed, we might as well go all out. The more people we can recruit, the higher the chances our plan will succeed. We still have time before the parade. All of you—get as many more to join as you can. Those who are unsympathetic with the Holy Warrior, those who want to get paid, those who aren't afraid to get their hands dirty, and really... Heh-heh—they don't even have to be human."

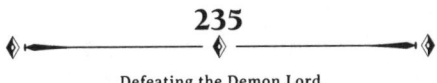

Sanya is now really hamming it up, but her performance absolutely nails it. The pathetic miscreants gathered before her collectively swallow lumps in their throats.

Will the demons they're up against actually fall for a plan like this? She has no idea.

At any rate, this is just how the mercenary Sanya Chatre rolls. She loves executing her duties with gusto.

§ § §

"These people are all destined to become priests who will someday save ten thousand souls each. In other words, guiding ten of them to becoming high priests will entail that you, Toudou, have saved a collective one hundred thousand souls."

"Isn't something pretty messed up about that? What do you mean by 'destined to save ten thousand souls'?!"

"That is...the revelation of God."

"W-wait up. If such people even existed, why does Nao even need to instruct them?! Just how will they supposedly save ten thousand souls?"

Although confused, Aria continues to object, and Rabi furrows her brow, sighing lightly.

"That's enough. If Toudou doesn't personally guide them, they will become completely useless to us. At present, they don't believe in God whatsoever—we can't afford them becoming a moot point."

Eve watches the scene unfold, struggling to contain her nausea. She is no longer capable of participating in persuading the people in question. If she opens her mouth, she will rain all forms of vituperation upon this outrageous folly. Of course, she would never directly address the Holy Warrior that way.

Why are Aria and the others making more competent and valid statements than Rabi (and of course, Ares, who came up with this plan)? Wasn't Eve and Grace's assignment to lead Toudou and his counterparts along the straight and narrow path?

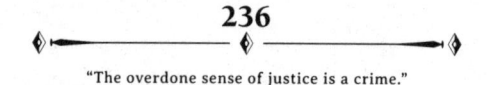

"The overdone sense of justice is a crime."

Fourth Report: On Encountering God

This assignment comes directly from Cardinal Creio, and Eve knew it would be oppressive and cruel from the very beginning. And when she was selected to be a part of it, she was racked with anxiety but also very proud. Assisting with two different legends of the Church of Ahz Gried—as a follower of the God of Order, there is no greater joy.

Nonetheless, the reality is sinking in. Oppressive and cruel was expected, but now the assignment is moving in a completely different direction from what Eve anticipated. She reached her breaking point when she was forced to take on the task of slowly adding cold water to the hot waterfall. Judging from Eve's intuition, that was already far off the deep end, but regarding the current assignment, even viewed in the most positive light—it's simply fraudulent.

The hero's party is unable to hide their bewilderment at the rite of alms that Rabi has presented—it's beyond logical comprehension. One unkempt man Rabi brought with her speaks in a drawl like some small-time gangster.

"*Gawd*? Listen, no amount of faith is gonna keep my belly full! I'm here for the gravy train, none of this gawd stuff!"

This prompts the two other people with Rabi to harass the Holy Warrior.

"He's just a kid. What can a kid even teach me?!"

"Damn straight! Fork over the cash and get outta my sight!"

Toudou, who isn't used to this level of verbal abuse, visibly deflates.

At any rate—this is all a ruse. Their supposed disparagement and contempt for God, alongside their shabby appearances... It's all part of the plan. Somehow, they will all be made to act like they're actually learning and growing as a result of following Toudou's instruction. What an absolute farce. Pulling wool over the eyes of the omnipotent Ahz Gried—simply unfathomable.

The training that Eve and Grace initially proposed is nothing like this. Their allegiance to the Church is being put to the test. Maybe Eve should just pull the plug and let every last secret out into the world—the thought enters her mind, and the only reason she hasn't taken action on it is because Captain Grace continues to maintain perfect silence.

Eve is merely Grace's attendant. The Sister General doesn't speak as a result of her vow to become closer to God through her human form. In return, Grace has always chosen a holy knight with a devout heart of faith to represent her.

There is only one rule: maintaining ultimate respect for Captain Grace's decisions. This is a matter of Eve's own discipline as a holy knight, too.

Fighting for prolonged periods against the roves of darkness through a human body as a representative of God is an extremely vicious task. Captain Grace's holy knight representative has always been on regular rotation, and some of them have failed in their battle against darkness, losing their lives.

Eve cannot comprehend it, but to the extent that Captain Grace keeps her lips pursed regarding these barbarous acts of treason, there must be a deeper meaning to the plan at hand. Cardinal Creio has been involved all along.

"We will prepare the curriculum used to share the Church's teachings on our end. Don't worry, Toudou's holy energy has already entered the realm required to provide others with guidance. Defeating the Demon Lord isn't the Holy Warrior's only role. Guiding people to the light—Toudou's predecessor also managed to complete the three ultra rites of Phimas while still only half-convinced of the Church's teachings, acquiring the power necessary to successfully defeat the Demon Lord of that era!"

"What?! Are you serious?!"

This is...nothing short of absolute fallacy. Holy energy and the capacity to lead others don't necessarily correlate, and the Holy Warrior's role is absolutely to defeat the Demon Lord. They are the foundation of hope for humanity, but they are not tasked with leading them. While on the subject, it goes without saying that the three ultra rites of Phimas are pure nonsense concocted by Ares Crown,

"The overdone sense of justice is a crime."

and there isn't any way the previous Holy Warrior could have undertaken them.

Rabi is taking advantage of the fact that no one at the Church has actually dug deeply into the history in this regard, allowing her to make any wanton claims she desires. Aria's and Limis's eyes are wide as saucers as they stand bewildered, yet they don't even feign to contradict Rabi. Both of them have received high-level teachings on the Church of Ahz Gried as members of the aristocracy, but they probably think it was all top-secret information held by the Church.

At that moment, Rabi suddenly looks directly at Eve. Reacting to her aggressive gaze, Eve speaks brusquely.

"...The room and teaching materials are ready. Leading others is the most fervent desire of any believer in the Church of Ahz Gried."

"...Teaching others will certainly lead to one's own faith being refined. The majority of high priests who take on disciples do it for this reason."

"Hmph... If you think you can, then go for broke! We can't wait to see what sort of enlightening teaching you highfalutin, honorable priests have in store for us!"

The way Rabi tacked on her next comment, making sure it sounded just and equitable, really makes Eve's blood boil. This is all an exercise in becoming a con artist.

Eve can only pray that this assignment is over as soon as possible. At this rate, her own faith is at risk of becoming obscured.

Prompted by Rabi, Eve leaves the room to begin instructing Toudou and the others. If anything is lacking in Toudou's way of teaching, it's Eve's job to indicate as much in place of Captain Grace. Eve always does her job the right way. Everything is for the honor of her captain.

When Eve passes by, Rabi addresses her in a hushed tone.

"Ares has something to discuss with you and Grace. You are to report to his room when today's teaching is complete."

"......Understood."

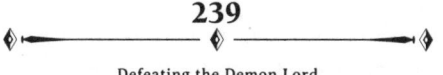

What could that possibly be about? Of course, Ares must already understand how Eve does not approve of this plan whatsoever. She's worried that he'll come forward with an even more absurd statement, but in reality, it's high time that she finally lets her sentiments be known.

§ § §

The current plan is markedly more important than any other we've had thus far. We absolutely cannot fail. At present, Naotsugu Toudou's level remains vastly lower than my initial expectations. According to my schedule, he should have already been level 60 by this point, but right now, he still has yet to reach level 50.

Entering a covenant with an elemental spirit, defeating a high-ranked demon—these are quality accomplishments that will allow Toudou to get along for now, but there isn't any substitute for being of high level. This responsibility falls directly on me. Once the Holy Warrior's existence becomes known by the public, Toudou and his party will be able to move a lot more freely.

Until now, their only allies have been the Church and the Kingdom of Ruxe, and directing their activities hasn't been particularly difficult, but with increased cooperators, instances will increase when the Church won't always be able to reach them.

Dispatching Grace and the holy knights was a curveball, but it really saved us. They remain key players. Everything happens for a reason.

It takes considerable time to increase in level, but it's also not the only way to make Toudou stronger.

"Mr. Ares... Please let me join, too! I want to offer my assistance in defeating the Demon Lord by depending on my faith alongside Toudou and the others!"

"No chance. You already had the fundamental aspects of the Church bashed into your brain by Gregorio, right? We don't need you, Spica."

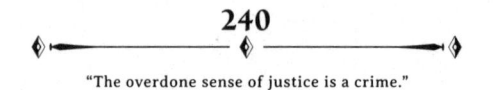

"The overdone sense of justice is a crime."

⚜ **Fourth Report: On Encountering God**

"No fair! No fair!"

It's evening. Because I can't predict what she'll do, Spica has remained tied to a chair during Toudou's ascetic training. As I rebuke her and organize information currently at hand, there's a loud knock at the door. It's Grace and Eve, who I sent for. Eve must have been who knocked. Even her knock sounds upset.

Grace is paramount to our plan, but Eve is a character of equal importance. She likely hasn't noticed it herself yet—but good God, Creio is really giving her the most troublesome assignments.

"Enter."

"...Excuse us. Rabi said you wanted to speak with us."

Grace is wrapped in an aura of silence, and Eve looks even more surly than when we first met. Perhaps my orders just simply didn't sit well with her? Holy knights that seek the deepest faith are often very straitlaced and stubborn. Nonetheless, at this rate, Eve will become a massive thorn in our side. I cough once and bark out an order.

"Your efforts are noticed. Begin with a report of current conditions."

"...We are carrying out your orders. Today...we oversaw the Holy Warrior teaching the holy creed to the ramshackle group of bonus characters in question, while looking, well, quite uncomfortable."

"And how are his prospects?"

"...While teaching requires some getting used to, I can't fathom that this exercise has any meaning. While perhaps presumptuous on my part, if this is to genuinely work, can you, Sir Ares, please tell me, if you may, what the holy creed actually means, to you?"

Eve's gaze rife with intention is bearing down on me. I meet her glance and assert with force.

"Eve Lucrao, you are...beyond the pale in your lack of comprehension."

"Wha—?!"

My assumption is spot on. This is also the reason that Creio discovered me to begin with when I was nothing more than a

241

Defeating the Demon Lord

commoner. According to him, the immortal knight's sidekick has always been of superior capabilities throughout the centuries, a holy knight of deep faith and serious intent. Even I can imagine the reasons for this.

I firmly believe that adjudication is also my role. I narrow my eyes and look down at Eve, continuing, "Calm yourself. You will understand soon. No matter how much it irks you. Prepare yourself thoroughly—tribulation is always sudden and swift, and God only puts those he chooses through such ordeals. Isn't that right, Grace?"

Eve quickly looks toward Grace, who doesn't react in the slightest. Nonetheless, as they've been by each other's side for so long, Eve's intent has clearly been communicated. Eve looks back to me with a stiff expression.

Even if she doesn't understand my words, she should quickly realize that a horrifying future awaits her.

"Eve, do you know the story of your predecessor?"

"Of course, I do. I know. Due to their age, the honored assignment was passed down to me—"

"Okay, and how about the person before? And then again, before them?"

"Well…"

Eve trails off. She clearly has no idea what I'm getting at.

"Did your predecessor truly…get so old they couldn't keep up with Grace anymore?"

"……"

Eve falls silent at my interrogation, while Grace simply stares at me. I can feel her gaze assaulting me even from deep within her thick metal helm. Maybe I said too much?

"Grace Godicent Trinity is a product of accumulated history. And regarding our current strategy—we don't require you to be on board with it. Right now you must simply comply. What I'm telling you must be easy enough to understand, right? Faith is not a matter of simply defending your creed."

"The overdone sense of justice is a crime."

Fourth Report: On Encountering God

Eve furrows her brow, but the disheartened look that was on her face when she first entered the room has disappeared. This is likely because she's realized that I'm not as insincere as she thought—and what's more, I have considered the scenario from every angle.

Regarding Toudou and company, as well as Eve and the others—we can now only believe in the divine protection of God.

There isn't anything else to say. I silently gesture for them to leave, and after a few moments of heavy silence, Eve speaks again.

"...Sir Ares. Captain Grace is stating that she would like to instruct the Holy Warrior in battle techniques. The Thirteen Rites of Phimas don't include battle training, but it will be necessary moving forward, and we plan to instruct him after the classroom lectures."

"...Hmm. Battle training, you say?"

It's certainly true that having Toudou receive battle training directly from Grace would lead to a vast improvement in her overall power. Grace's prowess has plummeted due to age, but the fact that she's a stalwart, storied warrior who has fought against innumerable forces of darkness is certain.

However, can we really afford to use up what's left of Grace on battle training? If the Holy Warrior's public debut goes off without a hitch, we might be in the clear, but if the parade is attacked as my fears tend to predict, and a potential assassin gets a bead on Grace, she will surely become a target as well. A real battle lingers imminently—using up Grace's powers in a mock battle would be an exercise in foolishness. The only reason I'm pushing forward with so many absurd ideas right now is to make use of Grace in the long run.

Nonetheless...Grace isn't so foolish as to not understand her own set of circumstances.

"Understood. I'll leave that up to you. Make sure Toudou works hard, in a fashion that doesn't derail any other parts of our plan, understood?"

"Mr. Ares...! Me too... I want to take the training, too!"

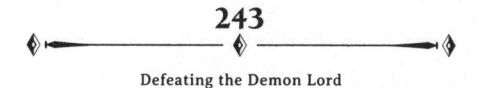

Spica squirms and offers her plea, but deep in her eyes, I can see the dusky flicker of the flame of battle-ready ambition. This fighting spirit is shockingly unsuitable for a follower of the God of Order, especially because her instructor and sparring partner is a sheer legend. Can I really trust Spica enough to make her a member of Toudou's party? Gregorio, you bastard... The way you educated this one is simply beyond the pale.

Just what level of trial by fire is required to make someone turn out this way? I'd love to ask him if I ever get the chance.

§ § §

Armor that was once light as a feather is now so heavy it prevents Grace from moving. A long time has passed since she lost her sense of omnipotence, which used to surround her body in an aura with each wave of blood gushing from the hordes of darkness she felled.

She can't help but think about how much time has passed. Before, when she wasn't yet known as Grace Godicent Trinity—she hasn't told anyone just how many years have actually passed. At this point, the days feel like they come and go at the speed of light.

Nonetheless, when exhaustively scouring her memories from up until now, she understands that she cannot help but feel the age that has settled in. It has been so long already since she stood at the front lines of battle. Even within the Church, only a scarce few know the true reason.

The holy knight order is intended to stand at the vanguard in battle against the Demon Lord Kranos. If only ten or twenty years... if the Demon Lord Kranos had appeared just ten or twenty years earlier...Grace would have been there, running in circles to dispel the forces of darkness.

But now she knows that it's simply no longer possible. Grace doesn't have the stamina anymore. And her inexhaustible supply of holy energy can't compensate for the way her body is breaking down. The fact that she couldn't leave peace behind for the next age

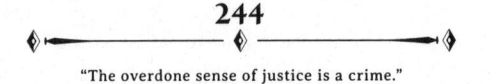

"The overdone sense of justice is a crime."

Fourth Report: On Encountering God

is the ultimate disgrace for a knight known as the symbol of immortality. No matter what, she cannot afford to simply push everything on to the next age, either.

Even if her battle prowess has become obscured, Grace is still capable of a great many things. Creio Amen is a man of insurmountable greatness. Ever since Grace was young, as Cardinal, he always found personnel that could carry the burden of the future.

Then there's Ares—Ex Deus—who remains young, which Grace can no longer claim, and has holy energy on par with her and a far more lucid mind than she did even in her former years. And the Holy Warrior, while still showing some uncertainty, has the universally recognized divine protection of the Three Deities and Eight Spirit Kings as a storied, upper-echelon hero. Finally, Eve Lucrao, a sincere holy knight who serves a vivid reminder of Grace when she was formerly known as the immortal knight.

Grace was the one who decided that she would participate in this assignment. The God of Death's footsteps are quickly approaching her. She knew that a day like this would someday come. Death visits all forms of life unequivocally, and even through the power of the God of Order, escaping it is largely infeasible. Even the Mad Eater, Gregorio Legins—who is said to have been released from the strictures of aging through a transcendental experience—will eventually die.

Inheriting power. This is the only way that humans, the weakest among a grand order of species, have managed to string along their existence, their souls.

The plan that Ares has established is beyond preposterous, even from Grace's perspective. She completely understands why it irks Eve's ire so much. At the same time, the plan has very solid reason behind it—including an unapologetic drive to reach its goal and a hell-bent level of thorough efficiency.

It serves to reason that Ares has accomplished everything through brute force up until now. And Grace has no right to refute Ares's plan, which is fundamentally predicated on kindness. Grace won this job from Creio with the intention of finding a place to die, but Ares is doing everything possible to push Grace back into the light, away from death. Everything he does is somehow for the sake of a better future. A young man, doing everything he can to reach the best result possible. To the extent that Grace is still mobile, she must fulfill her duties.

The Holy Warrior summoned by the Church's secret ritual, Naotsugu Toudou, is truly a human being on the straight and narrow. Toudou has the right mentality and sheer gumption needed to stand up to the training Rabi proposed, and despite how uncomfortable it has been, she never tried to run. The hero-summoning ritual calls on an individual with a certain disposition and gives them power. That disposition, in other words, is the individual's personality.

Not all that glitters is golden in this world. Even if the Demon Lord is defeated, we will be confronted with inevitabilities unrelated to the villainous demon race, including irrational realities founded in disgusting human traits. Yet especially when confronting these miseries, the Holy Warrior's disposition indicates they will retain a soul pure and white as driven snow. Naotsugu Toudou truly flowering in this regard is still a long way off, but she has the ability. And so do Aria and Limis, standing alongside her—

"Just who do they think they are?! They need to listen!"

"...I've never seen such a slipshod crew. Are they really fated to receive salvation?"

"A bunch of wet noodles."

The actor-believers have left the classroom, and Toudou and company are spewing vitriol, deep exhaustion worn on their faces. Despite the fact they're supposed to be acting, the actor-believers are a total joke. They're sleeping through class, for starters, hooting and hollering at every last incident, laughing their asses off regularly, and when chided for all this, they click their tongues, act sullen, and crumple into heaps onto their desks. Sure, it's Toudou and company's responsibility to teach them, but they didn't expect the crew to be assholes on this level.

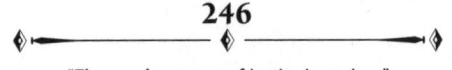

"The overdone sense of justice is a crime."

Fourth Report: On Encountering God

From what they've heard, in the world Toudou comes from, every person receives an education, and the literacy rate is essentially 100 percent. For the Holy Warrior, having grown up there—and for Aria and Limis, who come from upper-echelon roots and have received private tutelage since childhood, these Losers that Ares gathered are like people from a planet they've never seen before.

It's assumed that Toudou and company don't even know what to do. The curriculum that Rabi prepared for them to teach is exceptionally broad, and it's useless in rehabilitating such an irreverent bunch of students.

And there's another problem—the tasks that Grace must perform can't be completed by anyone else. As always, Eve is representing Grace and speaking to Toudou and the others. The longer they listen, the more her expression changes. Now, strength returns to her weathered face, and her eyes rife with determination have fallen upon Grace.

Grace passes on how to use holy energy and how to act as a hero. Even if it shortens her life—that is Grace's calling. She hasn't put her all into anything like this for quite some time. For this assignment, she won't resort to simply offering a counterattack, like she did the other day.

Grace inhales deeply and casts a holy technique, buffing her entire physical strength for the first time in ages, standing before Toudou and the others in a manner fully befitting the name of the immortal knight.

§ § §

Humans are a source of sustenance for vampires. Zarpahn has never been averse to skulking around human cities. Ruxe has rolled out the tightest security he's ever seen, but infiltrating it was still simple.

Vampires have a number of special skills. One includes *Charming Eye*, allowing them to control people's spirits just by looking at them. Even opponents of particularly high level aren't a problem, meaning that controlling just a few of the innumerable guards throughout the city was exceptionally easy. Ruxe is just too vast to prevent a single demonic entity from slipping through.

Zarpahn has formidable battle powers that eclipse any human being, and he can easily look exactly like one, joining their midst while going unnoticed. And above all else, he has the demonic gaze that can send humans into bewilderment. This alone is the primary reason that vampires have been natural predators of humans for eons. For Zarpahn personally, using a pathetic, weak human being as even a single pawn in his repertoire is unconscionable, but right now, obliterating the Holy Warrior has higher priority.

Zarpahn's particular set of special skills are especially well suited to strategies involving secret intelligence.

"The Holy Warrior... Ah yes. Humanity's hope... The Kingdom and the Church have been keeping him hidden—hidden even from us... I knew something was happening. Ever since that detestable sea demon was felled—"

"The sea demon is dead...? How the times have changed. Though I should scarcely be surprised that the man who felled me slayed that ocean recluse..."

Deep inside a lower-ranking aristocrat's residence in a corner of the royal capital, Zarpahn snorts while extracting information from the elderly estate owner. The man's eyes look like they're floating in heat-distorted air, and his enunciation is sluggish. Right now, his mind is incapable of thinking of its own will.

The demonic gaze that vampires have differs according to individual. In Zarpahn's case, he's able to steal his opponent's ability to make decisions and manipulate it freely. With this power, gaining total control of an aristocrat's residence that has paltry security to begin with is a simple task.

Zarpahn was imprisoned by Fahni, so he doesn't know anything about the current state of affairs. But it seems the man who defeated Zarpahn has made a mess of the Demon Lord's army. Kranos and his army must be struggling as a result.

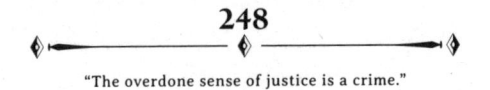

"The overdone sense of justice is a crime."

Fourth Report: On Encountering God

Zarpahn never really got along with Heljarl; he even resented him for his lofty position within Kranos's inner circle. Still, Zarpahn is not so narrow-minded that he can't recognize the sea demon's power. Born with the blessing of the ocean at his command, Heljarl boasted incomparable strength in any underwater battle. His ability to also control all sea monsters meant that his viability as a member of the Demon Lord's army was second to none. And he was destroyed.

Zarpahn doesn't know the gritty details, but the defeat of that abomination, who had successfully blockaded the entire ocean, entails a significant reduction in the Demon Lord Kranos's overall might. There is no doubt that right now, humanity has the momentum.

Timing the Holy Warrior's public debut right now can only be an attempt to make this momentum even more steadfast.

"But that's why...this is a perfect opportunity. Heh-heh..."

If Zarpahn can take the Holy Warrior, who defeated the sea demon Heljarl, and end him in a rain of blood... There isn't any better way to make his power known. Zarpahn has already engaged in battle with the Holy Warrior. He knows his human tricks and how he fights—he's felt it firsthand. Compared with any other demonic forces, he has a huge advantage. Yet...as Zarpahn stares at the stupefied estate owner and his servants, he narrows his eyes.

This is the perfect moment to strike while the iron is hot. Zarpahn can't picture a better time to attack the Holy Warrior other than the parade. He doesn't have any idea where he'll be until then, and if he can kill him at his public debut, it will be a performance for the ages.

Nonetheless, there isn't any chance the humans aren't already expecting this. They will be anticipating an assault—Zarpahn has complete faith that he can take out the Holy Warrior alone, but it wouldn't hurt to have a decoy, at least. Bringing a member of the Demon Lord's army inside the capital will prove difficult, but if they were human—that's a different story. He could control them with his demonic gaze, but because mesmerizing them chips away at their ability to make decisions, their battle prowess also plummets.

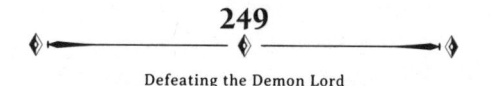

Drawing in a human from the anti–Holy Warrior establishment would be best, he thinks. There are so many humans traipsing about, and some of them must fit the bill. Using the aristocrat's influence, it should be easy to find one.

Most demons rely on brute force to make their attack, but Zarpahn is different. He will use every one of his faculties in order to kill the Holy Warrior. First, he must quietly chip away at the security levels before gathering some subordinates. Zarpahn will make them all taste the foulest form of desperation possible.

"Hmph… Just you wait, Holy Warrior Ares Crown. I will make you regret ever insulting me."

Zarpahn has been bestowed with a blessing from the God of Darkness, Lucief Arept. Now he smiles with deep joy as he gives new orders to the elderly estate owner.

§ § §

The holy knights are said to boast ironclad defenses, but this knight is particularly extraordinary in that respect.

Grace Godicent Trinity, the female knight obstructing Toudou's path, is markedly small in stature, but her majestic appearance makes her think only of a fortress—she is solid like a citadel and tranquil as raw, untouched nature. The light beaming from the joints in her armor, which is largely impossible to find anywhere else, is extolling the sheer prestige of her blessing from the high heavens.

Toudou is the one who wanted real-time battle training. She needs to get stronger, and not a second too soon.

"Hyahhhhhhhhhhhh—!!"

Toudou roars and leaps forward, rushing at the knight of legend. Her single slash imbued with fighting spirit from the holy sword Ex is easily blocked by Grace's massive blade. Despite the massive suit of armor she wears, the quickness of her movements and the power behind them makes Toudou pale in comparison. With each

"The overdone sense of justice is a crime."

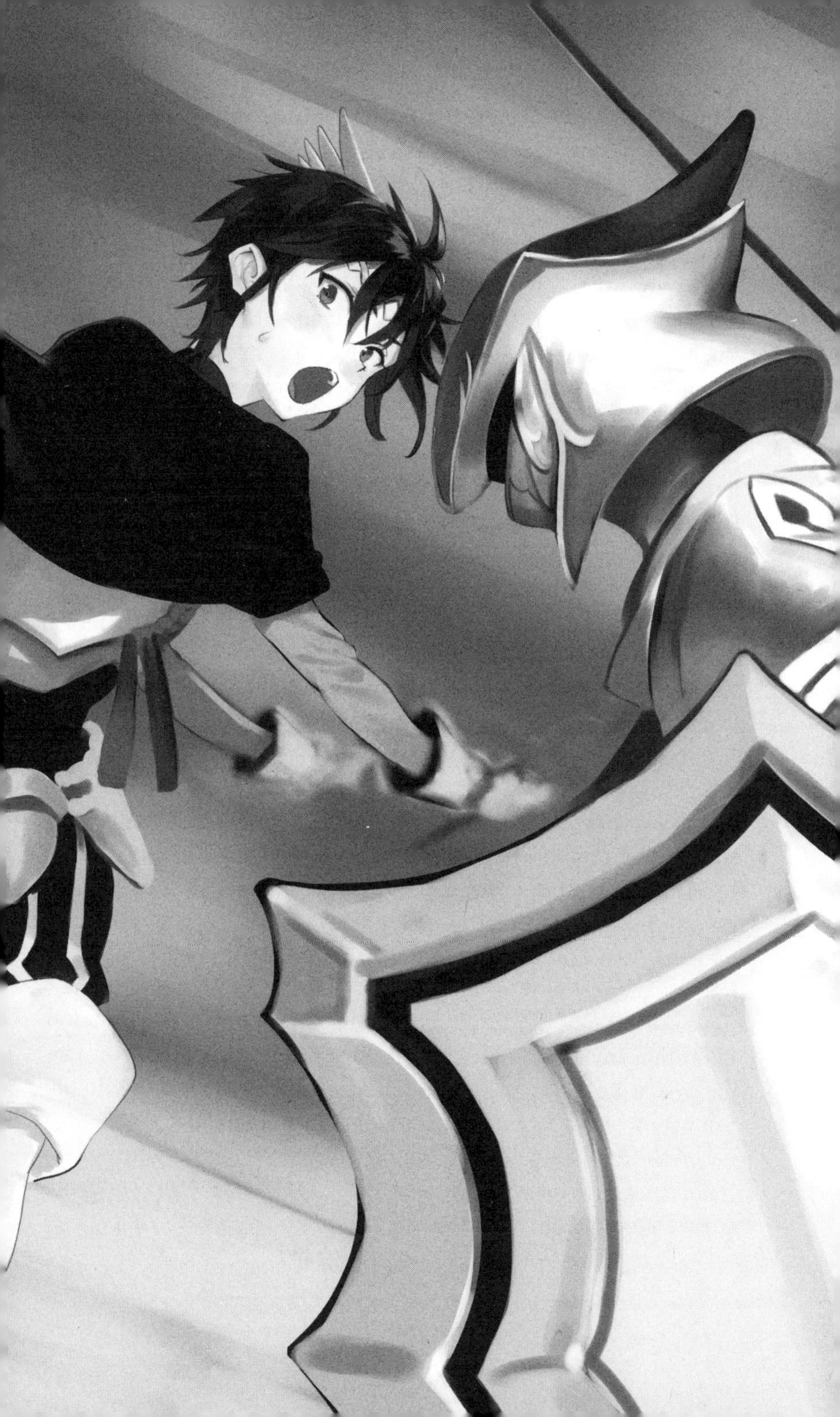

successive blow, the height of life force imbued in every fiber of her being is manifest. Any measure of mental or physical exhaustion is quickly overwritten with sheer fulfillment.

Even going after Grace's only weak point—her narrow field of vision due to the helm she wears—she still responds like she sees everything. She's toying with Toudou like a child.

Grace is strong. Unbelievably strong. The knight squadron leader who first taught Toudou how to fight was strong, too, but Grace is on a different level. Above anyone else, Toudou, who has the divine protection of Ahz Gried, knows this best. Grace Godicent Trinity has the direct blessing of God. The holy energy lying latent in her body is on a different order of magnitude. Among the people Toudou knows, Gregorio likely has the highest holy energy, but he doesn't even compare to this. Grace is the unbridled, pure might of heaven.

"...Even the hordes of darkness would put up a tougher fight."

"Tsk—!!"

Incredible. Toudou knew that her opponent was a being beyond the scope of human intellect, but that the divine protection of God can change a human being this drastically...!

Toudou feels her mindset shift completely. She can no longer hear Eve speaking. Instead, she simply pours her life force into each successive attack. As Grace fires a no-look arrow of light at Toudou, she chooses to intentionally respond by cutting it out of the sky.

This is training. An arrow of light might be effective against the hordes of darkness, but it isn't really effective against other humans. That said, taking the blow just because it wouldn't damage her would prove futile.

Even without words, Toudou understands. Grace is coming at her with many different techniques to tell her that this is also a viable way of fighting. She's also telling Toudou, who has the divine protection of Ahz Gried, that she can do the same thing, too.

Aria, who had been watching silently from the back the whole time, must have felt this divine intervention, too, and she suddenly speaks up excitedly, "Nao! Let me tag in!"

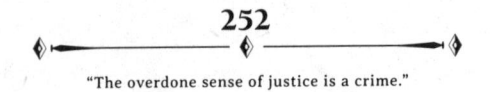

"The overdone sense of justice is a crime."

Fourth Report: On Encountering God

"Just a bit—just a bit more!"

"Sheesh, you guys flip-flop like nobody's business! You were just dead tired seconds ago."

"……"

Wings of light sprout from Grace's back, and she gains even more speed. She looks distinctly like an angel.

Bathed in light, Toudou can feel her own power surging within. The holy sword Ex, which had been dimming, also seems to beam with new light, she thinks.

Toudou inhales deeply and roars once again, flying toward Grace to attack.

§ § §

"Is that so? So he's actually showing palpable gumption?"

"Yes," Rabi tells me. "Boss, no follower of the God of Order could behold that scene and not be emboldened. The instructor is also fully engaged, from what I can see. We all know the opponent that Toudou is up against…"

I narrow my eyes. Grace Godicent Trinity, the immortal knight. She's essentially the Church's oldest form of propaganda. I have to give it to her, the storied hero—she really knows how to sell herself. Nonetheless, she's really bordering on excessive right now.

Judging from what Rabi's told me, Grace is using only high-level techniques during the current training. Grace's holy energy is higher than my own, but unfortunately, due to her aging and the exhaustion of all the battles she's been in thus far, her body simply can't keep up.

Grace claims she has only three years left, but the more she exerts herself, the more that time will contract. Stretching herself to the breaking point during Toudou's training and ending up passing away is the absolute worst possibility. Of course, in the public eye, this is still vastly preferable to her being tormented and slain by the hordes of darkness. Nonetheless, although her death is ultimately inevitable, we still need to be adequately prepared.

At any rate, I doubt I'll be able to stop her. Grace is stubborn, and she holds a special position. Also—she's not afraid of death. Worst-case scenario, if she can hold out until Toudou's public debut, the rest will be her own personal problem.

Rabi is boring her bloodred gaze into me while she waits.

"It seems like all is going well," I say to her. "This goes for Toudou, too, but if something happens to either Eve or Grace, report to me immediately."

"I understand that for Grace, but...Eve, too?"

"Don't pry. Keep just as close of an eye on her as you would Grace."

"...Yes, boss."

Rabi is decidedly useful. I never realized how much I'd appreciate a subordinate who would obey my orders solemnly without a single complaint... I'll keep her on board even after we defeat the Demon Lord, I think.

Judging from Rabi's report, there aren't any problems to be particularly concerned about right now. I can leave everything up to Rabi for the duration of the rite of alms without issue. The following rite of accession could prove problematic, but—as I begin to ponder the issue, I can feel Rabi looking at me like she wants to say something. I prompt her to do so, and she asks, with trepidation:

"Boss... Um... If it's not a bother, I'd like to ask, what exactly is Sanya doing right now?"

"...We are prepared for every last contingency. She's currently fanning the flames of sedition with the anti–Holy Warrior establishment. It's a dangerous assignment, but knowing Sanya, she'll pull it off without issue."

"...Huh. I have no idea what any of that means."

Sanya has been focused on playing her role as decoy. I've only received a brief report from her, but the strategy is going according to plan, and she's gathered close to one hundred people, I'm told. I don't know how many of those are getting paid to be there, but if possible, I need to borrow some bodies from the Church and get

"The overdone sense of justice is a crime."

Fourth Report: On Encountering God

them to thoroughly investigate the people involved. They might be able to provide further comrades, too.

However... It looks like we've struck out swinging in terms of advancing on Kranos, our real prize. Sanya has been giving orders to move in that direction, but the demons are on high alert ever since Heljarl was defeated... Or perhaps gathering a group with antihero sentiments so easily was unnatural for them, given the fact that the Holy Warrior is the manifestation of hope for all of humanity.

This is all coming together on the fly, truth be told... And they can't be that stupid. Without becoming too greedy, first we need to make sure Toudou's public debut goes off without a hitch, and then we should focus on successfully putting on a loud display of counterattack.

As I ponder our situation from every angle, Amelia, communications lead, sends me a message.

"Ares, I have a message from Sanya. We've been infiltrated."

"?! We have?!"

I immediately hone my senses to search for any sign of the hordes of darkness. When it comes to the presence of dark forces alone, I can detect them across a very wide area, but right now, I can't feel anything. Priests from the church are already dedicated to monitoring for any signs of the forces of darkness entering the capital. If something were to happen, I'd hear about it immediately.

"Yes. They are exactly human in appearance, but the scent is off."

"...It was the right choice to use Sanya. It's incredible that she performed exactly as predicted."

I had expected her to fail, but this result changes everything. If our opponent looks exactly human, but I can't detect any sign of the hordes of darkness, then they must be a human lookalike from a different species, or something else entirely? Kranos certainly has a convenient coterie of subordinates at his disposal. All ingress points to Ruxe should be heavily guarded, but...that's beside the point.

This has boosted my volition greatly. Even among the demons that the Demon Lord Kranos commands in his army, those who can take on precise human form are highly limited. He's clearly kept us guessing and made effective utilization of whoever they are while whittling down the cards he can actually play.

"...Boss, is something the matter?"

"I've got a fish on the line. It better be a big one—"

This is the royal capital Ruxe, a bastion for humanity. Assassination attempts have particular meaning precisely because they are ambushes. Assassinations that can be predicted are easy to respond to. Our opponent will easily take the bait for any strategy we plan, and if we give them an easy point of access, they'll attack without a doubt in their mind. As I smile broadly, Rabi looks at me with anxiety in her eyes.

Just then, another message comes through from Amelia.

"In addition—the man in question is a vampire, we're told. His name is...Zarpahn."

"Zarpahn...? That name... Zarpahn...?"

The smile immediately disappears from my face, and a chill rushes over my whole body.

"Ares, surely you haven't forgotten? He's that vampire you fought in the forest."

Amelia sounds like she's chiding someone who's absent-minded. Of course I remember!

Zarpahn Drago Fahni. It was my first mission supporting Naotsugu Toudou when we engaged in battle with this formidable vampire who has the divine protection of the God of Evil, Lucief Arept. In the end, he self-destructed in an explosion—or so I thought. I don't understand why he's still alive, but if he has some unknown powers, it could be interpreted that he easily was able to pretend that he self-detonated. And this also explains why I couldn't detect any trace of the hordes of darkness.

It's Fahni—the oldest of all vampires, and the one who has escaped the Church's clutches for the longest. Fahni is a bitter enemy of the

"The overdone sense of justice is a crime."

Fourth Report: On Encountering God

Church of Ahz Gried who all believers continue to hunt to this day. And the reason they're still alive is rooted in their special powers.

Upper-level vampires who have built up their powers over millennia can acquire certain abilities—such as Fahni's ability to conceal their innate darkness. This doesn't seem like a particularly noteworthy ability at first glance, but it's a thorn in the side for those in the Church who use Fahni's dark presence to hunt him.

What makes Fahni particularly dangerous is that they can conceal not only their own presence but also that of others. They can't keep this up forever, but so long as Fahni remains alive, there is a chance that some of the legions of darkness could go wholly undetected. I can't even fathom how many fellow priests have been taken out by Fahni's troops.

Every cell in my body shudders. A fearsome vampire—one I've already defeated—is back for more. Not only that—he is most certainly in close contact with the great Vampire Lord.

This is bad. Our opponent has now seen our hand. Furthermore, we can't detect his presence. Yet at the same time, we're very fortunate.

"Zarpahn... Heh-heh... He must be back for another round of torment."

"?! Umm... Boss...?"

Zarpahn Drago Fahni is a brilliant mind, but his thoughts are bound by his limited experience. And it's only been six months since our first encounter. I am still far stronger. If he's here alone, he's just a sucker coming to get his ass kicked once again.

Vampires live for a long time, but humanity has a storied history. We have studied them thoroughly. We have methods to contain their special skills, and if we subject them to torture, we might just discover the whereabouts of Fahni, one of our most bitter enemies.

This is a stroke of good luck. I need to warm up and prepare for what's ahead.

"Also, Ares... Zarpahn is convinced that Sanya is his ally, and he's really spilling the beans to her. Including about his powers..."

"...You can't be serious!"

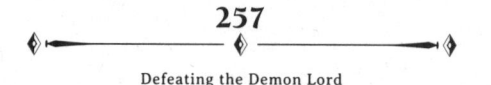

§ § §

Even if they look exactly human, determining they are indeed of inhuman ilk is as simple as peering into the primordial flame. A pale-blue, bloodless face; sharp, pointed eyes; and a thin physical stature that doesn't look strong at first glance. Yet Sanya's werebeast instincts are setting off alarm bells.

Zarpahn. Sanya could hardly believe it when another mercenary introduced him to her in the dead of night. Ares's plan is riddled with holes. It sounds interesting, and as his employee, Sanya has to follow orders, but she can easily imagine all the potential accidents that could occur along the way. For starters—why would a real-deal demon just show up out of nowhere like this?

But there's no doubt about it: This man *is* a demon—and a very powerful type, at that. There was something fishy about the look in the eyes of that mercenary who brought Zarpahn to Sanya. That was what clued her in to Zarpahn's identity.

Figuring out someone's identity and strengths before battling them is key—especially when that someone is a demon who can control human beings.

Vampires—those among the legions of darkness who possess fearsome abilities despite their inherent weakness to sunlight. Not even Sanya, a silverwolf werebeast, would want to fight these absurd undead beings. She certainly can't handle a vampire one-on-one. She's glad that her boss's strategy is going according to plan, but this is not gonna work out.

What should she do? Sanya is a mix of emotions: excitement over a new, powerful enemy and anxiety over realizing how bad this situation is. She narrows her eyes.

The vampire who calls himself Zarpahn sniffs heavily and speaks with arrogance. "That beastly smell... You...are one of us."

An eruption of thought explodes in Sanya's mind like a flash of light, and her heart pounds in her chest. The man in front of her— is clearly misunderstanding. And it's an exceptionally convenient

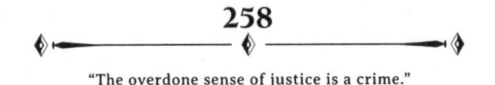

"The overdone sense of justice is a crime."

Fourth Report: On Encountering God

mistake for her. Sanya reflexively forces her wide-open eyes back to a normal gaze, and replies, stifling her voice.

"......Let's not go there. What does it matter, anyway?"

"...Very well. The true issue at hand is whether you will be of use to me."

Among humans, there is still a rampant level of prejudice against other intelligent species. If ten beast humans appear, seven are assumed to be demons. Conversely, that means that the remaining three must be of human ilk, but the man Sanya's facing hasn't even considered this possibility.

This is such a good opportunity. If Sanya can deftly manipulate Zarpahn's actions, she will definitely be able to make a greater case for her value to Ares. Not that this is a competition, but she might even one-up Rabi.

Sanya crosses her arms and reluctantly continues her spiel.

"All I need to do is eliminate my targets. I'll give you all the credit."

"...I don't need any favors. Tell me your plan."

It appears that Zarpahn intends to fall into lockstep. Is his intention of reaching an agreement with another species all due to the indelible charisma of the Demon Lord Kranos?

Sanya assesses her opponent's level of battle prowess. Infiltrating a human city alone means he must have incredible confidence. His eyes gleam bloodred, but his mind is pliant. Leaving this particular opponent unchecked will surely lead to trouble.

Sanya takes a deep breath and rattles off the detailed "strategy" that she practiced beforehand in case anyone demanded to know their plan.

"Our target is the Holy Warrior on the day of his public debut—it's not set in stone, but it's assumed to be within three weeks to a month from now. It will be heavily guarded against ambush, but if they intend to show the Holy Warrior's face to the public, the military forces they can deploy in the city are limited. We don't need to eliminate every last guard. All we need to do is kill the Holy Warrior."

"They won't be able to ignore numbers. Even the smallest fish will line up to get fried."

If Sanya was actually Toudou's enemy, she would have taken the same approach. Nobody knows where the Holy Warrior is under normal circumstances, and their security detail is guaranteed to be far tighter during a parade along the capital's main drag. Sanya is proposing the most effective strategy to make sure Zarpahn doesn't get suspicious. He is clearly impressed, his eyes wide yet arms crossed.

"A simple, yet reasonable strategy," he says. "But a month is too long to wait."

"We have no choice. We don't want to give time for security to bolster, but I can't determine when the public debut will happen. The Holy Warrior won't be revealed until all preparations are made."

"...I'll do something about that."

Now it's Sanya's turn to open her eyes wide in surprise.

The Kingdom of Ruxe upper-echelon elites, who summoned Toudou, will make the decision on when to hold his public debut. Changing it would require seizing the decision-making authority from a small number of those elites. This could never be accomplished through brute strength.

Controlling the top level of a dictatorship might yield results, but the Kingdom of Ruxe has a parliamentary system. Even with Zarpahn's demonic gaze, gaining control over one or two individuals wouldn't mean anything.

"...Understood. But really, is that going to work? You're all alone, right? Even if you can gain control, there are a lot of targets to manage. If it's going to be a tall order for you, I can certainly assist, so maybe we should hold off a moment."

Maybe Zarpahn has underlings? Even if so, powers to control human beings aside, entering the capital in large numbers would cause a scene. If the Kingdom's security happened to let through that many demons, they're as good as a sieve.

"The overdone sense of justice is a crime."

Fourth Report: On Encountering God

At any rate, this is not a great development. Ares has just two or three weeks maximum to get Toudou in top shape, and if her public debut is moved up, the plan will fall to pieces.

A look of worry creeps over Sanya's face, and Zarpahn snorts loudly. In that instant, Sanya can barely believe her eyes.

Zarpahn's entire appearance blurs. Wrapped in a lacquer-black robe, his entire form quivers like the moon reflected over water. Before she realizes it, two carbon-copy images of Zarpahn turn to face each other. Then they both look down at Sanya. Upon meeting their gaze, Sanya's mind becomes pure white noise.

This is— Sanya's never experienced this power before. She twitches her nose and ears to gauge her surroundings.

Truly unbelievable—this isn't a phantom illusion. Both Zarpahns are real, with actual physical bodies. Even using her refined silver-wolf werebeast senses, Sanya can't tell which is the original.

Zarpahn's life force has dropped a bit compared to when there was just one of him, but it hasn't plummeted by half by any means. Sanya reaches out her hand instinctively, but Zarpahn slaps it away.

"Remember this. My name is Zarpahn Drago Fahni, descendant of the legendary vampire Fahni. But I have surpassed Fahni: I possess the Manifold Horde. Soon, I shall be among the Demon Lord Kranos's inner circle. I am Zarpahn Drago Fahni, a vampire of manifold iterations."

There is undeniably the presence of a king in Zarpahn's proud demeanor. Sanya does everything she can to steady her breathing. Her mouth is dry. If she looked in the mirror, she'd see her own face nearly completely drained of color. Sanya has worked as a mercenary for a number of years now, but this is the most shocked she's ever been.

She rebukes her trembling tongue and speaks up again, hoping not to be compromised.

"R...right...... I'll, uh, remember that."

Manifold Horde. Zarpahn Drago Fahni, the Manifold Horde. She won't be forgetting anytime soon.

Sanya knew that upper-rank vampires have a number of inherent skills, but this—this power is on an entirely new level of insane. Even among elite vampires, surely one or two could contend for such power—of which just a portion is spent in creating a second physical form. What's more—this isn't a case of one person off-shooting into two.

It was Zarpahn, his real form, manifest as two beings. And most certainly—two beings are not a set limit. A vampire of infinite iterations. If just one is allowed to infiltrate, countless vampires could manifest to control the city. One vampire could take down an entire kingdom—that's just how incredible this power is. Just thinking about it for a moment, Sanya conjures infinite scenarios in which it could be used.

Should Sanya snuff him out right now? She considers the idea briefly, but it quickly leaves her. This is not an opponent she can match up against. If she tried, she'd be killed without even leaving a mark. She must remain faithful to her boss's command. Powers of this magnitude must come with certain restrictions. If that wasn't the case, Zarpahn wouldn't need to manipulate sacrificial pawns to begin with.

"Understood. I will leave the maneuvering to you, and I will take care of my own initiatives. If you think you're bordering on failure, get in touch immediately."

"……Hm."

Sanya can't hide her discomposure as Zarpahn's twain beings blur in the aether, again coalescing back into one.

Failure? There's no room for it. If it's just going to make Zarpahn suspicious, then she definitely shouldn't fail. Yet if she leaves Zarpahn to his devices, he will become a most repugnant foe in the battle to defeat the Demon Lord. At present, she still has an opportunity to take advantage of him. She must kill him while he is here in Ruxe. He still hasn't realized who Sanya truly is whatsoever.

If she were Ares, this is definitely what she would say next: "I'm so glad to have met you in this moment."

"The overdone sense of justice is a crime."

Fourth Report: On Encountering God

§ § §

"Are we finished...with the rite of alms?"

"......Yes."

Rabi nods, as cool as always. Toudou was preparing to leave for her instruction in her own room as she hears Rabi's confirmation, and she is dumbfounded. Until yesterday, there wasn't any such indication. For Toudou personally, she had just finally gotten warmed up.

She's realized that teaching the ten individuals in question isn't completely foolhardy. The ten people that Rabi brought to her don't have any previous study experience, but it's not like they're unintelligent. Toudou had her doubts on the first day, but the curriculum that Rabi prepared for the classes Toudou gave was clearly effective.

If she continues with other training soon, Toudou's chances to teach will be a thing of the past. It's not guaranteed that further training will actually boost her powers, and she remains doubtful if she's really the sort of magnanimous individual that is fated to save the lives of ten thousand people, but watching her pupils imbibe the content of her teaching like dry sand absorbing water was highly comforting, in the least.

Above all else, the live battle training that Grace assigned to Toudou is really beneficial—both in terms of how she uses her holy energy and how she composes herself. Grace is the best version of an elder leader that Toudou could ask for.

"...Why are we done already? Their instruction isn't complete yet..."

Toudou is long past the point of being dissatisfied with her current training. Toudou furrows her brow when asking Rabi, who replies blithely, "No, their instruction is adequate. They have ascertained the capacity necessary to teach others in the future."

"...What?"

Impossible... Certainly, they were continuing to absorb new

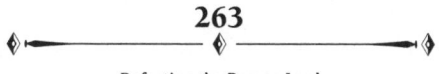

knowledge daily, but even from an amateur's perspective, they haven't acquired a true heart of faith. Not even half of the time initially dedicated to their teaching has passed.

Toudou thought it was inane to bestow real faith on them in just a week's time, but even if they had shown an unexpected level of knowledge absorption, there is a natural limitation to their progress.

Limis and Aria are equally confused by Rabi's sudden decree.

"??? Rabi, didn't you say we'd work until they all became high priests?"

"We've finally just managed to lay the most basic of foundations with them, you know!"

Rabi sighs quietly and puts her hand on the door. "Faith is not something that can be explained logically. At times, it can deepen suddenly, without explanation. Let me show you proof."

§ § §

One of the walls of the room that Toudou and company are using for instruction is made of a special material, allowing the interior to be viewed from an adjacent room. As I watch Rabi invite Toudou and the others inside, I sigh deeply.

"Zarpahn Drago Fahni. Zarpahn, the Manifold Horde... I never fathomed his powers would rise to this level."

Toudou and the others are still perplexed by the rite of alms coming to a sudden end—but the situation has clearly changed. The information passed on by Sanya last night is truly terrifying. In conception, every inherent skill that an elite vampire awakens to is utterly formidable. Yet Zarpahn's power that Sanya bore witness to is unlike any other—the ability to create an exact replica of his very being.

Vampires all have a number of special skills, and even among the hordes of darkness, their species requires special consideration whenever being dealt with. One of them multiplying infinitely is a

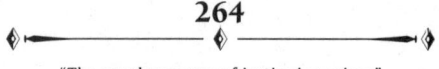

"The overdone sense of justice is a crime."

Fourth Report: On Encountering God

full-scale nightmare that alone could raze the entire Kingdom to the ground.

It's almost unfathomable, but if Zarpahn really does have such powers, then Zarpahn's self-destruction in the Great Forest of the Vale without hesitation makes a lot of sense, alongside his discovery and subsequent appointment by Kranos.

I must reward Sanya, who remained unflustered when giving me her report, despite her incredible achievement.

The details of Zarpahn's powers remain unknown. How many iterations can he conjure? Are each of them able to freely share information among one another? Are there limitations that come with additional iterations? How long do they last?

From what Sanya has gathered, Zarpahn's capacity to conjure new iterations of himself is far from inexhaustible. I tend to agree—if he could conjure as many as he wanted without limitations, then he wouldn't need cohorts.

And what's more—if Zarpahn's conjuring of iterations and Fahni's concealment were ever to coincide, our state of affairs would devolve into pure chaos. The God of Evil really chose one hell of an aberrant being to give his divine protection to. Compared with Stey, a careless dolt given divine protection by the God of Order, he's vastly superior. We absolutely must put an end to Zarpahn while we still have control over his actions.

Zarpahn intends to move up the date of the parade, I'm told. That will require manipulating over ten different aristocrats. In conception, if Zarpahn already knows our plan, there isn't any reason for him to take such measures.

This time, we will make sure our bases are covered. Zarpahn is rash and careless. This is proven by the fact that he believes Sanya is an ally, but this aspect of his personality is also readily understood by how he is so quick to show her his powers without any reason to do so.

We'll make him think everything is going perfectly, and then we'll strike at his most critical weak point and put an end to every last iteration alive. Zarpahn's greatest weakness is his own physical form. Even if he used most of his energy conjuring powers in the Great Forest of the Vale, his lack of battle experience was evident there. He can probably suppress most opponents he comes across simply through his powers and foundational abilities.

This entails an opportunity. Right now, we still have the chance to kill him. Even if he conjures additional iterations, we can pull it off.

Amelia is observing Toudou and the others with a sullen look as she says to me, "Nonetheless, Ares. You are certainly pushing it now, aren't you?"

"...It's our only choice to get him ready in time for the public debut."

In the next room, Toudou, Aria, and Limis are all utterly wide-eyed and trembling in the face of their students, who are busily clustered in a huddle. The Losers' behavior is completely different from just yesterday. Their shoddy clothing draped over their bodies has been replaced by common priest robes, and they have earrings that are the sign of faith worthy of priesthood hanging from their ears.

They're telling each other to fall in order and prepare to accept Toudou's teaching. Just yesterday, I finally believed Toudou was getting through to this group, but seeing them awaken to a deep sense of faith overnight would make anyone feel like they're dreaming. These measures were made possible because we prepared for the possibility of the pupils' faith awakening quickly beforehand.

Toudou approaches one of the Losers, who have suddenly become so pious, and asks, *"Wh-what...exactly happened in that one night—?"*

"Yes... Us folks, um, I mean, we distinguished individuals received a revelation from God yesterday evening, and now we've come to understand your teachings deep within our very souls. It was a very moving experience, as if being struck by a bolt of lightning."

"The overdone sense of justice is a crime."

Fourth Report: On Encountering God

"Wow... I—I haven't even understood these teachings from within my own soul yet..."

...Hurry it up, then!

Toudou is being a little too honest, and Amelia offers an apathetic comment.

"His heart's just not in it."

"He hasn't had a transcendental experience with faith yet, which happens to be the quickest way to acquire it. Encountering a life-threatening crisis is another speedy method, but alas—"

We don't have any spare Holy Warriors to try that out on.

All the Losers raise their hands in unison. It's a sign.

As they all bring their hands down, I offer up a prayer. My body is rife with lassitude. In the same moment, a stark white light rushes to fill the room. The dazzling glitter of light causes the Losers, who are likely the reason for it appearing, as well as Toudou and the others, to hurriedly look around the room, searching for answers.

This is a holy technique and a very upper-level one at that. A miracle only permitted by a small fraction of high priests—Create Sanctuary. When humanity convenes to build a church, this powerful technique is used by a high priest to help lay the groundwork.

Amelia looks at me and murmurs, "...Ares. Their holy energy... is no joke...despite their existence as profane beings."

"Forget about it."

"Personally, I really admire them."

...You call that admirable?

It's worth mentioning that we chose Create Sanctuary because it's a flashy, loud technique that is instantly recognizable as very high level at a glance. Toudou has no choice but to recognize the Losers' faith.

I need to flip a new switch. I slap Amelia on the shoulder and turn to leave the room.

"I'll leave the rest to you. I need to prepare what's next. Follow up on this situation accordingly."

"......Understood."

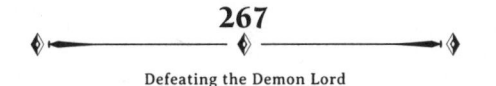

Next comes the final rite—the rite of accession. It's an encounter with God, a God who says that those who have not already reached him will never come close. We need to finish it quickly and turn our efforts to preparing for battle against Zarpahn.

The Holy Warrior's public debut is a storied legend. In eras past, each time the Holy Warrior appeared through hero summoning, the Church of Ahz Gried has hosted a parade called the Hero's Procession of Light. In addition to displaying the Church's authority and serving as a beacon of humanity's counteroffensive efforts, this ritual has certain meaning. It's not only limited to the hero—parades of a similar nature are also held for beings like Grace or the Saint.

For these reasons, although we understand we're being directly targeted, there isn't any option for us to not host the parade. To put it simply—we cannot achieve victory without the parade.

"It looks so peaceful in this light."

"That's because the capital hasn't actually fallen under attack yet."

With Amelia and personnel from the church in tow, I am surveying the parade route on the capital's main promenade. Zarpahn has pulled it off, it seems—the parade date has been changed, according to correspondence I've received from Creio.

It will now be hosted in ten days' time. Fifteen different aristocrats concurred to advise that the date be moved up. Although a number of Kingdom authorities were aiming to take a whole month to prepare for the parade, just as many spoke out in opposition, according to Creio, who sat in on the council. Those who spoke out in opposition looked totally off, he said. The majority of them were likely under the influence of Zarpahn's demonic gaze, I surmise.

Zarpahn's maneuvering in little to no time at all is astounding. The Kingdom was clearly unprepared, but for them to allow a demonic presence to infiltrate so easily—the aristocrats of Ruxe have clearly fallen far from heaven.

Above all else, if we don't take out Zarpahn soon, we are in

"The overdone sense of justice is a crime."

grave danger. At present, he has only managed to manipulate the aristocrats' decision-making, but he could have just as feasibly had them all killed. Zarpahn's Manifold Horde skill allows him to attack from many different angles simultaneously. Without even the adequate time to prepare, a being of Zarpahn's inherent strength could lay serious waste to our side.

Amelia shields her eyes from the sun and says, "Hey...Ares. Why don't we forget all this and run away together?"

"......"

"That was a joke."

Knock it off! Are you trying to give someone cold feet? Don't make me think you're under the spell of his demonic gaze, too!

I simulate the battle as I envision it while we walk. They say that numbers don't lie in battle, but Zarpahn intends to undermine this idea, completely alone, and he has the fearsome powers to make it possible. Yet his powers still entail a certain weakness...

Just as Sanya said, when he uses his power to conjure a second iteration, they are both of lesser capacity, albeit very slightly. In other words, they're not perfect carbon copies. The more iterations Zarpahn conjures, the weaker their respective powers become.

His weakness—is that he's a goddamn fool. His power is decidedly wicked, but the desire to fight through his own physical form is too high. Depending on the situation, a middle-class priest could even shut his iterations down through prism techniques.

Zarpahn's divine protection through Lucief Arept allows him to vastly reduce the majority of damage he takes, but it won't work for individuals like Toudou or Gregorio who have the divine protection of the God of War. His Manifold Horde iterations are only really suited for fending off weaker enemies.

Right now, Zarpahn thinks Sanya is his ally, and he's putting together his strategy while taking this into account. This means that we should be able to manipulate where he attacks from, to an extent. And we can put up traps. Truthfully, I already have Zarpahn in the palm of my hand.

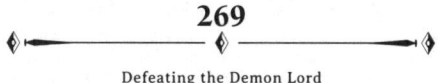

The biggest problem is what to do about security. Zarpahn is a fool, but he has the sense of reason and intelligence to ingratiate himself with Sanya. If we prepare too much military might, there's always the chance that he will balk at his assault or that he could keep some reserves ready for another day and attack in fewer numbers. In either scenario, we need to aim for complete annihilation.

Smaller numbers of highly skilled guards will accompany the actual parade. The additional soldiers that Stey is accumulating will be hidden in buildings along both sides of the promenade.

Amelia taps me twice on the shoulder and quietly leans in. "By the way, Ares," she whispers. "I thought vampires could only be active at night?"

"...If he hasn't already thought of that, he's even more stupid than I imagined."

That's a vampire's greatest weakness, now, isn't it? There's no way the Holy Warrior's public debut will occur at night, and he must be considering magic or some other means to summon dark clouds. As I furrow my brow, Amelia continues, like she's saying something top secret.

"But... What about the chance that he hasn't? Zarpahn doesn't seem that intentional with his strategy."

Amelia, what the hell...? Why do you look like you're having so much fun?!

"Maybe we should hold the parade at night? Or at least early evening..."

"You can't be serious..."

Why in God's name am I tasked with considering every last angle of a vampire's attack when I'm supposed to be simply supporting the Holy Warrior...? While our strategy hinges on inviting our opponent's attack, there are too many feasible critical lapses. But... Maybe she could be right? At any rate, Zarpahn's made the mistake of thinking Sanya's his ally, without any prodding from our side... I'll be damned.

"The overdone sense of justice is a crime."

✟ Fourth Report: On Encountering God

"...I leave it in your hands. Pass the idea to Creio."
"Yessir, boss!"

Thanks to the fact that we started moving early, even if the public debut is moved up, we should still be able to get everything ready in time.

"My name is Glacia...... I am a sacwed beast. Gawd tasked me with saving da Holy Warrior. My previous form was temporary......"

Glacia is wearing an oversize robe adorned with golden stitching. The white Glacia, who is wearing a crown of gold, repeats the lines she was taught with dead eyes.

"...Boss, don't you think this is a bit much for her?" Rabi asks, visibly concerned.

"Right. This isn't going to work."

"I am a sacwed beast—"

No matter what, proper acting seems to be a tall order for Glacia. Amelia tried her best, but this is what we're left with. It's not really a problem that we can simply fix. That said, the sacred beast doesn't actually have to do anything special, so we should be able to work with what we have. But we certainly can't afford to let Glacia slow us down.

"Be more convincing," I tell her.

"...You're really forcing this," Rabi says in exasperation.

Getting Glacia to properly act like a sacred beast might just be more difficult than actually defeating the Demon Lord. Currently, completing the rite of accession—somehow—is of the highest priority.

We still haven't touched upon three of the Thirteen Rites of Phimas: reaching the apex of light, spiritual discipline of the inner self, and encountering God. For us, they're all part of a singular narrative.

Know the light that the God of Order administers, know thyself, and become closer to the transcendental presence that is God. It sounds extremely simple, but the most idiosyncratic aspect of this ascetic rite is the fact that it doesn't have a clear goal, unlike the other rites.

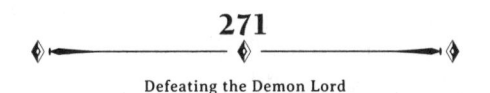

This training begins with establishing a goal. Successfully completing the rite of accession requires two things: absolute faith and a strong sense of conceit regarding that faith. And encountering God also predicates a certain level of ability.

In the past, when Gregorio was lost in despair, he somehow came to an understanding of his own faith and ability by feeling the presence of God nearby, and in this way, achieving the rite of accession could be claimed to be a crucial watershed for all priests.

Just now, I take out an item that I have been holding on to for a very long time and place it on the desk in front of me—a captivating crystal bottle holding a translucent, golden liquid. Rabi furrows her brow, staring at it contemplatively.

"What's this...?"

"To put it simply, it's a hallucinogen that disrupts and enhances the user's mental equilibrium. There is a high, high-percentage chance they will have visions of being wrapped in light."

".........For real?"

Rabi, you sound...off.

I tap the bottle a few times, which took much expended effort to acquire.

"It's a secret trick. This hallucinogen is prescribed by indigenous shamans to prepare subjects for encountering God."

"I am well aware of it, as well as the fact that due to the way it disrupts natural order, it is taboo within the Church of Ahz Gried."

At one time in the past, a great number of people appeared who used potions of this variety to force others into compulsory belief in their respective gods. The potions are theoretically meaningless in terms of increasing faith. For this reason, the largest religious organization in the land, the Church of Ahz Gried, determined that they were disruptive of the greater order and banned them.

The potion that I've prepared currently only causes high hallucinations and doesn't have any habit-forming properties, but it also doesn't cause particularly...positive effects. And furthermore, and

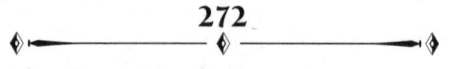

"The overdone sense of justice is a crime."

Fourth Report: On Encountering God

really at the crux, the greatest reason these potions are considered so taboo—is precisely because of the powerful effects they elicit.

If such a substance became rampant, faith would lose its meaning and all believers would be led down a path of delinquency. I cannot even imagine the tribulations of the pioneering souls who worked to control these potions when they started to spread, succeeding in almost wholly eliminating them.

Of course, I never drank the potion myself, but I have been keeping an eye on the viability of its effects.

"The taboo nature of the potion depends on how it's used. Arriving at a place of pure light through faith alone is exceptionally difficult. That is, without meandering along the line between life and death, you know."

"...May I contact the Church about this matter?"

I am acknowledging that it's a taboo, so don't go overboard with any unnecessary nonsense!

I myself don't want to use the potion to the extent possible, but seeing the light on the precipice of life and death and seeing the light with ease through the potion are essentially the same. We will, however...need to make sure that Toudou stays entirely quiet about this.

"...Understood regarding arrival at the apex of light. How about encountering God?"

"According to testimony from individuals who have achieved an encounter with God, it is easier to accomplish while in a trancelike state. Intoxication is one example... And achieving the encounter immediately after arriving at the apex of light is also fairly common, I've heard."

Rabi falls silent after clearly wanting to say something, but instead she casts her gaze aside and only says, "...I-is that so?"

She really knows how to keep unnecessary chatter to herself—one of the biggest differences between her and Amelia, who seems to always find the need to slip in a joke.

"Give this potion to Toudou under the pretext of being part of his rites. The effects will take place about one hour after imbibing. Get Aria and Amelia away from him. And do not speak of this plan to Eve whatsoever. It's too early for her to know."

Eve is already mentally exhausted from the ascetic training thus far... If she reaches breaking point and lets everything slip, I won't be able to look the other way.

"Yes. However, boss. Despite all these measures...umm...it's not guaranteed that Toudou will actually achieve an encounter with God, right? Of course, Toudou has Ahz Gried's divine protection, but as far as I know, God is very fickle."

Rabi speaks rife with trepidation. As a head-chopping assassin with her own divine protection, her understanding of faith runs undoubtedly deep. And she's right—God's purpose is so far beyond human comprehension. God doesn't intervene in a physical form to help humanity when they're up against the wall, and God also gives divine protection to unwarranted and outrageous beings.

I tap Rabi on the shoulder and whisper very quietly, just on the off chance anyone could be listening.

"Rabi—I will become God."

"Wha—?!"

Rabi covers her ears and hops back in shock.

I would never conjure a plan founded on betting odds. It's my job to bring in good luck.

Fate is rooted in results. Only after exhausting every last resource does fate rear its head.

Toudou's ascetic training will conclude successfully, I am certain.

All that's left is to welcome Zarpahn's ambush with open arms and slay him like a sacrificial lamb.

§ § §

Tension fills the small room. Unlike previously, Eve and Grace aren't present, and only Rabi has arrived. Her small body includes

Fourth Report: On Encountering God

slender limbs, thinner than Limis, but she's giving off a quiet, forceful pressure.

"Finally, we have arrived... The culmination of the three ultra rites of Phimas—the rite of accession. After Toudou completes this rite, he will be considered to have successfully completed the ascetic training of Saint Phimas."

"...It's really gone by quickly... I heard that it should normally take over ten years..."

"Yes, you're right... And the rites have all been so convoluted... Of course, they certainly have profound effects..."

Aria and Limis speak quietly among themselves. Toudou can only agree with one point they're raising. Certainly, the three ultra rites of Phimas have been nothing short of insane. At first, Toudou was highly doubtful if this was really the right path forward, but now, she's fully copacetic. Her holy energy has actually increased, and above all else, the battle training with Grace was so much fun. She doesn't have a single complaint.

Toudou swallows a lump in her throat and steadies her breathing while she waits.

Finally, Rabi says sternly, "However... Soon we shall commence the most secret ritual among all that the Church offers—and you alone shall take part. Please understand, Holy Warrior: No one other than you can know a single thing about this ritual."

"What?!"

Toudou's eyes are wide as saucers as Aria and Limis stand looking at her. They're both downtrodden knowing that they were made to accompany Toudou all this way only for this to be the end. The two of them remain composed and sigh quietly in tandem.

"...Hmph. I guess we don't have a choice. Nao—it looks like this is the end of the line for us."

"...Yeah, sad but true. It's the Church's decision. Stay on top of things, even without us, okay?"

This is an all too common experience in this world.

Rabi's gaze turns grim. "...For the record, all the ascetic training you've participated in so far is top secret. Don't speak of it to others. And also—rest assured, the rite of accession will not take very long. Or rather...only the chosen ones can achieve accession, meaning the results will be instantaneous."

A secret that only those chosen will be able to reach. These words alone cause a palpable sensation, both exaltation and dismay at once, to run up Toudou's spine. It's a similar sensation to when she was summoned to this land and first heard of the situation she found herself in.

Toudou clenches her fists and inhales deeply. She doesn't know what is going to happen to her, but she is more than ready. Rabi casts her bloodred gaze at Toudou and says, "Toudou. Please follow me. Aria and Limis—that's right. Glacia has become the sacred beast. Please establish a deeper friendship with her. That will complete the ritual with the sacred beast."

"Okay, got it... W-wait, what did you just say?"

Aria and Limis feel like very important information was just brushed over... They remain dumbstruck but can't find anything to say to Toudou, whose eyes have gone wide, too. Rabi simply twists around to face away from them and leaves the room. Toudou rushes to follow her.

Toudou is brought to a room rife with a peculiar aura. A large bed is pushed in one corner, next to a table where a glass filled with golden liquid rests. A parsimonious altar stands in the center of the room. The white walls of the room are lined with dilapidated old candlesticks.

Just what sort of ascetic training will take place here? As Toudou peers around the room with hesitation, Rabi coughs once before speaking.

"*Ahem*... The process for the rite of accession is simple. You will drink the Church's secret holy water to become closer to God."

"...What?"

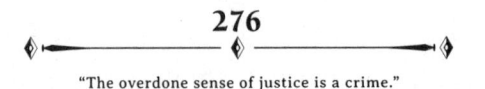

Fourth Report: On Encountering God

Toudou reflexively stares fixedly into Rabi's face. All the rites completed thus far were borderline absurd, but they all at least involved toil and hardship. Yet the final rite is...drinking holy water?

"You are not mistaken to be surprised. However, among all the priests who have participated in the three ultra rites of Phimas, the rite of accession has proven most difficult for the majority of them to overcome."

"...Even though all it requires is drinking some holy water?"

Toudou, too, is adequately hesitant to drink the suspicious liquid, but if the Church has prepared it for her, there isn't anything to worry about. Or maybe it just tastes extremely bad?

Toudou is vexed and can't gauge the situation at all. Rabi pushes her face close to Toudou and says with profound gravity, "Toudou. Coming closer to God means approaching death. This liquid is a secret trick, allowing whoever drinks it to instantly reach a mental state that would normally only be possible by completing a fierce and precipitous regimen of ascetic training. Mentally weak individuals are unable to withstand the sheer atmospheric pressure of God's existence. But you, Toudou, have the divine protection of Ahz Gried, so I believe you will be fine..."

"Oh, I—I see... I think I understand."

Toudou has a number of points of concern, but she's understood that she shouldn't drink the liquid without being mentally prepared. That said, she really doesn't have any idea how she should imbibe it...

Toudou is calming herself down through repeated deep breathing, and Rabi hands her the glass like there isn't any reason to give it second thought.

"Okay then... We're short on time, so chug it down."

"...That didn't seem very ceremonious."

"Pomp and circumstance are beside the question."

Rabi is acting all too glib, despite all her showy browbeating just earlier. Can Toudou at least get a second to prepare herself?

"Wait, maybe... Maybe I'm wrong, but is this going to take a long time? Things were unusually rushed toward the end of my teaching training, and hearing that Glacia is a sacred beast was really sudden, too..."

Is condensing the process of ascetic training this much really feasible, simply due to the reason that time is of the essence?

"Don't worry, just drink up. Toudou, the rite of accession is the most intense obstacle in all the three ultra rites of Phimas. I am not privy to how long it will take. We are out of time."

Hmm... Out of time, after all, is it...?

Rabi's eyes are dead flat. Toudou takes the holy water from her and brings it close to her nose to test it. The Church's secret holy water smells faintly of apples.

If Toudou recalls correctly, in her previous world, weren't apples called the fruit of knowledge...?

Toudou brings the glass to her lips under the pressure of Rabi's stern gaze. Her heart races.

"Drink up, great hero. The rest will become clear in due course."

Toudou closes her eyes tightly and gulps down the entire glass—instantly, a peculiar light floods her consciousness.

§ § §

"Get the Church prepared for the announcement. We'll spread word of Toudou's accomplishments far and wide: his battle training under Grace, the powers he's acquired by completing the Thirteen Rites of Phimas, and his successful defeat of the sea demon Heljarl."

"But he hasn't completed the Thirteen Rites of Phimas," says Amelia. "Rather, what Toudou actually completed were the *three ultra rites of Phimas*, which you came up with yourself—"

"It's all about appearances—even our budget! And what's more, this is part of our greater strategy in the battle against Zarpahn. We'll control the timing of the parade and limit where the battle will take place. Toudou and Grace will handle the fighting, and if it

"The overdone sense of justice is a crime."

Fourth Report: On Encountering God

looks like they're going to lose, we'll lure Zarpahn somewhere out of sight...and kill him. Even if he tries to flee."

"...Once again, those are not words befitting any priest I've ever known, but yes, understood."

Our cup is overflowing. I give Amelia an order and assess our framework moving forward. The three ultra rites of Phimas look like they'll be completed without issue. The rest all hinges on how well we can entrap Zarpahn, but at any rate, we must first deal with his powers. Assuming that innumerable iterations will manifest once one is killed, we will need to approach his annihilation carefully. Particularly, if he leaves one of his iterations behind as a contingency at home base before his ambush, we'll be in a heap of trouble after the fact.

These matters, including just how we'll get every last Zarpahn out in the open, are all dependent on Sanya's talents.

"I spoke to my papa, and he put in a good word for us! You can lead the knights, Ares, just like you asked."

"Mr. Ares! Please let me fight alongside Toudou and his party! This is my cross to bear!"

Stey and Spica are both in high spirits. In the end, they've both done exactly as I asked, and as long as they don't manage to bungle everything in the end, they really are accomplished individuals.

"Spica. I command you to be responsible for Toudou's defense. Fight with all you have, and don't say anything unnecessary. Stey, good work. You will join under Amelia's command. Amelia, make sure Stey doesn't do anything unusual."

Amelia pursues her lips as she replies, "Isn't that command... contradictory?"

No, dammit, it's not!

"The rest is up to you. Amelia—most beautiful and accomplished Amelia—you are now subleader. Keep in close contact, and if something happens, get in touch immediately. Keep me fully updated on every move!"

"...Yessir, most handsome and honorable Ares. Please watch as I, most flawless Amelia, complete my tasks with élan."

Defeating the Demon Lord

...Yeah, I get it. You've got one up on me—I fully submit.

I compose myself and bring out the mask that I've polished to a brilliant sheen. Considering when Rabi gave the holy water to Toudou, it's about time to make first contact. In place of the God of Order, Ahz Gried, who very rarely makes outward-facing appearances, I will give Toudou a real, proper lesson on just what the Holy Warrior is all about.

The holy energy at the source of all holy techniques is a complicated matter. In general, it's claimed that holy energy will increase as long as doctrine is followed strictly and prayer to God is not forgotten, but it's not all that simple.

Presently, there isn't any research being done within the Church regarding effective ways to increase holy energy. The outward-facing stance is that there aren't any shortcuts to faith, but the fact of the matter indicates otherwise.

It is precisely because there are ways to increase holy energy other than faith that the Church ceased all research participation to avoid complications. For example—if the power of a drug gives someone true belief in God from the bottom of their heart, are they able to glean holy energy? Considering such questions from the perspective of doctrine is very sensitive, and there are more problematic issues, too.

I don my mask and head toward the room where Toudou is isolated. The content of this ascetic training leaking to any member of the public would be a critical failure, so only myself and Rabi know what's about to happen.

The sun went down long ago, and a number of hours have passed since Toudou was locked in the room. The holy water in question is a type of hallucinogen. It breaks down human mental equilibrium and forces people to directly face their own spirit. If a good person takes the drug, they won't have any problems, but if someone of ill conscience takes it, their mental limits could be broken, leading to criminality—it's a dangerous drug.

"The overdone sense of justice is a crime."

✟ Fourth Report: On Encountering God

Powers of perception also plummet during use, so even if I speak to Toudou from a close distance, he shouldn't be able to discern my identity.

Arriving at the room, I readjust my mask and peer in to ascertain the aura. It's dead quiet. I breathe deeply and open all three locks on the door before erasing all traces of my own presence and opening it quickly and silently.

The room is in shambles—like a tornado has blown through. The altar is smashed to smithereens, and the bed has been split in two. The walls are laced with endless webs of fine cracks, some running with blood. Toudou is standing agape in the middle of the room. He's on both legs but barely staying upright. Both his eyes are open, but they're unfocused, and as proof that he himself created this disastrous scene, both his clenched fists are dripping with blood. His lips are parted askance—a querulous murmur escapes from them.

"I'm not...a bad person. Everyone else noticed, but they didn't do it. They couldn't. That's why I did. I knew that it wasn't the right way. But—everyone was wrong."

Maybe he's seeing visions from his past, before he was summoned? I always knew there was something wrong, ever since the time I saw him react so adversely toward men.

Mental self-improvement of one's inner world starts with facing the past. The holy water has the power to conjure the past, but it alone shouldn't produce results like these. I can only concur that Toudou was involved in some complicated matters before he was ever summoned here.

And what's more... Hmph... It seems like Creio has inevitably refrained from telling me something important. Nonetheless, getting over the past can only be accomplished by the individual in question, and caring for Toudou is not my business.

Toudou's disheveled gaze doesn't reflect my appearance. His consciousness is currently being flooded with a powerful light, I imagine. The demolished room is a sign of the battle he's fought against himself. This Toudou must never be shown to anyone else.

At the same time, to an extent, this means Toudou could be claimed the most suitable person to act as Holy Warrior. People who've had smooth sailing their entire lives often have a high sense of self-affirmation and excel in their capacity to mobilize others, but people who've experienced harrowing trauma exhibit explosive power when their backs are against the wall. It's not even a question, which is more favorable at current, when the Demon Lord's army has imposed such an inferior position upon us.

Clouded consciousness will snap back to reality through strong impact. I determine the best place to stand—behind the crumbling altar—and after putting the palms of my hands toward Toudou's wounded fists to heal them, I use a different holy technique as a wake-up call.

Holy Storm: a light powerful enough to cleanse the surrounding area of all forces of darkness—quite rare even among exorcism-related holy techniques—erupts with force and sends Toudou flying back into the wall.

This technique has been preferred by priests to show heathens the sheer authority of the Church. It hardly damages opponents that aren't members of the hordes of darkness, but the light it produces lasts for a while, making for an unparalleled flashy impression to the naked eye. Further, because the technique emits light from behind the caster, Toudou should only be able to see my outline due to the glare.

Toudou has fallen backward, and the light has returned to his eyes. He looks toward me. Before he becomes completely lucid again, I intensify my godlike presence and speak in the most sonorous voice I can conjure.

"Holy Warrior Naotsugu Toudou. I am the God of Order, Ahz Gried. It is I who discovered your latent power and summoned you to this world with my divine protection to become the savior of humanity."

"……? ...Mmph... Ugh... Huh?"

"And now, you have gained the power, the faith, to have a direct

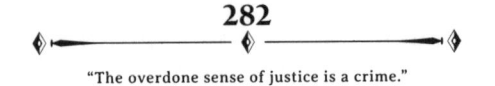

"The overdone sense of justice is a crime."

Fourth Report: On Encountering God

encounter with me. I have been waiting for this day. After all this time, you have proven you are exactly who I expected. The Holy Warrior is a beacon of hope. The greater your life force becomes, the more my own power, which has been in decline due to the God of Evil's increased influence, will return. This will directly lead to balance being restored to the human world."

While supporting my original scenario, I am stroking Toudou's ego and pushing a narrative that will encourage him to become even more incensed. The intense psychedelic experience he's been thrown into will disparage any seeds of doubt from sprouting in his mind.

"Now, after your successful defeat of Heljarl and your study under my eternal disciple, Grace Godicent Trinity, I will bestow even greater power upon thee. The power that wells within you will permeate your entire being, and as long as you continue to fight, I will continue to reside in your soul."

Toudou still doesn't have any idea what's going on as I proceed to cast the most powerful buffs I can on him. My holy techniques won't last forever, but ideally my claims will allow renewed power to permeate throughout Toudou even after the buffs wear off.

Toudou looks confused as he checks both palms of his hands. High-level buffs intended to increase physical strength can be so strong, they make the recipient feel nearly omnipotent.

"Now then, I will leave the salvation of this world to you. Don't forget—I am always by your side. And deliver the Demon Lord also unto salvation, for he has been cajoled and deceived by the God of Evil, Lucief Arept."

"W-wait... Wait a minute!"

Toudou cries out just as I was hoping to escape after my Godlike speech. I ponder whether to simply leave then and there, but it would look weird if God simply walked out the door, wouldn't it? I'll leave after putting Toudou back to sleep. I sneakily roll a sleep bomb that emits sleep-inducing smoke toward Toudou and wait for him to speak again.

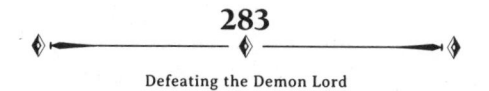

Defeating the Demon Lord

"Wh-why...have I...have I been chosen?! There were so many people much stronger than me in my world! What should I do now—?"

I would like to ask why you were chosen myself.

"...Act according to faith and faith alone. You were chosen because you are a human worthy of the Holy Warrior's path."

"F-faith and faith alone... Be more specific!"

Who in their right mind would ask that of God? I said to follow your faith!

I cough and give Toudou a more detailed indicator.

"...Take the monsters, demonic entities, and Demon Lord that unleash chaos on our world...and slaughter them all."

"...What?"

"Don't let a shred of the root of evil be left behind. And spare them not compassion. You are the blade of the God of Order that will bring hope to humanity. You must already understand. You must know of the immortal knight that serves by sacrificing their very being."

Continuing to fight without hesitation. That is what I am asking of Toudou. The Holy Warrior doesn't have any need for bizarre sentiments. The hero is nothing more than a weapon in human form summoned by the Church. Thanks to the exceptional power of the divine protection they are given, if they can become truly resolute, there is no greater defender.

At the end of the day, these are nothing more than the selfish wishes of myself and of humanity. I can't make such absurd demands of Toudou.

"The anguish you are mired in will only be truly dispelled once the Demon Lord is defeated."

Dammit—at any rate, I'm doing my best to ingrain our endgame goal into his consciousness. Doing as much is certainly better than not doing anything at all.

The smoke from the sleep bomb must have started working. Toudou's head starts to hang loosely and tremble. In Toudou's mind, this encounter will remain a memory stuck somewhere between a

284

"The overdone sense of justice is a crime."

Fourth Report: On Encountering God

dream and reality. This closely resembles all records of previous saints' encounters with God. The chance Toudou will find me out is very low.

Just as I turn around to disappear with the light, Toudou's voice rises like it's suspended in the heat of the room.

"A f-final...question..."

"...What is it?"

He has more questions? This does not bode well for the journey ahead.

As I sigh, Toudou asks a particularly unexpected question, his voice threatening to disappear into thin air.

"Are Stey...and Spica...and Rabi...really pious believers?"

§ § §

Toudou opens her heavy eyelids. She holds her throbbing, leaden head and slowly gets her bearings. Her memory slowly begins to come back. This is the room she was initially led to for her training.

Rabi is sitting beside Toudou and notices she's roused, turning her ruby-red eyes toward her.

"Toudou, are you awake?"

"Yes... Um... What is this place? Am I...dreaming?"

Although faint, Toudou can remember what happened after she was made to drink the holy water. A swelling light that threatened to erase her consciousness, followed by a long battle with spirits visiting from her past. And in the middle of the battle, a sudden visitor—

She feels like she was dreaming for a very long time. A long, terrifying, and bizarre dream. The room's appearance hasn't changed one iota since before she drank the potion. She has memories of the room being broken to bits, but now, it's back as it was. Her hands, which should be painted with blood, are completely free of injury.

If it wasn't a dream, then what was it? Just as Toudou considers this idea, she realizes something—her entire body is overflowing with power. She feels shockingly light, and her body is hot to the touch.

Rabi addresses Toudou, who is clearly confused.

"It appears...that exactly as I expected, you have successfully encountered God."

"What...does that...?"

She remembers. It's dim, but the memory is there. Looking back on it now, it's all quite hard to believe, but...it's not an exaggeration to say that the colossal power she now feels in her body now is divine...probably.

"But I mean... It's just, like, so different than what I imagined."

"......That's because God cannot be so easily understood by human beings. By the way, what did you find odd about the experience?"

"Well, just... The God of Order should administer...order, yeah? But the God I met—he told me all I should focus on is slaughtering monsters, demonic forces, and the Demon Lord. You think Ahz Gried would really say such a thing?"

It's simply an issue of perception, but in Toudou's mind, those are the words of an evil God. There isn't any mistake that Toudou has been summoned for the purpose of defeating the Demon Lord, but this portrait of the Holy Warrior is highly divergent from what she's heard from the Kingdom and the Church.

Rabi falls silent for a while with a perplexed look on her face before saying, "...Well, that is also a possibility. I think God was probably just in a bad mood."

A bad mood...? Does the God of Order also wake up on the wrong side of the bed?

The God Toudou met was so dry, almost sarcastic...and they really felt human. They emitted a holy aura, but without it, they could have just as easily been human. And what's more, when Toudou asked them about Rabi's, Spica's, and Stey's faith at the very end, all they did was disappear in silence. Leaving without responding is one thing, but up until then, they had at least thrown in adequate interjections during conversation—would an actual God really just leave? Considering the situation she found herself in, the God she

"The overdone sense of justice is a crime."

Fourth Report: On Encountering God

met was most certainly real, yet Toudou can't help feeling that there was something odd about them.

As Toudou falls silent in deep thought, Rabi rushes to say, "At any rate, the most crucial part of the rite of accession is now complete. Everything should come together in time for your public debut, and as a member of the Church, I am very relieved."

Toudou quickly switches up her frame of mind. The only reason she took on training at the Friedia estate's secret training grounds, alongside so many other efforts, is in order to become even a tiny bit stronger before her public debut. If she can just get through the public debut, her journey will begin anew.

Training in the capital isn't all bad, but for Toudou, staying on her journey to defeat the Demon Lord is far less vexing.

"Is the date set? I haven't heard anything yet myself..."

From what Toudou remembers, she was to be informed when the public debut is one month away. She sighs quietly, and Rabi addresses her indifferently without budging an eyebrow.

"It's in ten days. The Kingdom aristocrats have asserted that there isn't any reason to delay it further. We have little time. Soon you shall meet the sacred beast Glacia, and finally, we'll make any necessary finishing touches."

Fifth Report
On the Holy Warrior's Debut

Our hectic days have been filled with interminable changes. But soon, that will all be over.

A miracle has arrived to confront the Demon Lord Kranos. The Kingdom of Ruxe's successful summoning of the Holy Warrior, through the auspices of the Church, alongside many other meritorious achievements, has been announced quickly and, moreover, far and wide.

During this era, when many kingdoms are being encroached upon and a number have been completely destroyed, a ray of hope appearing has been largely received with positivity by Kingdom of Ruxe commoners. The announcement will soon make its way to other kingdoms as well. Rather—making sure this happens is the Church's responsibility.

The Holy Warrior is a double-edged sword. While the Holy Warrior of legend becomes a great source of power as the hope of humanity personified, repercussions in the event that they are defeated would be massive.

The character and personality of the individual summoned can also be problematic. This is one reason that Toudou's summoning has not been announced to the public thus far. In the case that Toudou was defeated before being publicly known, they would have an excuse, and if the Holy Warrior turned out to be a man of ill repute, they could easily deal with him. However, once his existence has been made known across the land, Naotsugu Toudou failing in any sense of the word will not be tolerated.

This is a matter of resignation—proof that the Church and the Kingdom of Ruxe have made up their minds to put the fate of humanity in the hands of the Holy Warrior.

Stey makes a half-hearted salute and says, "Holy knights and monks, one hundred total, have arrived!"

"Nice work. Deploy them according to our established plan."

"Yes! Leave it to me! Heh-heh... It seems that somehow, I have become a trustworthy girl, too!"

Mobilizing one hundred holy knights and monks, who are few and far between to begin with, in such a short time frame is a very tall order. We have the cardinal to thank. Why does Stey look so confident when all she did was use her father's influence?

"That must be a mistake—I think you mean to say 'convenient,' not 'trustworthy.'"

"What the—?!"

Stey freezes solid at Amelia's brusque statement. Probably not a good idea to say that to her, even if you're being dishonest...

Our battle-ready forces are more than adequate. We have myself and Grace, alongside the Kingdom's guard knights and soldiers from the Church. Toudou and the others have acquired more than enough battle experience. Even during an ambush, unless we absolutely drop the ball, there isn't any way Toudou will be assassinated.

Nonetheless, I wouldn't be so sure if we didn't have advance information. Zarpahn has the divine protection of the God of Evil, allowing him to greatly reduce the pressure on him during battle. With this power, we could have potentially ignored our innumerable counterattacks and simply gone in to take Toudou's life. Yet, now that we know this is the sort of opponent we're up against, we are able to implement a strategy.

Controlling information is the same as controlling the battlefield. We will absolutely not let him escape. Rabi has been working even harder than I have on Toudou's public debut, and she's been

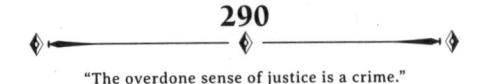

"The overdone sense of justice is a crime."

Fifth Report: On the Holy Warrior's Debut

incessantly assisting Toudou in the pursuit of her teaching, successfully getting her to grasp her role flawlessly.

Rabi says, eyes reproachful, "Yet, boss, was it really necessary to expound upon the fact that you completed the three ultra rites of Phimas in such a short time? Seems rash. You really did take it in whatever direction you pleased, and Toudou and the others have become quite suspicious."

"What's done is done."

The most important thing is whether facts will remain facts. Under the Church's tutelage, Toudou has received the immortal knight's teaching, alongside successfully completing the rites of Phimas and an encounter with God. Next, during the Hero's Procession of Light, he will be attacked by Zarpahn Drago Fahni and easily fend him off, defeating him to be recognized by the people with aplomb as the Holy Warrior.

The strategy is simple. We will limit the areas that Zarpahn can ambush and establish thick reinforcements in the surrounding buildings. Toudou will be supported quietly through holy techniques when engaging in battle with Zarpahn. If Grace and Toudou can successfully finish off Zarpahn together, that will be perfect, and in the off chance he escapes, we will stop him in his tracks with a barrier. This time, I won't let him escape alive.

The parade will be held in the early evening. This is a last-ditch measure to provoke Zarpahn into an ambush. It's not the same as midnight, but this time frame will also allow the vampire to move without limitations. The plan was set in motion through Creio, and there was very little opposing sentiment within the Kingdom. Zarpahn was certainly concerned with the time of day as well, which is why he worked to set the current plan in motion himself.

Our preemptive measures are nothing short of perfect. Yet we still have two concerns: whether Zarpahn will behave according to our assumptions and just how long Grace really has left.

Regarding Zarpahn, he still hasn't realized that Sanya is on our side, so we should be able to control his actions to an extent, but he hasn't exactly been completely forthcoming. Regarding Grace, we simply don't have any precedent to work from.

Nonetheless, there isn't anything we can do about these points now. At the end of the day, we are working behind the scenes, supporting a new chapter in the legend of the Holy Warrior. As an order of business, this is inevitable.

"Time to roll out! Leave no stone unturned!"

""Yessir!!"""

§ § §

Everything is going shockingly well. The announcement of the Holy Warrior summoning that has been brought to the Kingdom of Ruxe has everyone excited. With the parade looming, visitors from outside the Kingdom have spiked, and security has tightened, but this doesn't matter to Zarpahn, who's already infiltrated the city.

There's nothing to be anxious about. Sanya is offering her assistance, and the sacrificial pawns are all lined up. The parade has been set to early evening, which won't impede Zarpahn whatsoever. His demonic gaze wouldn't have worked on members of the Church, but he used it to dispatch a number of Ruxe elites under his control to collect information. If something happens, he'll be informed right away.

People are weak, yet because of this, they're prone to delivering low blows and ending up floundering drastically. There is also a reason that humanity remains proud of their prosperity and capacity to push back and defeat colossal demonic forces. Yet Zarpahn is aware of this and remains on guard.

Now, at the vacation home of one of the Kingdom aristocrats, in a stripped-down room that sunlight cannot enter, Zarpahn speaks to Sanya, who has the exact same goals in mind.

"We will create a diversion and scatter the guards. It will be a hassle to take out the Holy Warrior while trying to deal with ordinary grunts. From what I've heard from my aristocrat manservants, the

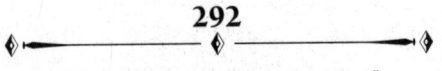

"The overdone sense of justice is a crime."

Fifth Report: On the Holy Warrior's Debut

Kingdom guards also include some special knights, including one human who extols supposed eternal life—Grace Godicent Trinity."

Grace's name is known far and wide among demonic entities. She is a formidable opponent who has been released from normal human life expectancy through the power of God. She has been quite dormant as of late, but she is still alive, Zarpahn has surmised. In terms of timing, this is both immaculate and horrendous. Taking on two different legends at the same time is an arduous task, but if Zarpahn can take out Grace at the same time as the Holy Warrior, he will be renowned as one of the greatest champions to ever live.

Sanya must not have understood what Zarpahn said, and her expression momentarily contorts.

"O-oh... Is that so? That knight... But really, taking her alone is one thing, but we have human support, and we have you, Zarpahn. We should be just fine, don't you think?"

"Hmph... You're soft. Even if we pull off an ambush on the Holy Warrior, he will not simply lie down to die."

Toudou and Zarpahn's battle in the Great Forest of the Vale. Zarpahn was not at full strength then, but he certainly wasn't taking it easy on him, either. If Toudou had just been summoned at that point—fighting him again now, after much time has passed, would certainly prove a vicious bout.

The name of the Holy Warrior that Zarpahn acquired through the aristocrats is different than previously. It's a fake name. From this fact alone, Zarpahn can determine that the Holy Warrior is not an opponent to be trifled with. Yet Zarpahn has ideas himself, too.

"We will scatter the defenses. If we attack a number of sections of the city at once, the soldiers will have no choice but to turn toward them. We will paint the parade red with despair."

"?! You intend to use humans?"

"...What are you saying, Sanya? The humans are only there to cause a stir. The guards won't even go on alert until demonic forces attack."

"...You are correct, that is my mistake."

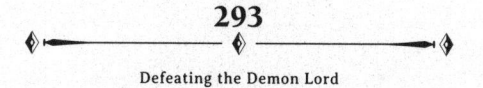

Has Zarpahn forgotten the name Grace? She is the guardian of humanity, and fearing her is entirely natural, yet Zarpahn is slightly disappointed. He needs the strongest allies he can find.

"Leave all matters of subversion to me. Don't dare get in my way."

"...Surely you'll at least let me know where you'll begin the attack from?"

"That won't be necessary. I'll say it again, but don't get in my way. I plan on recklessly destroying different parts of the city depending on the situation. I will aim for vital locations that the Kingdom and the Church can't simply turn a blind eye to. There aren't that many humans of high level, so I should be able to ravage the Kingdom thoroughly."

Humans are different from demons in that so many of them require protection. This is one aspect in which Zarpahn's Manifold Horde will shine.

As a smile spreads across Zarpahn's face, Sanya looks somber.

"Yet without you present, if something goes wrong, we might not be able to finish the Holy Warrior off. You become weaker the more iterations you manifest, right? Putting subversion on top of that—won't that limit the area of effect for your powers?"

"Hmph... You're so spineless. My powers can always come back to me, the one Zarpahn. That isn't a problem. As far as the area—it's not infinite, but my area of effect will be fine within the Kingdom limits."

"...Impressive, as always. I'm relieved to hear it. As long as you're there, we will be able to assassinate Grace, as well as the Holy Warrior."

"That's a given. Eventually, I will surpass my ancestor Fahni, you realize, right? You will be thankful for the good fortune of being able to plan this strategy with me."

The powers of a high-level vampire who has awakened are nothing short of sheer genius. Manifesting multiple iterations is already a very high-level power among all vampires, and Zarpahn is still growing. In the future, his area of effect will expand, and moments

"The overdone sense of justice is a crime."

of dwindling power will cease to occur. At that time, Zarpahn Drago Fahni will become ruler of this world.

"Understood, Zarpahn. For the task at hand, I will resign myself to supporting you in the fullest. I've done a lot to prepare on my end, too, but you clearly have a higher chance of successfully pulling off our strategy."

"......Hmph." Zarpahn narrows his eyes.

Sanya claps her hands and stands up. "Well then... I should attend to some miscellaneous matters, for the sake of our future ruler. Some of the pawns we've gathered are probably getting cold feet now that the Holy Warrior has actually been announced, and I need to make sure nothing leaks from those types. I'll triple-check them all and nip any problems in the bud..."

Sanya hurriedly leaves the estate. Zarpahn watches her in silence. He still doesn't know exactly whose army she's affiliated with, but she sure is a sharp werebeast. Even among the multitude of powerful subordinate species that have gathered under him, she is a rare breed.

Once Zarpahn joins the Demon Lord's inner circle, he will certainly keep her in mind.

§ § §

In the very back of the church of the royal capital, Toudou and her party are running over final preparations for the parade. Engaging in the three ultra rites of Phimas seems like a far-off, distant memory. It's only been a week, but the busy days were spent being called upon by the Kingdom and the Church and meeting with aristocrats.

It would be a different story if everything was directly related to defeating the Demon Lord, but being dragged around to be viewed by the inquisitive eyes of Ruxe aristocrats repeatedly was a difficult part of the arrangement, even though Toudou understands that it's necessary. Despite the physical toll that the three ultra rites of Phimas took on her body, Toudou almost preferred them in comparison, given how they led to her capacities increasing.

Those days are now behind her. Once the Hero's Procession of Light is complete, Toudou and her party will again set out on their journey to defeat the Demon Lord. Not only will they receive the full backing of the Kingdom, their journey will no longer be confined to domestic affairs. The Kingdom of Ruxe isn't the only nation that has suffered at the hand of the Demon Lord Kranos. Addressing all those affected is the true meaning of the Holy Warrior's existence.

After completing final confirmation of the parade route, Toudou and the others return to the room they've been provided. Aria and Limis look very tired—they're not particularly adept at the face-to-face meetings they have been taking part in.

Toudou wants to change the mood, and after sighing once, smiles and says, "I still can't believe that Glacia was a sacred beast—what a surprise…"

Even looking back on it now, Toudou remains shocked by her meeting with Glacia, who now has snow-white hair thanks to Rabi. All three ultra rites of Phimas proceeded too quickly, including Toudou's encounter with God.

"I've never heard of a sacred beast," adds Aria. "This must have also been the guidance of God."

"Hard to believe there's any sacred beast that's this hungry all the time…," Limis says incredulously.

"……"

Glacia—still in the white robes given to her by the Church—doesn't say anything. Her trademark appearance somehow instills a sense of calm.

Come to think of it, the party has been acquainted with Glacia for quite some time now. Spica is currently working for the Church, but she will apparently be rejoining Toudou's group. Encouraging news, although Gregorio's influence on Spica remains a concern.

Soon, Toudou will set out on a new journey and get a fresh start. She has cleared the three ultra rites of Phimas, successfully encountered God, and boosted her physical and mental capacities.

Toudou takes a deep breath to focus her mind—practically an

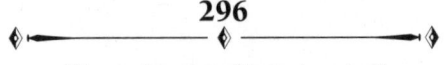

"The overdone sense of justice is a crime."

Fifth Report: On the Holy Warrior's Debut

old habit by now—when there's a a quiet knock at the door. The only people who know where Toudou is staying before her public debut are members of the Church.

She answers the door, and a young female holy knight enters—Eve Lucrao, Grace's right-hand woman, sounding as insincere and brusque as always.

Eve wasn't involved with the final rite of accession, so Toudou hasn't seen her since completing the rite of alms. Eve's role is to communicate Grace's wishes, and although Toudou hasn't spoken to her much, she can tell that this holy knight is honest and has good intentions.

"It's been a while, Eve. What's going on?"

"Captain Grace—wants to speak to you, Sir Toudou—about future endeavors. Please—come with me."

Toudou wonders if Grace have has another training regimen in mind, but the Holy Warrior's shallow hopes are soon dashed.

"An attack by demonic forces...?"

"This is highly reliable information."

The information provided by Eve indicates that a cohort of the Demon Lord is planning to aim for Toudou in an assassination attempt. Captain Grace remains as stoic and stalwart as a giant tree. An attack in the capital of Ruxe, which has rolled out the tightest security measures in all the land, would normally be a huge deal, but Grace doesn't seem even slightly perturbed.

It's almost hard to believe, but a follower of the God of Order would never tell a lie. Aria and Limis have very severe looks on their faces.

"In that case, we must inform the Kingdom populace immediately—"

"No—that will not be necessary. Although we are facing a demonic infiltration, the Church would like to show the Holy Warrior's powers off to the fullest extent on this occasion."

"Huh...?"

Toudou stares wide-eyed at Eve. The holy knight doesn't appear to be joking.

Eve continues providing information in a solemn tone, including the enemy's strategy and their plausible attack routes. It's unclear how she ascertained this intel, but she certainly has fine details. Most shocking of all, the enemy plans to attack vital locations in the capital. Even if Toudou survives, any severe damage dealt to the capital's functionality could tip the scales of warfare in Kranos's favor.

"The demonic being that will attack has a particularly troublesome set of powers. The Church is of the belief that we absolutely cannot let him escape from our midst. However, pawns of the enemy are also interspersed in the Kingdom's upper ranks, and the majority of the reinforcements the Church has prepared must be allotted to vital locations and for protecting the populace. The knights of the Kingdom only put us at a disadvantage against the hordes of darkness, you see—in other words, it is necessary that you take out the demonic forces in question alongside a few select elite members."

If the enemy figures out the security measures that are in place, then all is lost. The same goes for if the capital's vital locations go unprotected—or if Toudou dies.

This will be a ferocious battle. Toudou's holy energy has increased, but no one can be sure of exactly how much. As Toudou swallows a massive lump in her throat, Eve speaks to her in a sonorous and beautiful tone to confirm her intentions.

"Failure is not acceptable in the face of demonic opponents. Naotsugu Toudou, achieving victory is the practice of eliminating all possible sources of defeat. Captain Grace once told me this long ago—sometimes we must make the decision of forsaking the weak. Do you have the intestinal fortitude to continue guaranteeing victory, no matter what the cost?"

The Holy Warrior is the hope of humanity. This reality has become manifest for Toudou, seeping deeply into her soul. She stares back into Eve's eyes.

"The overdone sense of justice is a crime."

Fifth Report: On the Holy Warrior's Debut

"Of course—I will never lose."

Toudou doesn't hesitate for even a moment. She has traveled across many lands thus far. Everything on her journey has become a source of power—her battles, victories, losses, and training. Her gaze is imbued with powerful life force as she invokes her destiny. Eve nods.

"In that case, all is well. There are only two things left we have to give you. The first is a holy relic. Because you are no longer able to wear the holy armor Fried, we have this new armor for you to fight in—"

Toudou's eyes go wide as Grace passes a bottle to her. It contains a strange, shining silver liquid. It's far too inorganic to claim it's magical, but it sparkles almost like it's alive. It certainly doesn't look like armor. Aria is visibly dumbfounded in amazement. She just might know what this liquid really is.

Toudou carefully accepts the bottle as Eve continues.

"The other is the power of the immortal knight, Grace Godicent Trinity. This is a momentous ritual that has only been performed once before in the history of the Holy Warrior. Previous Holy Warriors have inherited the power of the immortal knight, alongside her determination, and successfully defeated the Demon Lord that plagued our world. Toudou, you have already participated in live battle practice with Captain Grace, but now—you will fight her once again to experience every last ounce of her power. Your shining blade, imbued with the universal divine protection of the God of Order, will rip through any shred of doubt in the present, past, and into perpetuity, becoming a beacon for humanity—"

Grace had been standing silently, but now, she abruptly steps forward. Toudou and the others all witness Grace's massive arm ensconced in armor pushing Eve, who had fallen silent, from behind. Eve's eyes flare wide in shock, her expression more than appropriate for her young age. Her voice shakes.

"?! C-Captain Grace, what does that...?"

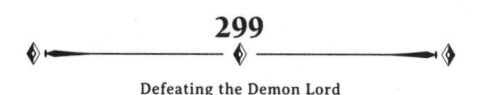

"……"

"...I understand. No, it is an honor. It would be dishonest to say that I have not been impressed by the speed at which Toudou has grown. Toudou—"

Eve regains her calm, dignified composure and looks at Toudou with her crystal-clear eyes.

"My apologies, but Captain Grace has opted to designate me as your opponent in succession. Captain's true strength has not yet waned, but I have watched her in the closest proximity for a long time. I don't believe my existence will be lacking in terms of your opponent in succession—please humbly accept these conditions. This is a first for me, but Captain—is looking toward the future, according to her wishes."

This really must be a first. Eve's expression is tainted with anxiety, and she's stiff.

The future—Toudou could never understand the gravity of these words used by a knight who is fated to never die. Yet if Toudou can't live up to the challenge, what sort of Holy Warrior is she?

"I don't mind whatsoever. Let's do it—let's show everyone the future."

Toudou hasn't engaged in battle with Eve at all thus far, but she has a decent idea of her strength. Eve is certainly not lacking. Toudou unsheathes the holy sword Ex, always hanging at her side. Eve's eyes are wide with shock.

The holy sword is beaming brightly, belying the fact it was ever fading. It is the embodiment of pure light.

§ § §

A bloodred sunset has painted over the entire sky. Quietly, yet certainly, a thick heat hangs over the royal capital, permeating it. Vendor stalls line the streets, which are packed with people. The enthusiasm filling the street is reminiscent of a true festival, the kind that hasn't been seen since the Demon Lord's invasion began and kept everyone's spirits suppressed.

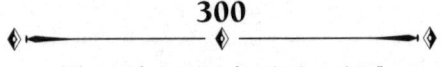

"The overdone sense of justice is a crime."

Fifth Report: On the Holy Warrior's Debut

Nonetheless, there isn't any other way today could play out. Today will be a day that lives on in legend—because today, the summoned Holy Warrior will march throughout the capital. Toudou is legitimately good-looking, and when he begins parading throughout the city, the frenzy is expected only to intensify. If Toudou walks alongside Grace, it will be nothing short of a triumphal hero's return.

I look down from the second floor of a house on the central promenade that Toudou and everyone are scheduled to march down, and I sigh. The time has finally arrived.

I have endeavored to make the best of our situation until now, but just considering what will happen if we fail, I can feel a headache coming on.

"It seems that somehow, someway, Sanya has not been found out."

"Yes, it seems so. She has been sending regular communications, and Zarpahn must really be an optimist."

"Even those with formidable special powers can be optimistic, I guess. But he is no fool."

I was dumbstruck when Sanya told me that Zarpahn plans to attack vital locations by using his innumerable iterations. It's certainly a potent mechanism, but a demonic being using such a backdoor tactic, and especially given Zarpahn's personality—I would have never expected it. If Zarpahn played that hand and we didn't have any preemptive intel, the Kingdom of Ruxe would have been in dire straits. And even now that we understand his strategy, responding with effective countermeasures is proving difficult.

What I've been able to accomplish is getting Stey to prepare soldiers and asking the guards that were set to protect Toudou to inconspicuously gather in the vital locations. We can't prevent Zarpahn's intentions of pulling the guards apart, but even if Toudou is able to fend him off, if the city is left in ruins, it will not look good.

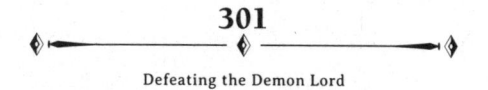

However, the information Sanya's provided is not all bad news. The area of effect of Zarpahn's powers encompasses the entire capital. This is a frighteningly large area, but it also means that if we close off the capital, there won't be any chance of letting Zarpahn escape. We have already begged Creio, and he has put up a powerful barrier around the entire capital in order to not let Zarpahn out. This is not a level of warfare power that is normally employed to trap one single opponent, no matter how powerful they may be. Zarpahn is nothing more than a rat in a trap now.

I truly can't believe he's become such a pernicious thorn in our side.

The street suddenly erupts in a murmur. Toudou and the others have likely appeared at Ruxe Kingdom Royal Castle. The Hero's Procession of Light is scheduled to begin at the castle before heading down the central promenade and traveling throughout the city. As I narrow my eyes at the cries of joy, Eve, standing nearby, speaks.

"Sir Ares. Why must I remain separated from Captain Grace?"

"Have you not heard from her directly?"

"...Huh?" Eve's eyes grow wide.

That Grace... It's a real pain in the ass that she can't communicate with other people. And Eve must have fought Toudou instead of Grace; the girl has terrible judgment.

I remain silent, and Eve must get the message. She purses her lips.

I narrow my eyes again. Just as I look in the direction that Toudou and company are set to approach from, I can see the head of the parade come into view.

§ § §

Toudou looks down from a balcony of Ruxe Royal Castle at a group of people in the courtyard. They're gathered in the semi-darkness, and the heat billowing around them in waves makes Toudou's soul stir. The sensation continues to travel from her fingertips to the top of her head. She can feel her body and mind swelling to repletion. It's evident that the power surging within her is now manifest. It's very similar to the omnipotent feeling she got from her encounter with God.

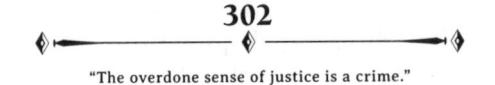

"The overdone sense of justice is a crime."

Fifth Report: On the Holy Warrior's Debut

What...is this? It's not an illusion.

"Nao, are you okay?"

"...I can't believe there's so many people... I'm nervous all of a sudden."

As Aria and Limis speak uneasily, after joining the group, Spica interjects to explain.

"Well, that's because the hero summoning is a deep-seated secret of the Church and will serve as a ray of hope that will eliminate Demon Lord Kranos's current oppression..."

However, the three girls don't seem to feel the same odd power that Toudou can. The magic relic—summetal armor—that she was given by Grace is a very strong armament, although in a different way from the holy armor Fried. The armor transforms freely to conform to the exact shape of the wearer's body, and it can even expand in front to build a protective wall. With practice, it will likely be able to evolve to help maintain maneuverability or even perform attacks. At present, Toudou is wearing this armor, with a special robe over the top from the Friedia estate, which has the power to prevent detection. The robe is as black as the abyss, and it's not particularly suitable for the Holy Warrior, but without paying special attention, the summetal armor will stick to Toudou's body, and the robe is necessary to hide her curves.

Toudou was not particularly on board with the parade idea at the beginning, but now, her sense of duty as the Holy Warrior is percolating rapidly. She heard from the Church that demonic forces will be attacking soon, and Toudou doesn't feel like she can lose. She can feel her razor-sharp synapses firing. The Kingdom's announcement—a notification of the Holy Warrior's summoning—is occurring on schedule, but she doesn't even hear it.

The throngs of people gathered occasionally erupting in a murmur is likely due to their surprise in hearing of Toudou's meritorious achievements. These reports have likely been manipulated by the media. But her next achievement won't be.

"Nao, you're on."

Toudou returns to herself as Limis speaks to her. She is pushed from behind and steps out to the front. So many eyes filled with expectation. Infinite gazes are centered solely on Toudou. She had decided what to say beforehand, but before she realizes it, her hand is gripping the holy blade on her waist. A sharp metal scrape erupts into the air, and the wind rushes. A pillar of light beaming from the blade ascends into the sky.

The holy sword Ex. The sign of the Holy Warrior—a blade of light gifted by the God of Order.

Naotsugu Toudou makes her proclamation naturally.

"I am—the Holy Warrior."

A moment of silence—then the crowd erupts into cries of joy.

The Holy Warrior is summoned from another world by God for support in times of human crisis. Alongside her stands the immortal knight, who has protected humanity since time immemorial, Grace Godicent Trinity.

A frenzied rush envelops Toudou and the others as they are guided forward by the gallant knights of Ruxe. The central promenade of Ruxe is unbelievably crowded and lively—as if every single resident of the capital has been strung out into the street like a puppet.

Streetlights illuminate the city alongside valiant music playing, and the parade has indefatigable swagger as it marches forth, both emanating power and holiness. Following after it, one would think that every line of people marching in the parade is imbued with the pure, powerful light of the God of Order. There isn't any sign of the jeering or heckling they had been concerned about. This glorious procession will serve as the quickest method to communicate to all the other kingdoms that are suffering at the hand of Demon Lord Kranos.

Toudou has the blessing of the Eight Spirit Kings and the Three Deities. She feels like her entire physical form has been exchanged for a new one. Her senses are honed and clear, and she can perfectly

"The overdone sense of justice is a crime."

Fifth Report: On the Holy Warrior's Debut

see every last face that's pushing toward her. This sensation, which can't be described through mere words like "a change in consciousness," could perhaps only be aptly indicated as an evolution.

The crowd loudly exclaims the names of Grace, of Toudou. Their voices become a wave of sound that resounds throughout the capital. The procession begins with Ruxe knights leading the way, followed by Toudou and Grace riding upon pure-white steeds so that the populace can see them well, with Aria, Limis, and the others taking up the rear. Even behind them, although largely out of sight, the Ruxe Army, separated into individual branches, is also following behind.

Yet Toudou can't afford to focus on the parade alone. She focuses her synapses as she manipulates the reins of her horse. She remains constantly aware of her location. Among the infinite gazes laid upon her, she calculates which could potentially be rife with enmity.

She finds one—it's certain, they're looking at her. Among the swelling fervor of the crowd, a single gaze sticks out because it's so cold. Aria and Limis don't seem to notice, but Toudou can feel a tingling sensation, the determination to fight, stemming from the gaze.

The parade hits a ninety-degree corner. They're almost at the point of attack the Church has indicated. Just how will their opponent attack Toudou and the others, who are protected by the Kingdom of Ruxe's knights?

Just as Toudou considers every angle, she hears an unforeseen, strange sound from within the cries of joy. It's a querulous groan that she would never, ever notice under normal circumstances.

Toudou looks up and quickly checks to the right and left. A scene unfolds in her field of vision—the tall buildings on either side of the road are wrenched in half and begin to crumble down upon her.

§ § §

Something isn't right. This was made clear when Zarpahn checked out the ceremony that occurred before the parade started. The Holy Warrior that raised the holy sword looks a lot like the man who defeated him previously, yet they're obviously a completely different person. For a moment, he thought they could have been a decoy, but the light emanating from the holy blade is most certainly a miracle only possible by the true Holy Warrior.

Zarpahn remains shocked and looks to Sanya for an answer. But she doesn't give him the response he is looking for. It seems inevitable that the Holy Warrior who defeated Zarpahn and called himself Ares Crown is not actually the real hero of holy divination.

Or could there be two Holy Warriors that have been summoned? At any rate, Zarpahn no longer has the option to call off his attack. His order from Fahni is to extinguish the Holy Warrior—although they have not been indicated by name.

The Holy Warrior is a formidable opponent. From what Zarpahn can see, he's far advanced compared with that man, even judging from his divine protection alone. When put alongside Grace, they form the greatest enemy Zarpahn has ever fought against without question.

Zarpahn does not underestimate Demon Lord Kranos. When the war began, Kranos gathered the demonic forces that pledged their cooperation to teach methods for assaulting humanity. Humanity's greatest strength is their power in numbers. In other words, when assaulting a human kingdom, chaos should be created so that nobody can properly take command.

Zarpahn destroys the buildings through his own attack and falls upon the Holy Warrior. Humans are weak. Simply reducing their structures to rubble leaves them incapable of fighting in many instances. The commoners flocking in the streets cry out in despair.

It's exactly as he planned. If even a strong opponent rushes to save the citizens, they'll expose a certain weakness or two. Zarpahn will take advantage of this—and kill them.

Just as Zarpahn considers his plan, the cries of despair turn to shouts of joy. Zarpahn unconsciously swallows a lump in his throat.

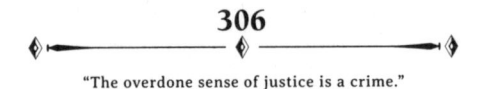

"The overdone sense of justice is a crime."

Fifth Report: On the Holy Warrior's Debut

The buildings that should have crumbled due to their foundations being laid to waste have somehow maintained their original positions without falling. White walls of light have risen from the ground to protect the citizens and the street, propping up the buildings that were on the brink of total collapse.

This is...the power of Grace's holy technique. Zarpahn's planned ambush across a wide area has been thwarted. Creating such a miracle with only a moment's notice proves her formidable level of proficiency. Yet holy techniques can't be used without limit.

Zarpahn must determine the outcome right now, at this moment. He launches himself down from the roof of the building he was hiding on, which should have collapsed. He transforms his fingernails into claws and plans to slash straight for the neck with one swipe. As he envisions his success—an acute pain rips through his own stomach.

"Geh—?!"

A silver tentacle has pierced him in the belly. Zarpahn's divine protection of Lucief Arept provides a supreme barrier that mitigates damage from all attacks. Yet right now, this absolute defense isn't working. Zarpahn grips the tentacle and looks up. Pure rage erases any sensation of pain. A determined set of powerful black eyes are staring down at him. The tentacle is extending from underneath a lacquer-black robe. There are only very few who can break through a barrier Lucief Arept has devised.

"Ho...ly...War...rior—!!"

"You must be Kranos's puppet."

A cold, clear voice, accompanied by a steady gaze rich with fighting spirit. Feeling the power of light emanating forcefully from the Holy Warrior, for a moment Zarpahn completely forgets about the existence of the Ares Crown he loathes so much.

This is the Holy Warrior—the universal enemy of demonic forces everywhere, and the being that Fahni is most afraid of. Zarpahn suddenly remembers his compatriot that was supposed to use humans to help attack alongside his ambush.

Sanya... Where is Sanya? Why isn't she here yet? Did an unforeseen accident occur?

No—it doesn't even matter. There's no denying that his ambush has been thwarted, but there is still an absolute gap in the power between demonic forces and human beings. His strategy will roll on. Sputtering blood, Zarpahn smiles deeply at the Holy Warrior and activates his powers.

"My name is Zarpahn Drago Fahni. Zarpahn, the Manifold Horde. And your life, Holy Warrior, is mine for the taking."

The humans walking by him with indefatigable swagger like they own the damn place only have strength in numbers. What does that mean when a vampire hell-bent on eating them alive acquires the same strength?

Two of Zarpahn's duplicates rush at the Holy Warrior and Grace in perfect unison. Then, the silver tentacle stuck in Zarpahn's abdomen pierces his brain, and the other Zarpahns lose consciousness.

§ § §

"Wh-wha— Gyahhhhh!! What the hell are these things?!"

"We're under attack!"

The stately parade has been transformed into a hellish scene of agony and pandemonium. I watch quietly from the window. Zarpahn Drago Fahni's doubles have already infiltrated the street.

The Manifold Horde—I'd heard the rumors, but this is truly a terrifying power. I was racked with a formidable chill when he brought the buildings toppling down. If Grace hadn't created the walls, a great number of citizens would have been gravely injured. She really understands humanity's weaknesses. Standing next to me, Eve looks ready to leap out the window at any moment. The only thing stopping her is my command; right now, my authority to give her orders comes directly from Cardinal Creio.

"Sir Ares..."

"Not yet. Do not mistake our order of priorities."

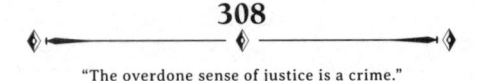

"The overdone sense of justice is a crime."

Fifth Report: On the Holy Warrior's Debut

The battle is still in flux. Above all else, we must remain in the shadows—and absolutely cannot mistake our order of priorities. Stey and Amelia are casting holy techniques with all their might to support the Ruxe knights. The wide-area buffs that top-tier priests can cast grant so many different powers in situations like this. Of course, Amelia is coming through, but watching Stey conjure prayer fervently while wiping sweat from her brow, I am quite glad that I properly kept her on board all this time.

Regardless of his abilities, Zarpahn is still a high-level vampire with the divine protection of Lucief Arept. Yet the elite knights of Ruxe, when boosted by powerful buffs, will definitely be able to hang against him. And when this creates an opening—the Holy Warrior will slip in to slay him.

Naotsugu Toudou has risen so greatly in power, he could be called a completely different person. I was shocked when he appeared in the robe that prevents detection, but his appearance is hardly an issue given how brightly he is now shining. Rabi's eyes are wide as saucers and her face pallid as she watches Toudou moving like a man reborn. His power is clearly imbued with the existence of God. Although he also has the divine protection of the God of War, just six months ago he wouldn't have been able to even get near Zarpahn, but now they don't stand a chance against him. He is using the phantasmagoric shape-shifting armor, which was just given to him, perfectly well, while thrashing a number of the upper-level vampires at once. His blade is truly a beacon of hope manifest.

The Ruxe knights, who have been thrown into utter confusion, are beginning to coalesce with Grace and the Holy Warrior at their center. Spica, who joined at the start of the parade, is also fighting back against Zarpahn's iterations with all her might.

I exhale loudly in wonder. We have been scrapping for all we're worth thus far, but I'm finally starting to see concrete results. I haven't particularly prepared anything—but it doesn't look like I'll even need to join the fray this time.

The holy knights that laid ensconced in the vital locations also seem to be holding their own against the Zarpahns. Our preparation is paying off in spades.

Just as I breathe a sigh of relief, the Zarpahns' target switches from Toudou and the others to the citizens panicking in a rush to escape. They must have sensed the citizens' disadvantage, as they fall upon them to suck their blood and transform them into vampires through their powers of darkness. They're clearly hell-bent on creating more chaos.

"Stey, Amelia. Can either of you use holy techniques that are effective against vampires?"

"...Erm... Y-yes."

"Of course!"

Amelia seems to have used most of her holy energy, but Stey... What a little whippersnapper. Vampiric transformation is a horrifying power, but there is an amount of lag before the person in question transforms into a vampire. If the proper holy technique is used quickly, they can be treated. Conversely, the more that are afflicted, the stronger the Holy Warrior's influence becomes, which is a certain silver lining.

Perhaps due to our current dominance in battle, Eve speaks calmly.

"What...incredible power. Even with the holy sword, the last time I engaged Toudou in mock battle, he was nowhere near this strong..."

"...You must have heard of it. The legend of the Holy Warrior's awakening."

A turning point exists when the Holy Warrior's level of strength increases greatly. The Church calls this an awakening, and when it occurs, the Holy Warrior's physical strength, holy energy, sensory perception, and magical power all receive individual boosts, embodying the greatest level of might attainable in the quest to defeat the Demon Lord. This awakening has been experienced by nearly every Holy Warrior throughout history, and the only one to not receive it was an exceptional Holy Warrior who was already infinitely powerful upon summoning.

"The overdone sense of justice is a crime."

Fifth Report: On the Holy Warrior's Debut

"Is this the infamous—? Does that mean, that your three ultra rites of Phimas, Sir Ares, were only—?"

"Precisely."

Those were simply rituals to quicken Toudou's awakening. Sure, they were a bit overbearing, but we didn't have time to spare, and we needed to consider Toudou's equilibrium with grace, too. The fact that we couldn't simply pursue the most ideal reality is largely due to the Church's unfortunate ineptitude.

Eve is staring in amazement while Amelia is clearly uninterested, and Stey's mind is a complete blank. And yet—Rabi's eyes are rife with awe and a sliver of hope.

She must have realized the Church's deep secret. It's just as I expected. There isn't a more troubled existence than that of an intelligent yet timid werebeast.

The capital has already been sealed off by a powerful barrier. Even if Zarpahn resolves to retreat and tries to use his demonic gaze to manipulate another human, the barrier can't be bypassed. A barrier strong enough to hold in an upper-echelon vampire will not last forever, but it should be enough.

Up until now, I've mostly been running around in a huff to make sure everything succeeds, but our strategy at current is airtight. As I nod while observing Toudou and Grace fight, I notice that something isn't quite right.

Zarpahn's momentum—it isn't waning in the slightest. According to Sanya's information, he should be getting weaker as he uses his power, but from what I can see, the Zarpahns multiplying before my eyes aren't changing whatsoever.

"...This isn't good."

My strategy is hinging on the Zarpahn's iterations becoming weaker and weaker. Yet the rate of weakening I'm witnessing is nothing like what Sanya had reported.

I focus my gaze to observe the Zarpahns. The aura of darkness welling from within them is easily ascertainable. I have a definite hunch. Given these unforeseen developments, I bite my lip.

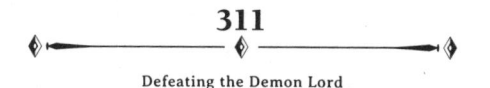

"...Zarpahn's getting extra support, I can see...from Lucief Arept."

Receiving power from God and having a grand awakening is not limited to the Holy Warrior alone. Within evil beings also dwell the powers of evil.

Will Toudou really be able to defeat him, given his just-recent awakening...?

Watching Zarpahn and Toudou collide head on, I quietly grip my mace.

§ § §

Toudou's body is light as a feather. Power wells within her as she grips the holy sword Ex, which she controls like an extension of her own body. The demonic attacker that calls himself Zarpahn is a formidable foe. He moves with the speed of wind and has the pure brawn to lift a massive hunk of rubble up with one hand, alongside species power, not the least of which is his ability to shapeshift.

This is all par for the course for a vampire according to what Toudou's already heard, but he's still completely different from what she imagined. More than likely, Toudou would have been at her wit's end fighting him up until just a few days ago. Yet at current, through her divine protection of the God of Order, Toudou is irrefutably capable of taking on more than one iteration of Zarpahn at once, despite his powerful status as demonic fiend.

A burst of flame from Garnet pushes the Zarpahns back; Spica is wielding a giant cross. Toudou's holy sword Ex rips with ease through the dark barrier surrounding each Zarpahn that falls upon them, turning their bodies to ash. On both sides of her peripheral field of vision, a surreal scene unfolds as the buildings supported by Grace's walls of light begin to sway and tremble.

"Get the people to safety! We can take it from here!" Toudou yells to the Ruxe knights, the protectors of the Hero's Procession of

"The overdone sense of justice is a crime."

Fifth Report: On the Holy Warrior's Debut

Light, who continue fighting back against their countless attackers despite the chaos.

The capital citizens are hesitating to escape on the central promenade. The Zarpahns are focusing their attack on Toudou, but if the citizens are dragged into the fray, they will not be able to escape without grave injury. The Church has instructed them to evacuate, but Toudou can't be too careful.

"These are forces of evil divine protection! Only Toudou can take them out!" Spica cries.

Toudou fends off Zarpahns attacking from behind while ripping through the bodies of many others raining on her from the sky. She can't even fathom how many she's already laid to waste.

Toudou knew of her enemy's skills beforehand, but Zarpahn's strength and sheer numbers are far greater than she expected. Toudou isn't struggling to fend them off at current, but Aria, Limis, and Glacia can only manage to push them back. At this rate, they'll be overwhelmed.

Grace remains their finest ray of hope, and she's devoting all her energy to the walls of light keeping the buildings on both sides of the promenade from crumbling down on top of them. Toudou protects Grace at her rear and continues to mow down the waves of Zarpahns that fall on them.

Above all else, if the buildings fall, so many will perish. Toudou has chosen to protect the people over her own self. If she is not the savior of humanity, then what else is she?

Toudou feels like a flame is burning within her. As if letting a massive burst of energy loose from within her, she continues to be completely absorbed in laying wanton waste to the vampires—using her sword, holy techniques and magic. Nonetheless, there isn't any sign of their number dwindling.

An attacker that doesn't even feign to dwindle in number is the embodiment of despair. Toudou is met with unquantifiable amounts of murderous rage, infinite bloodred ablaze boring into her. The enemy's momentum only continues to soar.

Somehow...someway...she must break through and create an opening. In that moment—the tandem movements of the Zarpahns hell-bent on attacking Toudou and the others all cease in unison.

Toudou's eyes are wide in amazement. The formidable demonic beasts all look down at their hands and croak in unison.

"Gwa-ha... Mwa-ha-ha... What worthy strength. Is this a blessing from the God of Darkness?!"

Toudou sees a dark abyss in each vampiric form. The noxious miasma of dread threatens to suffocate her. Zarpahn is becoming even stronger—just as Toudou was emboldened by the joyous cries of the people.

There are just a few citizens left that the Ruxe knights have not yet evacuated. They collectively swallow a lump in their throats.

The dark tremors rising from within their bodies, prevalent to the naked eye, are more than proof of Zarpahn's status as humanity's natural predator. While his hands have stopped from attacking for a moment, the sense of death and despair he emanates has not wavered in the slightest.

Over ten Zarpahns gather in one location. Seeing so many of the same face grouped together is nothing short of an agglomeration of malaise.

"Geh-heh... Heh-heh-heh... With this power, I will transcend Fahni and Kranos. Pitiful humans, you will become the cornerstone of my new dynasty."

Zarpahn speaks blithely, and then the figure of each gathered blurs—and becomes one.

Toudou has been caught unaware. The combined Zarpahn stomps on the ground and cracks the earth in two before rushing toward the Holy Warrior. His eyes are glaring ominously, with a deep smile on his face. His speed and power are on a different order of magnitude than just moments before.

Toudou gasps. The tentacle that shoots from her armor is immediately evaded by Zarpahn, who doesn't skip a beat. His movements are simply next level now—but nonetheless, at present, Toudou can

"The overdone sense of justice is a crime."

Fifth Report: On the Holy Warrior's Debut

still manage him. She composes her stance and grips her blade. Her opponent must also be at full strength—even with her sword in his face, Zarpahn doesn't show any signs of slowing down. As he encroaches upon Toudou, her holy sword Ex splits him vertically like a section of bamboo. Then—the Zarpahn that should have been bisected smiles wryly and disappears into thin air like mist.

Toudou stops in her tracks. Atomization must be just another special power that vampires have. But now, Toudou's left her backside open, and she quickly whirls around. She immediately sees Grace defending her and taking attacks from Zarpahn. The sharp clash of metal against metal—and then Grace crumples over and is blasted backward.

"—?!"

"Tsk." Zarpahn clicks his tongue. "Stay out of my—"

Aria, Limis, Spica, and the others attack the vampire. Yet he easily evades the blades and magic raining down upon him. His unadulterated physical prowess is simply on a different level. That said, when Toudou sees an opportunity, she quickly runs around and catches Grace just before she's crushed by a falling hunk of debris.

"Grace... But why—?"

Although she always looked massive before, now Grace is like a piece of driftwood. She's not bleeding from underneath her lacquer-black armor, but taking a physical blow of that magnitude head-on, there isn't any way she's uninjured. Anyone wearing normal armor would have been ripped to shreds like wet tissue paper.

Toudou can feel Grace's life energy vastly depleting. Her heartbeat is slow, and she doesn't have the power to stand. Yet Grace remains silent and slowly moves her arm wrapped in her gauntlets. Her fingers gradually rise up, and extending from them are the walls of light, which still refuse to waver.

Maintaining these walls requires an extreme amount of concentration and colossal holy energy. While keeping them up, Grace still defended Toudou and sacrificed her body in the face of Zarpahn's

315

Defeating the Demon Lord

attack. Toudou can't even begin to fathom how impossibly difficult this would be.

Toudou begins to sob as Grace takes her hand. It's clear that the immortal knight doesn't have any intention of lambasting Toudou for being unprepared. Even without words, Grace's intentions are clear to Toudou. The power of light pours into Toudou through her steel gauntlets.

Toudou understands. Grace intends to instill every last ounce of power currently used to keep herself alive into Toudou. Everything— is for the sake of dispelling darkness and saving humanity. This is the equivalent of Toudou inheriting Grace's life.

"What a troublesome development. Yet now, order has been reversed. If I...kill you, it's over."

Zarpahn, who took on every last attack thrown at him through the power of the God of Evil's divine protection, bores his hateful gaze into Toudou. Grace's hand goes limp, and the walls of light that were protecting everyone disappear into thin air. Yet, the rubble does not fall to bury the entire promenade. Zarpahn's eyes are wild with shock.

"You...!!"

Toudou stands. A new set of bluish-white walls now stand to support the buildings. Their brilliance is different from the power Grace used—they closely resemble the light of the holy sword Ex.

A strand of tears falls from Toudou's cheek. Her breathing is collected, as usual, and her spirit is as clear as the heavens without a single obstructing cloud. Toudou's level of supplication has reached a level where she can now summon powerful walls of light in moments of near destruction.

Now, Toudou truly understands. The Holy Warrior, the hope of humanity, must inherit the will of the people. And now, Toudou has succeeded to take over Grace's will.

"I am the one who put up these walls. And I will be the one to kill you. With Grace's will now as my inheritance. And I will destroy your Demon Lord."

"The overdone sense of justice is a crime."

Fifth Report: On the Holy Warrior's Debut

"...What fun. You're dead."

This is now a war by proxy between the God of Evil and the God of Order.

As Toudou points the razor-sharp tip of the holy sword Ex directly at Zarpahn, he loses all color in his face. He must now understand. Even with the power of the God of Evil, he doesn't stand a chance in the face of Toudou, who has directly inherited the power of the immortal knight.

Now Toudou even has the power to destroy Demon Lord Kranos.

The battlefield falls deathly silent. Ruxe's knights, alongside all of Toudou's compatriots, watches attentively as the moment of final justice lingers in the aether.

Zarpahn stomps on the ground, and in the same moment, Toudou rushes forward.

The holy sword Ex was forged to ward off evil. It's emanating light as pure as the sun, and there isn't a single being of darkness that could ever withstand its power.

The innumerable ungodly iterations used to launch Zarpahn's assault are vaporized in an instant when greeted with this powerful light. Phantasmagoric wolves and bats erupt from within them, but they also instantly billow into dust. Zarpahn's face contorts into sheer rage and indignation, but it's too late. None of his attempts at evasion, interception, or escape have a chance against the immortal knight and the Holy Warrior.

Toudou slashes diagonally with the holy sword Ex, cleaving Zarpahn in two.

Epilogue
Setting Out Anew

The assault on the royal capital now lives on in historical infamy for creating much chaos before the incident finally came to a close. The citizens of the Kingdom have come to truly understand the Demon Lord's formidable powers while simultaneously ascertaining a strong sense of relief at just how strong their protector of humanity truly is.

Grace Godicent Trinity, who stayed the course to protect humanity against all odds without ever raising her voice, alongside the Holy Warrior, Naotsugu Toudou, who inherited Grace's power and will to slay a heinous demonic vampire and become a new hero.

The elites of Ruxe are still in the throes of mayhem since the member among those who proposed to change the date of the parade, who was manipulated by the demonic foe, was made evident. They'll likely remain flustered for some time, but now, the contingent of aristocrats who didn't take Demon Lord Kranos's threat seriously have certainly garnered a real sense of imminent crisis.

In my room, I report to Creio on our most recent sequence of events.

"You really went overboard, Ares. I hadn't even heard a number of these things."

"Yet—we completed our goal. Toudou achieved his awakening and put a definite end to Zarpahn. There couldn't be any better result."

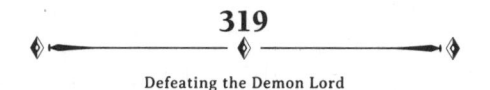

"There are a portion of commoners who were injured, and a section of the holy knights that you set into motion through Stephenne have become widely mistrustful. They believe you knew of Zarpahn's assault beforehand."

"Tell them this—'If that's the case, what did you do to help?'"

My job remains supporting Toudou in his quest to defeat the Demon Lord, and to this end, it's not my duty to maintain common order or save every last human being.

This is an issue of roles and responsibilities. Saving the citizenry is a job for the Ruxe elites, and the reason they failed lies solely in their own ineptitude. In this regard, Grace deviated from her role in the slightest—but really, that's not our concern.

As far as I have ascertained, Toudou's reputation is on the up and up. His name will be known throughout the entire world without incident. Sanya has also successfully completed her job of taking out the trash, and in my eyes, this is as perfect of a result that could be asked for.

The only problem left—is Rabi.

"I see—knowing when to let go is necessary in such serious matters, is that it? Ares, you can really be overly dry."

"If you wish to bring those I have let go back into the fold, I don't have any qualms. As long as they stay out of my way. I have my hands full considering Toudou's next move. He's become...almost too powerful now."

With power comes great responsibility. The Holy Warrior's awakening can lead to incredible feats, but simply acquiring power doesn't mean he'll remain prepared. And of course—the vast gap in his power compared with party members like Limis and Aria will also become a major issue. My head hurts just thinking about it.

At any rate, given his current state of prowess, at least we don't have to worry about him dying from being such a weakling. A small concession.

Creio falls silent for some time before finally sighing deeply.

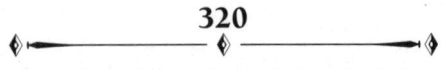

"The overdone sense of justice is a crime."

Epilogue: Setting Out Anew

"Hmph... Well, forget it. You have succeeded meritoriously, Ex Deus. May our lord Ahz Gried bless you today."

Our communication cuts out. I have succeeded, is that so...? I understand what Creio was pointing at when he spoke. In truth, Creio is even more dry than I am, and it seems that this time around, he's become a bit sentimental.

The strategy we employed included a number of issues that should have resulted in much more than minor fault-finding, from both the perspective of doctrine and humanitarianism. The fact that Creio hasn't said anything about it shows that the cardinal is overwhelmed.

My call finished, Sanya pipes up while massaging one leg thrown out in front of her.

"Damn, our recent strategy has me beat. I was scared shitless."

"You really came through for us. Without you, Sanya, the number of casualties would have had at least another zero tacked on. We can't make your achievements known to the world, but you should be proud."

Sanya and Rabi performed exceptionally well in our strategy. Of course, Zarpahn turned out to not exactly be the sharpest knife in the drawer, but regardless, I am expecting continued valuable contributions from them.

Sanya purses her lips and casts me a sidelong glance. "Gee, I'm so flattered... Sheesh... Think I've earned a bit of a bonus?"

"How much do you want?"

"It's j-just a joke, boss. You look like you're gonna kill me dead."

This is how I always look.

Honestly, my estimation of Sanya has legitimately skyrocketed. Her greatest achievement was not being won over to Zarpahn's side. Silverwolf werebeasts are infinitely loyal to their leaders, but at the same time, there's a heavy emphasis on their sheer power. When I saw how Sanya wasn't even fazed by Zarpahn's mind-blowing Manifold Horde skill, I knew she had grown to fruition. And now—I can really exploit her loyalty.

"You did well to resist betrayal. Even if you did and were found out, given your position, you could have easily escaped."

Sanya looks positively vexed. "Wha—?! That's messed up, boss. You didn't fully believe in me?!"

I believed in her, of course, but projecting the absolutely worst-case scenario is a boss's job. Sanya gets up from the couch and rushes close to me. She takes my hand gently and smiles broadly before speaking again.

"And anyway...you're so much tougher than me, boss. You killed Zarpahn, right?"

§ § §

A few kilometers from the scene of the assault, in an abandoned factory kept that way for times of unforeseen need, I stand with my mace, Wrath of God, in one hand—dripping with blood—over a man groveling on the factory floor.

"Act like you mean it. You are bestowed the power of Lucief, yet you're timid like a lamb... You're a disgrace to the Fahni bloodline."

"Hrngh... Ungh... You... Ares...Crown..."

Zarpahn looks up with blood-riddled eyes, propped up by his right arm. The power surging within him is on a different order of magnitude compared to when we fought in the Great Forest of the Vale. This is predicated on the fact that he has the power of the God of Evil now, but it is still an astounding rate of growth.

Luring him in was simple. Zarpahn became fixated on me, now wearing a mask, far easier than even Toudou or Grace. Just showing up was enough to lure one iteration in without any issue. And after one was pulled in, gathering the rest was a cake walk.

Toudou's awakening was so much greater than expected. He could probably take down Zarpahn now, even if Zarpahn had his own awakening. Nonetheless, I would never entrust fate to another being. Anything I can do myself, I will, that's for damn sure.

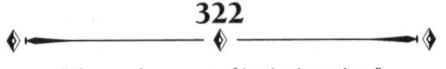

"The overdone sense of justice is a crime."

Zarpahn stands up. He's barely damaged, although I put plenty of power behind my blows. What a hard-headed chump.

"I was waiting for the day we'd meet again."

"Hrngh... The same, goes, for you, Ares! This day, a day of revenge—oh, how I longed for it!"

Zarpahn stomps on the ground and rushes toward me to attack. He is imbued with the power of the God of Evil. He's nearly on my level, and I've been strengthened with a buff to my physical prowess. The ground ruptures from his stomp, and a single swing of his arm causes a tempest. Yet his baseline in terms of battle tactics is the exact same as the Zarpahn I fought before.

The single Zarpahn instantly multiplies into five. But it's not an issue. I'm used to fending off enemies—from multiple sides at once. I swing my mace repeatedly while humming to myself.

The first emotion that erupts onto Zarpahn's face is anger. This is quickly followed by doubt before shifting to fear. Zarpahn Drago Fahni, even with the divine protection of the God of Evil, could never take me down. I crush his head against the floor with my mace.

"You still lack such basic understanding. The future cannot be left up to the power of God but rather must be carved out by one's own volition."

This is why anyone who wholly depends on the power of a God is weak. A defensive barrier will cause anyone to become neglectful of actual defense or evasion, and any increase in power without an accompanying demerit causes human beings to fall into depravity.

This is why Toudou remains comparably weak, despite his incredible divine protection, and why Zarpahn is crumpled in a heap before me, even though our physical prowess is actually on the same level.

"I'll say it once again. You cannot be at full strength just yet. Pull your iterations together, Zarpahn. You are lacking in desperation. Come at me with intent to kill or die. We will decide everything right here, right now. Or instead, will you continue to run for eternity?"

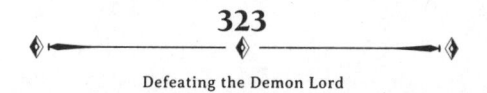

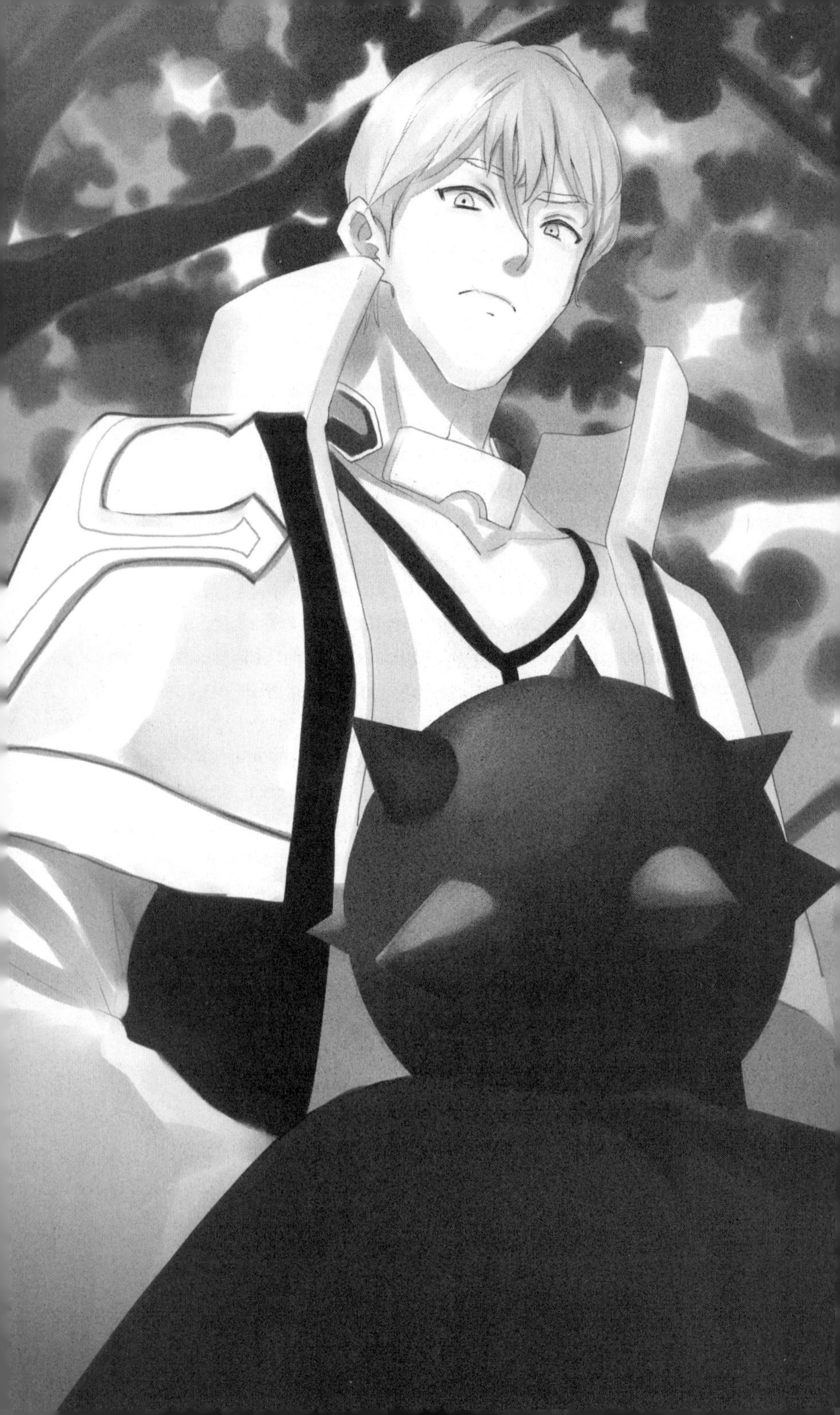

Epilogue: Setting Out Anew

A lack of divine protection must be supplemented with intelligence. And a lack of power requires polishing one's skills. Between someone who is born strong and a weakling that works hard to refine their skills to become stronger—even with the same end result—their repertoires are completely different.

As I look down at him with utter scorn, Zarpahn's expression breaks down.

"Wha... Whatever... No king would feign escape while being looked down on like this! Ares Crown—exactly as you wish."

Zarpahn's power surges even further, and energy black as the abyss spills from his being. He's gathered his iterations back into one. I feel like I'm staring directly into hell. A normal person would feel like their soul has been compromised just getting close to him and could even face full-blown cardiac arrest. As Zarpahn becomes intoxicated with his excess of power, the anger leaves his face, and he regains his composure.

"Ah... Ahhh... I feel so good... What an incredible feeling, Ares. I must thank you, after all... Without you, I would have never made it this far."

Zarpahn's power has reached a dreadful level and, without a doubt, surpassed mine, even at level 93. I grip my mace and sigh deeply before speaking to Zarpahn again, who's now in a trance.

"Zarpahn, it's hard to put into words, but you are truly an imbecile."

"...What?"

Becoming easily provoked would be careless, and putting too much faith in my own physical strength would be a mistake. You should never fight an enemy in their own territory or mistake the source of your own power.

This abandoned factory—I worked so hard to prepare this place as an execution site, to put Zarpahn to certain death.

Zarpahn's eyes are wide, and beams of light stretch from all corners of the factory to envelop him. I activate a barrier a few meters wide around his feet, and a wall of light completely entraps him. Zarpahn rushes to claw at the wall, but the light only burns his hands as he cries out.

"Hnrgh—! What is this...confounded madness...?!"

Zarpahn is truly a dimwit. Didn't he realize that I was slowly controlling exactly where he'd end up standing during our entire fight?

Barriers get even stronger the smaller the area they encompass. The barrier I've conjured with the help of an ancient relic held by the Church can't be broken, even with the divine protection of the God of Evil. It goes without saying that I've also imbued the barrier to prevent all forms of teleportation magic.

I move toward Zarpahn, mace in my hand. He cowers from me and burns his back on the barrier, howling fiercely. I don't need a holy sword or anything to destroy a member of the hordes of darkness. With just a bit of time to prepare, they're easily trapped. Fahni had a nose for such tactics, but Zarpahn has clearly not inherited it.

"You seem to underestimate me, but I will not do the same to you. Tell me where Fahni resides, and I will spare your life."

I imbue my voice with life force and pressure, and Zarpahn's eyes are wide as saucers.

§ § §

Zarpahn Drago Fahni was truly a formidable man. If he was just a bit more experienced, a bit more wary, he could have become the Church's public enemy number one. Our ability to take him down is entirely due to the blessings of Ahz Gried.

Zarpahn proved quite useful in allowing Toudou to show his authority as the Holy Warrior, so in hindsight, we couldn't have really asked for a more suitable opponent. Not that I'd ever want to fight him again.

Sanya's eyes go wide hearing my story. "Wow, so you let him live? I'm surprised that you would cut a deal with him."

"...It's not transactional like that. He didn't even give up the

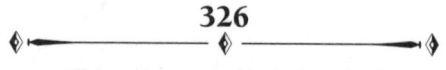

"The overdone sense of justice is a crime."

location, and if he does, I won't have any use for him. Letting him live would only be asking for pain without a single gain."

"...Yikes."

If a vampire that the Holy Warrior theoretically put an end to was found wandering the streets, we'd all be in for a world of trouble. If I spent time on him, he would inevitably cough it up, but I refuse to again mistake how dangerous he can be.

That's one major foe down for the count. Given Zarpahn's level of power, Fahni obviously feels like they were completely betrayed. We should be satisfied with that for now—I'm nothing if not humble.

"You all worked very hard. We'll take a little break."

"Hmm, I feel like I've heard you say the same thing, and quite recently... Did Amelia and Stey go somewhere?"

"They're taking care of some tasks for the Church. Don't worry about it."

Priests have priestly duties to attend to. For Stey in particular, I've asked her to deploy the holy knights, and she's probably now dealing with the responsibility of taking their verbal abuse. Surely her father can intervene to help her again.

"Doesn't sound like they're on a break," Sanya says exasperatedly. "And what about Eve?"

The second I turn to answer, Rabi, who has been sitting silently as a stone next to Sanya the whole time, pipes up instead.

"......Boss, would you mind if I spoke with you for a moment?"

We change locations. I knew I had to speak with Rabi, even if she didn't say something first, and I had a room ready. In the church hall of worship, we enter together; a single elderly nun is bowing her head low before a statue of the God of Order.

Rabi and Sanya have the same master, but they are completely different types of mercenaries. Sanya is quick to act over contemplating, while Rabi really ponders the situation before jumping into it. And Sanya has the potential for betrayal, while Rabi's potential for any treason is very low. That's why I gave her a relatively heavy role of responsibility this time around.

Rabi looks at me like she wants to say something. She's the one who came to me in the first place, so I prompt her to speak.

She breathes a small sigh and stays quiet for a few moments before saying resignedly, "Those training methods you came up with... I couldn't help thinking they were wrong this whole time. But my feelings changed when I saw Toudou at the parade. Boss, I don't have even the slightest intention to defy the Church. Yet, now I know...the Holy Warrior—he transforms people's supplication and faith into power, right?"

So she's finally realized. Actually—she's clearly had a hunch for quite some time. She just didn't say anything because she's so very timid. And now, she's bringing up the topic because she has finally made up her mind to stay the course on this ship, no matter what. The only reason she didn't bring it up in front of Sanya is because she considers her a friend.

Rabi continues, "That's why the public debut was necessary. And that's why you emphasized the results rather than the process of the three ultra rites of Phimas. You gave the Holy Warrior dignity and gathered even more faith in him, and that made Toudou even stronger."

"Yes, that's right. But, Rabi, you are still slightly mistaken."

Everything happens for a reason. For example, the raison d'être behind the Holy Warrior's awakening is the necessity of the holy sword Ex. The immortal knight is founded in the Church's deep secret. Performance is vastly affected by whether you know or don't know these facts. And that's why we needed an accomplice.

And further, these secrets must never, ever be known by the demonic forces that oppose us. I put my lips close to Rabi's ear and whisper, "The Holy Warrior isn't the only one capable of gathering supplication."

"?! Wh-what...does...?"

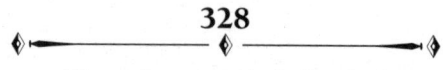

"The overdone sense of justice is a crime."

Rabi's eyes grow wide and her voice trembles. She must have understood.

I realized the secret of this power in childhood; this is why Creio scouted me.

The holy sword is a symbol of the Holy Warrior for the purpose of efficiently collecting supplication. The most important things are a strong name and a symbol. This is all a system. Power begets additional power in systematic fashion. The principles that past oracles with the Church of Ahz Gried reached have been quietly passed down throughout history and amalgamated to become the world's largest religious organization.

And for all intents and purposes—the same is true of the power of the God of Evil. Zarpahn failed to notice this. In a sense, this is all a war of attrition between the God of Evil and the God of Order.

The nun offering prayer raises her head and walks toward us. Her white skin is riddled with cuts. Her body is like driftwood, and her eyes are half-closed. Rabi, who is still trembling from having just been forced to learn of the Church's deepest secrets, stares in wonder. The elderly nun looks up at me and speaks feebly.

"I no longer have a place to die."

"Thank you for your many years of servitude," I tell her. "The torch has been passed. You should find somewhere safe to watch the future from."

The elderly nun narrows her eyes and moans loudly. Rabi's ears twitch rapidly as she continues staring slack-jawed at the nun. That's no way to look at someone who has fulfilled their servitude.

"?! Huh?? I-is that...voice...?!" Rabi yelps. "It couldn't be—"

"I've...been fighting...from age thirteen...to age one hundred and fifty," the elderly nun tells me without paying any mind to Rabi. "I thought...I could keep going."

"...No average person could ever pull that off. That's why Creio respects you so deeply."

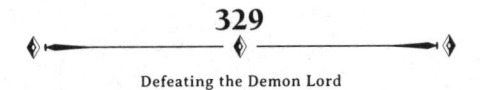

Rabi is simply an outsider from this nun's perspective. Just as this woman believes in me, I, too, believe in her. Although I don't know her name...

One of the nun's eyes opens wider, exposing a silver iris. A single tear falls from the corner.

"I never imagined...this burden would...fall onto her...without me dying..."

"The elites don't have enough respect for the aged. Instead of forcing someone so old to fight until their death, making someone young take their place is much more effective. If you still have any regrets, then you be the one to impart your skills and experiences to her. She's your daughter—you brought her up under your care."

Acrimonious words, if I do say so myself. Yet no matter how much I console her, she can't get her life back, and any comfort I offer her would merely be an insult. She's a martyr—the Church's longest-serving zealot of all time.

She's in a completely different headspace from the average person. Dedicating your entire life to the Church would easily keep your mind distracted from reality.

Rabi's face is white as a sheet. She looks back and forth between the nun and me, whispering in a trance.

"Clad in lacquer-black armor, the protector of humanity—bathed in God's influence, she who has obtained immortality, she who will never fall but continue fighting to save our world... Never speaking a word, her face unknown to all—that is Grace Godicent Trinity. Then—w-wait, that means Eve is a...a...a...*demon*...?"

Rabi is quivering and stuttering. Poor thing.

From the very beginning, the Church of Ahz Gried has followed this method of gathering prayers: A noble woman of the cloth who vowed to continue fighting in God's name. The knight of legend who never removes her armor, never saying a word—merely laying waste to the legions of darkness forever, for the sake of the Church and humanity.

The immortal knight—the untouchable Sister General.

All God's creatures, great and small, will be visited by death, but there is a method to escape it.

"The overdone sense of justice is a crime."

Epilogue: Setting Out Anew

"Thank you...young whippersnapper."

The elderly nun leaves the hall of worship. She's quite lively even though the supplication consolidated in her body should be gone now.

Eve Lucrao is respectable, straitlaced, and has watched Grace more closely than anyone. Above all else—she is young.

The nun who just left has a similar personality, I've been told. I'll bet that Eve will do a good job filling the role.

"Rabi, you're going to keep working for me for even longer."

"Ye...yessir, boss!" Rabi says, clinging desperately to my arm. Her eyes are brimming with tears. "I have absolutely no intention of objecting, I just feel like crying for some reason."

§ § §

The radiant sunlight shining on Toudou and her party seems to be blessing their latest departure.

Three days have passed since the assault on the parade. The hero's party is surreptitiously gathered in front of Ruxe Royal Castle. In a first for this group, all preparations are in order; the goods provided by the Kingdom of Ruxe are stashed in a magical horse-drawn carriage. Aria and Limis's equipment, basically in tatters from their arduous journey, has been upgraded, and Spica has rejoined the party. This same carriage felt spacious when the group first set out, but with the addition of Glacia and Spica, it's now feeling a bit cramped—in a good way.

"Ugh, you were so insistent about leaving as quickly as possible...," Limis grumbles icily.

"Sorry...," says Toudou. "I just can't sit still, you know?"

"Well," says Aria, "most of these aristocrats' invitations are bound to be nothing but trouble anyway..."

Following the Holy Warrior's striking debut—complete with an assault by demonic forces—aristocrats from the Kingdom of Ruxe and other lands have sent Toudou a veritable mountain of invitations. The majority of them, just as Aria says, were sent purely out of self-interest by those enamored with the Holy Warrior's might. But Toudou can't spare even a moment on these solicitations. She has a mission—to defeat the Demon Lord. And what's more, this mission is no longer hers alone.

Toudou no longer possesses the God-given power she wielded at the very end of Zarpahn's assault. She is still leagues stronger than ever before, but that divine strength was handed down to her from Grace—a temporary miracle.

Grace Godicent Trinity—the holy knight who has protected humanity for so long.

She passed her might on to Toudou before collapsing, at which point the Church took her away. Toudou hasn't been told what happened to Grace after that, but she can't imagine the immortal knight will ever be able to fight in the same way again.

The news doesn't appear to have made the rounds just yet, but Grace's defeat in battle will certainly put humanity in another predicament. She devoted her entire existence to protecting the people, which makes her far more noble than Toudou.

Therefore, as the successor of Grace's wishes, Toudou must bring light back to this world without delay. Toward the end of Toudou's training, Grace said she would use Toudou and Eve's mock battle to show them the future.

Now Toudou finally understands what she really meant. Grace probably knew that she wouldn't be able to fight much longer. She must regret not being able to speak to Eve at the end. Eve respects Grace from the deepest reaches of her being, and she conducted herself with such strength and sensitivity. Her master's defeat must have her crestfallen.

Yet even if Toudou and Eve met again, Toudou wouldn't have the right to console Eve; Toudou was the one Grace protected before collapsing in battle.

Toudou will repay her debt of gratitude by saving the world. Now that her identity is public knowledge, the Demon Lord's army

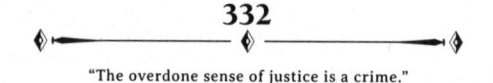

"The overdone sense of justice is a crime."

Epilogue: Setting Out Anew

will narrow their attacks on her. And with Zarpahn defeated, an even stronger demonic foe will strike.

And Toudou wants nothing less.

God commanded her to destroy the Demon Lord and all demonkind. She has more than a few opinions about maintaining order through the act of killing, but if her enemies are anything like Zarpahn, she can't afford to stop pursuing their demise.

Once everyone is in the horse-drawn carriage, they make their way to pass through the castle gate. There isn't anyone here to see them off. Toudou turned down all their offers.

Ruxe remains in chaos after Zarpahn's assault. Toudou couldn't possibly ask them to trouble themselves further.

The next time Toudou passes through this gate, light will have been restored to this world—that much is certain. Filled anew with resolve, she and her party take their leave.

A human figure is waiting just next to the gate, and Toudou falls speechless. She looks like she's been punched in the face; her chest tightens. Spica's eyes are wide as saucers.

There stands a holy knight, dressed in unforgettable lacquer-black armor adorned with golden crosses.

Toudou can scarcely believe it. Beneath the knight's cold metal armor lies hidden a sacred, tranquil interior and palpable might. This female knight carries a massive sword and shield—neither of which she had during the parade—and stares silently at Toudou.

"You're...still alive," Toudou says.

"……"

As always, Grace doesn't reply. For some reason, this makes the Holy Warrior irrepressibly happy. Grace isn't an immortal knight in name alone—she stands before the party without a trace of the wounds she suffered just recently.

And above all else—the sheer life force emanating from within her armor is vastly higher than it was even before the assault on the parade.

Grace begins walking forward. Every single movement Toudou

has ever seen her make has been heavy, rife with historical presence. But now, she moves with astonishing weightlessness.

It's hard to believe that Toudou thought Grace would never fight again after the battle against Zarpahn. There was never any need to worry.

Grace stands before Toudou, whose eyes are suddenly filled with tears. And then—Grace slaps Toudou on the back. This is no doubt Grace's own rallying cry for the hero.

Holy knights are born protectors. As long as Grace lives, Naotsugu Toudou will be able to concentrate all her energy on defeating the Demon Lord.

There's no need for words—Toudou has received so much from Grace. Now, she wipes the tears from her eyes and smiles.

"It's time for us to go."

Toudou's journey has only just begun.

§ § §

The carriage that Toudou and the others are riding moves away from the Kingdom. Grace watches until they disappear from view. Toudou still can't believe it—seeing her was like a scene from a dream.

Thinking back on it, Ex Deus had given Grace a number of hints. At the time, Grace's power of observation was terrible, and even though he was so close to her, she didn't realize the truth, and she didn't even realize that the insinuations he made repeatedly were all coming from a place of warm-heartedness.

Now, Grace is confused—yet someday, she'll realize if this is a dream or a nightmare. Grace is an immortal knight destined to continue fighting to save humanity forever. No human being has ever seen her face. She may have some time ago forgotten that she is even human.

Grace herself cherishes the deep respect that comes with this noble cause, yet if the tables were turned, the reality is so grim,

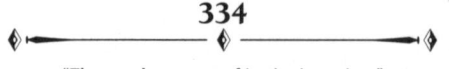

"The overdone sense of justice is a crime."

Epilogue: Setting Out Anew

it would be hard to call it superior or virtuous. Grace was never able to tell her friends or family goodbye. She has no idea what she should do next. She is not allowed to even shudder in fear, much less attempt to forget her reality.

And if asked why—the Grace that she knows in her own mind has never been able to show that side of herself. She realized this the first time she was given the armor—it may bestow magnificent levels of power, but it can't imbue the wearer with faith.

When Ares brought his proposal alongside the armor to her that fateful day, he told her that she had a choice and that Creio was skeptical of the idea of an immortal knight. Yet regardless, Grace was unable to nip the idea in the bud.

She couldn't tolerate the idea of erasing a long-standing legend that she herself admired, and she thought that the next member was already chosen.

The Grace standing here now is likely stronger than the Captain Grace of a few days ago. Her battle experience is still limited, but her body moves freely, and she has power bestowed from God that wells within her. For some time, this Grace's duties will be different from that Grace—they'll be much more attack-focused. This makes her excited but also afraid.

Can this new Grace really take on the same responsibilities as the incredible Captain Grace?

Suddenly, she hears a voice from behind her—the rare voice of a friend with whom Grace can actually converse.

"If you want to show your face, just come see me. I'll order you around while I'm at it."

"……"

"You really are over the top. That's fine. Whoever came up with this idea was insane, but you're the one who chose to continue the line."

Ex Deus comes with a gaze that could kill and excessive accomplishments—more than anyone—made in forging his own legend.

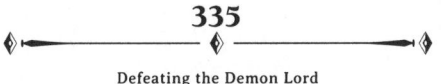

Some holy knights spoke poorly of him (in fact, Grace did, too), but Grace now understands why their captain never entertained such ideas. Ex Deus might have a cunning gaze, and he might spew vitriol with the best of them, but his words come from a place of compassion. Him being specially selected for the cause of defeating the Demon Lord makes perfect sense.

An elderly nun, as worn as a piece of driftwood, stands next to him. Grace has never met her before, but she knows who she is. She's spent more time than anyone by Grace's side and has the most respect for her, too.

Grace's eyes well with tears, but they can't escape from underneath the seal of her armor.

Ares Crown gives an order.

"Go now, Sister General, protector of humanity. Your power is needed more than ever."

From there, Grace Godicent Trinity takes her first step.

Special Story
What Happened to Amelia

"Sorry to bother you right after your plan went off without a hitch, but Amelia really seems to be down right now. Managing your subordinates is also a boss's job. Look after her properly."

I instinctively furrow my brow in response to Creio's words, which are coming after I finished giving him my full report on our successful implementation of the plan to take down Zarpahn.

"Amelia? What for?"

"Hmph... Well, she seems vexed by not making any significant contributions again."

...Just what does she have to worry about?

Amelia Nohman is a truly accomplished priest. Her personality leaves something to be desired, but she's high level and can use holy techniques as well as magic, alongside an advanced capacity for dealing with administrative tasks. She never cowers in fear, no matter who she's up against. On our journey, if I didn't have Amelia obeying me implicitly from the very beginning, I would have probably ended up working myself to death from lack of sleep. Of course, Amelia was the cause of a few problems, too, but nonetheless, it goes without saying that she's been a huge help.

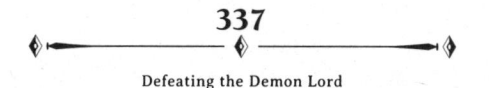

It's true that Amelia hasn't been as directly involved since Rabi and Sanya joined us, and she doesn't really stand out on her own like Stey does. Her main responsibilities include contacting the Church and administrative tasks—they are a bit drab—but she's truly an unsung hero. At the end of the day, such sober, straightforward work is crucial to coming out victorious. If Amelia, who accomplishes these tasks without complaint, doesn't understand her own importance—then we certainly do have a problem.

Actually, though... Thinking twice, on our most recent sojourn, Amelia...really didn't do anything right—she lost at the casino and ended up forcing Toudou to shut himself in. Well, let's not dwell on the past... The long story short is that she's a valuable member of our crew.

Just then, I hear a loud bang from outside the door. Amelia must be back from the errand she was running.

There's nothing else I can do about it. I'm hesitant, but we can't afford Amelia leaving us, not now. I guess I should ask her what's up...

I stand and walk to the door. As I put my hand on the knob, I come to an abrupt halt at hearing voices from the other side. I furrow my brow and concentrate on listening. The voices come through clearly.

"...Boss, leave that job up to Amelia! She was bored anyway."

"*Cough, cough...* If it works for you, boss, maybe Amelia should go?"

This...this can't possibly be happening.

"Ares! Isn't it Amelia's turn yet? She's always ready to go at the drop of a hat!"

"...Ares should really depend on Amelia more—she's always been so faithful."

All these voices belong to Amelia. She's changing inflection, but her slightly low voice for a female is unmistakable.

I realize I'm still on the call with Creio and speak into my magic communication device.

"...She's vexed about not making contributions, is that right?"

"Hmm... Spica is...well, no good. She has...certain idiosyncrasies—"

Amelia tries to imitate Spica but fails, and now she's perplexed. I can't believe that she's actually being this ridiculous, even when I'm not around... And to be honest, I can't perceive any level of vexation...

338

"The overdone sense of justice is a crime."

✟ Special Story: What Happened to Amelia

After a moment, I hear Creio on the line.

"...Yes, and she sounds exhausted. You really should take care of her from time to time."

"I'm fairly confident this is just how she is. I've seen her in this state many times."

"...Take better care of her every once in a while."

The call cuts out.

Creio, what the...? Does Amelia have some dirt on you or what?

Threatening a cardinal is some next-level bullshit... But I wouldn't put it past Amelia.

I sigh deeply and open the door. After I enter, suddenly, Amelia stares up at me before pushing her hands to her eyes.

"*Cough, cough...* I've caught a cold... And I think I'm blind, too!"

"...Wh-what do...you...?"

Rabi pulled this trick... Where did Amelia learn it? Rabi wouldn't tell her.

I'm at a loss for words as Amelia changes her expression and says, "Sexual harassment is a breach of contract. I'll have to report to the cardinal."

It was necessary conduct in the line of duty. I am not at fault in the least.

"...Is something wrong with you?" I somehow manage to compose myself to ask.

Amelia replies with a dead-serious look on her face.

"I am dispirited because I was not able to make valuable contributions, and you, Ares, continue to refuse to notice me. Touch me like you did to Rabi."

She looks serious but the tips of her ears are burning red. So she *is* embarrassed.

...Amelia's such a tricky one; she's just hard to employ. Her contributions might not be noticeable, but her presence certainly is, and she really does play an active role.

What else could she possibly want from me?

CHARACTER DATA

NAME: Eve Lucrao

ABILITIES
- **Physical Strength:** High
- **Endurance:** High
- **Agility:** High
- **Magical Energy:** Regular
- **Holy Energy:** Very High
- **Will:** High
- **Luck:** Regular

【Level】: 65
【Occupation】: Holy Knight
【Gender】: Female

EQUIPMENT
Weapon: Crossblade (a cross-shaped sword wielded by holy knights)
Clothing: Holy Knight's Armor (a symbol of holy knights affiliated with the Church)

EXPERIENCE UNTIL NEXT LEVEL 5,523

A member of the holy knight order and right-hand woman of Grace, the immortal knight. A very capable young lady who can intuit Grace's intentions. Accompanies Grace on both weekdays and holidays. Her interests include: Grace. The person she respects most: Grace Godicent Trinity.

NAME: Grace Godicent Trinity

ABILITIES
- **Physical Strength:** ???
- **Endurance:** ???
- **Agility:** ???
- **Magical Energy:** ???
- **Holy Energy:** ???
- **Will:** ???
- **Luck:** ???

【Level】: ???
【Occupation】: Servant of God
【Gender】: Female

EQUIPMENT
Weapon: Holy sword Grace (a lacquer-black blade carrying the weight of time immemorial)
Clothing: Servant's suit of armor (lacquer-black full body armor; prohibits any peering through)
Other: Shield of Black Light (lacquer-black tower shield)

EXPERIENCE UNTIL NEXT LEVEL ??????

One of the emblems of the Church, Grace is both the immortal knight of myth and the captain of the holy knight order. A peerless figure who never stops fighting to protect others. As long as Grace exists, humanity will never fall. She doesn't have any hobbies. Her favorite thing in the world is peace.

AFTERWORD

TSUKIKAGE

Thank you so much for picking up this copy of *Defeating the Demon Lord's a Cinch (If You've Got a Ringer)*. It's been quite a while—this is Tsukikage, the author.

I'm sorry to have kept you waiting. It's been four and a half years since the previous installment, but I am very glad to deliver this new volume detailing Ares and company's adventures.

During those four and a half years, a lot happened in my life, both regarding writing and otherwise. The time really flew by, and if I imagine the high schoolers who became fully fledged members of society during this time... It really was quite the hiatus.

This is the edited and revised fifth installment of the series, which was originally published on the website Kakuyomu. After departing from Cloudburst in Volume Four, in this volume we return to where the party's journey started—Ruxe, the royal capital. In terms of the entire story, this is a definitive homecoming.

I won't detail the story here, but new members join the fray, and Ares goes even harder in his rampage than ever before, creating a whole new powered-up comedic story that I think you'll enjoy. I spent a lot of time smiling and laughing while writing this volume, and if you smile or laugh while reading it, that will make me so happy.

From my perspective as a writer, I had always wanted to do a volume focused on the capital. In this volume, I was finally able to

Afterword

reveal the secret of the Church, which had been warming on the stove for quite some time. This was a huge relief. For *Defeating the Demon Lord's a Cinch (If You've Got a Ringer)*, I always consider editing and calculate back from there in the writing process. While the story in this volume represents a homecoming to the capital, it's also a major turning point, and the latter part of the story begins from here.

Until now, Toudou's journey itself was a secret, but her travels will now begin in the public eye. Ares's troubles were largely centered around guiding Toudou as well, but his trials will take on a different form—please look forward to it!

Also, the publication of this novel was put on hold for a while, but the manga adaptation by the artist Renga Kijima has now been published through Volume Five as of April 2022. (Talking about the comic release of the previous volume in the afterword really makes me realize how much time has truly passed.)

In the manga, the party is currently in Golem Valley, where Stephenne—who makes her mark on this volume, too—goes on a rampage. The female characters are meant to be adorable and action-packed, and this really comes across in the comics well, so if you're interested, please give them a look. (As the author, Ares's stern expressions that generate comedic moments are a favorite part of mine.)

In conclusion, I must continue to acknowledge everyone who's supported me on this journey.

Despite the long hiatus since Volume Four, the amazing illustrator bob continues to provide incredible drawings. Thank you very much—seeing Ares depicted for the first time in a while was very moving.

I must also thank my editor, Wada, who put so much effort into preparing this volume for publication, alongside everyone on the editorial team at Famitsu Bunko, as well as all other related parties.

"The overdone sense of justice is a crime."

Afterword

I owe a massive debt of gratitude to you all! I will endeavor to complete the next volume more quickly. (I always say that.)

Above all else, thank you to everyone who waited so long since the publishing of the last volume for continuing to support this series. I express my deepest gratitude to you all.

I drew Limis just for fun.

HAVE YOU BEEN TURNED ON TO LIGHT NOVELS YET?

86—EIGHTY-SIX, VOL. 1–11

In truth, there is no such thing as a bloodless war. Beyond the fortified walls protecting the eighty-five Republic Sectors lies the "nonexistent" Eighty-Sixth Sector. The young men and women of this forsaken land are branded the Eighty-Six and, stripped of their humanity, pilot "unmanned" weapons into battle...

Manga adaptation available now!

WOLF & PARCHMENT, VOL. 1–6

The young man Col dreams of one day joining the holy clergy and departs on a journey from the bathhouse, Spice and Wolf. Winfiel Kingdom's prince has invited him to help correct the sins of the Church. But as his travels begin, Col discovers in his luggage a young girl with a wolf's ears and tail named Myuri, who stowed away for the ride!

Manga adaptation available now!

SOLO LEVELING, VOL. 1–8

E-rank hunter Jinwoo Sung has no money, no talent, and no prospects to speak of—and apparently, no luck, either! When he enters a hidden double dungeon one fateful day, he's abandoned by his party and left to die at the hands of some of the most horrific monsters he's ever encountered.

Comic adaptation available now!

THE SAGA OF TANYA THE EVIL, VOL. 1-12

Reborn as a destitute orphaned girl with nothing to her name but memories of a previous life, Tanya will do whatever it takes to survive, even if it means living life behind the barrel of a gun!

Manga adaptation available now!

SO I'M A SPIDER, SO WHAT?, VOL. 1-16

I used to be a normal high school girl, but in the blink of an eye, I woke up in a place I've never seen before and—and I was reborn as a spider?!

Manga adaptation available now!

OVERLORD, VOL. 1-16

When Momonga logs in one last time just to be there when the servers go dark, something happens—and suddenly, fantasy is reality. A rogues' gallery of fanatically devoted NPCs is ready to obey his every order, but the world Momonga now inhabits is not the one he remembers.

Manga adaptation available now!

VISIT YENPRESS.COM TO CHECK OUT ALL OUR TITLES AND...

GET YOUR YEN ON!

Yen ON
Yen Press